Cicuta virosa (Poison Hemlock)

THE
CONFESSIONS
OF
YOUNG NERO

ALSO BY MARGARET GEORGE

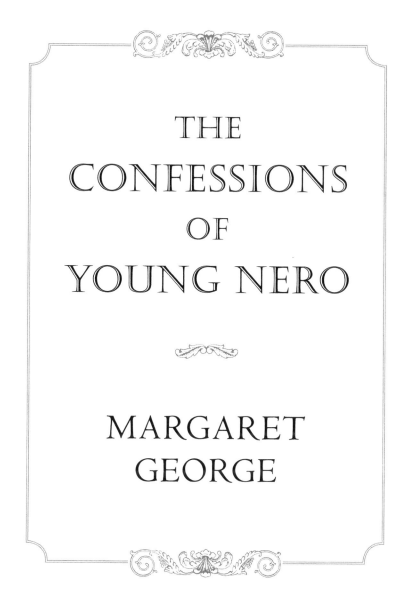

THE
CONFESSIONS
OF
YOUNG NERO

MARGARET
GEORGE

BERKLEY
New York

BERKLEY
An imprint of Penguin Random House LLC
375 Hudson Street, New York, New York 10014

Copyright © 2017 by Margaret George

Poetry from *Sappho and the Greek Lyric Poets*, translated by Willis Barnstone,
used with permission from Willis Barnstone.
To quote the lines from Sappho, by kind permission of the translator Tony Kline.

Library of Congress Cataloging-in-Publication Data

Names: George, Margaret, 1943– author.
Title: The confessions of young Nero / Margaret George.
Description: First edition. | New York, NY : Berkley Books, [2017]
Identifiers: LCCN 2016024945 (print) | LCCN 2016031052 (ebook) |
ISBN 9780451473387 (hardcover) | ISBN 9780698184763 (ebook)
Subjects: LCSH: Nero, Emperor of Rome, 37–68—Fiction. | Rome—History—Nero,
54–68—Fiction. | Emperors—Rome—Fiction. | BISAC: FICTION / Historical. | FICTION /
Biographical. | FICTION / Literary. | GSAFD: Biographical fiction. | Historical fiction.
Classification: LCC PS3557.E49 C66 2017 (print) | LCC PS3557.E49 (ebook) | DDC
813/.54—dc23
LC record available at https://lccn.loc.gov/2016024945

First Edition: March 2017

Printed in the United States of America
1   3   5   7   9   10   8   6   4   2

Cover design by Emily Osborne
Cover imagery: *The Consummation of Empire* from *The Course of the Empire* by Thomas Cole, 1836; *The
Remorse of Nero After the Murder of His Mother* by John William Waterhouse, 1878; Coin, Nero and
Agrippina, Roman Empire, AD 54 © The Trustees of the British Museum / Art Resource,
NY; Smoke © BortN66/Shutterstock; Mosaic border © ariy/Shutterstock;
Gold laurel wreath © Nick Kinney / Shutterstock
Endpapers: Cowbane, Cicuta virosa Illustration (1831): Florilegius / Contributor/SSPL/Getty
Images; Texture: alfocome/Shutterstock Images
Book design by Laura K. Corless
Genealogy chart created by JoAnne T. Croft, designed by Laura K. Corless
Maps by Laura Hartman Maestro, based on sketches by Margaret George

To my granddaughter
Lydia Margaret
who is (I like to believe) descended from the great warrior queen Boudicca

MY THANKS

To Bob Feibel, who many years ago made a suggestion: "Have you thought about the emperor Nero?" and to classics professors Barry B. Powell and William Aylward at the University of Wisconsin–Madison, who translate, advise, and help me keep company with Nero.

To Claire Zion, my insightful editor, and Jacques de Spoelberch, my forever agent, for their excitement and wholehearted support of the idea of telling Nero's story.

THE GENEALOGY OF THE IMPERIAL HOUSE

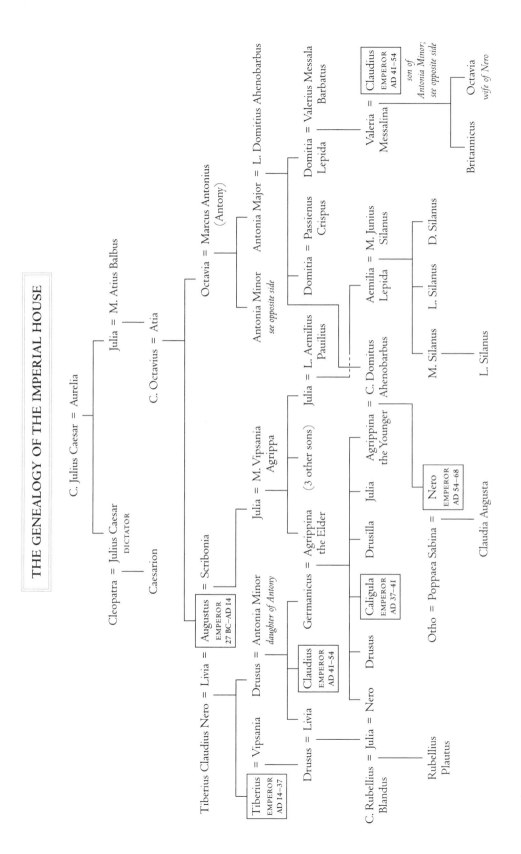

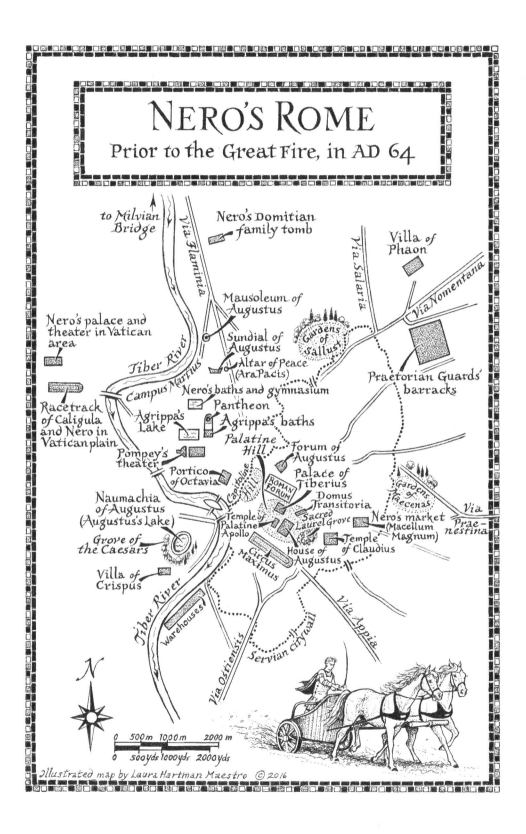

NERO'S ROME
Prior to the Great Fire, in AD 64

to Milvian Bridge

Via Flaminia

Nero's Domitian family tomb

Villa of Phaon

Via Salaria

Mausoleum of Augustus

Via Nomentana

Nero's palace and theater in Vatican area

Tiber River

Sundial of Augustus

Gardens of Sallust

Altar of Peace (Ara Pacis)

Campus Martius

Praetorian Guards' barracks

Racetrack of Caligula and Nero in Vatican plain

Nero's baths and gymnasium

Pantheon

Agrippa's Lake

Agrippa's baths

Palatine Hill

Forum of Augustus

Pompey's theater

Portico of Octavia

Capitoline Hill

ROMAN FORUM

Palace of Tiberius

Gardens of Maecenas

Via Praenestina

Naumachia of Augustus (Augustus's Lake)

Domus Transitoria

Grove of the Caesars

Temple of Palatine Apollo

Sacred Laurel Grove

Nero's market (Macellum Magnum)

Villa of Crispus

Circus Maximus

House of Augustus

Temple of Claudius

Tiber River

Warehouses

Servian citywall

Via Ostiensis

Via Appia

N

0   500m 1000m   2000 m
0   500yds 1000yds 2000 yds

Illustrated map by Laura Hartman Maestro   © 2016

LOCUSTA

This is not the first time I have been imprisoned. So I am hopeful that this is a sham and that the new emperor, Galba, will soon need my unique services and quietly send for me and once again I shall be treading the palace halls. I feel at home there, and why shouldn't I? I have provided my timely services for those in power for many years.

By trade I am a poisoner. There, why not say it? And not any old poisoner, but the acknowledged expert and leader in my profession. So many others want to be another Locusta, another me. So I founded an academy to pass on my knowledge and train the next generation, for Rome will always be in need of poisoners. I should lament that, should say what a pity that Rome must descend to that, but that would be hypocritical of me. Besides, I am not convinced that poison is not the best way to die. Think of all the other ways a person may die at the hands of Rome: being torn by beasts in the arena, being strangled in the Tullianum prison, and, most insipid of all, being ordered to open your veins and bleed yourself to death, like a sacrificial animal. Bah. Give me a good poison anytime. Did not Cleopatra embrace the asp and its poison, leaving her beautiful and stretched out upon her couch?

I first met the late emperor Nero when he was still a child, still Lucius Domitius Ahenobarbus, the name he was born with. I saw him at the low point in his life, when he was an abandoned child at the mercy of his uncle Caligula. (Now, that was someone who gave me a lively string of business!) His father was dead, his mother, Agrippina, had been banished when he was not even three years old, and his uncle liked to toy with him.

I remember he was a likable child—well, he remained likable all his life; it was a gift—but timorous. Many things frightened him, especially loud noises and being sent for unexpectedly. Caligula had a habit of that—sending for people in the middle of the night. He once forced me to watch a nocturnal theatrical performance in the palace, featuring himself as Jupiter. Sometimes it was harmless, like the playacting; other times it ended with the death of the helpless person he had sent for. So, Nero—let us call him that to avoid confusion, just as I call Caligula Caligula rather than Gaius Caesar Germanicus—was precocious in recognizing the danger of the serpent in his uncle.

Ah, such memories! Here in my cell I find myself returning to them, helping the hours to pass, until that moment when Galba sends for me with a task. I know he will!

II

NERO

The moon was round and full. It shone on the flat surface of the lake, which was also round, making it appear that the moon itself had expanded and enlarged itself there. It rose golden from the encircling hills but soon was a bright white ball high above.

It illuminated the wide deck of the ship. I was to sit beside my uncle and listen to him intoning praise to the goddess Diana, whose sanctuary was on the shore of the lake and to whom the lake itself was sacred.

I remember the flame of the torches that threw a flickering red light on the faces around me, in contrast to the clear bluish-white moonlight bathing the wider scene. My uncle's face looked not like a human's but like a demon's, with a burning hue.

These are all impressions, memories that swirl without being attached to anything. The reflection on the water—the torches—the thin, reedy voice of my uncle—the nervous laughter around me—the chill in the air—

I was only three years old, so it is no wonder my memories are disconnected.

Then his face shoved up into mine, his silky voice saying, "What shall I do with the bitch's whelp?"

More nervous laughter. His rough hands grabbed my shoulders and hauled me up, my legs dangling helplessly.

"I shall sacrifice him to the goddess!" He strode over to the rail and held me over the rippling water. I can still see the undulation of the reflected moonlight, waiting for me. "She wants a human sacrifice, and what more worthy than this kin of mine, descendant of the divine Augustus? Only the best for Diana, and perhaps a propitiation for the lapse of Augustus, who preferred to worship her brother Apollo. There you go!"

And I was flung out over the water, landing with a splash, cold, cold, and I sank, unable to swim or even cry out. Then strong hands grasped me, pulled me mercifully out of the water, and I could breathe. I was hauled onto the deck, where my uncle stood, hands on hips, laughing.

"Better luck next time, eh, Chaerea? You are too softhearted, to rescue such flotsam. Anything born of my sister can come to no good."

III

As I sat shivering next to Chaerea I could see down the whole length of the huge boat, see the light dancing on the mosaic-covered deck, the moonlight shining on the white marble cabin. The madman who had thrown me in the water now paced up and down, laughing. Not until I was older did I hear such a laugh again, and it was from a captive hyena, whining and mewling in its cage.

Let me off, let me off, let me off this boat, I prayed, to what god I knew not, just whatever god was listening.

"Come, lad," said Chaerea, putting his huge arm around my shoulders. "You should walk, warm up." He pulled me up and marched me up and down the deck, until feeling returned to my numb feet. We passed the rowers, whose heads turned as if on stalks to see us as we passed. One or two smiled. The others looked like the statues that were placed here and there on the deck.

"The shore is close," said Chaerea, holding me up and pointing to it. "Soon we will be back on it."

How I got back and when I got back I do not know. I have told you, my memories are wispy from this early age and do not join together to make a whole; rather, they are like pieces of cloud drifting through the sky of my mind, each portion separate and contained. But the horrible memory of the boat ride is burned into my mind.

My little bed in my aunt's home, where I lived, was narrow and hard; I can feel the rough linen when I think about it, but cannot see what else is in the room. I know the place was in the country because I heard roosters crow in the morning and I remember gathering eggs, still warm, from a bed of straw. I also remember many kinds of butterflies, and flowers on tall stalks, although I know now those were weeds.

I called my aunt Butterfly because one of her names was Lepida, which means elegant and graceful, and she was very pretty. Her hair was the reddish color of copper with a bit of dust on it, not the bright shiny copper that has just been polished. She was my father's younger sister and told me stories about him—he who had died before I could know him—and about their ancestors. When I told her how the sun made her hair glow, she laughed and said, "Bronze hair is in our family. I can see little glints of it in yours, too, even though it's mainly blond. Shall I tell you the story about how it came to be that color?"

"Oh, yes!" I settled in next to her, hoping it would be a long story.

"Well, long ago one of our ancestors saw two tall and handsome young men standing in the road."

"Were they gods?" I guessed. Whenever tall strangers appeared out of nowhere, they were gods.

"Indeed they were—the twin gods Castor and Pollux. They told our ancestor that the Romans had won a great battle, and to go to Rome and tell everyone. To prove that they were gods and telling the truth, they reached out and touched his beard, and it turned instantly from black to red. So from then on the family was called Ahenobarbus—Bronze Beard."

"Did my father have a red beard?" I wanted to know more about him. I wanted to hear that he was a hero and famous and that his death had been tragic. I later found out he was none of the above.

"Oh, yes. He was a true Ahenobarbus. Another unusual thing about our family is that all the men have only two personal names—Lucius and Gnaeus. Your father was a Gnaeus and you are a Lucius. Your grandfather, also a Lucius, was a consul but also a chariot racer. A famous one, too."

I had little ivory play chariots, and I loved racing them against one another on the floor. "When can I drive a chariot?"

Aunt Butterfly cocked her head, smiling. "Not for a while yet. You have to be very strong to race chariots. The horses pull the reins from your hands unless you hold very tight, and the chariot bounces and you have to be careful not to fall out, which is very dangerous."

"Maybe I could have a little chariot, pulled by ponies?"

"Perhaps," she said. "But you are still too young even for that."

I do remember this conversation about the chariots and the red beards. But why I was living with Aunt Butterfly, and what had happened to my mother and father, I still did not know. I knew my father was dead, but I did not know about my mother. All I knew was that she was not there.

Aunt gave me two teachers. One was named Paris and he was an actor and a dancer. The other was named Castor and he was a barber. He shaved the beard of Aunt's husband (who did not have a bronze beard but a regular brown one) and sewed up cuts and did other handy things. Paris was only for fun. I could not see that he did anything but act and pretend to be someone else. First he would tell a story— usually it was about a Greek, because they seemed to have the best stories—and then he would pretend to be those people. In real life, he was dark and not very tall. But when he played Apollo, I swear he grew tall before my eyes and his hair lightened.

"No, little one," he would say, laughing. "That is only your imagination. It is the actor's job to make you see and hear things inside your own head."

"Does an actor do magic?"

He glanced around; a frightened look flitted over his eyes. "Of course not! The magic happens only in your own thoughts."

It was not long before I learned that practicing magic was forbidden, and that there was just such practice going on in that household.

I n some ways it was odd to be the only child in the household. I did not have anyone to play with except Paris—who was childlike in many ways but still an adult—and the children who were slaves. Aunt did not like my playing with them but she could not be watching all the time, and what did she expect me to do? Let me say it: I was lonely. Lonely as in alone, as in solitary, as in set apart. Aunt kept stressing that being set apart was a special thing, a glorious thing, but it only felt like a punishment to me. So I found freedom in playing with the slave children my own age, and freedom in acting out the parts Paris taught me. Sometimes I was a god; sometimes I was a girl (I would be Persephone to his Hades—and we always used the proper Greek names, not the Roman ones of Proserpine and Pluto); sometimes I was an adult. On the stage—in actuality just the courtyard—I could be anyone. In real life, as Aunt kept reminding me, I was the descendant of the divine Augustus and must remember this at all times. But, as Paris informed me, I was also the descendant of his adversary Marc Antony, and Marc Antony was a lot more fun than the stolid and dull divine Augustus.

"Antony went to the east, to the lands that speak Greek, and to Egypt, and reveled in music, flowers, wine, and the Mysteries of Dionysus. He commanded a great fleet of ships and had a wife named Cleopatra, queen of Egypt. He—"

"Ruined himself, and disgraced himself as a Roman," cut in a sharp voice. We turned to see Aunt's husband, Silanus, standing in the doorway. It was doubly frightening because he was rarely at home. He stepped over to me, bent down, and looked me in the eyes. "Let Paris tell you the whole story, then. Go on, Paris!" He jerked his head up toward the trembling tutor.

"Uhh . . . he fought a great sea battle against Augustus, at Actium, and he lost."

"More than that, he fled back to Egypt, rather than falling on his sword as any self-respecting Roman general should do," finished Silanus. "Before he had defected to the east, he had married Augustus's sister. He left two fine daughters behind, Antonia the Elder and Antonia the Younger. You are descended from both of them. Never forget you are the heir of the *Roman* Marc Antony, not the debauched and debased Greek one."

He was so fierce about it I nodded just to get him to look away. Finally he did, standing up and telling Paris to get back to his regular lessons with me, and none of that Greek nonsense.

After he was safely gone, I said, "But what happened to Marc Antony back in Egypt?"

"Augustus pursued him there and he died. He is buried in Egypt, not in Rome. Now, Egypt is a very interesting place—there are ancient ruins and huge pyramids—many tombs—and all in all, not a bad place to lie for eternity." He whispered to me, "Antony had other children in Egypt; Augustus brought them back here and raised them as Romans."

"Did it work? Were they good Romans?"

"As far as anyone could tell. The girl grew up to be queen of Mauretania, and her son came to Rome later. He would have been your cousin."

"What happened to him?"

"Caligula had him executed—because he dared to wear royal purple in the emperor's presence. Now do you see how lucky you were that he only threw you overboard? And that he let someone rescue you? And only laughed about it?"

Aunt Lepida fetched me from my room one blustery day, beaming and carrying a child in her arms. She put the little creature down, where it teetered and took halting little steps, burbling and speaking nonsense.

"Someone for you to play with!" she announced. As if I could play with this baby, who could barely walk and could not talk. "My grand-daughter Octavia!"

So this was what she preferred for me rather than the slave children? What was I supposed to do with her? I bent down to look closely at her, and she reached out and pulled my hair. Then she started crying. An unpleasant little bundle she was. Then I saw another woman behind Aunt, peering over her shoulder.

"Is this your little cousin?" she asked the baby, as though she actually expected it to respond. When it didn't, she addressed me. "Why, little Lucius, I do believe you have the family wavy hair! Very desirable! As do I," she said, fluffing up her curls. "We are first cousins, you know—very close!" She bent over and kissed my cheek. The deep fragrance of crushed iris wafted from her. Her voice was low and warm. "I am Octavia's mother. I hope you will grow fond of one another."

Aunt Lepida looked on possessively. "My daughter, Messalina. Although she is married and a mother, there are only seventeen years between you."

"I envy you, out here in the country," Messalina said, with her syrupy-slow voice. "I miss it."

"She lives in Rome with her husband, Claudius—the brother of your illustrious grandfather Germanicus."

"He must be very old, then," I blurted out.

Messalina laughed, and her laugh was as enchanting as her voice. "If you meet him, you must never say so!" Even as young as I was, it did not escape me that she didn't argue the fact.

"Well, so we have visitors—family visitors?" said Silanus, striding into the room.

"Yes, family visitors," purred Messalina.

"Family visitors are the best kind," Silanus said. Why did they keep repeating "family"? And why did the proper and self-disciplined consul seem flustered? "It has been a while—too long—since you have visited us. But it is hard to extricate oneself from Rome. I understand."

"Not so hard if one truly wants to." She moved closer to him. Only I saw it, because her feet were right beside mine. It was only a minute move.

"I am sure that Claudius appreciates having you nearby," said Silanus, moving almost imperceptibly back. Why were these adults scuttling about like crabs, albeit slow-moving ones?

Octavia let out a wail and a slave came to pick her up.

"Let us share some heated wine," said Silanus. "These days we crave warmth."

They retired to another room, and left me to myself.

I t was hard to keep the family—to use Silanus's seemingly favorite word—straight. There was so much intermarrying that everyone seemed related to everyone else. One of my favorite rooms housed a number of busts of ancestors and I liked to study them, so I could link a face with a name. Since they were all dead, I would never meet them, but at the same time they seemed as alive as anyone else, since they popped up in conversation all the time. "The great Germanicus"—"Antonia the Elder"—"Marc Antony"—"Octavia the Younger"—you would have thought they lived down the road.

In the hushed shadows of that room, which seemed seasonless to me— the marble floor was always warm in winter, and slippery-cool in summer, but the air was always the same—the busts presided over that little kingdom. They were all of white marble, except the one of Marc Antony, which was a dark purply-red porphyry. He had a lot of tousled curly hair and a thick neck and I imagined the rest of his body to be stocky. He looked different enough, in his dishevelment, that I would never mistake him for anyone else. His daughter Antonia the Elder was on a nearby stand. He had never seen her as an adult; the last time he had seen her she was a baby like Octavia. The busts were immobile, forever apart.

I studied her face carefully. I wish I could say that my grandmother had been beautiful, but she was plain and forgettable. It would be hard to remember her no matter how many times you met her. They say her younger sister, my great-grandmother on the other side, was much prettier. She died just around the time I was born. Perhaps someday I would see a bust of her and I could compare them.

The family god, Germanicus, had a larger bust set apart from the others. He was handsome and youthful, and youthful he would remain in our stories, dying while he was governing far from Rome. Like all people who die before they have fulfilled their promise, high achievement was bestowed upon him as if he had actually earned it. I heard people lamenting the death of the noble Germanicus and bemoaning that he was cheated of his destiny to become a great emperor. But who knows, really, what sort of emperor he would have been? Promises turn sour and watched buds do not always open to reveal a lovely flower. Death saved him from being found out.

There were many others, going further back—several Luciuses and Gnaeuses of the Ahenobarbus tribe, and their wives who had left little imprint on their descendants. As they seemed to belong to the very misty past, I did not trouble myself to study them.

IV

Days passed very slowly at Aunt Lepida's. I cannot say they were all the same, because what Paris taught me changed, and sometimes it was golden and sunny outside, and other times dreary and chill and we stayed indoors, warming ourselves by braziers. But the variation was small, and there was little excitement. I could spend hours playing with my chariots, sprawled out upon the floor, and no one took notice.

The olive harvest was one thing that broke up the even march of the days; it happened in autumn, and I was given the task of following the slaves who picked up the fallen olives and making sure none were left on the ground. In truth, it was just something to keep a little boy busy, but it made me feel very important as I searched the ground for a telltale rounded shape. Many were bruised or had been trampled, and the sweet, heavy smell of their oil hung in the air.

"It's liquid gold," said the overseer. "More useful than real gold. You can eat it, light your room with it, dress wounds with it, smooth dry skin with it, cook with it, dip bread into it—truly a gift from the gods. Without it what a tasteless world it would be. And your aunt would be the poorer, too. Olives may not have the lure of gold, but they are a much more reliable source of income."

There was a commotion behind us and I turned to see Aunt Lepida walking with a man, who lurched and swayed as he approached.

"Poseidon's balls! It's Claudius!" the overseer gasped. Then he turned to greet them, with a smile as slippery as the olive oil he extolled.

"Yes, it's a fine harvest this year," Aunt was telling the man, who looked around vaguely, plucking at his cloak.

"I—I—yes, I see," he said. His eyes took in the grove of olive trees, stretching across the hills. The sun was striking them at an angle, giving their green leaves a silver-gray sheen.

The overseer bent low. "We are honored, O prince," he said.

I looked around and saw everyone else bowing, so I did, too.

"You need—need—need not bow to me," said the man. He reached down, took my hand, and pulled me up. "I am your g-g-great-uncle Claudius, the b-b-brother of your grandfather Germani—Germanicus."

I almost laughed but stopped myself in time. But was this a joke? Everyone said Germanicus was the ideal of manhood, and that bust Aunt kept made him look like Apollo, but this man was a shambling wreck.

"So we treasure him all the more," said Aunt Lepida, taking his arm. He looked bewildered. "He is all we have left of that paragon of a soldier."

"I am not a r-relic!" Claudius burst out.

"No, you are my beloved Messalina's husband, and nothing is too good for her."

Oh, Messalina—that woman who had exuded more ripeness than the olives all around me. That odd woman with the uninteresting baby.

"She is—c-coming," said Claudius. "She was delayed in Rome but is f-f-following me."

"I am grateful you are bringing her," said Aunt. "I have seen her seldom of late."

"The n-n-new baby makes demands. So I seldom see her, too." He smiled.

Suddenly Aunt bent down as if she had something of great interest to tell me. "Lucius, you have a new cousin—a little boy named—what is it, Claudius?"

"T-Tiberius Claudius Germanicus," he said. "G-Germanicus to pre-serve the precious name and show that the line goes on."

And that is how I first heard the name of that future rival to my life and my standing.

Just then Claudius gave a shudder and reeled against the overseer, almost knocking him over. His eyes rolled upward and his mouth went slack.

"Shh, shh . . ." Aunt wiped his forehead and stroked his face. Then, turning to us, she said, "He has these fits but they pass quickly. Take no notice."

As if we could not! I stared at his blank face, his gaping mouth. It was as if a spirit—one of those the cook talked about, demons that took control—had entered him.

Then it passed, as Aunt had said it would. Claudius blinked, closed his mouth, wiped the drool away with his hand. He looked around to orient himself.

"A noble name," said Aunt, continuing the conversation as if nothing had happened.

They returned to the house, Claudius leaning on her.

"Nothing to envy, is it? The poor sod," said the overseer. "Even if he is Germanicus's brother. How did that happen, anyway? Was his mother unchaste, or do the gods just like to play with us?"

"You are speaking of my great-grandmother," I said, with all the dignity a child can muster. Then I laughed. "So I must choose the idea that the gods toy with us for their amusement."

I went back into the house, just in time to see Messalina bustling into the hall. She had the little girl with her, as well as a bundle that I presumed held the new addition.

"Oh, Lucius!" she said, rushing to me and enveloping me in her ample bosom as if we were dearest friends. The bundle—which smelled bad—was crushed between us and let out a howl. "Here is your new cousin, Tiberius!"

I looked at the little face and tried to smile. What I mainly wanted to do was extricate myself from her grasp. "Very sweet," I said.

Messalina pulled Octavia over to us and hugged us all together. "Is there any greater joy than cousins? How fortunate we are to have each other." Then, abruptly, she let us go and stood up. Her voice changed as she called for a slave to come and tend the babies. She clearly meant to include me, but I shuffled off to one side and went to my room. As if I belonged with these infants!

I amused myself playing with my chariots and trying on the miniature dramatic masks Paris had made for me, enjoying the quiet. It began to rain and the soft patter of the drops outside was lulling. Eventually I put my head down on my arms and drifted away in sleep.

I had no idea how long I had dozed when I awoke, but it was getting dark outside. I heard soft footsteps outside my door; someone was looking in. I kept my eyes closed and pretended to still sleep. Then I heard the person leave and, in a voice I could just barely hear, report to people in a nearby room that it was safe to speak. Then a murmur of voices rose, some speaking at the same time so I could not separate them.

What was so secret that they needed to make sure I—or anyone else—could not hear? The idea of such a secret enthralled me and I crept out of my room as quietly as I could. I dropped to my hands and knees so I could inch along, feeling my way, and be out of sight if someone looked.

They were gathered in the library room, encircling the glowing brazier. Aunt sat on a stool, as did the infirm Claudius and a woman I had not seen before, but the others were standing. Having seen them, I ducked back out of the doorway, where I could hear just as well. In the brief moment I had glimpsed them everyone was gesturing and the men were pacing.

". . . he cannot be truly mad," was the first thing I heard, followed by: ". . . it comes and goes."

Then: "Lately it has been coming quickly and going slowly."

"If it did not affect others, no one would care if he wishes to dress as Jupiter or connect his palace to the Temple of Jupiter on the Capitoline. But the murders are mounting. There, I've said it—the murders are mounting. The fact that I can say this as a plain fact is shocking."

They must be talking about Caligula. I could certainly attest that he was a murderer—he had tried to murder *me*.

"Keep your voice down. The slaves—"

To my annoyance they spoke more softly.

"He was ill and I thought he might not recover. But he did. And . . . should anything happen to him, who would replace him? His only child is a baby girl, and he has not adopted an adult as his heir."

"It is truly not safe to speak of this. Even here. Spies might be anywhere."

"Then we are controlled by him and might as well admit we are helpless. Is anyone safe? He strikes at random."

"No one is safe. Not even anyone in this room, relatives that we are. We know he kills relatives—ask Ptolemy of Mauretania. Except that he cannot speak."

I jumped to my feet and rushed into the room. My fear and loathing of Caligula overcame my caution and I cried out, "I can speak! I can speak! He tried to drown me!"

They all turned to me in shock.

"Lucius!" said Aunt. "You must return to your room. Go back to sleep."

"It is t-t-too late," said Claudius. "He has already h-h-heard and is too old to forget. But h-he has honor and will keep what he has heard to himself. Isn't that r-r-right, Lucius?" His head twitched when he spoke but his words were commonsense.

"Yes, sir. And none must repeat my words, either. But he took me out on his boat and tried to offer me to Diana. He called me bad names and threw me in. A soldier saved me."

"Do you think the soldiers are still loyal to him?" asked Messalina.

"The P-Praetorians are traditionally loyal to the emperor," said Claudius. "But if they should turn . . ."

"I have heard that he belittles them and mocks them," said Messalina. "Will they endure it?"

"That depends on how m-many of them he humiliates," said Claudius. Another commonsense answer.

"I might suggest another way, if you are willing to follow it. I assume that is why you have called me here." The unknown woman I had seen earlier now rose. She had dark hair and was striking in her posture and composure. "My professional name is Locusta, and for safety's sake I will not tell you my real name. I specialize in making an ambrosia that has carried many to Olympus, although I cannot say whether, once there, they are turned into gods or not."

"In other words, a poisoner!" said Messalina. "We would not stoop to such methods. But . . . can you name some of your . . . successes to prove your point?"

"Of course not. I am not that stupid. So far I have a clean record and have never been convicted. But only a fool would advertise her hand in what passes for nature. You would have to trust me. I could, of course, do a demonstration for you on an animal of your choosing. And you can order a slow, intermediate, or quick-acting agent. It depends on what sort of . . . event . . . would most suit your purpose."

"We might do that," said Messalina.

"I cannot be a party to this!" said Claudius. "I cannot even l-listen to it. My ears have heard nothing. Swear it!" He looked around the room at each face, ending with mine. "Even you, little Lucius. I have h-heard none of this."

"Great-Uncle Claudius, you have heard nothing that has been spoken in this room. You were not even in the room!" Let us go one better.

"So it is," he said, limping away down the passage to the dining rooms. "Messalina, we will return to R-Rome sh-shortly."

"Yes, my love," she called after him. "Rome," she said. "These days, we never know what is waiting for us there."

"Do not fret yourself, my dear," said Aunt. "You are safe as Claudius's wife. Caligula keeps him as a pet. He enjoys humiliating him more than he would enjoy killing him."

Messalina, tight-lipped, nodded. "And Silanus is safe, too," she said. "We can be so thankful for that."

Locusta came over to me. "Well, little boy, you were brave to come into the room and say what you did, even if your knees were shaking. I saw it. But only the brave can do it anyway, no matter how hard their knees shake."

"It was true. And I hate Caligula. He should not be allowed to do to others what he did to me."

"Ah, but who will bell the cat?"

"I am not sure what you mean."

"It is a country saying. A council of mice met to decide what to do about the tomcat who was on the loose. They agreed the best plan was to attach a bell to his neck so they could hear him coming and hide. It was a fine plan—but it needed a mouse brave enough to risk his life jumping on the cat."

"I see." No one would dare to attack Caligula. "But the ambrosia . . ."

"Clever lad. That would be the same as putting out a dish of milk for the cat, but to get it he must pass his head through the bell loop. The hand that set up the trap is nowhere near when the trap is sprung." She sighed. "Still, if they don't want my services, well, they will just have to take their chances with something more dangerous."

V

They say that where you are when you hear of a life-changing event is forever burned into your memory. You can recall every little detail and, at the same time, you cannot fix the larger picture—like a dream, where the little things are clear but the bigger meaning or location is a mystery. Thus it is that I remember being in a garden, watching two white butterflies dancing around each other, with the rest of the setting a blur, when I first heard the scream—"Caligula is dead!"

Who said it? I do not know. Where did the voice come from? I do not know. I stood rooted, watching the butterflies. Caligula was dead, Caligula was dead . . .

I must have run back into Aunt's house. I must have been told then that the emperor was dead, murdered by those who hated him—which left a lot of suspects. But the assassins had been captured, and their leader was none other than Cassius Chaerea, the man who had rescued me. I must have been told then that the new emperor was Claudius. Because I came to know all these things, but I have no memory of how I learned them. I remember the joy I felt in knowing my torturer was gone.

The change in the household was immediate. Aunt was now the mother of an empress—Messalina, barely twenty years old. The Praetorian Guards had proclaimed Claudius emperor, as one of the few surviving members of the imperial family on hand. They did not have time, nor did they wish to bother, fetching someone from further afield.

"He tried to refuse," Aunt said, with a shake of her head. "And rightly so, because he hardly is very majestic. But the blood in his veins is royal, and that was what mattered."

"And Messalina is empress," I said. "You must be proud."

"Indeed I am, and so is Silanus, that his stepdaughter is in such an exalted position."

And now I felt more than ever like an outsider, a poor ward of this elevated family. My father dead, my mother gone, and my inheritance from my father seized by Caligula, so that I lived on Aunt's charity. Would she now cast me out as an embarrassment?

I was the last thing on anyone's mind during this upheaval; I became invisible, and happy to be so. Sometimes I hid in the room with the ancestral busts. They calmed me; I am not sure why. Because they and their troubles were gone? Because they stared out at a world that had gone past them? Antony could not know what had become of his Roman daughters, whether they had even survived into adulthood, let alone his children with Cleopatra, or that the Senate had stripped him of his honors, forbidden any celebration of his birthday, and ordered all his official statues removed. Death bestowed a blissful ignorance upon him and allowed him to be free.

We were not free. As we learned more about what had happened, fear ran through the household, so thick even a child could taste it. Caligula had been struck down by his trusted guards, led by Chaerea, hacked and left gushing blood like the flamingo he had personally sacrificed earlier on that day. His wife and baby daughter had been killed, and the rampaging assassins went looking for other members of the imperial family. I may have been saved because of my lowly status in Aunt's household, far from the Forum. The story was that they almost killed Claudius, too, but he was saved by some other Praetorian Guards, who found him cowering behind a curtain.

"I would doubt that story if I were you," whispered Paris to me.

"Claudius is more clever than he likes to appear." When I looked blank, he said, "If Claudius was accidently found, it was because he had arranged to be found."

A chill ran right down my spine. So even Claudius was a snake beneath the cover of his amiability and ineptitude? "Do you mean that he—arranged it?"

Paris shrugged. "Not necessarily. But if he knew of the plan to kill his nephew, he made sure that he would profit by it."

"What have they done with Caligula?"

"Took his body and gave it a quick burn, then put what was left of it in a shallow grave in the Lamian Gardens. They say his ghost's screams ring out nightly from that place."

Claudius assumed the purple and added the names Caesar Augustus to his birth names. In the early summer Messalina invited her family to the palace, the first time we would step foot into it. I hoped that going there would banish the nervous fears I had, the dreams of Caligula's ghostly form invading my room that refused to fade away. The new emperor would protect me, not hunt me down.

Like so much from that time, my memories are in little pieces. The slow trundle of the cart bearing us to Rome . . . the entry into the city, the mass of buildings crowded all together, some red brick, others gleaming white marble . . . the litter that I was put into, that bounced all the way . . . the hill it climbed, so that I was pitched backward . . . alighting in a cool green garden on the flat top of the hill . . . the sprawling building before us.

"Tiberius built it," said Aunt. "The divine Augustus was content to live simply in a small house, sleeping in the same little bedroom for forty years, on a low bed with a thin coverlet." Was there a whiff of disapproval in her voice about his successors' way of living? If so, it vanished when Messalina appeared and invited us inside.

She seemed different. She was enveloped in swaths of silk, and her hair was dressed with pearls and gold threads.

"My dear mother," she said, kissing her cheek, but in a formal manner.

"Silanus." She looked a long time at him before she held out her hand and said, "I am joyous to welcome you." Silanus bowed stiffly.

"Lucius," she said, bending to look at me. There was none of the sticky warmth she had exuded at Aunt's house. She was sizing me up anew. "You should not wear green," she said. "It doesn't suit you."

"What color should I wear, lady?"

She narrowed her eyes, thinking. "Red, perhaps. Gold. Definitely not purple."

A warning even I understood: *Do not think of climbing higher than you already stand.*

The first room we entered was so high ceilinged that I could not see where it ended above me. Walking through it took a long time; the marble was slippery underfoot. Then there was another room, then another, then another. Open windows framed fluttering green leaves and ushered in soft breezes, rich with the scent of box hedge and mint. The whisper of Messalina's silks drew us on.

At length we reached a chamber that opened onto a gigantic balcony; from it the great city spread out below. I rushed to the balustrade, barely able to see over it. Far below was a huge open area, a long thin oval.

"What is that?" I asked.

"Lucius!" said Aunt. "You should stay with us until you are called to do otherwise."

"It is all right," said Messalina. "He is just a little boy, and they can hardly stand still." She came over to me. "That is the Circus Maximus," she said. "They race chariots there."

Chariots! "Oh, when?"

"They have them all the time," she said. "It makes a dreadful racket."

"But you can watch them from here?"

"Yes, but you have to have good eyes—it's not close."

I was longing for an invitation to see a day of races but dared not ask. She did not offer.

Claudius joined us. Unlike his wife, he did not seem different, except that he now wore purple.

"It is w-with great joy that I welcome you," he said, shuffling forward.

Everyone bowed.

"I have been in this p-palace at many different s-stages of my life," he said. "So in many ways it is like coming h-home. But whenever one moves into someone else's house one tries to make it his own. So there are ch-changes. And I will undo some of Caligula's decrees, which I hope will p-please people." He turned to me. "There is a s-special event I wish to invite you to."

My heart rose. Was it the chariot races?

He turned and murmured something to Aunt. She nodded.

Claudius then said to me, "It will be a surprise. The true end of something, that will make you happy." Then, in a most unimperial manner, he winked.

A servant entered quietly and offered a tray of golden goblets filled with a refreshing cool drink. I stared at the goblets, at the intricate designs on them. The gold felt heavy in my hand. But such a heavenly heaviness!

To be an emperor, then, was to drink even your simplest refreshments from weighty gold goblets. It was to see the chariot races whenever you pleased from the privacy of your dwelling. It was to have fleets of servants waiting to hear your bidding, then sliding away silently to fulfill it.

"Lucius looks tired," said Messalina suddenly. "Perhaps he should lie down." Before I could protest that I was wide-awake, she grabbed my hand and placed it in the palm of a servant, who then pulled me away, through more long rooms, and finally into a room with a couch spread with silk. It was plain I was to lie down and pretend to rest.

Slats of sunlight came through the shutters, but the room was cool and otherwise dark. I could barely make out the decorations on the walls—red and black designs framed by deep yellow backgrounds. From somewhere in another of the cavernous rooms came soft flute music.

To be an emperor was to lie upon such couches in such rooms and hear sweet music wafting in from secret places.

Why would Augustus have preferred his little house, his narrow bed with plain linen like mine at Aunt's house? He may have been divine, but dare I think he may have also been foolish? At least in earthly things.

The gentle warm air passing over me died as the afternoon wore on. Then the flute faded away, replaced by notes of such pure beauty they could only come from Apollo himself—a rippling, golden, liquid sound. I lay utterly still, as if by moving I might cause it to cease—was it a dream? But it was not, and I knew I must approach its source and hear it even more clearly and directly.

I stole through the rooms, drawn on by the sound. Finally I reached the room where it originated. For long moments I stood outside, my eyes closed, drinking in the sound. I did not want to look inside, for fear of who I would see playing. Paris had told me many tales of enchanted music that lured people to their doom. The player was always a demon or a god in disguise. But finally I had to stick my head in and look.

A slender young man was standing before the window, holding a large instrument—his left arm supported its flat bottom while he touched strings from behind, and at the same time he plucked strings from the front with his right hand, holding a pick. The instrument was shaped like an incomplete circle, with flourishes at each end. The notes played with the fingers were soft, while the ones with the pick were clear and sharp, together making a melodious and complex waterfall of sound. Suddenly the musician was aware that someone was in the room, and he jerked his head around to see me.

"I—I am sorry, I just wanted to hear more." My knees were shaking—not from fear but from the abruptly stopped divine music.

"I am only practicing," he said. "The cithara is a stern mistress. She will not yield her music easily, or to just anyone. She makes us all suppliants first."

I could see that only an adult could play it; it was too large and heavy for a child. I made up my mind in that instant that I would learn to play it as soon as I was able.

"Who are you?" he asked.

Of course he would be puzzled. I was too old to be Messalina's son and too bold to be a slave. "Lucius Domitius Ahenobarbus," I said.

"The emperor's great-nephew," he said. "We all know about you."

"You do? What do you know?" How curious that this musician knew of me.

"Well, in truth, we know about your lineage but nothing more than that. We don't know, for example, whether you like mullet better than lamb. Or whether you can swim."

"I prefer mullet," I announced. Swim . . . the mention of it made me shudder.

He gave a flourish with his deft right hand and the magic sound came out of the instrument once again. Then he stopped. I waited, but there was nothing forthcoming.

"Thank you," I said. "Perhaps when I am older you could give me lessons."

He smiled. "If you remember. And if I am still here."

Slowly I made my way back to the resting room, the day ordinary again.

VI

The summer was a hot one. My little room at Aunt's house was stifling; I told her I felt like a loaf of bread baking when I lay down.

"I suppose you want a slave to stand over you and fan you," she said. "We can't spare any."

The bean plants were drooping in the fields, and the morning glories that opened at dawn shriveled up before noon. The fishponds were drying out, and the fountains ceased running, their silent stone spouts gaping like open mouths. It was the time of the Dog Star, when the mad star rose and brought in the searing heat of midsummer. Romans fled the city, some to the coast and some to the mountains, if they had homes there. We sat out under the trellis with its wilting canopy of leaves, but it was no cooler than being in the house.

A message came from the imperial palace. Aunt seized it eagerly, hoping that it was from Messalina. She heard from her seldom, although Silanus was often summoned to Rome. But her face fell. "It's for you, Lucius, and Silanus," she said. "The emperor wants your company for a trip. Where, he doesn't say. Once again I am not invited, but my husband is!" She turned to me. "Best get ready. Apparently he is already on his way."

• • •

Claudius arrived shortly and I clambered into the carriage beside him, Silanus following. So far Claudius had not extended the promised invitation to watch the chariot races, but this proved he had not forgotten me.

"Where are we going?" I asked eagerly.

"To lay ghosts to rest," said Claudius.

"But where—"

"Trust me," he said. "Did I n-not tell you I would surprise you?"

Silanus was looking around with more than idle curiosity.

"My wife is not here," said Claudius.

"I can see that, sir," said Silanus.

"I hope you are not d-disappointed," said Claudius.

"No," replied Silanus. "Although I always enjoy her company."

Claudius grunted. The carriage rumbled on.

After several hours we began climbing a fairly steep hill; when we crested it I could see that it was the lip of a big circle—and in its center below was a glittering lake.

A round lake . . . reflecting the sky . . . calm and unmoving . . .

And in it floated two enormous boats, shaped like stingrays.

I gripped the arms of my seat. Claudius reached out and took my hand. "Do not be afraid," he said. "Today they perish."

The carriage began its descent.

We stood on the dock, and the monsters floated before us. I saw again the hideous bronze animal heads that had burned in the torchlight, boars and wolves marking the place of each rower. I could see the white marble cabin that I had gazed upon in the moonlight. All the things that had haunted my dreams now loomed before me, stripped of their magic. The harsh sunlight had banished the mystery of the moonlight, burned it off.

Claudius held up his arm. "Strip and sink them!" he ordered a large company of workmen gathered there. "Take all the v-valuables off. Then tow them to the middle of the lake and sink them."

Claudius bent down and took my hands. "The S-Senate wanted to condemn Caligula, declare his memory legally damned—*damnatio memoriae*. Mad and cruel as he was, I could not allow someone of my b-blood to be dishonored publicly. But I am doing the same th-thing, on my own accord. He will be removed from the official lists, his statues taken down, his name erased from m-monuments. And these t-tokens of his folly, waste, and cruelty will be destroyed. Tonight is the dark of the moon. Diana will not be offended—she c-cannot see our deed." His words were hard to hear over the hammering and splintering coming from the doomed boats. The men began tossing the bronze animal heads onto the shore. Each snout had a big ring.

Claudius bent down and examined one. "Fine workmanship," he said. "Do you w-want one?"

I recoiled. "No! Destroy them!"

"We'll m-melt them down," said Claudius, turning one over in his hand. The tusks of the boar scratched his finger.

As the sun set, the disabled boats gurgled and sank beneath the surface of the lake. There were bubbles and ripples and then all was quiet. "Gone," said Claudius. "Now, little Lucius, you must no longer fear the water."

We were quiet on the way back. But halfway there, we were met by a company of horsemen and a contingent of Praetorians.

"He is here," said Claudius. "T-take him. Transport him to Rome." He turned to Silanus. "You are under arrest for c-conspiracy against my life. I h-have been expecting you to strike during this journey. That is wh-why we have been closely followed all day by my guards." He nodded to the guards. "Take him away."

Silanus shrieked, "I have done nothing! Nothing! I am your loyal subject!"

Claudius just looked at him sadly.

"Then I shall speak!" he cried. "Ask your wife! Ask Messalina! She has pursued me for months. Trying to get me into her bed. I refused, and this is her revenge!"

"T-take him away," repeated Claudius.

The guards stepped up to the carriage and hauled Silanus out, dragging him over to a horse.

"She's a whore!" yelled Silanus. "And a murderer, if she kills me for this! For rejecting her—I, her stepfather. Filth, filth!"

"For slandering my w-wife, you deserve to d-die," said Claudius.

Before my eyes, the company of soldiers took Silanus away. I heard him yelling and then—silence.

Claudius turned to me, affably. "Lucius, I will return to Rome here at this f-fork in the road. I have an escort to take you b-back to your aunt's. And a letter to give her explaining wh-why you return alone." He thrust it into my hand.

My joy at seeing the objects of my torture vanishing beneath the waves was short-lived, now eclipsed by the terror that gripped Aunt's household. She had collapsed upon reading the letter, shrieking and running to her bedroom, only to sink to the floor sobbing before reaching it.

"Silanus, Silanus—what did he say?" she kept asking me, clutching my arm. The sight of my revered aunt reduced to a whimpering lump begging me—me—for information terrified me. And I was hard put to answer, for it had all happened so swiftly.

"He—he cried out that he was innocent." It was all I could remember.

"Of course he is innocent!" She wiped her eyes, pulled herself up to a sitting position. "But who accuses him? Claudius talks about a dream that both Messalina and his freedman Narcissus had that—that proves his treason."

"Silanus said that Messalina wanted revenge on him and this was her way."

"Revenge? But why? I thought she was fond of him."

A brave Praetorian spoke up. "Too fond," he said. "Silanus said she tried to seduce him, and when he refused, she promised to ruin him."

Her eyes wild, Aunt clutched her head. "No, no. It cannot be."

But it was. Soon the entire story was out. Not the seduction part, for presumably that took place in private. But the plot to damn Silanus, which rested on complicity between Messalina and her tool Narcissus. Each had come separately to Claudius troubled by a dream in which Silanus would come secretly armed into Claudius's presence to assassinate him. The credulous Claudius had believed that their having the same dream proved it was a true warning. In truth it only proved they were good actors and collaborators.

The motive was despicable. Could Messalina's vanity really demand such a human sacrifice, one that would make her own mother a widow? It was my first, and most brutal, lesson in what lengths to which evil people will go, and for what flimsy reasons. I have never forgotten it, nor let down my guard since. Let them call me cruel. Better that than dead.

Aunt took to her bed for several days, while the sham of a trial was being readied. Then she rallied and one night sent for me. I was ushered into the room with the busts, where she and a man whose face was veiled stood before an altar with smoking coals.

She seemed like a statue herself, exuding no warmth and little movement. She had died and been resurrected in a new form, this shell before me.

"We have decided on a course to save Silanus." Her voice had no intonation. "The only possible way to save him. The emperor puts stock in dreams, does he? Even other people's dreams? How much more will he listen to his own dreams, then. We know a way to send him a dream, a specific dream that will show him the truth." The silent man next to her nodded. She gave him no name.

"It is well-known that an innocent young mind is the best receptacle of dreams," the man said, with a voice like sand shifting across desert wastes—subtle, quiet, murmuring. "That is why we have selected you, Lucius. We will show you a painting. Stare at it, imprint it on your mind. Then inhale these vapors." He tossed grains of something onto the coals. A hiss of steam rose, then a sharp, bitter smell.

"That will seal the image into your dreams. Go silently to your bed, lie down, and do not move until morning. The image will seek out Claudius while he dreams, push the other dreams aside, and lodge in his mind."

This itself seemed a dream—the room, dark save for two torches and the glowing coals; the busts barely visible in the gloom, watching; these wraithlike people taking my hands and leading me to the altar.

I wanted to cry out, "No! No! I won't do it! Keep my mind free of your magic!" But like a sleepwalker, I submitted to the ritual. I bent over the coals and inhaled the smoke, making myself dizzy. I gazed on the painting, showing Silanus's likeness turning away from Messalina, who was grabbing his tunic and trying to pull him onto a couch. A second depiction showed him kneeling loyally before Claudius with no knife or weapon.

"Now," murmured Aunt, turning me around, "I shall lead you back to your room and put you to bed. Keep your eyes closed the entire time. Do not open them again until morning."

To my knowledge, I did not dream of either of the images, although I have seen them many times in my own mind since. I hoped that somehow, by the magic Aunt had invoked, they had flown to Claudius anyway.

But they had not, for Silanus was executed soon thereafter.

VII

The household never recovered—indeed, how could it? Yet we had to continue on our same everyday paths, while Aunt drifted through the rooms, ghostlike. Once she clasped me to her, whispering, "I have no child; my daughter is not my daughter. Lucius, you are my son now," but she never said it again. Paris and I went on with my lessons, some the proper ones and others the interesting ones. Needless to say, there were no invitations to the palace, and I knew I would never see a chariot race or hear the sounds of the cithara again. There would be nothing but this plodding, placid country life. The sun would go round and round over rolling fields and rustling forests, the seasons blur into one another, but at each turn of the year the same earth would be beneath it.

I was left unsupervised much more than I had been before the "incident" (as we referred to it, to tame it and let us go on). I could spend much time not only playing with my chariots but also painting my crude little pictures and making clumsy pots from clay. I even persuaded Paris to find me a little flute so I could learn to play simple melodies.

The quiet was in some ways soporific, in others like soil in winter, nurturing what will burst through in spring. The very sameness, peace, and routine allowed me to plant the seeds that would bloom later in my life, but they needed time to develop. There is no rushing creativity. It must have firm roots.

. . .

I was sprawled out on the floor, painting the flower I had plucked earlier, now wilting. It had not lasted long. Dimly I heard footsteps coming down the corridor but that meant nothing to me. There were murmurs, strange voices, but that also meant nothing. It must be a merchant making a delivery of some sort.

"So this is how you treat him!" said a low, loud voice at my door. I looked up to see a strange woman standing there, staring at me.

If I say she seemed to take up all the space in the doorway, is that hindsight? She was not fat, not even hefty, yet she was formidable. I thought of the Amazons that Paris had told me about. Was this what they looked like?

Her hair was pulled from her face, with neat rows of curls on either side. Her nose was straight, her lips both curvy and small. Her eyes were wide set and direct, and they were focused on me. She had the face of Athena.

"I have taken good care of him," said Aunt. "To me, he is my son."

"Oh, so you would treat your own son to a small room with a hard bed, shabby clothes, and low-class tutors? An actor and a barber? How could you, to the grandson of Germanicus and the great-great-grandson of the divine Augustus?"

Were my clothes shabby? I had never noticed. And Paris was wonderful. Life without Paris would have been unbearably boring. "That isn't fair!" I said. "I love my tutors. They are good to me. And Aunt is good to me, too."

"Hah." The strange woman laughed, but it was not a real laugh. "That's because you know no better. But why should you? You are just a child. So young you will soon forget all this."

Even then I thought it sad that, if I were so young, I already had so many memories I longed to forget. Caligula. The boats. Silanus. The magic. Now this lady wanted me to forget the good ones, too.

"Do you have no other greeting for him than that?" said Aunt. "You hardly deserve the name of mother."

Mother! Oh, no! I had no mother, at least none I knew. She was only a name, someone who had disappeared. She did not even have ashes, like my father, who rested in the Domitian family tomb. She was not real.

"And you do? With that murderous slut for a daughter? The gods forbid that you should influence my dear Lucius any further." She bent down and looked me straight in the eyes. "I am your mother. I have come to take you home."

And thus my sojourn at my aunt's house ended as abruptly as Silanus's life. I was whisked away without even a chance to bid farewell to Paris and Castor, deposited like the object I was in a new house with a new woman who called herself my mother, and expected me to, too.

The new house was in Rome, halfway up the Palatine Hill, on the far side of the imperial dwellings. The woman—Agrippina—talked incessantly all the way into Rome. She seemed to be talking to herself rather than to me because she did not look at me but stared straight ahead.

"At least I have managed to find a house," she said. "Caligula took all our property, the furniture, too, and sold it. Stripped us. Uncle Claudius has kindly restored it, but of course he couldn't get our old house back. Nonetheless, this will do. Anything is better than that wretched island my brother sent me to." She sniffed. "Of course I shall make a show of properly interring his ashes, but I'd rather throw them in the Tiber."

Oh, yes, she was Caligula's sister. It was hard to keep all these connections straight. But knowing she shared his blood was frightening to me. Would she also go on mad rampages?

The litter stopped and we alighted. We stood before a house situated midway up the hill, cypress trees framing its entrance, and a formal garden surrounding it. Agrippina marched toward the door, hardly glancing at the shrubs and flowers on each side. I trailed along, watching the bees burrowing into the peonies until she called out, "Stop dawdling!"

The entrance led into a light-filled atrium, the floor of shiny marble, the ceiling high and divided into ivory and gold coffers, with an opening to the sky in the middle. Directly below it was a little pool. I went to inspect the pool and dipped my fingers into the water. It was shallow, with a blue mosaic on the bottom that made it appear deeper. I looked up at the sky overhead, marveling at seeing the clouds floating past, almost part of the ceiling.

"Come along!" said Agrippina, pulling my hand. She hurried me out of the hall before I could see what the wall paintings depicted in their gaudy hues of burnt yellow, rusty red, and bluish green. Now I was marched down a passage that gave out onto an enclosed garden ringed by rooms. Some workmen were sitting in an arbor in the middle, but they leapt up as we arrived.

"Idle? Nothing to do?" said Agrippina. "Have you finished already?"

"No, but we were having a rest and a snack," said one.

"I don't pay you to snack," she said. "Get on with it."

She went into one of the rooms near the garden and ushered me in. It was small, and its main light came from the door to the garden, but it had a proper bed, a lampstand of many oil lamps, several three-legged tables, a small couch, and a chest.

"They have managed to get this ready, at least," she said. "This will be your room, Lucius." For the first time she knelt down, eye level with me, and really looked at me. Her voice changed. "You cannot know how I thought of you all the days I was in exile. My only child, far from me, at the mercy of relatives. I did not know if I would ever return. The list of women in our family who have perished in island exile is frightening: Julia, Augustus's own daughter and my grandmother; Julia the Younger, her daughter; my own mother, Agrippina, for whom I was named. I was meant to be next. But here I am, and you are with me. We will never be separated again. We will never be at the mercy of anyone again. I promise you that, on my honor. I will do everything on earth to keep you safe, and to make sure I am by your side to protect and guide you."

Her wide eyes continued to hold mine. They were gray, like—like Caligula's. A little shudder ran through me. Could she feel it?

"I am yours, and you are mine. The two of us against the world. But I will never be bested again. So do not fear, little one. You may lie down in safety." She pulled me to her and held me so tightly I could hardly breathe. Her body was strong and solid, and as I rested against it, I felt it could indeed shelter me from all storms.

Children are resilient. For a little while I missed Aunt, but I was soon absorbed in my new life in the heart of Rome. The big house that we lived in became more luxurious every day. Painters were busy in the atrium and reception rooms; couches with tortoiseshell feet, tables of Moorish wood, bronze tripods with ornamental tendrils, and inlaid braziers were carried in on the shoulders of muscular workmen. Then came the works of art—marble sculptures, bronze busts, mosaics. Some of the marbles looked so much like living people I watched them carefully to see if I could detect any breath.

"Greek," said Agrippina. "They aren't good for much else, but their statues can't be bettered. You can always tell the Roman copies from the originals." She saw me frowning.

"If the Greeks are not good at anything besides art, why did you appoint Greeks as my tutors?" I had two—Anicetus and Beryllus.

"I should have said they are good for only two things—art and scholastic studies."

Only the two most important things in the world! "Agrippina," I said, "those are—"

"You must stop calling me Agrippina," she said. "I know in some ways we are still strangers, but you must call me Mother. If you do not, then you will never think of me that way. Anyone can call me Agrippina, but only one person in the world can call me Mother. And I expect him to do so." Then she hugged me, kissing my ear.

Days passed and gradually the grand house began to feel like home. Familiarity seeps in and takes root and even luxury seems commonplace—is this not the way everyone lives? Slaves hovering to take orders from Mother, and even from me; flowers out of season, grown under glass in greenhouses; floors heated by steam underneath so that my little feet were never cold, even when I could see frost on the juniper hedges outside. My new tutors were attentive but in awe of me, I could tell—such a difference from Paris. Anicetus was a burly young Greek freedman from Greece itself with a broad and seemingly open face, quick to laugh and quick to oblige. Beryllus, from Palestine, was quieter and more standoffish. Both were ardent partisans of Greek studies.

One day as Beryllus was drawing a big chart of all the characters in Homer, with lines connecting them, Anicetus said, "You need to see them!" and, taking my hand, led me into the big atrium. It was a clear day and sunlight was pouring in through the open skylight, illuminating the room.

"There! Who is this?" he said, stopping in front of one of the large wall paintings. A swirl of blue-green enveloped an angry-looking muscular man with a trident.

"Neptune," I said.

"We are speaking of Homer!" said Beryllus. "You must not use Roman names for the gods. His proper Greek name is Poseidon. Poseidon!"

"Why is he so angry?" Or were the gods always angry at something or someone?

"He had a grudge against Troy," said Anicetus. "But we needn't talk about why. And look, here is Troy." He led me to the next painting, of a great city with high walls and towers, on the top of a hill, with a wide plain stretching away on all sides and down to the sea. A number of ships were anchored by the shore, with a little city of tents nearby. "This painting is incorrect. There should be many more ships—a thousand of them! But of course the artist could not paint them all. Yes, a thousand ships went to Troy to fight the Trojans."

"Why?" It seemed a basic question.

"To bring Helen back," said Beryllus, sighing, as if he could not imagine anyone not knowing the story.

"Who is Helen? And why did they want her back so badly? Would not one ship have done?"

"Who is Helen?" Anicetus closed his eyes and smiled. "Helen is beauty. Helen is everything you want and cannot have. Helen is what you have lost and must find. Helen is that which cannot be possessed."

"In his long-winded way, Anicetus is trying to say that there is a real Helen and a Helen of the mind," said Beryllus. "The real Helen was the queen of Sparta in Greece, married to Menelaus of the family of Atreus. She ran away with the Trojan prince Paris—or was she kidnapped? So her husband and all his kinsmen and subjects went to Troy to rescue her. They fought a ten-year war and eventually won. Troy was destroyed."

"Completely?" That lovely city I was gazing upon—no more?

"Completely," said Anicetus. "But a Trojan man, Aeneas, escaped the burning city, carrying his aged father on his back, and eventually came to Italy and through his descendants founded Rome. So in that way Troy lives on."

I was now standing before the next painting in the series, which depicted Helen being recaptured by Menelaus. He grasped her wrists, dropping a nasty-looking sword to the ground. His eyes were focused not on her face but on her rather substantial breasts. "She isn't so beautiful," I said. Her face was not more lovely than others I saw often.

"No artist can capture her beauty," said Anicetus, defending the painting. "It is impossible. Besides, this person has never seen her, so how can he be equal to the task? This serves only as a stand-in, a substitute."

"What did she look like?"

"Homer does not describe her," said Beryllus. "He only describes how others respond when they see her. That is enough."

"Do you know why?" Anicetus knelt down so he could speak directly to me at my level. "Listen. This is important. It is because each person has his own idea of what true beauty is. To describe beauty in detail is only to fall short in convincing another person. That is why Helen is queen of the mind. Of your mind, of your imagination."

"Besides, Homer never saw her, either," said Beryllus.

"Especially since he was blind," said Anicetus, laughing.

As we walked away, I kept looking back at the painting of Helen, willing her true image to appear, to let me glimpse her. But the painting stayed the same.

The rest of the series showed the Greek and Trojan heroes I was later to know so well: Achilles, Agamemnon, Odysseus, Patroclus, Hector, Priam, Hecuba. And then there was a small panel showing a different sort of man. He wore trousers and a peaked hat and used a bow and arrow. It was the last painting on the wall.

"That is Paris," said Anicetus. "The cause of the whole thing!"

I stepped closer to see better; the light from outside was weaker here in this corner. The man had a noble face; he was gazing straight out from the walls of Troy to the plain, pulling his arrow back, aiming for the enemy below. "No wonder Helen ran off with him," I said.

"Lucius!" said Beryllus. "Paris is not a noble character. In fact, he is a coward."

"Why?"

"Because he does not fight as the others do, in manly duels with sword and spear. He hides safely behind the walls, killing from a distance."

"But if the object of war is to kill the enemy, what difference does it make how it is done? And is it not more sensible to kill from afar without endangering himself?"

"Someday you will understand," said Beryllus. "You are too young now."

"Who is he aiming at?" I asked. I could not see who the target of his arrow was going to be.

"Achilles," said Anicetus. "He aimed at the one spot where Achilles was vulnerable."

"He killed him?"

"Yes."

"So the coward killed the mightiest of the Greek warriors?"

"Yes. So it often is in life. A lesson for you."

"No, the real lesson here is that being a keen archer is a valuable skill. And new ways of doing things can be better than the old."

Beryllus shook his head. "You are too young to understand."

VIII

The seasons had turned again before an invitation came from the imperial residence. It was high summer, just before the Dog Star would rise and everyone would flee Rome for cooler places.

"About time," said Mother. "There is a message in this, of course. That bitch knows that *I* will now know she considers us the lowest on her horizon. The last guests before the exodus to the imperial villa in Baiae."

"Why would she feel that way?" Messalina was strange, but we had done nothing to make her dislike us.

"We threaten her. Not by what we do but by who we are—we have the blood of the great Augustus himself, which they do not. And beyond that, we have the blood of Aeneas, and beyond that, Venus."

Aeneas! "Is that true? We really are descended from Aeneas?" I did not care about Augustus.

"Yes, the Julian line comes from Aeneas. Long, long ago, of course. And Aeneas was the son of a mortal man and Venus herself." We were sitting together on a couch and she pulled me closer to her. "Anchises was so handsome even the goddess was swept away with love for him. So you carry within yourself a bit of Venus herself, and you will be as handsome as Anchises when you grow up." She then ran her hands over my back and lightly over my jaw, turning my face to hers. "Oh, so handsome," she murmured, stroking my cheek.

Whenever she did this I felt both a melting inside and acute embarrassment. I twisted away. "I will be glad to see Great-Uncle Claudius again," I said, sliding off the couch.

Mother smoothed her hair. "Don't talk too much when we are there. Let me do the talking."

This time the trip to the imperial residence was a short one, as we were already on the Palatine. It was thick with houses on the slopes; the top was reserved for the rulers and for the gods. Augustus and Livia had had their dwelling here, next to the Temple of Apollo. Nearby, the cave where Romulus and Remus were taken in by the she-wolf was honored. But Tiberius had not been content with such humble quarters, so he'd built the sprawling Domus Tiberiana, which survived more or less intact, if looking old-fashioned.

"Stand straight!" said Mother, pushing the small of my back as we approached the entrance. "Stand tall like the son of Aeneas!"

I threw my shoulders back and marched in beside her.

"Ah, the lady Agrippina," said the slave ushering us into the imperial presence. "Welcome. And welcome to young Lucius."

"Agrippina!" There was a rustle, and Claudius shuffled into sight. He held out his hands to Mother, and she gripped them, bowing low.

"Up, up! I am the same uncle who h-held you as a child," said Claudius.

She rose. "Oh, I remember, Uncle. I remember."

Together they went into the chamber, me following. It was not the same one I had been in with Aunt. This one was smaller, its wall paintings duller, and it faced in the opposite direction from the Circus Maximus. In fact, it did not even have a balcony, but it did have a large window opening onto gardens blooming with stately white lilies, tall blue larkspur, and clear yellow crown daisies hugging the ground. In the middle was a score of rosebushes, and their sweet scent stole through the window.

"Things have changed for us all," Mother said. "Your change elevated you to the purple. And so you were able to bring me home again. For that I should fall at your feet and cover them with kisses."

"P-please d-don't," said Claudius. "I could not do it fast enough. I have been r-reversing all the deeds of Caligula that were wrong. Bringing home the exiles. Rescuing the leaking t-treasury. And a h-hundred other things."

"And soon my extraordinary husband will be a conqueror." Messalina had appeared, seemingly out of nowhere, and slid to Claudius's side. She looked at us, murmured a hasty welcome, then said, "Did he not tell you? He plans to invade Britain. To finish what Julius Caesar started." She gazed on him adoringly.

"Is this true?" said Mother. She could barely keep the shock out of her voice. How could crippled old Claudius command troops?

"Indeed it is," said Claudius.

"I have urged him to it," said Messalina. "The brother of Germanicus can do *anything*."

"N-not anything, my dear," said Claudius. "But I h-have good generals and I can leave the hard part to them."

"As long as you return safely to me," purred Messalina. "Dear Agrippina," she said, "welcome back to Rome. I trust you have quite recovered from your years in the wilds of Pontia?"

"One never recovers from a false accusation—or, I should say, forgives it. But as for the island itself, yes. I had the ghosts of other unfortunate ladies to keep me company, and the cape that bears the name of the enchantress Circe is not far away."

"All the ladies who perished there had a touch of the enchantress about them, to be sure. Pity she did not save them," said Messalina. "But we must celebrate your rescue!" She clapped her hands and a slave appeared with a tray of gold goblets. "Only the finest wine, diluted with melted snow."

She clapped her hands again and a nurse brought in the two children. They were bigger now—Tiberius Claudius was walking, although unsteadily, and Octavia was taller and looked more solemn. "My darlings," said Messalina, shepherding them toward Claudius. "And here are your dear cousins—Agrippina and Lucius. Do you remember Lucius?"

What a stupid question. They could hardly remember me. But they nodded dutifully.

"We invited you here today so you could be the first to see the honor being bestowed on Tiberius Claudius," said Messalina. "Dear Claudius, show them."

Now it was Claudius's turn to call for an attendant, and his secretary Pallas came in, bearing a rosewood box. "Here you are, Imperator," he said, handing the box to Claudius.

Claudius flipped the lid off and took out a shiny new coin. "I am issuing a sestertius in Tiberius Claudius's honor," he said, holding it up. "I name him here 'Spes Augusta.'"

"'The hope of the imperial family,'" said Messalina. "He will carry on our line."

The object of this honor paid no attention and stumbled against a stool. Everyone laughed. "What an adorable child," said Mother.

I had found the time only boring; I was disappointed not to hear cithara music again or be invited to the Circus. It had grown hot in the room as the sun reached the middle of the sky, and I was glad to leave. But we were scarcely out of earshot on the path back to our house when Mother let loose a stream of venom.

"'The hope of the imperial family,'" she hissed. "We shall see about that! We shall see! There have been many 'hopes of the imperial family,' but none succeeded to the purple. That baby will have to live a charmed life."

"I am sure they will take good care of him," I said, eager to change the subject. "Do you think Great-Uncle will let me watch the Circus from his balcony someday?"

"If he does, do not stand too close to the edge," she muttered. "Not if Messalina is nearby."

•　•　•

We passed the steamy month named for Augustus, then passed his birthday the next month, a date when the cooler weather came in—traditionally ascribed to his benevolence. The breezes that came in our windows were refreshing rather than wilting, and at last we could sleep well, after weeks of tossing and turning on damp sheets.

Lying in my bed I could see the sickle shape of the moon, caught on a spear of cypress tree outside. A soft wind was caressing me, passing over the bed. I had had a good lesson that day with Anicetus, learning about Egypt and the pyramids and the Nile, whose source was unknown. Crocodiles . . . there were crocodiles lurking there, in the papyrus marshes . . . I wanted to see a crocodile . . . were they ever brought to Rome?

I was riding on the back of one. It was bumpy and slimy, and it was hard to hold on. It glided through tall reeds. It turned its head to speak to me, showing its teeth. I could not understand its language.

The language . . . someone was whispering. I came awake suddenly. The breeze had fallen; the moon had disappeared. It was utterly still in my room, dark except for one oil lamp in the corner.

Now there was movement. Two shadowy shapes came toward me. I lay rigid, stifling my breath. Closer, closer. One was bending over me, his hands reaching for me. Under my pillow there was a scratching sound, a wriggling, then a scaly thing sliding. It felt like the crocodile. But that was a dream—or was this a dream?

A hiss. A slither. Then the lash of a tail that caught me in the face. I rolled off the bed and saw the men scrambling away, waving their arms, flailing at the apparition. Then they fled, knocking over a lampstand.

At the sound, Mother rushed into the room. "Guards, guards!" she yelled. "Cut off the entrances. Let no one escape!" She turned to me. "Lucius, what happened? Light!" she ordered two slaves who had followed her in.

They brought lamps and held them up over the bed. "Look!" Mother said, holding up a long, crinkled, milky tube. "A snake was here. It scared away those assassins." She stroked the snakeskin. "I will have this made into a protective bracelet that you must wear always. For surely as the gods live, this creature was sent by them to protect you from those intruders."

"But why were they here?" I did not understand.

"To make sure you will never be Spes Augusta. For you have more right to it than anyone else. As long as you live, that is."

Her face was set like flint. "Now the duel is set. But, my lady Messalina, no one has ever bested Agrippina. No one. And no one ever will."

She frightened me more than the men. I knew even then that to be her enemy was to perish—and that being her son would not exempt me.

IX

As soon as it was daylight, slaves came into the room and began gathering things up. They stripped my couch of its linens and blankets, carried out the chest with my clothes, and threw my toys into a basket.

"We leave immediately," said Mother, bustling into the room. "We are not safe here."

"Yes, Mother," was all I could say. I had just begun to get used to the Palatine house, to relish the shaded view out of my window, to anticipate how the light slanted in at different times of day.

"The household gods! The shrine. Don't forget them!" she barked at the slaves.

By noon we were trundling south toward Antium, where Mother's villa lay. The land lay quiet and golden; harvest was almost over. Towering above the trees, graceful and soaring, were the arched stone aqueducts that brought Rome its lifesaving water.

"Don't look so downcast," said Mother. "You will love the villa."

It was growing dark before we pulled up in front of an opulent colonnaded building. As I climbed out of the carriage, I could hear the crash and roar of the sea below a nearby cliff. Slaves threw open the bronze doors, and we entered an imposing vestibule, then an even greater atrium. This was no mere country home; it was more like the imperial residence of Claudius. In fact, it *was* an imperial villa. Many members of the ruling families had stayed here.

"Guards—I want guards stationed all around the villa," said Mother. "And bring us some food!" The slaves scurried off to do her bidding.

We sat alone before a round table of polished marble, with bronze feet shaped like lions' paws. Several oil lamps flickered from the lampstand nearby, and Mother picked at the grapes heaped on the platter the slaves set before us.

"Decent," she said. "Sweet enough."

I was eating them eagerly; I was so hungry and thirsty anything would have seemed delicious. There were cheeses and bread and a bowl of figs and apples; the fruit was sweet and fresh. There were also cold pork slices and pickles.

The room around us felt cavernous. The meager light from the five-lamp lampstand did not reach into the corners of the room, and we were surrounded by gloom. Only one side of Mother's face was illuminated, making her look like an unfinished statue.

"Mother," I said, "I feel like we are in Hades!"

"Whatever do you mean, you odd child?"

"It's chilly and dark and the only light comes from flickering flames," I said. "I always thought that Persephone and Hades sat at a table like this, alone in their black palace, with the flames jumping and glowing around them."

She laughed. She laughed so seldom that it was a surprise to hear it. "At least we have food and you needn't worry that if you eat any of it you can never leave. Poor Persephone—if I were to barter my future, it would not be for mean little pomegranate seeds."

"What would you barter it for?"

She looked thoughtful. "An astrologer gave me that choice once, so I know my price. Sometime I will tell you of my decision. But now I must speak of other things. We have come here to escape Rome. After what happened last night, we are not safe there, not until we have a powerful protector. I can get one, but it may take time. In the meantime, there is this beautiful villa. I will give you the room, the very room, in which you were born." She put down the grape cluster and took a drink from her wine goblet. "Let me tell you of your birth." Her face grew dreamy, her voice faraway. "You were born feetfirst," she said. "It was a difficult birth and a bad omen. But the rest was favorable—more than favorable—blessed. It was just dawn, and although no ray of sun had yet fallen into the room, as you were held up, a glow surrounded you. The sunlight struck you and bathed you in gold. It was an omen, a miraculous sign, that the sun touched you before it touched the earth. I knew then that your destiny was the highest there could be."

I was holding my breath. It was like one of those legends that Anicetus told, from a world filled with divine signs and prophecies and omens. But . . . perhaps we only imagine them in our own world, or try to fit them into a story we have heard.

I had not had any such signs—or had I? What of the snake the night before?

"First I must grow up," I said.

"Yes. That is our first duty—to make sure of that." Speaking as softly as she was, the sound echoed feebly and died away in the dark corners of the room.

The bright morning light stole into my sleeping chamber, setting the night to flight and banishing the image of Hades and the underworld. In the daylight the room was cheerful and colorful. Before long Mother sought me out and took me through the rooms where we would be living. There were many more, closed and shuttered, beyond what we would need for now. She ushered me into a spacious, light-filled room with a balcony that faced east. "This room is yours, Lucius. It is where you first came into this world, and it is where you will live now."

Should I have some secret recognition of it? "I will be happy here," I promised her.

"Yes, Lucius. Be happy. Happiness has not been the lot of our family up until now, but for you it can all be different." She moved softly to me and put her arms around me; she caressed my face, stroking me as if I were a kitten. "Dear, dear Lucius," she murmured, her eyes closed. I found it reassuring, comforting. I truly had a protector. But at the same time I wanted to wriggle away. The reassuring feelings were tinctured with something dark and I pushed them away.

Anicetus and Beryllus arrived a few days later, along with more household slaves. Household goods were not needed, as this villa was so stocked and adorned it put the Palatine house to shame. I roamed the rooms, coming upon one sublime statue after another. On the wide terrace facing the sea was a depiction of struggling men entangled in the coils of a giant serpent.

I stood in front of it trying to trace the twinings of the coils. The man was straining with all his power but was unable to free himself, and the two younger men were caught and helpless.

"Magnificent, isn't it?" said Mother. "We stole it from the Greeks. Well, not really *stole*—but borrowed, shall we say? It is a Roman marble copy of a Greek bronze. What I'd give for the original! It's probably in Delphi."

"Who is it?"

"It's Laocoön, the high priest of Poseidon in Troy, and his sons. They tried to warn the Trojans not to take the horse into the city, but Athena sent sea serpents to strangle them and silence their warning."

Why didn't Poseidon protect his priest? I didn't like Poseidon. But I would never voice this aloud, since I might have to travel on his sea. Outside, I could hear the sounds of his realm, the crashing waves. Later that day I explored the cliff above the sea but did not dare try the path leading down to it. It stretched out to an empty horizon, but Anicetus had told me that if I were a bird I could fly directly to the island of Sardinia. And that if I wanted to fly a bit to the left I would come very soon to the small island where my mother had been exiled.

"Not much to see there," he said. "Very bare. No natural springs for water. A fine natural prison."

I never wanted to behold it. I changed the subject. "Is there a temple in Antium?"

"Oh, yes, a very big one, to the goddess of fortune. There's even an oracle associated with it. Not as famous a one as the sibyl at Cumae or Delphi, but much more convenient, I daresay. There's also a shrine at the place where the son of Aeneas, Ascanius, landed once."

"I want to go there!" I said.

"I'll ask permission to take you—if you finish your studies today and tomorrow without fidgeting."

Although I am prone to restlessness, I kept it in check while I listened with what I hoped were wide eyes to Anicetus explaining about the monumental historical work by Livy, which in reality I found very dull. But there was a prize to be had at the end of it, one I wanted. And so I endured the recitation of *Ab Urbe Condita Libri—Books from the Foundation of the City*.

True to his word, Anicetus took me into Antium, which was a tiny town compared to Rome. Nonetheless, the temple would have been worthy of any city. The thick pillars encircling the sanctuary on its platform were of golden stone. Throngs of people were gathered around it, some worshipping and others simply selling goods from stalls. Many specialized in offerings for the goddess, flowers and sweet incense.

"Here!" one aggressive vendor called, waving a bunch of narcissus and violets. "Her favorites!"

Anicetus bought one, saying we needed something to offer her, but we must save our coins for the oracle. The statue of the goddess of fortune was to be pulled out of the dim sanctuary, where one of her acolytes would bring out a little box with wooden tokens in it. One by one the people seeking the goddess's pronouncement on their fate would take a token and read her prediction.

"This is not the goddess of blind chance, or of cruel randomness, but of the hidden will of fate, which is a fixed thing. It is hard to explain the difference, but it is there."

"Is my fate already fixed, then?" I asked. "And whatever I do, I cannot alter it?"

"That is what some say," he said. "But the gods are notorious for changing their minds."

We shuffled up, waiting our turn. I saw people staring at us; word must have gotten out that Mother was back in Antium. But I did not want to be associated with her; I wanted to be invisible, seeking the oracle on my own.

The man just ahead of us received his token and scurried away to read it in private. Now I faced the stern visage of the goddess on her pedestal. Was that truly what fate looked like? No softness, no yielding, no mercy? Anicetus gently tapped my back; I should move forward to the little chest.

It lay on a wooden table, its lid open. It was not large; even my child's hand did not have much room inside it. I plunged my fingers down and felt the slippery wooden tokens inside. They made a dull clacking as I touched first one, then another. Was whichever one I chose also fixed, so that my fingers would go there of their own accord? They closed around one and I withdrew it. Then I turned away, leaving my place to the next suppliant.

Clutching the token, I led Anicetus to a shady place beyond the vendors. Once we had stopped, I opened my sweaty palm to see Greek writing on the token. I still could not read, either Latin or Greek, so silently I handed it to Anicetus to read and translate.

His brows furrowed. Was it something dire? Oh, why did I take that one? Why not the one next to it instead? Oh, why, why?

He gave a crooked smile. "Well, this is a puzzle. It says, 'There is no respect for hidden music.'" He shook his head. "The oracle is obscure today. But she is known for that. So, little Lucius, you must make of that what you will. Interpret it as best you can. As for me, I can make no sense of it."

After that we visited the shrine set up on the seashore to Ascanius, my ancestor. There was a little cove beyond the rocks; the sea pounded them but even at high tide did not reach the statue of Ascanius, looking noble. Was it because he was grandson to a goddess? I should have felt stirred by this tribute, but all I could think of was the saying on the token, which felt as if it was burning in my palm. *There is no respect for hidden music.* Whatever it meant, my life would be governed by it.

X

The idyllic days rolled on; even in winter the villa was beautiful; sometimes spray from the sea carried as far as the windows facing the cliff if the wind was stiff enough, coating us with a fine salty mist. My lessons continued and I fancied I could feel my head expanding with everything I was learning, like a melon swelling on a vine. They taught me the letters of the Latin alphabet until I could shout them out in order upon command. That being mastered, I then was taught to form the letters—a step on the way to being able to write and then, finally, to read. They gave me a wooden board with the letters incised into it, so I could practice tracing their shapes.

"No, no, Master Lucius!" Beryllus grabbed the stylus out of my left hand, switching it to my right. "Use this hand!"

"But it is not as comfortable," I said.

"The right hand is the correct one," he insisted.

I didn't like using it; it was awkward for me. But when Anicetus agreed with Beryllus, I gave in. "Normal people use the right hand," he said. "Let no one say you are not normal in every way! Switch the bracelet to your left wrist so you can write more easily with the right hand."

I pulled off my gold spiral bracelet and moved it over; inside, protected by a crystal, was the snakeskin from the creature who had frightened off the intruders. True to her word, Mother had commissioned a bracelet of it and made me wear it, to remind myself of the miraculous delivery from harm.

"When you master this, you will start on the wax tablets."

"And then we will begin to teach you to read."

Read! It seemed a reasonable bargain in exchange for forcing myself to use my right hand.

By the time it felt natural to draw and form letters with the right hand, spring had come to the villa. A sweet warmth touched the gardens, coaxing them to put forth tiny new green leaves on all the shrubs. The earthy tang of fertilizer rode the breezes as gardeners spread it around roots and plant beds. That anything so foul could give rise to the perfume of flowers was a great mystery. I liked to stroll through the gardens, asking questions about what would grow here and when it would bloom. The gardeners were very patient with my questions, telling me where some of the plants had come from and superstitions connected with them.

"The yew, here"—one gardener said, nodding toward a hedge—"is used by the Furies. It has a poison inside the needles. And yarrow is what Achilles used to heal wounds." He pointed to the newly sprung stalks. "We still use it for that. Crocus, violet, iris, hyacinth, narcissus, and rose are sacred to Persephone, because that is what she was gathering when Hades grabbed her."

He gestured toward the bushes, not yet ready to bloom. "The king of flowers is the rose, of course," he said. "But to be honest, they grow best in Alexandria. That is why they are imported here by the shipload."

There was a scuffling and scratching from the base of one of the rosebushes, and he exclaimed, "So he's up! Now we can know that winter is truly gone." He bent down and picked up a large tortoise with handsome yellow and black markings. "Have you had a good winter's nap?" He rotated the creature, turning him to face me, then tilted him to show

PATER PATRIAE carved on his underside. "He's an old fellow, been here, so they say, since the days of the great Augustus. It was when Augustus was staying here that a commission from the Senate offered him the title Father of His Country. So perhaps Pater here was marked to commemorate that day."

Augustus again! Was there no escape from him, even here? Would his shade dog my footsteps no matter where I went?

I dutifully patted the animal's scaly head and hurried back to the house.

Inside, the filmy silk curtains had been drawn back to allow the spring sun into the rooms. I heard voices from the large chamber that overlooked the sea, but I gave them no mind, until Mother's voice rang out.

"Lucius! I can tell your footsteps from a thousand others. Do not sneak past, but attend me in here."

I crept into the high-ceilinged room to see Mother, dressed in her best, ears weighted with jewels, likewise her neck, standing beside a tall, gray-haired man. He turned to see me and smiled, setting down a goblet.

"This is my precious son, Lucius Domitius Ahenobarbus," said Mother. Her tone was sweeter and more unctuous than I had ever heard it. She must be up to something. "In taking me to wife, you will be taking him into your heart."

The man came forward and took my hand. "It will be an honor," he said. His eyes were a warm brown and kindly. But he was old!

"What do you mean?" I asked Mother. "Who is this?"

"Do not be rude!" She turned to the man, ignoring me. "Crispus, you must not think I have not taught him manners."

"I am sure it is a shock," said the man. "A stranger is suddenly dropped into his life." Now it was Mother who was ignored while the man spoke to me. "I understand that, and I do not expect you to let me take your father's place. But in time I hope we can be friends."

I did not know what to say, so I only nodded.

"This is Gaius Sallustius Crispus Passienus," said Mother proudly. "A consul ten years before you were born, a senator, an adviser to Caligula and now Claudius. A very important man!" She hooked her arm through his and looked up at him adoringly. To his credit, he did not blush or simper, merely patted her hand. "We will be married in a fortnight. He has come down to meet you and for us to spend time together away from the eyes and spies of Rome."

"One is never away from the spies of Rome," he said, casting a glance at one of the slaves standing duty. "But what fun would it be without them?"

I decided then that I liked him.

They were married quickly, with the blessing of Claudius, who had ordered Crispus to divorce his wife so he could marry Mother. I was startled to learn that he could be ordered to do such a thing and comply happily—or seemingly happily. Within just a few months, he was appointed proconsul for Asia and sent to Ephesus; Mother announced her intention to join him there. She seemed girlishly giddy to be going far away, barking out orders for her trunks and traveling cloaks. I was torn between wanting to see the east with her and having the freedom of being here without her.

"Can I go?" I asked wistfully as I watched her sorting through her toiletries to choose what to take.

I expected her to keep sorting without looking up, but she stopped and looked hard at me. "Why would you want to, little one?"

"I have heard tales of it," I said. "Anicetus and Beryllus tell me of the Temple of Diana there, one of the seven wonders of the world. And there is another of the wonders nearby, the Mausoleum of Halicarnassus."

"Are you especially devoted to Diana?" she asked. "And to mausoleums?"

"No, but I want to see the biggest and best of anything; the temple is the biggest, and the mausoleum is the best."

"We have a famous mausoleum in Rome."

"Augustus's? It is not beautiful as Anicetus says the Halicarnassus one is."

"Anicetus! I wonder what he is teaching you." She frowned as if she were remembering something. "I would not let you set foot in the east," she said, "no matter how many temples and mausoleums there are. My father died there under mysterious circumstances. Our ancestor Antony came to ruin there, and died by his own hand. It is dangerous to venture there. It corrupts the brain."

I looked at her heaps of jewels and cosmetics being readied for the journey. "Then why are you going?"

"To protect Crispus. I do not want anything to befall him, far from Rome with no witnesses."

"You care for him, then?"

She got up from her stool and came over to me. "Of course I do," she said, as if there was no question of it. Then she knelt down and embraced me. "But not as I care for you, and you care for me. No one, no husband, can come between us. Never." She began stroking my hair in that way I found both exciting and repellent, and kissing my cheek. "I have done it all for you," she whispered fiercely. "Marrying him. Going to Ephesus now to safeguard him."

I wriggled out of her disturbing embrace.

"We needed a protector, Lucius. A man, a wealthy and powerful man, to keep enemies at bay." She touched the gold bracelet. "Never forget. You and I are surrounded by danger. But Crispus makes us a sturdy fence."

After she departed, I felt a great sense of both freedom and unease. I had not realized how much of a presence she had had even when she was not actually in a room, and being suddenly relieved of its brooding weight made the days lighter. At the same time, her talk of danger made me skittish. If she thought I stood in danger, why had she left? And why had she not appointed some weathered soldier to guard me at all times? Instead, the open villa seemed to invite trespassers. Before long, a message came from Mother while she waited in Brundisium for a ship to Ephesus—that I should move to Crispus's villa on the other side of the Tiber, where it would be better guarded. She must have had the same thoughts I did. So back to Rome I went.

It was not Rome proper, but an area across the Tiber where many gardens and villas lay, as it had more open spaces.

If I were writing this as a history I could not say, "These were the happiest days of my life," because I would instantly be countered by the retort, "Surely being emperor gave you happy days beyond those available to ordinary men." But I would counter that the only things unavailable to an emperor are the pleasures and freedoms of an ordinary man—or boy. And the days I spent at Crispus's villa, with little supervision, are sacred memories to me.

Mother was gone. Crispus was gone. Even Claudius was gone, attacking Britain. I had only Anicetus and Beryllus to mind me, and Rufus, a legionary soldier, to guard me. I still needed a guard against the possible machinations of Messalina. But Rufus was unobtrusive and, best of all, nonjudgmental. He never said, "Master Lucius, you don't want to be doing that," or "That is inadvisable," or "I shall have to report that to the lady Agrippina." No, he looked the other way and stayed discreetly in the background while I roamed the Janiculum Hill and its shady, leafy gardens, floated toy boats from the muddy banks of the rushing Tiber, climbed overhanging branches and swung back onto the shore, dropping into the rushes. Caesar's old villa and its grounds were near Crispus's and I liked to wander there, thinking about Caesar and the days Cleopatra lived there with him, scandalizing Rome. He had given his gardens to the people of Rome, and those who had condemned him were happy enough to stroll on his grounds and enjoy the spoils: a lesson here?

Farther up along the banks of the river were the huge villa and gardens of my grandmother Agrippina the Elder, inherited by Caligula. He had built a private racetrack there, set with an obelisk imported from Egypt, where he held chariot races. It was still in use by special permission; teams not well-known competed there rather than at the Circus Maximus. The crowds were smaller and the charioteers less expert, but for me it was bliss. My reward for doing well at lessons was always the same: an excursion to the races. Anicetus enjoyed them as much as I, so I never had to worry that he would tire of taking me.

For years I had played with toy chariots, had seen wall paintings of chariot races, but the real thing was beyond my imagining. The parade of drivers in their chariots slowly circling the course, warming up, the dust rising behind them, the spokes of their wheels glinting; the snorting and prancing of the horses, sometimes all the same color, other times a mixed team; the shouts and cheers of the crowds. Then they would take their places at the starting gates, awaiting the signal to begin, impatient and twitching and pawing the ground. And in an instant they were off, moving so fast it was hard to distinguish one from another. By the time they got to the first turn they had begun to separate, and usually at that first turn, one would smash against the wall, or against another chariot, causing them to careen off the course. I could hardly breathe when that first turn came, but then came the next turns, each more dangerous. Only when the race was over and I was dizzy did I realize I had cheated myself of air.

Sometimes the racers had two horses, other times four. Anicetus told me rarely there were six and that he had heard someone once raced with seven, although he wondered where the seventh horse was attached.

There were other exercise grounds nearby, too, where men could compete in contests not popular in Rome. We would stroll over to them and watch the athletes wrestling, running, and boxing, in a small arena with special fine sand from Alexandria. Here there were no cheering crowds, no money changing hands, no betting or attention. These competed for the sheer challenge and joy of the sport itself, and they seemed different from the popular charioteers. Anicetus and I would sit comfortably and watch, Rufus leaning against a pillar in the background. I was taken with the skill of the athletes and their beautiful bodies. What a pity that they had so small an audience and so little appreciation.

"That is here in Rome," said Anicetus. "In Greece it is different. They are revered there, and the national games—the Panhellenic Games—have the same excitement as the chariot races and gladiators do here. Boys train for them from about—well, your age. Their dream is to go to Olympia or Nemea or Isthmia or Delphi, compete there, win crowns."

"Crowns? A kingdom?"

Anicetus laughed. "No. Perishable crowns of leaves. Olive for Olympia, wild celery for Nemea, pine for Isthmia, laurel for Delphi. They wear them only for a day." He paused, looking carefully at my expression. "But that's just the beginning. Winners are honored in their hometowns all the rest of their lives—they even get free dinners—and with a statue where they competed. On their tombstones they turn their wilted leaf crowns into stone by having them carved there. The highest honor is to have won all four contests, and then you have all the crowns carved on the tombstone. They call such a winner a *periodonikes*, a circuit winner. It is very difficult to do this."

"What do they have at these games, besides racing?" It was obvious there would be races. And wrestling.

"There's boxing, and javelin and discus, and long jump. In various combinations, and even chariot and horse racing. But besides that, at Delphi there are poetry, drama, and music contests, all sacred to Apollo."

I found myself trembling, so eager to see such a thing, a wish from half-formed dreams of what I loved and what excited me. All together! Not only the body, but the mind! "I want to compete someday," I said. "I want to, I must!" I wanted to leap up and join the men on the sand right then.

"I am sorry to say, you are not eligible," said Anicetus.

"Of course I am not eligible now—I am not old enough, I would lose!"

"You are not Greek," he said. "You must be Greek to compete. Sorry, dear Lucius."

An older spectator, dressed only in a tunic and sandals, edged his way toward us. He hesitated, then spoke to Anicetus. I was pouting in disappointment and barely noticed him.

"Please forgive me," he said. "I could not help overhearing you. I am a trainer—I train Romans now—but once I was *periodonikes* and I can explain more about the games, if the lad wants to hear."

I jerked my head around and stared at him. He was not a large man, but he was wiry, and even though his face was lined, he moved with the ease of a big cat.

"It doesn't matter," I muttered. "I cannot compete in them."

"But you can follow them; you could even sponsor an athlete in Greece. It is very expensive to train and then travel to the competition sites. Some very gifted athletes never have the chance to compete because they cannot afford it." His voice was gentle, persuasive. "Besides, in a few years' time, who knows? The rules may change. You could train hoping that will be the case. If it isn't, you would have done something valuable for yourself. Honestly, the Romans—they simply don't understand sports. They just want to watch, not participate: Watch the races. Watch the gladiators. Do nothing themselves!" He gestured toward the competitors. "Of course, there are still a few, and I am in demand for training them. But I would be honored to have you, such a young one, with no bad techniques yet to untrain, as a pupil—what is your name?"

"Marcus," I said. I did not want to give my real name. I didn't want either fear or fawning. "And this is my tutor, Anicetus. A fellow Greek."

Immediately they started speaking Greek, which I could just barely follow, knowing only a few words. Anicetus was animated in a way I seldom saw him, discovering his countryman. Finally they quieted down and Anicetus said to me, "Would you like to train in the Greek sports?"

He had to ask? "Yes, yes!"

"Then Apollonius here will train you. Twice a week? After our reading lesson? Here? What should he bring, Apollonius?"

"A tunic he does not mind dirtying, that's all. We have the oil and strigils here. A headband if he sweats a lot and wants to keep it out of his eyes."

"Agreed!" Anicetus said.

We fairly danced home. I would say that was the happiest of all the happy days of my youth, happier even than when I actually trained with Apollonius. For the event is never equal to the anticipation, and I was so pumped full of anticipation I could have floated.

laudius was back. He had followed his victorious army across the sea and into Britain, claiming it for Rome. It is true that almost a hundred years ago, Caesar invaded Britain, likewise claiming it for Rome, but he had not set up anything permanent there.

Upon his return, Claudius told tales of fierce warriors in the wilds of Britain, with matted hair, painted faces, and ugly rites of human sacrifice, which the people of Rome loved to hear. In spite of the fact that he was there only sixteen days, and his generals had done all the fighting, he was granted a Triumph to celebrate his victory in his military venture, and I was invited to join his family in the imperial box. If Mother had been here, I would have had to go, but as it was my tutors could beg off, saying I was too young to truly appreciate it or to endure the lengthy ceremony. Of course, that did not stop us going to watch it ourselves, standing with the crowds, seeing it as they saw it.

A Triumph has a very set and traditional route: it begins outside the old walls of Rome and then winds its way through the Forum and finally up to the Temple of Jupiter on the Capitoline—about three miles. Booty and spoils are displayed for a few days beforehand in the Campus Martius; we went to look them over.

The Campus Martius was an open field west of the Forum long ago, where soldiers drilled and children played games; but now it was filled with civic buildings, temples, theaters, and baths. It still felt more spacious and airy than the crowded Forum and houses in central Rome. Strolling about in it was a pleasure rather than a fight to make one's way.

We found the flat, paved square where the war prizes were being displayed on stands and tables, guarded by fierce-looking soldiers. To my disappointment, there was little to see. There were stacks of hides, oblong ingots of tin, piles of rough yellowish stones, bowls of tiny pearls, and, snarling in cages, enormous dogs. I jumped back from one when I saw foam dripping down between the bars.

"What is *this*?" asked Anicetus, likewise pulling back.

"The broad-mouthed war dog from Britain," the soldier said. "Very precious. Much better at fighting than the Greek Molossian."

I edged up closer. The dog had retreated into the shadow of the cage and I could see nothing but the white bared teeth and hear a low growl like distant thunder.

"They will be in great demand here in Rome," he said.

Anicetus gestured toward the display tables. "Where is the rest of the treasure?"

"This is all there is. There is not much of any worth in Britain. Just territory."

"I gather the yellow lumps are amber?"

"Yes, good but unpolished. But the pearls over there are a disappointment—small and dull of color. And, oh, are you in the market for slaves? The people make lovely slaves. There's a tent of them over there"—he pointed—"filled with the most beautiful blond children. Really, sir, you should see it! I think they will be sold for a bargain after the Triumph. But first they will have to march in it. We have to have *something* to show, after all the expense of going there."

We wandered around the grounds, peeking in the tents, fingering the meager goods on display, and listening to the blunt comments of our fellow visitors.

"Waste of money!" a fat man muttered. "What was the point of bothering with it?"

"It's the first new province in ages," said his wife.

"Hardly worthy of the name," he said. "We ought to name it Ridiculania."

They meandered off, after glancing at the slave children. "We don't need any more, Quintus!" said his wife. "They look appealing on the stand, but once you get them home—"

Two men in tunics were fingering the hides. "Greasy and stiff," one said.

"I like the color," his companion said. "It won't show the wear."

"Neither does an old goatskin."

"This stinks worse than a goatskin." He dropped it back onto the table. "Is our emperor going to load these on carts and parade them around?" He laughed heartily.

"What did you expect? Cleopatra?"

"Don't they have a queen there? I thought they did."

"Yes, I heard something about one. I guess we didn't capture her."

"Or maybe she stank worse than the hide! So no general wanted to get near her."

"Ignorant fools!" whispered Anicetus. "Listen well, Lucius. These are the famous 'people of Rome.' They know little and care less, as long as there are free amusements and food."

We looked in the tent with the British children, some almost adult. Their coloring was what stood out in the dim light—many had golden hair and eyes like the sky in October; a few had rusty red hair instead.

I tugged at Anicetus's cloak. "Do you think Helen had such hair?" I said.

"Homer does not tell us what color her hair was," Anicetus said. "But perhaps he did not know. Since she was the daughter of a god, I imagine her hair must have been like gold."

"We wouldn't need an extra slave, would we?"

Anicetus laughed. "I suppose we could buy one, but it is like getting a puppy. It has to fit into the household and be trained. From the looks of these, they are quite wild and would take a lot of work." Seeing my disappointment, he said, "There are sure to be some on sale after the Triumph, and Claudius may reserve a few for us."

The day of the Triumph was clear and fine. We hurried across the river to take our places in the Forum early enough to get a good view. Anicetus said it was best to position ourselves near the end of the processional route; that allowed us the widest perspective. Festive garlands draping the buildings ruffled in the slight breeze. We found a place where no one could block my view; I could hardly wait to be taller and not have to worry about such things.

We stood on the Via Sacra right in front of the House of the Vestals; the way narrowed here and that would give us a close look at the parade as it passed. It was slowly making its way through the Triumphal arch just outside the Campus Martius, skirting the Tiber, inside the Circus Maximus, making one circuit of it, then to the Via Sacra, and finally to us. We could guess its progress by the roar of the crowd. First it was far away, then it grew louder and louder, and then the first of the procession burst into view. Ranks of toga-clad senators and magistrates marched abreast, followed by trumpeters, their horns blaring. Rumbling behind them were the carts laden with the spoils of the war, such as they were, along with paintings of various battles Claudius had supposedly fought in.

"Of course, he wasn't there at all," said Anicetus. "But that's the privilege of artists, to put in what isn't there and to remove what actually was. Or, perhaps I should say, it is the privilege of the emperor to rearrange the truth."

I watched the canvases swaying as they passed, showing Claudius clad in battle gear, vanquishing quavering barbarians, with eleven kings kneeling before him in submission. Someone behind me laughed. Then another, until the whole section was giggling and guffawing. A soldier turned a stony look at us.

"Claudius has come to believe it, so I hear," said a low voice nearby.

"He has changed the name of the Roman colony there to the 'Colony of the Conquering Claudius.'" More stifled laughter.

The miserable prisoners marched next, laden down with chains. There was no leader or ruler to parade out, so they made do with captured warriors and their families. The golden heads of some of the children I had seen the day before were visible behind their parents.

"Many years ago Augustus marched the children of Antony and Cleopatra in his Triumph in golden chains," said Anicetus. "They had to walk behind a painting of their mother dying of snakebite. Or so they say. But Augustus did not drop them off at the Tullianum prison to be executed. That would have been unpopular. So he took their hands and let them walk with him up to the sacrifice at Jupiter's temple."

"What happened to them?" I had heard whispers, hints, from Mother, but never the whole story.

"Augustus's long-suffering sister, Octavia, took them into her household and raised them. How jolly that must have been—Antony's brood of half siblings all under one roof. But Augustus, as always, had a deeper plan—to turn them into good Romans by immersing them in a household steeped in Roman virtue."

"Did it work?"

"It seemed to. No one has heard of them, or their descendants, challenging the throne. The girl was married off to another political prisoner, Juba of Mauretania, and lived out her days there. The boys? One died young; the other became a soldier and served in the army of Drusus in Germany. I heard that he lived to a great age. In fact, he might even still be alive, although that would make him—hmmm—in his eighties."

Before I could probe further, a great cry went up. The emperor was approaching, surrounded by lictors in purple tunics, clouds of incense, and musicians piping flutes and strumming harps; the delicate sound wove itself into the incense, a caressing of the senses.

Claudius rode in a special Triumphal chariot, pulled by four horses. He wore a purple toga painted with gold stars, his brow was crowned with laurel, and in his hand he held an ivory scepter with a gold eagle. He looked magnificent, godlike.

"Costumes are magic," said Anicetus. "They can turn anyone into an emperor." He ruffled my hair. "Even you, Lucius."

Then I saw them—Octavia and little Tiberius Claudius standing in the chariot beside their father, smiling and waving. From time to time Claudius picked them up to give them a better view and, holding Tiberius up, exclaimed, "Behold Britannicus! I bestow my new title upon him, my beloved son!"

Anicetus was taken by surprise. "I knew the Senate had named Claudius Britannicus, but I had not heard about this. So Claudius wants the world to know that this is the next emperor—even if he is still learning to talk."

"It's bad luck," I said. "It makes the gods target him. They don't like people being too sure of their future."

"When did you become such an expert on the gods, Lucius?"

"Since I've heard the stories of what they do. You cannot trust them."

He made a mock silencing motion, then clapped his hands over his ears. "Don't let them hear you!"

I lost interest in the gods as I saw Messalina inside a carriage that bumped along behind Claudius, her eyes searching the crowds, her head held high and haughty. I ducked away lest she see me. Coming to Messalina's attention was never good. I stroked the gold bracelet I still wore with the snakeskin inside, protection against her wiles.

More carriages followed, carrying the generals who had actually won Britain.

Then came rank upon rank of the regular army, then white oxen with gold-painted horns, driven by priests. These were to be sacrificed to Jupiter up on the Capitoline Hill, where Claudius would also dedicate trophies of war.

His chariot had stopped at the foot of the steep street leading up the hill. He dismounted and, supported by two men, went up the incline on his knees. By this point I could not see anything, with so many taller heads surrounding me, but I heard the gasps of the crowd and the comments.

"Did he fall?"

"He's so fat and clumsy."

"He'll never get up there at this rate."

"He's imitating Julius Caesar, you blockhead. Caesar went up on his knees to show humility for his victories, not because he couldn't walk!"

Anicetus put his hands on my shoulders. "Let's leave now, before the crowds crush us. It's over."

I was glad to follow him out, sliding between people, always being careful to keep my footing on the uneven stones. The excitement of the occasion was still high, and people looked dazed. It was their escape from the dreariness of everyday, and a reminder that Rome ruled the world, even if they themselves ruled nothing. It was an escape even for the ruler himself, who could put aside his human limitations for one day.

XII

My everyday life, however, continued to be an adventure. I looked forward to my training with Apollonius, all the more so because it was something I had secretly arranged and it had nothing to do with making me into a noble Roman. Instead, the wrestling moves and holds took me back to Greece, back to the land of the gods and the demigods. The running united me with all those who had run in Olympia or Delphi. There was no way to measure the speed of a race once it was over, and so each race stood on its own, forever. I was faster than most boys my age and delighted in crossing the finish line ahead of them. Best of all I liked overtaking them. In the long jump, Apollonius taught me how to swing the weights and propel myself farther. It did not come naturally to me, but with patience I improved.

No one in the training grounds knew who I was. I had taken another name—I called myself Marcus and gave myself a familial name not connected to anyone of importance. No one ever came to watch me, except Anicetus, so people assumed I was an orphan or a ward; in any case, not anyone of importance. I loved the freedom of being nobody. I think all children want this freedom. That does not mean they would be content with it forever.

Apollonius was around forty years old and had been in Rome since he was thirty. He came from the Athens area; his last competition was at Nemea, when he was in his midtwenties. He had competed in the *stadion* and the double *stadion* and won both.

"And that was the most exciting day of my life," he said. "I look back on it and say, 'That day I gave my utmost.' Very few people can say that. Perhaps soldiers in battle, but few others. I can remember the names of all the other contenders, where they were at the start, at the halfway point . . ." He sighed, embarrassed. "Any athlete can do the same. In some parts the race is a blur; in others, as clear as a perfect glass vessel. At the moment of finish, we are as close to gods as we will ever be. Then we fall back to earth . . ."

"To win the *stadion* is to be the champion at any one meet," I said in awe. The *stadion* was the original event at Olympia, a short race that could be run on only two or three breaths. The man who won that could call himself the fastest man in all the world—that day.

"Yes, and a good one to retire on. Younger athletes would surely appear the next cycle. There are always younger ones and faster ones coming up from behind you. Being beaten is something one never gets a taste for. So I was content to watch the games after that; once I was no longer competing, I could observe more keenly what others did right—or wrong. I began to train men, to teach them what I had learned. In running, though, although technique can help—pacing, how to move the arms, how to hold the head—speed is something you are born with. Strength can be bestowed through training regimens, but speed—no one knows the mystery of speed and why one man has it and another not. I see that you have it. Be careful not to squander it."

His words puzzled me. "How could I squander it?"

"By not using it. By neglecting it. Or by hiding from others the gift of having it."

"Outside the competition track, I will have little opportunity to use it." And once it is known who I am, I will have no opportunities at all, I thought.

Instead of arguing, he sympathized. "More's the pity. But attitudes are changing here in Rome. If they were not, I would not be in such demand." He waved his hand toward all his students practicing in the palaestra, the wrestling yard. "Now, about wrestling—you have a gift for that, too, because it relies as much on balance and timing as on actual strength, and like running, those are gifts you are born with—or not. Hercules is the patron of wrestling, Hermes of running. Those two endeavors are from the gods."

But not from the noble Romans, I thought. "The aristocrats of Rome will never taste those delights," I said. "They do not bestir themselves to do anything beyond wallow in the baths. And only soldiers exert themselves or feel sweat on their brows. Romans are so crass."

Apollonius laughed. "The Greeks are not all as noble as you imagine. It is true the four main competitions—Olympia, Nemea, Isthmia, and Delphi—give only a wreath, a palm, and inscribe the name of the winners. But there are hosts of other contests held all over Greece in which money prizes are given, and not just to the winner, but to the others, even down to fifth place. There are many entertainment events, like torch and boat races, and even donkey-cart races. And musical and poetry contests."

"Music contests!"

"Oh, yes. They have trumpet and herald contests, but the most prestigious are the cithara singers. They compete at Delphi but also at many lesser festivals, and at those they earn huge amounts of money!"

"If only we had those at Rome, instead of gladiator and wild-beast shows." The sweet memory of the long-ago cithara player in the palace came back to me.

"Do not berate Rome so," he said. "Nothing can equal the Circus Maximus for chariot racing."

I had yet to see it. I would have to persuade Anicetus to take me, as an invitation from Claudius would obviously never come.

"Enough talk, young Marcus! No more dallying! Now go into the changing room, smear on the oil, and get ready for training! I'd say today we should concentrate on the jump. I have some new brass weights for you . . ."

Τhe days passed in a dreamy mix of athletic training, exploring the lush public gardens around the villa, and wandering by the banks of the Tiber as the wind stirred the rushes growing out of the mud. I thought of the stories of babies put into baskets and sent to their fates, usually because they were the offspring of a god and a mortal, like Romulus and Remus and Perseus. I found myself peering into the tangle of rushes and half expecting to find such a basket, although I told myself those were just myths. Still, I was looking for something miraculous to come into my life.

No one now claimed to be the child of a god, but in many family lineages there were gods. In my own there was Venus, hundreds of years ago. But what would it feel like to be half god, not just a long-ago splinter of one?

There was never anything in the rushes but birds' nests and drifting sticks and leaves. But a miracle came into my life from a different direction.

He is still alive," said Anicetus one day when we finished with our lesson. "I daresay the one thing that will lure you from Apollonius today is a visit to a very old man."

I drummed my fingers. I had been looking forward to practicing the *trachelizein*, the neck hold in wrestling. I was close to mastering it. "An old man?" As if I cared about an old man.

"A very old man. His name is Alexander Helios."

Alexander Helios . . . Alexander Helios . . . I thought hard but came up with nothing. A Greek man, obviously. "An old philosopher?"

"Come now, Lucius, you know more than that!"

Helios . . . "A priest of Apollo?"

"Think *cousin*, dear boy. Think of the many marriages of Marc Antony. He married both Octavia and Cleopatra, besides a couple of other women first. There were children from each—of course there would be, knowing Antony. You descend from Octavia. Alexander descends from—"

I gasped. "The boy in the Triumph? Cleopatra's son?"

"The same. The very same. We were wondering about him, yes? Well, I have found him."

"Where is he?"

"Not absurdly far from here. If we hurry, we can see him this afternoon."

"If he marched in Augustus's Triumph, how old do you think he is now?"

"Old." Anicetus laughed, then finally added, "I would guess mideighties."

I did not dare to ask how Anicetus had found him. It seemed too good to be true, but I knew Anicetus had ways. How fortunate I was to have him for a tutor!

It was a bit of a trudge, going across the Tiber and all the way to the Caelian Hill where he resided, but I would have walked ten times as far. The son of Cleopatra! Someone who had witnessed firsthand all the Roman history that was only that to me, history. To have sailed away from Alexandria, seeing the lighthouse growing ever smaller and vanishing beneath the horizon. To have seen the living Augustus. To have served under Drusus as he pushed across the Rhine into wild German territory.

We reached the gentle hill and began to climb. Large houses lined the street, their painted windowless walls offering no glimpse of what lay inside, slender tops of cypresses betraying private gardens within. Finally, near the summit, Anicetus halted in front of a smaller house that looked out of place among its neighbors.

"Umbrella pine at the corner—house is ocher colored—"

Gingerly he made his way to the door and knocked. A slave answered it and confirmed that this was the house of Alexander Antonius.

Of course! In Rome he would have taken his father's family name. Helios would have been long discarded as foreign.

Anicetus talked, gesturing in his disarming way, and soon the slave was nodding along with him and opened the door for us.

"Please tell the honored master that his cousin seeks to meet him," said Anicetus, as he gripped my shoulders and turned me to face the slave. "This is Lucius Domitius Ahenobarbus, grandson of Antonia the Elder and great-grandson of Antonia the Younger, your master's half sisters." Soon we were standing in the atrium, awaiting the man himself. It was a long wait, and while we stood there I looked around. The house was modest, the decorations spare. This for the son of a queen? But a long-ago queen, a queen who had lost her realm.

"Don't ask too many questions," whispered Anicetus. "Let him do the talking. He might find it tiring, and so we should not tax him."

At last a man appeared at the far end of the atrium, leaning on a slave. He looked thin and delicate, but not weak. As befitted a proper Roman, he had obviously put on a toga to welcome his unknown guests. Approaching us, he nodded and held out his hands.

"Welcome, my cousin," he said, addressing me. Then he turned to Anicetus. "How did you find me? I fancied I had been quite forgotten in Rome. If you ask anyone, I daresay they would tell you I was dead." His voice was not the quavering, reedy rasp I expected but still strong.

"Some did," Anicetus admitted. "But I was persistent."

We adjourned to a private reception room and he ordered refreshments to be brought. "The kind for special guests," he told the slave, with a wink.

Then he settled himself on a couch and looked at me, still standing before him. "Do you like history, boy?" he asked. "And please sit down. Take this stool."

"Yes, sir, I do like history. But being who I am, I cannot escape it, so it is all to the best that I do like it."

"Being who you are? And who is that?"

Anicetus looked at me, indicating, *Tell him what you know, what you have been taught.*

"I have a double dose of Marc Antony, having him for both a great-grandfather and a great-great-grandfather, and a single dose of Augustus, having him for a great-great-grandfather. I have also a dose of the noble Germanicus, and—"

He laughed. "Enough, enough. It is a wonder your blood flows at all—with all those doses I would think it clogged."

"Sometimes it feels that way, sir."

Now the slave appeared with tall goblets filled with fresh juice of the pomegranate, mixed with crushed apples. A tray inlaid with mother-of-pearl followed, heaped with dark-skinned grapes.

"You will have to clear it out. Filter out all those ghosts and keep only that which is you."

"I fear it is impossible to strain out one's ancestors, sir."

He sighed and put his goblet down on the veined marble top of a three-legged table. "Wise beyond your years, then. But make it so that your descendants brag of your blood that flows in their veins. Look forward, not backward."

I felt disappointment seep through me. Did that mean he had erased all the things I was longing to hear about? I sipped my juice and made a study of looking down into it.

"Of course, at my age I can only look backward. But for the longest time I tried not to," he said.

Relief! He was going to share his past!

"Still, Iphicrates had a saying—'My family history begins with me, but yours ends with you.' It's not a bad motto to have," he went on.

"Tell me about Augustus!" I asked. That seemed safest. No one could take umbrage at that, or suspect a trap, or hesitate to speak freely.

"Augustus . . ." He cocked his head and ransacked his memory. He had fine features—a thin nose, high cheekbones, shapely lips. If I squinted, I could make him younger and see what a handsome man he had been. He looked nothing like the bust of the beefy Antony. He must have gotten his features from Cleopatra. It was impossible to tell what color his hair had been, or whether it was curly, straight, thick, or thin. It had vanished into only a few sandy wisps around his ears.

"Augustus . . . I first knew him as an enemy, the man who killed my parents and stole my country and took me as a prisoner and spoil of war to Rome. I was only ten years old then, and although in truth he was quite young himself, he seemed like a monster to me. I did not know what he would do to us—to my sister and brother and me—but I never imagined he would let us live. For months we waited to see what he would do to us, kept guarded in a villa outside Rome." He stopped and helped himself to one of the grapes. Clearly the memory was such a distant one that reliving it was not threatening, and he savored his treat. It seemed rude to interrupt, so I waited.

He resumed. "It was the middle of summer, the hottest time of the year, when we were summoned to be in his Triumph. His henchmen brought out heavy gold chains and weighed us down with them. We were instructed to walk slowly before his chariot. For hours, it seemed, we walked through walls of people staring at us, behind the canvas with the painting of our mother. But there were no jeers for us; there were cheers for Augustus but silence for us. When the procession reached the foot of the Capitoline Hill, I took a deep breath and braced myself. We would now be separated and taken to the dungeon and killed, like all royal prisoners of war paraded in a Triumph."

He was recounting this so calmly. Perhaps the terror of it had worn away, even the memory of the terror.

"I felt our mother and father watching us. I prayed to be strong, not to disgrace them with crying or cowardice. And then—Augustus stepped out of his chariot, came over to us, and took our hands. He had us march up to the Temple of the Capitoline Jupiter with him, help lay his Triumphal laurel crown at his altar. Then he commanded one of his slaves, 'Take them to the house.' He put his hands, his very gentle hands, on my shoulder. 'You have a new home now,' he said."

He reached for another grape and settled himself farther back on the couch. "And that is how we came to live with Octavia, his sister, in a house full of cousins. Our two half sisters were near our age—Antonia the Elder and Selene and I were around ten and Antonia the Younger was eight; little Ptolemy was youngest of all, at six." He took a long drink from his goblet. "So the five of us became close. Octavia was the kindest stepmother I could have imagined. She welcomed us and never treated us differently even though we must have been a constant reminder of her husband's desertion."

"What were they like, my grandmothers?" I asked. I was descended from both Antonias.

He smiled. "Both admirable in every way, especially Antonia the Younger, who was also comely to look upon. I am sorry that you just missed knowing her. She died just about the time you were born." He looked at Anicetus. "Did you not tell me that he was born the year Caligula became emperor?"

"Indeed he was," confirmed Anicetus. "In December."

"The lady Antonia died in September," said Alexander.

Tactfully he did not say how she died—by her own hand, although some said Caligula had poisoned her. In any case, she had been so disgusted by the degradation she saw around her that she was eager to leave and join her beloved husband Drusus, waiting for her almost fifty years.

"What happened to all of you afterward?" I asked. I knew that Selene had been wed to Juba of Mauretania and become queen there. But the rest?

He related Selene's marriage, then added, "Of all of us, she tried hardest to keep the Ptolemaic dynasty alive. She built a city much like Alexandria, calling it Caesarea, and issued coins with her name of Cleopatra on them. But, in the end, her lineage did not last. There are no descendants of Antony and Cleopatra left. My brother Ptolemy died young and unwed. Augustus married me to a plebian woman, the best way to ensure my family line would cease being aristocratic. But in any case, we had no children. I never sought a place in Roman politics; instead I joined the army and served with Drusus in Germany."

He pulled himself to a sitting position. "I made an honorable name for myself; I served with distinction and had the privilege of being in the army that crossed over the Rhine, although we could not hold the territory beyond it." He laughed. "Even that was a long time ago. When I was sixty, I retired. That was when Tiberius was emperor. Then I faded into obscurity, so that by now you had a hard time finding me."

"You have seen so much," I said in awe.

"Yes, the procession of life that has passed before me is a long one. I saw Augustus grow old and die; likewise with Tiberius; I have outlived all my siblings and cousins. I feel as old as one of the mummies in my native country. I fancy I must look like one, too."

"Oh, no, sir!"

"You flatter me, cousin. But the gift of flattery is not a bad one to have. Well, I have survived and even had a commendable life. I trust my mother, if she is looking, is satisfied with that." He glanced up at the ceiling. "Mother, we cannot all be rulers."

"Tell me of her!" I blurted out. I wanted to hear something personal about her.

He shut his eyes for a moment, and kept silent so long I feared he had gone to sleep. Finally he said, "I remember her voice best of all. It was low and melodic, like a harp."

As he described it, the sound of the cithara floated in my mind. I could hear it once again, clear and divine.

"When she spoke, I wanted to hold my breath. It was that magical." He shook his head. "But something more concrete than that? She was not very tall. She had a pet monkey she was fond of. She was good at figures—she could add sums quickly in her head. She laughed easily, and her laugh was an extension of her extraordinary voice."

Now he fell silent, as if he could not think of anything else to tell me. But I want to know more! I thought. I want to hear everything about her.

"I will give you something to help you picture her," he said, summoning a slave. The man scurried off, then quickly returned with a sandalwood box.

Alexander held it out to me. Inside was a pile of silver coins. "Take one," he said.

I reached in and grasped one. It was a heavy one, and the portrait on it was the lovely profile of Cleopatra.

"This is a tetradrachma from Ascalon," he said. "Made when she was very young, before she met Caesar, before she met Antony. You can see what she looked like then. It is yours."

I clasped it. "Truly?"

"I cannot think of anyone who would treasure it more. Besides myself, of course, and I have others."

"How did you know I would treasure it?"

"Because you sought me out. Because you are the only one who has ever asked me these questions. Everyone else steered clear of the subject, but you embraced it."

Slowly he drew himself to his feet. The visit was over. I saw how tired he looked.

"I apologize for wearying you," I said.

"On the contrary. You have breathed new life into me," he said. "I feel more alive than I have in some time." He put his arm around my shoulders. "Cousin, I am glad to have met you." He opened my palm and pressed down on the coin. "Take good care of her. I surrender her and her dreams and ambitions into your safekeeping."

XIII

Then, suddenly as a cold blast of early winter descending on flowery fields, my idyll of freedom ended.

"Master, they have returned," said Anicetus. "They have docked at Brundisium and will be in Rome in ten days."

Back. Mother was back. Instinctively I pulled my ivory model chariot closer to me. I would have to hide it; I knew she would not approve of such toys. I smiled—or tried to. "I am relieved that they have returned safely. That part of the world has proved deadly for too many—I think especially of Germanicus."

Anicetus's eyes danced. "Alexander the Great? Crassus? The list is long." I noticed that he left Antony and Cleopatra off it.

A sturdy, creaking carriage drew up to the villa and they alighted. Mother was swathed in a palla of piercing colors—yellow, scarlet, and lapis—in intricate patterns of the east. For that one instant she was a stranger, and I saw her beauty as a stranger would. Not only was her face beguiling, but her posture and stance said, "I am *somebody*."

She was looking around as if to ascertain what had changed—for the better or the worse. Crispus stood behind her, not judging, just seemingly joyous to be home again. He looked up and saw me in the window.

"Lucius!" he called. "Come down here at once so we can know we are truly home." Mother was silent. When I came out the door, Crispus swept me up in his arms and said, "Have you kept it safe for us? Yes, I can see that you have!"

After he put me down, Mother came over and bestowed two cool kisses on my cheeks. "Dear son," was all she said before turning to march into the house.

Crispus had been appointed consul for the coming year, so his time had been cut short in Ephesus. Still, it was such an honor that they could hardly regret it. Mother seemed especially pleased—more than Crispus himself—at her upcoming high status. Soon the house was swarming with guests at various entertainments they gave. They dove back into Roman society like a boy eagerly jumping into a summer lake.

It wasn't long until the inevitable invitation came from Claudius to attend him at the palace before proceeding to the gladiatorial games together. I had no interest in going, except to hope that the cithara player would somehow be there among the musicians. I did not care to see Octavia or the newly named "Britannicus," and I especially did not want to see Messalina. But children's wishes count for little, and I was dressed in my boy's purple-banded toga and given many unnecessary instructions about how to act. Anicetus winked at me and said, "Just don't tell Messalina she looks fat. Otherwise you will be fine."

"Is she fat?" I asked. I did not remember her being particularly so. Of course, he was out and about as a free man and had probably seen her in passing lately.

"The life she leads is hardly very healthy," he said. I pestered him to tell me what he meant, but he shook his head.

"Let's just say she does not always watch what she eats." Then he laughed at his incomprehensible (to me) joke.

So now I would have to watch keenly to see what she ate. It gave me something to do. And off we went to the palace, all jostled together in our carriage, until we switched to litters for the climb up the Palatine.

There were effusive and insincere greetings once we arrived. Messalina pretended to welcome Mother and me; I pretended to be pleased to see Britannicus and Octavia; likewise they pretended to be glad to see me. Only Claudius and Crispus were obliviously congenial.

"Savior of the east!" Claudius said, smiling at Crispus, who responded, "Victor of Britain!" to Claudius.

"Ah, we h-have much to celebrate," said Claudius. "When I have such f-faithful stewards as you, I know the empire is well guarded."

Soon we were back in the large reception room I remembered. A subtle perfume filled the air from curved glass bowls heaped high with red and white rose petals. The entire room now had a rosy hue from the filmy silk window covers that dimmed the sun's glare.

Mother spoke first. "We regret not seeing your Triumph, Uncle."

"It was mag-magnificent," he said. "We invited young Lucius to view it with our party, but his tutors said he was too young."

Of course I could not betray that I had seen it all. I merely hung my head sadly.

"I have been thinking of replacing those tutors," Mother said. "They were adequate for an infant, but not for such a young man as my Lucius is growing into."

No! She could not take Anicetus and Beryllus away from me! But the truth was, she could. I was, as always, powerless.

Crispus jumped into the awkward conversation gap. "'Britannicus'! An honorific is no small thing. There have been so few of them—Africanus, Asiaticus, Germanicus, and now—Britannicus! How generous of you to bestow it directly on your heir without wearing it yourself for very long."

At that, the child leapt into the circle and bowed and capered. He reminded me of a monkey. Everyone billed and cooed and the silly thing grinned all the more.

Just then I caught Messalina glaring at me. She had been watching me rather than her son. I gave her a watery smile, thanking the gods that she could not hear my thoughts. I also thought, fleetingly, that she did not look fat, and puzzled about what Anicetus had said.

"I could not w-wait for h-him to have it," said Claudius. "I will enjoy it all the m-more seeing him wear it. Now he truly is 'the hope of the dynasty.'"

"We all await his greatness," said Mother.

Then all thoughts of Britannicus and Messalina were vanquished for me, and I was rewarded for enduring this tedious event.

"My musicians," said Claudius, as three entered the room, and one— oh, praise to the gods!—was the cithara player. He was clearly the main performer, and he was flanked by an aulos player and a panpipe player. They all made obeisance to Claudius and then took their places in a little alcove and began to play.

The sound of the cithara was both piercing and sweet at the same time, like an indescribable joy. It was no wonder I had not been able to reproduce it in my memory, for it was impossible to capture. One could only listen to it, in rapture.

But to my annoyance, the company kept talking. Inane conversation and comments, and the shrieks of Britannicus as he capered around, almost drowned out the divine sound. I ached inside for the musicians, who had to stand heroically through this insult to their art. I wanted to yell and smack the audience. Someday when I was an adult—oh, this joined the list of all the things I longed to do—I would.

I had to fight to hear every note, and when it was over, Claudius merely said, "Th-thank you, Terpnus, for entertaining us." That must be the name of the citharoede. Now I knew it and would never forget it.

"M-my dear," Claudius said to Messalina, "do they perform in any of the plays you have seen? You go so often to the theater."

She swiveled her rather thick neck and looked at Claudius from beneath her eyelashes. "I have not noticed them, if they were there."

"Tell me, Messalina, what plays are you most fond of?" asked Mother.

"I like Plautus and Terence," she replied. "And sometimes Ennius. Why do you ask?"

Mother sighed. "I have been away awhile and need to know what is being performed these days. I suppose, though, it depends more on the actor than on the play—would you not agree?"

Messalina shrugged. "One actor is the same as any other to me."

At that, Crispus laughed, and so did Mother, who said, "How fortunate for them."

Claudius frowned. "What is so f-funny?"

Messalina giggled girlishly. "I have no idea," she said. "Give it no mind, dear husband."

The gladiatorial games we were to attend were the last of the celebrations of Claudius's victory in Britain. I had never attended one, although in our rambles through Rome Anicetus and I had watched crowds pouring into the amphitheater of Taurus, rushing like a restless river downstream into the entrances. Everyone attended the games— broad-faced men in togas, young servants in tunics, old wives and nubile maids, and even the Vestal Virgins, who had their special section. But Anicetus did not like them.

"They are nothing but executions in costume," he said. "In Greece they are not permitted. We are not barbarians."

His prejudice made me curious, and so I was wide-eyed as we entered the amphitheater, which was packed with spectators, all of whom rose and cheered the arrival of their emperor. Handkerchiefs waved and a chorus of song rang out, greeting him. We were escorted to the royal enclosure, which permitted us the best view of the spectacles. Half the audience was in white, as togas were required for the upper classes, all sitting in the same reserved areas. Higher up in the stands the colors were mixed.

I wished someone were there to whisper in my ear what exactly was happening and what it meant. I was seated with the annoying Claudian children, far from Crispus, who would have been the one most likely to have explained things to me. As it was, I was left to puzzle over what I saw before me.

The center of the amphitheater was spread with raked sand. Around one side of the rim of the highest tiers spokes projected; over them a silk awning was spread to shade the spectators. It could be moved or unfurled by long ropes, worked by sailors from the Roman fleet.

Claudius settled himself on the royal couch spread with purple; he himself had put on his imperial toga with gold embroidery, and on his head he wore a gold wreath. Messalina lounged on an adjacent couch weighted with gold and pearls. Another couch beside them seated Crispus and Mother; we children were relegated to a bench in front of the royal one and down one step. The royal enclosure had the comfort of small tables and dainties to eat and drink, with slaves standing by to fan us. Even with the sun's direct rays shielded by our canopy, it was hot, and the tall sides of the amphitheater cut off all breezes.

Beside me Britannicus squirmed and Octavia fidgeted. This was going to be a long afternoon. "Have you attended these before?" I asked Octavia.

"No," she said. "Father was away and Mother never went to them, so I did not have to."

Britannicus was playing with toy gladiators, one dressed like a Thracian and the other like a *hoplomachus*. He moved their arms about and made groaning noises. A slave, on Messalina's orders, shushed him.

Just then I was spared further make-conversation when a commotion down on the arena floor drew all eyes. To the sound of trumpets, a long cortege of effigies was emerging from the door, followed by purple-draped statues of the gods. The effigies were of the late emperors; as they passed, Claudius rose and the crowd cheered, acclaiming the living one. Quickly following was a wagon with the program of fights listed on a large board, then slaves carrying the swords, shields, and helmets of the gladiators. Next came carriages with gladiators, who stepped out and were greeted with a roar of welcome. They then paraded around the arena, raising their arms and whipping the crowd up into raucous cries for action.

Officials brought out a large urn and drew lots to assign fighters their partners. Then they inspected all the weapons, making sure they were in good order. Dull swords were replaced with sharp ones and the helmets and shields were likewise inspected. Now all was ready.

But I was not ready—not ready to see men actually die while I was looking, while the crowd was yelling, while Claudius was calmly eating pine nuts. In the first pair, the crowd demanded one man's death and Claudius agreed. The loser took the stance of kneeling, grasping the knee of the victor, and baring his throat. Without flinching or wincing he remained still while his opponent drove his sword into his neck. Slowly he leaned back, spurting blood, and soon lay in its pool on the sand. The crowd cheered.

Two figures approached. One was dressed like Hermes, his skin painted violet, carrying a red-hot caduceus. He poked the man with it to assure that he was really dead and not just unconscious. Then followed a man in a dark tunic and high black boots, wearing a raptor-beak mask. This was Charon, lord of the dead. He swung a long-handled mallet and smashed the man's head. The underworld had officially claimed him now, and slaves loaded the corpse on a litter and took it out through the door designated for the dead.

Crispus sensed our discomfort and moved as close to us as he could. Leaning over, he whispered, "It is a custom. The man was brave."

"What will happen to him now?" I asked.

Crispus shook his head. "They will attend to the body, remove its armor, and take his blood."

"What?"

"Gladiator blood is highly sought after. They will sell it after the games. People think it is a tonic and a cure for certain illnesses."

How disgusting.

Now the next pair had come out, and Crispus settled back into his seat. These were a net-fighter who used only a net and trident to defend himself, and no armor at all, with an opponent who carried a large shield, a short sword, and wore a conical helmet. The task of the net-man was to entangle the other; but the smooth helmet made it difficult for the net to catch. Against my will I found the different defenses of the men made exciting watching. The man with no helmet and no armor was vulnerable but had freedom of movement, while the encumbered man was more protected. It truly was a test of skill.

In the end the net-man fell, but only after clever fighting and an exhaustive chase. According to custom, he had to kneel and submit to the judgment of the crowd, but the crowd loved him and cried out, "*Mitte!* Free him! Send him back!"

Claudius stood and looked calmly about. Then he turned his thumb down and said, "*Jugula!* Cut his throat!"

He then munched on his pine nuts as the man died, his uncovered face contorting with pain.

After that I only wanted the day to be over. Claudius continued to condemn every net-man who fell, regardless of what the crowd wanted. By the end of the day the sand in the arena was pink, since the blood spilled on it was raked over and over, but finally it was saturated and there was no clean sand to be seen.

In the litter on the way home, I sat rigidly while Mother chattered on. But Crispus noticed my silence and asked me what was troubling me.

"Claudius!" I said. "He was so cruel. He did not even acknowledge what the crowd wished. He ordered so many killed!"

"Only the net-men," said Crispus. "That is because they alone of all the gladiators do not wear helmets, and so Claudius can watch their faces as they die." He took a deep breath. "He likes that."

XIV

Crispus was kept busy with his consular duties, and I found that I missed him when he was not home. He wore his office as easily as he wore his toga, that voluminous garment that had to be draped a certain way and needed a helper to do it. It surely was the most uncomfortable covering ever devised for a man; I envied women who were spared the duty of wearing it. But Crispus never seemed overwhelmed by its folds and yardage and he never seemed ruffled by whatever debates were going on. In the evening, at dinner, he often spoke of the day's deliberations in an amused manner, while imitating some of his shrill colleagues in the Senate.

"They puff and pant like old roosters in a barnyard," he said, taking a sip of his wine while sprawling carelessly on the dining couch. "Such a bluster. Such a dither."

"What exactly were you deliberating today, husband?" asked Mother, picking at her food. I could almost see her ears pricking up.

"Claudius is pushing his Ostia harbor project," he said. "He is, of course, meeting resistance. It is a worthy goal, to improve the facilities for the transport of grain to Rome, so naturally he is criticized for it. Now, if he had decided to make a law dictating only red leashes for dogs, everyone would have applauded."

"Where does Statilius Taurus stand?" Mother asked.

Crispus shrugged. "My fellow consul, as is his nature, tries to float downstream with whichever current buoys him up."

"Sometimes that is the only way," said Mother.

"That depends on what your goal is," said Crispus, reaching for a hard-cooked egg in sour sauce. "To survive, or to achieve?"

"Both," said Mother.

"But discussing the harbor and grain transport can hardly be very captivating to young Lucius here," he said, leaning on his elbows and turning to me. I was pushing my boiled endive and cabbage leaves around on my plate. They were limp and unappetizing. "Is it?"

"I do not lie awake thinking of them," I said, and Crispus laughed.

"So what do you lie awake thinking of?"

I hated to say in front of Mother. "I think of music. I would like to learn to play an instrument."

Mother made a dismissive noise.

"I would also like to practice chariot racing."

"A fine ambition!" said Crispus. "Tomorrow the Senate does not meet, so I shall take you to the Circus Maximus." He held up his hand when Mother made a sour face. "Yes, I will, and as consul of Rome, no one dare forbid me, not even my wife, the highest censor there is. Would you like that?"

"Oh, yes!" I had waited so long for this.

Setting out with Crispus was always an adventure. He said this should be a boys' outing only (Mother pouted) and I asked if Anicetus and Beryllus could come, too. Most consuls would not want to be seen with Greek freedman tutors, but Crispus was different. Most consuls would also want to be surrounded by other high-ranking officials and march into the stadium with them. But not Crispus. We were accompanied only by bundles of food, seat cushions, and sun hats. He gave us all bags of money so we could bet.

"It's my gift. I am celebrating—well, something! There is always something to be celebrated if you look for it." He grinned as he handed us the bags.

There is always something to be celebrated if you look for it seemed a good motto to adopt for life.

"Now, I think it would be only fair, since there are four of us, if we each bet on different teams. That way one of us is sure to win." He looked as eager as a little boy himself and I thought how young he looked, even though he was elderly. He had unruly hair and restless movements and a face that seemed youthful from a distance and only revealed its lines and sags at close range. He must harbor youth somewhere within him, bottled in his inner core like a fire.

I wondered what dictated who stayed young and who did not, and whether I could know in advance which category I would fall into. Was there anything I could do to change it?

After crossing the Tiber, we were still a long way from the Circus when we could hear the hum of a crowd that grew louder and louder the closer we got to the area. First it was the murmur of bees, then the buzz of wasps, then the roar of a waterfall, and finally what I imagined an earthquake would sound like. Then we rounded a corner and suddenly were caught in the midst of the surging crowd. Crispus took one of my hands and Anicetus the other, and we clumsily waded through the people and finally into the stone seats reserved for senators, closest to the track.

Crispus made a show of arranging his toga with its senatorial stripe before being seated. "In case anyone tries to evict us, since this is for senators only, I shall remind them that a consul has special privileges and can bring all the guests he likes. And that one of his guests happens to be a descendant of the divine Augustus. That should shut them up." He looked mischievous as he said this, just loudly enough that everyone around us could hear him.

Because Crispus was who he was, we were able to take seats in the first row, with the best view. He had selected the section at the first turn, near the Triumphal arch, where the most dangerous and demanding stint of the races occurred. Although I had seen the Circus at a far distance from the balcony of the palace, its true size was overwhelming once I was in it. The temple and elaborate roofed royal enclosure was far away on our left, back near the starting line. The Egyptian obelisk Augustus had erected in the middle looked short and stunted against the high banks of seats.

The crowds were filling all the seats now; the noise built to a roar. Beside and behind us, senators and guests were hurriedly staking out their places.

"My esteemed colleague," a raspy voice said over my shoulder. I turned to see a man who looked for all the world like a pig—pink and hairy, with shiny skin.

"Statilius Taurus," said Crispus. "Greetings. Who do you support?"

"The Blues," said the porcine man.

"Lucius, may I introduce my fellow consul?" Crispus said to me. "Statilius, this is Lucius Ahenobarbus, Agrippina's son."

"Agrippina and I are great friends," said Statilius. They were? He nodded at me. "Who are you supporting?"

"The Greens," I said.

"The Reds," said Anicetus.

"The Whites," said Beryllus.

"That way one of you is guaranteed to go home happy," said Statilius.

Trumpets blared—or tried to. The crowd was so loud they could barely be heard. A procession was starting at the far end, much like the one in the arena—images of gods, marching officials, display carts. Then came the chariots! There were twelve of them, three of each color.

"This first race of the day is the most prestigious," said Crispus, speaking directly in my ear, and even then I could barely hear him. "It's traditionally for four-horse chariots."

The chariots made a long, slow circuit of the track, their drivers waving to the tumultuous cheers of their partisans. Each man wore a tunic of the appropriate color so we could distinguish them easily from afar. Finally they entered the starting stalls, and, upon the dropping of a white cloth by the head official, in the box at the starting line, they broke out and the race began.

I had seen the races at Caligula's track and so I knew they had to make seven circuits of the arena—that meant fourteen turns around the turning posts, chariots skidding and trying to force others against the wall. Turn too sharply and the chariot might overturn; turn too slowly and be left behind. Let your opponents get too close to you and you will be forced to either fall back or outrace them in a confined space; see your opponent rounding the turn ahead of you, you could try to overtake him on the outside but that called for extraordinary speed as you would have more ground to cover. I felt myself trembling with suspense as they headed for that first turn, directly across from us. One of the Blues was ahead, followed closely by a Red, and as they approached the turn, the Blue came too close to the post, hit it, and flew through the air, landing in the pathway of oncoming chariots. Some jumped the wreckage, throwing their charioteers out; others went around it. The Red chariot was far in the lead now, due to the pileup. Four slaves rushed out with a litter to remove the driver of the Blues; others grabbed the horses' reins and cleared the track of animals and chariot debris. In the end the Red chariot won, with no more suspense after that first turn. No one could catch him, even if their horses might have been faster on a flat track.

"Why, Lucius, you are shaking," said Crispus, his hands on my shoulders.

Unaware, I had been straining every muscle as I watched; now the tension drained away and I felt limp. "I felt as if I were in a chariot myself," I said.

"You must relax. If you go on this way, we will have to carry *you* out on a litter when the races are over."

Just then a senator arrived, and he tried to sit beside Statilius, but there was no room, so he asked if there was any space by us. We had to push close together but managed to accommodate him. "You've missed the first one, Gaius, although it wasn't exactly gripping," said Crispus.

It wasn't? My heart was still pounding.

"I heard. Crash at the first turn, which pretty much decided all the rest of it." He had a melodious voice and, as I looked more closely, I realized how handsome he was. He had features like the ones Augustus had appropriated for his statues—the real Augustus was not the Alexander-like figure of his coins and portraits. But the memory of the real one was fast disappearing. Thus art triumphed over reality.

"Gaius Silius," said Crispus, "this is my stepson, Lucius Ahenobarbus . . ."

Another race followed, this one dull—the chariots were slow, one of the horses pulled up lame, and the drivers did not show much emotion. Perhaps they were holding back after the casualties of the previous race.

The third race was a fast one, with horses from Africa and Spain, and a Blue winner. The next featured six-horse chariots, which made for a fine show, although there were fewer chariots and overall it was slower.

"The more horses there are," explained Crispus, "the slower the race will be. The combined power is cumulative, but the speed is determined by the slowest horse—the faster ones cannot be added to it."

Before the fourth race, a leathery-faced Praetorian Guard paced in front of our section, greeting the senators by name. He walked stiffly and seemed to have trouble turning his neck.

"Crispus Passienus." He nodded toward us. "Might I ask if you have any extra room?"

He could see for himself we did not. We were already jammed together, so tightly that I could feel each breath Crispus or Anicetus drew. But Crispus said, "Oh, yes."

Why? Did the man wield hidden power? Later I was to learn he was not just a Praetorian Guard, he was prefect—head—of the Praetorians.

"For you, Rufrius Crispinus, there is always room," continued Crispus.

Rufrius laughed. "Not for me. I will be pacing outside the seating area. For my wife." And at his elbow stood a woman beyond mortal beauty.

Her hair was of an amber color, tumbling curls of it. Her skin was luminescent. Her lips, full and curved, were the delicate blush inside a seashell.

Instantly we made room for her. She settled herself next to me.

"Poppaea," he said. "My wife." He had already said that. Did she render even her husband clumsily grasping for words? So one would never be accustomed to the presence of a goddess?

Now I was trembling in earnest. I prayed she would not notice. I steeled myself, told myself to stop.

She was quiet. She said nothing. Was that preferable to speaking? Which would have been more unnerving?

Another race was under way, and blessedly, I could turn my attention to that—or try to.

At the end, she finally spoke. "I am disappointed," she said. "My team did not win."

"Which team do you support?" asked Crispus.

"The Greens."

Oh, the same as me! "I do, too. Perhaps in this next race—"

That afternoon I entered into paradise—gazing straight ahead at the most skilled chariot racers and sleek horses in the empire, and out of the corner of my eyes at a woman who was the personification of beauty. I barely dared to move, lest it all vanish and I find it was only a dream.

Not until we were out of the crowds and well on our way back home did Crispus say, "I need not ask if you enjoyed it, Lucius. Now, do you think you have recovered yet?"

"Yes," I lied, knowing that if recovering meant I would be the same, the answer was no; I would never be the same again after what I had seen. "The horses—" It seemed safest to speak of them.

Crispus explained the differences between those from Africa and those from Spain, saying that the African ones were stronger, the Spanish ones lighter and faster. He then ventured into the people we had met, noting that Gaius Silius was reputed to be "the handsomest man in Rome" but he wore it well, and that Rufrius was known for his old-fashioned manners and was recently married to the young Poppaea, the daughter of another Poppaea, reputedly "the most beautiful woman in Rome."

"The young Poppaea may surpass her mother," said Crispus. "Then what a Greek drama would unfold. It's an old theme—the beautiful mother loses her place to her daughter. I hope no one gets killed!" He was laughing, making light of it.

"I cannot imagine that her mother is more beautiful than she," I said. "Tell me about the family."

"They are from Pompeii; the daughter is fourteen. Her husband, as you saw, is much older."

"Menelaus!" I cried. It all came clear now—I had seen Helen of Troy, and I understood the Trojan War, and young Paris and how he had stolen her from old Menelaus.

Crispus shook his head. "Do not let your imagination run wild," he said. "Rufrius is not Menelaus, and there are no heroes walking the earth who are like those in *The Iliad*; there never were, except in the mind of Homer. If you look for them in those around you, you will forever be disappointed."

XV

Time passed. I grew. I flourished in my schooling—history, rhetoric, oratory, poetry—in my music, and in my athletics. Especially in the latter—as every day passed to make me taller or stronger, I got better.

Apollonius never wavered in his dedication to training me. He faithfully kept all our appointments, and if I could not get away because of sudden demands by Mother, I would manage to get word to him so he would not wait for me.

He had developed an ingenious device for measuring my speed for running events, to see how much I was improving. He had me run my best down the field, while he let water run through a funnel into a bowl. When I crossed the finish line, he stopped the trickle of water and set aside the amount in the bowl, transferring it to a vial. The next time I ran, he would use only that saved water in the funnel—if I finished before it had all run through, then I was faster than the last time. On the other hand, if the water had finished before I did, I was slower. The biggest challenge was keeping the water in a closely stoppered bottle for the next time, making sure none of it evaporated.

Although I was a respectably good runner, I was a better wrestler. Apollonius said that was because my balance was so good and I was blessed with superlative timing.

"Now, if you also had the muscles of a muleteer, you would be as great a wrestler as the legendary Milo of Croton." He laughed.

Milo, many times an Olympic champion, was so spectacular that some believed he had to be the son of Zeus—no mortal could achieve his feats.

"I don't fancy carrying a bull around," I said. Milo was claimed to have carried an adult bull on his shoulders. "But Anicetus told me he was also a musician and a poet, and he studied with Pythagoras. For that, I envy him."

"You are wise," said Apollonius.

"Marcus? Wise?" Crispus had found us. He often came to watch us train, and he kept my secret about my name.

"When it comes to wrestling," I said. "But I admit I know little of the Senate or suchlike."

"Oh, neither do I!" Crispus's tenure as consul was over. But in truth he was still very much a presence in the Senate. Nonetheless, he showed great interest in my athletic training, encouraging it and coming to watch me train and compete in small local meets, without revealing our true relationship. "It is much more interesting to learn about Milo of Croton than about who is voting for what." He turned to Apollonius. "When is the next meet?"

"There is a race at the next full moon. *Stadion*, double *stadion*, wrestling."

Crispus whistled. "Better train harder, then."

He was leaning up against the fence separating the palaestra from the lawn. As I looked at him, I realized he was using the fence for support, and his arms were drooping. "You are working too hard," I said. "You need a rest."

Instead of his usual wide grin, his smile was a wan imitation of it. "You are right," he said. "I am run-down." Trying to make light of it, he said, "No running in the competition for me." As the sun hit his face, I saw with dismay it had a greenish cast.

◆   ◆   ◆

Crispus declined bit by bit. His strength never returned; it ebbed away in spite of the directions Mother gave to his physician and the cooks. After a month he was unable to rise from his bed, and his eyesight began to fail.

Mother was distraught; I was frightened. Crispus could not leave us; he could not desert us! He was my protector, my friend, my teacher. I could not imagine life without him. I also imagined that if I wished it hard enough, I could reverse whatever it was that was eating away at his vitality.

I forgot my lessons; I forgot my training. I did not dare to leave the villa, as if my presence there could prevent any ill fortune. I took to roaming parts I seldom ventured into, shadowy rooms and empty corridors, dank storerooms. It was there, one afternoon, that I saw the figure of a woman bent over a workbench, arranging bottles and vials.

I did not recognize her. If she was a member of the household, she must be new. I stepped into the room. "Hello," I said.

She turned to answer me. Something flitted across my memory. I had seen her before. "Hello," she said cheerfully.

"Are you new?" I asked cautiously.

"I am here to help the lady Agrippina, with the illness of her dear husband."

The voice. The voice. Where had I heard it?

"She called for you?"

"Yes. I am often called to help when physicians have come to the end of their knowledge."

"And is that—is that what is happening here?"

"I fear so. None of my remedies are working. I feel quite helpless."

"He can't die!" It was close to a howl.

She sighed. "He can. And he will."

"No!"

"I have seen too many die before him to mistake it."

"But what is it?"

"I cannot say. It is mysterious. As if his body suddenly said, 'Enough.'"

"Bodies don't do that!" I cried. "Something must be making him die."

"You are young and haven't lived long enough to know. In fact, bodies do decide to die, and we never know why. Only the gods—"

"I curse the gods!"

She looked alarmed. "Don't do that. Never do that."

"Why? What can they do that is worse than this?"

She shook her head. No one had to bend to talk to me now; I was too tall. She looked straight at me. "Now, I know how young you are. But keep your innocence as long as you can. Let them hold their cruelty back so you don't see the full extent of it for a while." She brushed her hair back, and with that movement I almost knew her. Almost. Then it slipped away. "Go upstairs. Be with him. Stay with him till the end. I heard him calling for you once; I know you are a comfort to him."

XVI

LOCUSTA

I was horrified when I turned to see young Lucius standing behind me at my workbench. I had been so careful; usually I had my wares delivered by a slave to Agrippina so I would not be seen on the premises. She had warned me that Lucius was deeply fond of Crispus but she assured me that he would suspect nothing.

"He's a dreamy boy, spends most of his time thinking about the Trojan War, or his athletics, or paintings and music. He doesn't notice much of what goes on in the real world."

But she was wrong. I could sense that he was acutely aware of the world around him, and that he would be devastated by Crispus's death.

I tried to prepare him. I also tried to disguise my voice and keep my face turned away, hoping he would not recognize me. It had been years since I'd met him at Lepida's, and he'd been a small child then, but just looking into those intelligent eyes told me he had stored away the encounter somewhere, and it might awaken in his mind.

I cursed myself that I had needed to prepare something on-site. I should have used something else. This was the second potion, to speed the action of the first. Agrippina had ordered that it be slow acting, so as to look natural. But now he was far enough along that it was time for the finale.

I was surprised when Agrippina had contacted me. After all, they—she and her family—had declined my help to remove Caligula. But I had not shown my disappointment at the time; it would have been unprofessional.

Now my professionalism was taxed again. I wanted to grant Lucius's wish, be like the goddess Atropos, who can decide not to cut the thread of life after all. I could still reverse the effects of the drug. But that would harm my own reputation. A poisoner whose poisons fail to work is a poisoner out of demand.

But what I could do was give my victim a reprieve. Let him recover slightly, enough that Lucius could talk to him, say good-bye, so he would not feel that he had been robbed even of that opportunity.

As for Agrippina, she could just wait a while longer for her desired outcome. She had said that he had outlived his purpose in her life, as well as living way too long anyway. "Sixty years is long enough to do anything you want to do, do you not agree? Anything you have not done by then, you are not *going* to do." She lifted her chin slightly, having passed judgment and pronounced it easily.

"But why now?" I asked. "He is not harming anyone, and he seems to give you your freedom to do whatever you like—at least, that is what I have heard."

"His money and status gave me protection against that whore Messalina and her plots against little Lucius and me, but now that Lucius is older, the danger is past. He's become a pest, an encumbrance. So I'd like to have his money without the bother of his presence."

Her ruthlessness brought out the same in me.

Why, lady, I could easily poison you as well. Remove you from the world. Lucius would be better off under someone else's care, since you do not love him or respect his feelings. Of course I would not do that—unprofessional, and I was hired only to kill Crispus. But I was tempted. She was a loathsome creature.

But a poisoner does not have the luxury of moral choice. We are just instruments, instruments of those who hire us. Ours not to question. Ours not to disobey.

XVII

NERO

I should have rushed, but instead I walked, slowly. I did not want to enter the room and see Crispus in any state but robust health. Somehow I felt if I did not enter the room, then nothing was happening to him, nothing could happen. But my feet took me closer and closer, and then to the threshold.

I peered in. Light poured from the window behind his bed, dazzling me. I blinked and only then did I see the shrunken figure in the bed, the body making a long white mound under the covers. I came closer and moved out of the blinding sunlight. Only then did I really see him.

His eyes were closed, his lips moving slightly as he breathed in and out. Smoking pots of herbs stood in the corners, making a haze in the room, as if a veil had been drawn over him.

Should I wake him? It did not seem right. But to never speak to him again—

He stirred and his swollen eyes opened. "Lucius," he said. I had to bend close to hear him.

"I am here," I said.

"Lucius," he repeated, as if too weak to say more than just that one word. Then, "I did not go to your competition. Did you win?"

The competition . . . it seemed so long ago. I had not won anything but the wrestling. "I did win one thing," I said. "I wish you could have been there." Immediately I wanted to smack myself for saying such an insensitive thing. "But I know you would have been there if you could," I hurried to add.

"You must keep on trying," he said. "Always keep trying."

I wanted to throw myself on my knees and cry out, *Without you, it will be hard to keep trying. You alone of my family cared what I did.* Instead I just said, "Yes, sir."

He struggled to raise himself up on his elbows but lacked the strength. From his supine position he said, softly, "You know I must meet the Boatman soon, although I am not sure I believe in him." A slight smile pulled at his lips. "I hope I recognize him. But he is sure to recognize me. Remember me, Lucius. Remember me, as I will remember you as the son of my old age."

Don't leave me! I wanted to moan. *Don't leave me!* But how selfish could I be? How could I hinder his departure like that? "And I you as the father I had at last." I took his cool hand and squeezed it.

"Let go of his hand," a voice hissed. Mother. "He might have something catching!"

She was standing in the doorway, slender and still. Then she glided over, took my hand out of his, covered his hands with the sheet.

"If he has something catching, then you should not touch him, either," I said. I knew the mysterious illness that was claiming him was not something that would seep into me, and somehow, I knew that she knew it, too.

"I am careless of my life when my dearest husband needs me, but I must preserve yours," she said. She patted his covers tenderly. He looked at her a moment, then closed his eyes again.

"It is time for the afternoon dose," she said, reaching for a small bottle on the nearby table. She poured a bit out into a tiny glass. It looked perfectly clear, like rainwater. A slave came forward and helped raise Crispus up so he could swallow. She poured it slowly into his mouth, which he had obediently opened.

"There, dear one. Rest," she said.

I stumbled out of the room and into the dim hallway, then sank onto a marble bench around the corner. My heart was beating as fast as if I had run a double *stadion*. But at the end of that race, I had entered another world. A world without him.

I do not know how long I sat there. Fright and a detached calmness alternated in me. Finally the waves of emotion smoothed out and I returned to the world. Only then did I notice the low voices in the hall around the corner.

"Three more, I would say."

"How long?" This was Mother's voice.

"Five days? You wanted it to be slow."

"Yes, yes."

"I only did what you requested."

"I know." The voices were getting closer. I just sat there.

Rounding the corner were Mother and the woman I had seen in the basement. They stopped dead when they saw me. Mother recovered first.

"My dear Lucius is as upset as I am," she said. "This is such a blow."

"I know. I spoke to him earlier. It is I who urged him to come upstairs."

"You?" Mother looked surprised. "Locusta, I wish he had not had to see the suffering. That is what I would have spared him."

Locusta. Then it all came back, swimming out of my dark deep sea of memories. The woman at Aunt Lepida's, the woman I had burst in upon when they were all having their secret meeting. Long ago, when Caligula was still alive.

The poisoner! Would she remember me? Would she know I now remembered her? "I—I—I have to go!" I said, rising as slowly and deliberately—no sign of panic, of alarm—as I could. I walked stiffly down the hallway and then, when I was around the next corner, I took off my sandals and ran as fast as I could to get out of sight of them.

Where could I go? I rushed out of the house and into the garden, then put my shoes back on, pulled open the gate, and ran out of the grounds. The river. I would go to the river, hide by the banks. I had to be alone, where Mother could not see me—and I could not see her. The murderess! My mother was a murderess.

The banks of the Tiber were dry, with weeds and thornbushes guarding the waterline. It had been some time since the waters were high and the banks overflowing. The wind was sighing gently, making the dry stalks rustle and murmur. I sank to my knees and started crying, my sobs blending with the kindly sound of the wind.

I was completely alone in the world now. The one person who should have been my protector was a murderess!

I stayed there until it got dark and the air grew chilly. I stayed there until I had got used to the knowledge that had driven me there in panic and despair. I stood up and made my way back to the house, a thousand years older than the boy who'd left it.

XVIII

From that day on I entered into an almost dreamlike state, where I could see what was going on around me but I did not care, or it did not seem real. Crispus's funeral, and the cremation, and the laying of his ashes to rest in his family tomb. Mother pretending to mourn, whispering softly and veiling herself in black. There were athletic competitions, but I did not care if I won or not, and my legs were sluggish. There were lessons with Anicetus and Beryllus, but I did not retain much. I really did not care about chariot racing, so when the long-sought invitation came from Claudius to view the races from the palace, I said I was ill and could not come. Mother was angry with me, but she could not prove I was not ill and I lay listlessly on my bed, never wavering from my story.

It was sweet to float along, caring for nothing, yearning for nothing, feeling nothing. I had reached the state that some philosophers strive for, with no effort on my part: detachment, unswayed by the world beyond me.

But slowly unwanted thoughts crept in, seeping through the barrier of protective blankness I had put up around me. They came at night, when all was quiet except for the sounds of owls in the trees around the villa and the distant rumble of carts through the streets of Rome across the river. At first they came softly, lapping around my sleep. My mother's face began to appear in dreams, coming closer to me, kissing me, then suddenly melting into a skull. I would wake up shaking and covered in a cold sweat.

My mother was a murderess. She had cold-bloodedly killed her husband. Who would be her next victim? Who else might she have killed, that I had not accidently stumbled upon? My father? No, she was far away on her island by then, exiled. Her reach was not that long. But could she have employed that woman, that Locusta?

The thoughts came more boldly, as I lay awake in the darkness. Here was the horrible truth: I came from a family of murderers. Caligula had tried to kill me. Messalina had tried to kill me. It was rumored that Caligula had murdered Tiberius, smothered him with a pillow. There were questions about the death of Germanicus; again, poison was suspected, with Tiberius in back of it.

This blood of murderers was coursing through me. Was a murderer inside me waiting to get out?

"There is no such thing as 'the blood of murderers,'" Anicetus had said, in one of the few lessons I had paid attention to since the death. "That is only in Greek plays."

But I felt I was living in a Greek play. They must have been based on something real. And then the most forbidden of all thoughts came: would she murder me? Immediately I told myself no, no, mothers do not murder their children, but then I remembered Medea. But that was only a legend, a Greek play, not real . . .

Gradually those thoughts lost their grip on me, as every thought will, sooner or later. I learned to live with the knowledge I had; people can get used to anything, even horror, and it begins to feel normal. And the thought that I had inherited the blood of murderers seemed less threatening than that my mother, a proven murderess, might kill *me*. Thus we make peace with ourselves and our weaknesses, for there is always someone worse to focus on.

I grew; birthdays came and went. When I was nine Claudius celebrated the eight hundredth anniversary of Rome's founding by holding a festival of games, the Ludi Saeculares, and one of the events was the

Troy game, a traditional equestrian exhibition for boys too young to be soldiers but old enough to ride. Both Britannicus and I were chosen, and Mother went on and on about it.

"It will be your first public appearance," she said. "We must make sure it is auspicious."

"We?" I asked. "Will you ride along with me, then?"

"Don't be impudent. Just listen. This is the opportunity to show your princely demeanor. Riding and horsemanship were traditionally part of the education of a prince, but now that there are no princes—except you—"

"And Britannicus," I reminded her.

"Yes, Britannicus. But he is only six and will look like the child he is, perched on a horse too big for him."

I shrugged. But I allowed her to dress me any way she pleased, if that would satisfy her. I must satisfy her whenever I could. The game itself was a ritual pageant that required a certain level of horsemanship, which by that time I had attained. It was unfair for poor Britannicus to have to participate at all, and not surprisingly, he did not do well. My performance, however, received thunderous applause. So they told me. I was quite removed in my mind, even while my body executed all the movements.

Mother was gloating, and Messalina was glowering. I knew that Messalina's hatred counted for more than Mother's approval, at least as far as my immediate safety went.

"There was simply no comparison between you," Mother crowed. "You, a fine youth just on the brink of manhood, he, a timid, awkward little child. The crowd knew it; the crowd has chosen you over him."

It was the same crowd that cheered for the Greens one day and the Blues the next. I put no stock in it. I had done my part. It was over. Now I just wanted to steal away back to my room, withdrawing again into my private world.

"Claudius has sent you a token," she said. "Something to remember the games with." She held out a small gold ring with a carved intaglio carnelian. It showed a young man on horseback. "He said he was proud of you."

That was generous of him, I thought. I pushed the ring onto my little finger and surprised myself by hoping very much that it would fit. It did.

"He said it was Germanicus's as a child, and that it belonged with you."

"He is kind," I said. "I shall treasure it."

"Your grandfather would be pleased."

But now I really had to get away. I felt myself about to cry and did not know why.

Life continued in its predictable yet plodding trudge through the year, brisk and rainy spring giving way to dusty dry summer, on to golden autumn and then to stinging sleety winter, and so to my tenth birthday.

"You chose the worst time of the year to be born," Mother complained.

"You are the one who chose that," I reminded her. "I had nothing to do with it. Besides, the weather may be bad but it's the best time of the year otherwise, because right around my birthday it's Saturnalia." I wished it could be Saturnalia all year long, instead of just seven days.

Saturnalia, when they sacrificed at the Temple of Saturn in the Forum, then unbound his statue, thereby symbolically unbinding the cords of custom that confine us, was celebrated just two days after my birthday. For those few days each year, everything was turned upside down. Togas were replaced by loose Greek party dress, slaves traded places with their masters, free speech for all was allowed. Some people disguised themselves and roamed freely; others indulged in gift-giving parties, and drunkenness abounded.

But what intrigued me wasn't the license of drunkenness but a larger license, a license to transcend our borders, to burst out to freedom. I began to see a meaningful connection, a calling, in that it followed so closely upon my own beginning.

"It's a dangerous time," my mother said. "People pretending to be who they aren't—"

"Or, perhaps, revealing who they really are," I said.

After the brief fun of Saturnalia, the year lapsed back into boring rhythms. At one point, when the leaves were first opening on the trees, while the wan and crinkly ones of the previous autumn still lay beneath, I wondered why the trees even bothered. Such effort—such toil required to sprout all those leaves, and for such a short time. Such was my ennui.

But the tedium was shattered in the autumn in the most sensational way. Our lives broke open and rearranged themselves around a singular event: Messalina's spectacular folly.

Having just turned ten at Saturnalia, and still living a sequestered life, I did not know about her lovers. Neither did Claudius, although apparently all of Rome did. When he was off in Ostia inspecting his new harbor, his wife was going through a public "marriage" ceremony with her latest lover, the new consul Gaius Silius.

"The handsomest man in Rome," Mother mocked. "What a fool."

Gaius Silius . . . that man Crispus had introduced me to at the Circus! The one I thought looked like Alexander the Great. "Who?"

"Both of them." She smiled. "And both executed."

"What? Messalina has been executed?" Claudius had executed his own wife?

"She was ordered to commit suicide but was too cowardly. So a soldier had to do the deed. Her mother was standing by, urging her to be brave and do it herself, but no—"

Poor Aunt Lepida! First her husband was killed by the scheme of her own daughter, then the daughter herself brought disgrace. Painful as it was, she was better rid of this evil. For Messalina was pure evil.

"Claudius could bring himself to order this?" The doting old man did not seem that decisive, and he had been Messalina's toy.

"Well . . ." Mother rolled her eyes. "He signed the papers when he was drunk, and when he woke up the next morning and asked to see her, alas, it was too late."

"You mean that his secretaries hurried the orders through before he could remember what he was doing?"

"You are showing some political acuity, my boy. Perhaps you are not hopeless after all."

Messalina was executed in the autumn and only a few months later, on New Year's Day, Mother married Claudius.

Yes. I have put it down in the simplest words, for what can any more words add?

It was shocking—it was against Roman law for an uncle and a niece to marry, but Mother took care of that, having Claudius persuade the Senate to vote to allow it.

How did she manage the rest of it? A handsome freedman lurked around the villa often enough to give rise to rumors that they were lovers, and this freedman, Marcus Antonius Pallas, was Claudius's secretary of the treasury and had Claudius's ear. He supposedly whispered into it that the lady Agrippina would be the ideal fourth wife for him, uniting the Julian and the Claudian royal houses and putting an end to the discord between them that began with Tiberius and Agrippina the Elder. But the real reason was that Mother befuddled him with lover's caresses and, using her excuse as his niece to enter the palace freely, sat on his lap and toyed with him, arousing the old goat's lust. He was fool enough to call her in speeches "my daughter and foster child, born and bred, in my lap, so to speak." Everyone was speaking of it, I had no doubt.

I was so ashamed I wanted to shut myself in my chamber and never look upon either of them again, but that was impossible. Mother would punish me, and her wrath was not to be taken lightly, if I wanted

to live. I was forced to attend their wedding and stand by while the
hypocritical guests wished them good fortune, happiness—and children.
That was the only time I felt solidarity with Britannicus and Octavia,
who winced when the words were pronounced. Being older than they,
I just managed to keep my expression blank and not join them in the
grimace.

That night I returned to the villa but Mother stayed in the palace,
spending the first night of the new year in the shaking embraces of the
elderly Claudius. Of course I did not witness this, nor did I allow myself
to picture it, but I could not banish the memory of his tremulous,
spotted hands when he lifted her bridal veil. Only as I lay in bed, in the
villa now vacated by Mother, did the enormity of what had happened
almost crush me into the pillow. Mother was now the empress. She was
the most powerful woman—no, the most powerful person—in the
empire besides Claudius. I ran my fingers over the ring he had given me,
remembering that he had been kind to me. Suddenly I felt very protective
of him, for he was now in Mother's clutches and at her mercy. Her
husbands did not have a long life expectancy.

Soon there was the obligatory gathering at the palace to celebrate
the emperor's newfound happiness. There was no way I could not go,
and so I resigned myself. I felt strangely abandoned in the villa—in
both senses of the word—and almost looked forward to going where
there was life and noise.

Tall blazing torches lit up the entire perimeter of the grounds, and
closer to the building itself, guards held smaller ones, and panpipes and
tambourines welcomed the guests as they approached the great bronze
doors. So many years past, I had gone in these very doors, nervous and
afraid, the first time we had been summoned to meet Claudius. Oh,
what changes—now I walked in as a member of his family, and the
cruel Messalina reigned here no more. It was my first taste of revenge,
and I liked the flavor.

The buzz of assembled guests carried way out to the farthest rooms;
a slave escorted the most recent arrivals down long hallways and finally

into the cavernous room I remembered. It still looked enormous to me, even though I was no longer a small child. The yellowish light of hundreds of suspended oil lamps made the air golden and changed the color of the gowns—grass green looked like moss, red turned orange. Braziers were making the room almost uncomfortably hot, and I followed the stream of cooler air to the balcony. At night the Circus Maximus below twinkled with torches placed all along the track, making a starry oval.

There was a knot of people at one end that I assumed clustered around the newlyweds. Suddenly I felt very awkward. I was now tall enough that I did not get lost in crowds, but I did not know how to start a conversation, since I didn't recognize anyone. A slave pressed a goblet into my hand and that gave me something to hold, but still I looked around hoping to see a familiar face. Anicetus, as befitted a mere tutor, had melted away and I was on my own.

Just then a voice behind me said, "Are you looking for someone?"

I turned and saw a strapping man. Even the long sleeves on his ornamented tunic could not disguise his muscularity. "Only for someone I might know," I said.

"Why are you here by yourself?" he asked, although he was polite enough not to add, *where you so clearly do not belong.*

"My mother is the bride," I said.

He laughed. "You needn't look so sad about it. It's I who should be sad, and look, I'm cheering them."

He had bright blue eyes that stayed clear even in the yellow light. I asked—as I was meant to—"And why should you be sad?"

"Because although your mother and I are old friends, and remain so, when the emperor brought me back from an exile imposed on me by Caligula, it was only on the condition that I do not enter the royal palace."

"But you have," I said. "You are here."

"Ah, to be forbidden something is to make the desire to do it bloom.

Claudius will not see me—I'll be careful to stay here in the back—but it gives me an opportunity to speak with some others, which is always helpful for business. I shall leave after I have done that."

"What is your business?"

"I breed racehorses."

I almost gasped. "Racehorses! Where do you breed them?"

"I have big estates in the very far south."

"I love horses! I love racing! Oh, this is the best thing that has happened to me—meeting you."

He laughed, crinkles around his suntanned face. "Better than your mother becoming empress?"

"Yes," I said stubbornly.

"You are obviously a singular individual, Lucius."

"How did you know my name?"

"I told you, I am a friend of your family. I was in your father's household. I even knew your grandfather, another Lucius. Now, *he* was the man obsessed with chariot racing and horses! You must have inherited it right from him."

People were edging up to us and I could see him looking for his business contacts. "What is your name?" I asked. I wanted to be able to meet with him again, anywhere but inside the palace. Racehorses!

"Tigellinus," he said. "Just don't mention it in front of Claudius."

Someone tapped him on the shoulder and he was gone.

Now I was back in the milling crowd, but it did not seem so alien. I saw a darkly beautiful young woman slipping through the people, handing out goblets. She must be a slave. I held out my hand and she replaced my empty goblet with a full one.

"Juice for you," she said. Up close she was even more beautiful.

"I can drink wine," I said stoutly. I sipped the contents. "But I like the sweetness of this juice. Thank you. Do you serve Claudius? Where are you from?"

"The province of Lycia. My father was captured and executed for resisting the Romans. You must not think we were always slaves." She looked directly at me, not as a slave would do.

"I do not think anything," I assured her. "I merely wondered where your ancestral home was."

"Do I look so foreign?"

"Not foreign, but not Roman, either."

She smiled and glided away with her goblet tray, duty calling. I watched the curve of her back as she disappeared.

Perhaps I should leave. I had met a racehorse dealer and a beautiful woman. Things could only get worse now.

Before I could turn to go, a hand clapped itself on my shoulder, and a smooth, polished voice said, "You should join the imperial family." The hand did not move and its owner began to steer me toward the front of the room. Then he stopped. "Allow me to introduce myself. I am Pallas, secretary to the emperor." I turned to look at him. He had the polished looks to go with his voice, a very sophisticated demeanor. "You have me to thank for your mother's marriage."

He should have said, you have me to blame. "And why so?" I asked. Had he been the one to advise her to crawl up into Claudius's lap?

"My advice was heeded, that is all I can say. What passes in the councils of the emperor must, of course, remain private." He laughed, an odd, detached laugh. "I think it is the most beneficial choice for everyone. I like to see the emperor happy, but with his happiness founded on reality."

As we came closer to the emperor, the number of important persons rapidly increased.

"Rufrius!" said Pallas, stopping before someone who was, at last, familiar. It was the Praetorian prefect who had the immortally beautiful wife I had met at the Circus. Was she here? I did not see her.

Rufrius recognized me. "A big change for you," was all he said.

"Indeed, sir."

We continued on, then Pallas abruptly steered me to the right. But it was too late. The person he wished to avoid moved and stood right in front of us.

"I see you have young Lucius in tow," he said. He had a long face and dark features. There was something serpentine about him.

"Nothing so sinister, Narcissus. I am just helping him through the crowd."

"You have me to thank for this, Lucius," he said.

Him, too? How many people had engineered this wedding? "I am not sure exactly what you mean, but in any case I should be grateful."

He laughed darkly and bowed, then stepped aside.

"What he meant was, he was the one who had Messalina executed. He is the secretary for correspondence, and in that role he ordered her death, since Claudius was hesitating."

"But that's treason!"

"He claimed Claudius had signed it and, in his cups, Claudius did not remember."

"But why did he do it?"

"Because it was necessary. Ah, here we are!"

Opening before us was a slightly raised platform, draped with jeweled rugs from Arabia and flanked by slaves wielding frothy feathered fans languidly moving up and down. Resplendent before this backdrop stood Claudius, wearing the purple toga of the emperor, a gold wreath on his head, and enormous emerald bracelets on his wrists. He stood like a sturdy barrel beside Mother, who suddenly, frighteningly, looked as I had never seen her.

She seemed to burn with an inner fire that suffused her face, turning it into a goddess's. All of the long history of Rome looked out of her eyes, cold and pitiless. Aeneas, Romulus, Scipio Africanus, Pompey, Augustus, Germanicus—all within her, all driving her forward.

It was Claudius who spoke, not her. "Dear Lucius," he said. "I w-welcome you as a son, and you must look on me as a f-father." He held out his hand to draw me up to the platform. Mother did not look at me.

The jeweled carpet was pebbly under my feet, and I was hit by a wave of musky perfume from the fans. I took my place between them. Mother put her hand on my shoulder. But she still did not look at me. "It is my honor to do so," I said.

Looking out from the platform I saw a swarm of senators nearby. They had come in their senatorial striped togas lest anyone not recognize their status, regardless of how uncomfortably hot it was in the room. They were of all ages and shapes—decrepit and bald, portly and sleek, glossy haired and robust, sharp nosed and emaciated. So these were the men who were held in such esteem and believed they were running the empire? Perhaps it was true that there was safety in collective wisdom. Or perhaps wisdom was dulled by being parceled out between so many. Thus they could be either a shackle to the emperor or his invaluable guide.

On Mother's other side stood Britannicus and Octavia, formally dressed for the occasion. They both looked miserable, probably for the same reason I did. Octavia, being older, hid it better than her brother. Our ages were now eleven, nine, and almost eight. We had to stand for hours acknowledging the well-wishers who filed past. The senators each spoke and introduced himself, but although I am gifted with the ability to remember names and faces, there were so many new ones all at once I would never be able to remember them all. Next, court officials made their way past, then former provincial governors, then officers in charge of the Roman city, then officers of the guard, then "Friends of Caesar" clients, and finally down to the official tasters.

Finally Claudius held up his hands.

"We are grateful for your w-wishes. We are blessed in having your l-loyalty and blessed in our union. Now the great Julian and C-Claudian houses are joined. We are one family. And to cement this, the empress and I are p-pleased to announce that another wedding between our houses will follow shortly—that of her son, Lucius Domitius Aheno-barbus"—Mother grabbed my shoulder and hauled me back toward her—"and my daughter, Claudia Octavia." He extended his hand to her and pulled her over beside me. Mother grasped our hands and forced us to clasp them together.

The room felt as hot as Vulcan's furnace and the heat lapped over me in waves. I could not believe it, could not be sure of what I had heard. Mother had arranged this without even telling me? Marry Octavia? No, I would not! She was only a child, but one I had found unappealing since her infancy. And I was still a child. I wanted nothing to do with marriage or girls or—or being part of this playacting. And I was forced to stand there, humiliated in front of the entire room, living a lie. Being a liar. Pretending to be what I was not.

A great cheer went up. My face pulsated with anger and shame. Beside me, Octavia looked down at the floor.

XIX

I was ready to begin my Greek lesson with Anicetus, who had commiserated with me but warned me not to voice my anger and distaste outside the room—more playacting, more lies! I could not stand it. But he said, "You must stand it. It is your inheritance."

"What, being a liar?"

"Hiding your true feelings. The higher in the aristocracy, the less open anyone can be. In your family, honest feelings must not be exposed." He tactfully did not say, *because they could be fatal.*

"There will come a time, Anicetus—I swear it to you—that I will be free to say and do exactly as I wish and to hide my true self no longer."

He smiled. "Even the emperor cannot do that. Perhaps the emperor can do it less than anyone."

"Then what's the point of being emperor?"

A shadow fell across the open door. Mother. I had not seen her since the horrible night at the palace a week before.

"Anicetus, what are you teaching him? I hear no history, only rebellious and foolish ideas."

"They were my ideas, Mother." I turned to face her.

"He encourages them."

"I am capable of generating my own ideas. And here's one you won't like: I won't marry Octavia."

Her eyes widened.

"And next time, you might ask me first before you pledge me to something that affects my entire life."

"How could I ask you? You were not there when Claudius suggested it. He changes his mind by the hour, so I dared not let him wait. My dear, do not distress yourself about it. It would not happen for a long time."

"I don't like her! I never have!"

Now she looked genuinely puzzled, not pretend-puzzled. "What does that have to do with it?"

"Everything! How could I live with her, hold her, kiss her"—the thought was repulsive—"or anything else?"

She laughed, relieved. "Is that all? It's such a minor thing. You need not see much of her. You can have mistresses for *that*, and see Octavia only on formal occasions."

"I won't live a lie like that!"

"What silly ideas have filled your head? What sort of a wife do you envision, then?"

"I don't envision a wife at all. I'm only eleven years old, Mother. But if I did—I would want someone I could love to madness, someone who was myself, only better, someone I could never get enough of looking at."

She gave a dismissive grunt. "You have been reading too much mythology." She glared at Anicetus. "Greek rubbish. Jason and Medea, Orpheus and Eurydice. You see what happened to them! And what about Paris and Helen—the love you want destroyed all of Troy. We don't want the same for Rome—do we?"

"I won't marry her!"

"We shall see. It isn't now. In a few years, you may feel differently. I am sending the packers to the villa tomorrow. You are moving to the palace. That is your home now."

•   •   •

I should have been used to sudden changes; I had had so many of them in my life. But a person can choose two responses to this: he either develops no attachment to things around him, knowing he is bound to lose them, or he develops strong bonds with them and resists being separated. I was of the latter outlook.

I walked through Crispus's villa, appreciating the wall paintings against their red background, the view from the shaded balcony, even the way the branches of the pine tree outside my window scratched the shutters on a windy night, holding them all dearer to me than ever before. The palace beckoned, frightening and echoing with a mixture of memories, mostly bad. I felt that I was crossing over into a chasm, and all that was lacking was Charon to ferry me.

At least my people were coming with me: Anicetus and Beryllus, Alexandra and Ecloge, my nurses since childhood, now attendants, and many others. The day came and all my prized possessions were loaded onto a cart that rumbled the short distance to the palace.

For most people, life changes slowly and imperceptibly from one day to the next; their life is on a continuum that reveals its turning points only in retrospect. But as I stepped across the threshold of the palace, not as a guest but as an inhabitant, I understood just how momentous the change was.

Instead of one room, I had a suite of them, with views of the Forum from one and of the garden from another. Instead of plain black and white mosaics, I had a floor of red and green marble. Instead of lampstands, I had gold sconces that held resin torches to illuminate the room. And the bed—rather than the narrow linen-covered one I had grown up with, a couch with ebony legs and pillows of swan's down awaited me.

On the round citrus-wood table stood a silver ewer and tray. The walls were pale ocher and painted with garden and sea scenes in green and blue. On the far wall with southern lighting, three mosaics of pigeons, laurel, and roses looked almost real, their details meticulously rendered.

My beloved possessions looked like shabby cousins here: my miniature chariots, my well-worn copy of *The Iliad*, even my gold snake bracelet. They sat, forlornly, on a marble display stand. Standing all by itself, much larger than my old one, was a marvelous bronze model of a two-horse chariot; the horses were leaping and I could swear I saw the chariot wheels turning, so realistic was it.

"How do you l-like that?" Claudius was standing in the doorway, smiling. "It is my w-welcome to you."

"It is beautiful, sir. It takes my breath away. Like the real chariots do."

"I know you l-love the races," he said. "If you l-like, I will buy you your own horses to r-race in the Circus."

"Truly?"

"Yes." Claudius limped over to me, his tunic swishing. He put his heavy hands on my shoulders. "I know th-this is not easy for you. But I will try to make it so, and tell you th-that I am p-proud to have you in my family."

"I am most grateful."

"Changes are wrenching, I know that. I h-have lived through too m-many of them. But we have to l-learn to step over them."

He was right, of course. He had survived his changes, and I would survive mine.

My plain coarse wool and linen clothes were replaced by silk and wool so fine it floated. My boy's toga, rough and dull, was replaced by a new one, clean white and with a true purple stripe at the hem, not the inexpensive substitute dye. My thick-soled shoes, used to running over stony ground, were replaced by soft kidskin. For the first time, large polished bronze mirrors were available in my room, so I could become aware of my appearance. The ordinary olive oil I had used on my skin was replaced by the prized golden liquid from Liburnia. I remembered the stories of mortals who had ascended to Mount Olympus, there to partake of nectar and ambrosia and become immortal, their earthly trappings replaced by celestial ones, and now I was acting this out in real life.

For Mother, it was only a restoration: she had been born into such status, and now she was merely picking up her discarded life. Daughter of a presumptive emperor, sister to another, now wife to another. I said as much one day as she reclined on one of the many day couches in my suite.

"And, next, mother to another." She reached her arms out over her head, stretching like a cat. At that moment I thought how feline all her movements were and always had been.

Oh, was she about to announce a pregnancy? It should not have induced such a sickening feeling within me, but it did. I was used to having her all to myself, being her only child. She was a murderess, a cold and often frightening presence, but still I possessed her in a primal way, to be shared with no one else.

"That is blessed news, Mother," I said politely. I possessed her and yet all our words were formal, the true essence always unspoken.

She stretched again and then sat up, hugging her knees. "I thought it would be. I am telling you first, before anyone else." She smiled.

"And when is this to be?"

She sighed, got up from the couch, and sauntered over to the table where there was always fresh-pressed juice in its pitcher. She took forever pouring it out into a fine green glass, and then sipping it slowly.

"Very soon," she said. "Perhaps next month."

"But—" She was as slim as ever.

She doubled over laughing. "Oh, your face!" She turned and came over to me, taking it in her slender, cool hands. "Oh, the expression! It is worth a million sesterces." She kept laughing. Finally she said, "It is the emperor who will gain a son, not I." Then she dropped her hands.

"Claudius has agreed to adopt you. You will become his son. You will take a new name. You will, by doing this, be the next emperor."

"But—" First my home and freedom were stripped from me; now my very name and family?

"Why do you think I married him? So I could be empress? No, it was so *you* could be emperor."

"But—"

"Stop muttering 'but' like an imbecile! Of course, if an imbecile could not be emperor, then Claudius would not be one. But you are no imbecile, no, you are smart—too smart, sometimes, for your own good. So smile, Lucius. Smile. Your fate is coming for you."

"My fate—" I had thought to fashion my own, not receive it from her.

"Both our fates," she said. "After you were born, I consulted a Chaldean astrologer. He looked at your chart and said you were destined to become emperor, but that you would kill me. I said, 'Let him kill me, as long as he rules.' That is true. Had I wanted to avoid our twin destinies, I could have killed you as a baby. It is easy to kill a baby; you just smother it and it looks natural. Babies die all the time. So I held you in my arms and knew I could do it, but I did not. And here we stand, here we are."

"It will not come to pass."

"What part? The emperor part or my death?"

"Your death. I could never, I will never, kill you. I am no murderer."

"Like me? You do not know yet. Murderers do not plan to be murderers; it just happens."

"It won't to me. And the emperor part may not happen, either. There is Britannicus."

"We will take care of that." She held up her hands. "And not by murder. It won't be necessary. The age difference will be enough. You will soon be declared an adult. You are only two years away from it."

"Three years," I said, correcting her.

"I can make it two. Claudius will listen, and permit the ceremony earlier."

"You have thought of everything."

"Of course."

She was formidable; to outsmart her would be difficult. But I had no doubt that sometime in the future, I might have to.

She kissed me good-bye, leaving me reeling.

Adopted. By Claudius. A prophecy that I would be emperor, kept secret by her all this time. I lay down, afraid if I did not, I would fall to the floor.

XX

The adoption ceremony was set for the end of the month of February, following the ancient nine-day Parentalia holiday that honored dead ancestors with wreaths of flowers. Mother made sure that the busts of my father, Germanicus, Augustus, and Antony were all festooned with flowers that had been grown under glass in the palace gardens. She arranged them lovingly, smiling.

For me it was different. I felt I was deserting these ancestors, especially my father, although I had never known him. I could not hum as she did. I noticed that she gave the best wreath to Germanicus and the scantiest one to my father. When she had left the room, I put my hand on my father's bust and whispered, "Forgive me, Father."

Most of the adoption ceremony was done by lawyers and magistrates and followed a set ritual. They did not require my presence and that made it a little more bearable.

The documents had been witnessed by the required seven witnesses and were inscribed on fine parchment, now rolled and awaiting the emperor's seal. It sat on a high marble stand in the reception hall of the palace, where the Senate, imperial administrators, and Praetorian prefects now waited.

Mother and I were to enter at one end, while Claudius and his children were to enter at the other, meeting just before the table. She took my hand and guided me out, as Claudius limped toward us. He swayed more than usual that morning.

We stopped. The table with its rolled scroll sat waiting.

Claudius reached over and took it. "This day you all w-witness that I have acquired a new son." He unrolled the parchment and read the terms of the adoption.

It was very quiet in the room. Then he got to the heart of the document.

"Lucius Domitius Ahenobarbus, son of Gnaeus Domitius Aheno-barbus, from t-today henceforth you are Nero Claudius Caesar Drusus Germanicus and the s-son of Tiberius Claudius Caesar Augustus Germanicus." He put it down and hobbled over to me, embracing me.

"Nero, my son," he said. "But you have always been, in a s-sense."

Nero. I was Nero. Lucius was gone, evaporated.

The hall exploded with noise. People cooed and cheered and congratulated us. *Nero, Nero,* I kept hearing. The new name rang out—or perhaps I just heard it floating above all the noise. Claudius sealed the document and handed it to me. "It is yours, my s-son." Mother embraced me. Octavia approached and said softly, "Welcome, brother." Britannicus just stared, then blurted out, "You won't get 'Britannicus' away from me. It's already mine!"

Claudius overheard him and said, "There is only one Britannicus and th-that's you, my dear."

Mother smiled as if she agreed.

Now the eating and drinking began, but I pushed the proffered trays away. I was too mobbed by people pressing up to speak to me to eat, anyway. "Nero, Nero," they were all saying. What they were thinking but not saying was, *Our next emperor.*

Mother brought a worried-looking middle-aged man over to me. He bowed low—something I must accustom myself to from now on.

"This is Lucius Annaeus Seneca," said Mother. "An old friend from my earlier days in Rome. He is a brilliant philosopher and rhetorician, and he will be your new tutor."

"It is my honor," he said. He had a deep, rumbling voice. I would also have to get used to everyone considering it an honor, no matter what it was.

"I look forward to learning from you," I said. Let the ritual exchange be correct.

Before he could say anything further, I turned away. I did not want to discuss lessons now. I had just become someone else, and that was all I could manage to think about.

Mother clasped his hand and held it for a long time before following me. "You needn't trail me, Mother. I can make my own way."

A stocky man with choppy blond hair appeared at her side before I could get away. "Congratulations, Nero," he said, with the clipped accent of southern Gaul. "We all salute you."

Now Mother had another introduction to make. "My son, this is Sextus Afranius Burrus, another old friend of mine."

He merely nodded. He was not, apparently, the sort to make toadying talk.

Many senators came up to greet me, but a trumpet sounded and Claudius held up his hands.

"Es-esteemed guests, I wish to m-make another announcement. To honor this day, I am issuing a new g-gold coin, with the bust of Nero and 'Princeps Juventutis.'" He held up a drawing of it. "It w-will be ready by the summer."

My profile on a gold coin. The title "Young Prince." A Caesar.

Nero, Nero, Nero, they were all calling me.

I collapsed back in my room as soon as I could decently get away. Fortunately Claudius, unable to stand for long, left the hall early, releasing the rest of us to scatter. I rushed across the wide expanses of the palace, feeling like a hunted animal. Let no one accost me or stop me until I reached the safe privacy of my rooms.

I flung myself on the couch and caught my breath. The curtains around the windows were still. The ewer stood in its usual place, doubtless filled with the same juice. The mosaics had not changed—as if they could.

I held out my hands. They had not changed, any more than the mosaics had. My arms—they were the same. Yet I had become someone else—not on the inside, but on the outside. I had become someone else through the power of a piece of parchment and one man's pronouncement. I felt no different. I felt entirely different.

"Worn out?" Mother's voice came from the doorway. She had opened it and come in without permission. A flitting thought: now that I was a Caesar, did she have the right to do that? "You must get used to it." She glided over to me and sat down on the couch, crowding me. She caressed my forehead, pushing my hair back. "But I admit, it was a demanding day. Almost like the day you were born. That day was demanding for me, and your rebirth as Nero was demanding for you. So I forgive you for running away at the end." She leaned down and kissed my cheek. Then she kissed me again. "You are a handsome boy, and soon to be a handsome man," she said. "I never told you before, because people who are told that too early become vain. But it is true."

"Or is it suddenly true because I am now a Caesar?"

She got up. "Don't be cynical."

"I must have got it from you. I have learned from the master."

"Rest up. There will be a family dinner later to celebrate."

"There always is. A family dinner, I mean. Now, Mother, I really do need to rest."

Thus I dismissed her. And lay in the darkening room, exultant and confused.

I had been to "family dinners" before, but then I had been relegated to the children's table while the nine important grown-up people dined from the couches. Now *I* was the important one, the one being honored. I was to dress in my lightest, finest clothes, make sure my wavy hair was flattened into an austere Augustan coif, wear the gold ring Claudius had given me, and bring my own linen napkin.

The family apartments within the palace were a labyrinth of rooms, with lower ceilings and a more intimate feeling. In the dining room the three couches were drawn up in the usual horseshoe shape, while the children's table was set off to one side. When I arrived, Claudius and Mother were already reclining on the left-hand couch, with Claudius at the upper end in the host's place. The first place on the adjoining middle couch, to his left, was the place for the guest of honor, and he waved me to it. As I climbed up onto the couch—I was tall enough now that I did not need a stool—I had to grab the slippery covering to keep from sliding back. Finally I slid into my place.

"T-tricky, eh?" Claudius said. "You will get used to it."

I was embarrassed that my first formal dining experience was so obvious. I felt my face growing red. All I could do was nod.

The other spots were filled by senators and, at the lowest-ranked place, the top of the right-hand couch, the tutor Mother had introduced me to earlier. Now I noticed that the plates were all of gold and that the napkins varied: Claudius's was Tyrian purple, and the senators' had the broad senatorial stripe. The goblets were priceless murra, a translucent stone. If one crashed to the ground . . . ! I would have to make sure it wasn't I who dropped one.

At the children's table Britannicus and Octavia sat demurely, but every so often Britannicus glared at me. I studied Octavia, taking advantage of her modest downcast eyes. She was not unattractive in features, but there was no animating spirit in them. Suddenly I had a thought—I was now Claudius's son, and she was my sister, so it would be illegal to marry her. A wave of delight spread over me. I did not have to marry her!

Claudius took the floor, as it were, saying, "I w-welcome you all to our table, where we are ce-celebrating the addition of Nero to our family."

Everyone dutifully raised the murrhine glasses, filled with the best Setine wine, and murmured, "We salute you!"

They then began chattering with one another and I used the opportunity to study them to sort out their names and looks. I would not learn of their politics as it was the height of bad manners to discuss politics at dinners—or perhaps it was just practical protection against spies. Seneca, the tutor, at the low end of the couch, was a rumpled sort, the type who would never look put together no matter how long he spent at it.

The slaves were circulating, pouring more wine, and then the various courses of the dinner followed. As this was masquerading as a simple family dinner rather than an imperial banquet, there were only three courses, and one of them featured country fare—to show how down-to-earth the emperor was? But the finale was nightingale in rose petals, something that would never be found in the country.

The conversation drifted from the charioteer who was today's darling to the problem of the Druids in Britain to poetry and even that most banal of topics, the weather. As we were nibbling the sweet figs and cakes of the final course, a senator suddenly said, "Let's have some philosophy! We've got a famous—or should I say infamous?—philosopher at the table. Seneca!"

The disheveled man looked up with dignity, making one forget his wrinkled clothes. "I hardly think one can consider weighty philosophical matters while the stomach is digesting."

"You're a Stoic, right?" the senator persisted. "Can't you perform in all conditions? Isn't that what Stoicism is all about? To be indifferent to your surroundings?"

"It is a little more complex than that," said Seneca.

"You must have mastered that 'indifferent' challenge, as your life has proved. We should learn from you."

Mother took that opening to say, "Seneca is going to be the tutor of Nero. He does indeed have much to teach."

But the senator was not to be deflected. "Much to teach, indeed!" He rolled his eyes.

"Publius, these innuendoes are an insult to our guest. S-stop at once," said Claudius. "We have chosen him to t-teach our son, and that is all the proof anyone needs of our c-confidence in his character."

"What about me?" Britannicus's shrill voice rose from the other table. "Can I have him for my tutor, too?"

"No, you have your own tutors."

"Baby tutors! Why can Lucius have him, and I can't?"

"*Nero,*" said Mother, her voice icy. "His name is Nero."

"Well, I know him as Lucius."

"That is no longer his name." I recognized Mother's tone now as her most dangerous, the one that said, *That's enough. Stop or you will be sorry in a way only I can make you sorry.*

Britannicus clapped his mouth closed, but when Mother's head was turned he said, "He'll always be Lucius to me."

"Th-that's enough," said Claudius. "You are being impertinent and r-rude to your brother. Leave the t-table, go to your room, and await your punishment later."

Britannicus threw down his napkin and ran out in tears.

"Father," I said (how odd it felt to say that, how unnatural), "do not be harsh with him. Why, even I will have trouble remembering all my names." I attempted to make light of it.

"That's my dear son," said Mother, using the beguiling voice she kept in reserve. "He is just too tenderhearted, and of course he loves his brother. But, one cannot overlook things that cross a boundary of protocol."

Seneca chuckled and, in a movement almost imperceptible, shook his head as if in amusement at us mortals.

Finally the ordeal was over and I was back in my room. I could rest at last, drifting off to sleep and putting a close to what was the most extraordinary day I would ever have. Or so I believed.

XXI

Before I was to meet with Seneca, I assured Anicetus that nothing would displace him in my life. He just smiled and said, "That would be my hope. But now that you have been elevated"—he stood on his tiptoes—"you may see things differently."

"No," I said. "No!"

"I will continue to function as your instructor in everyday life, then. I daresay you will not get much of that from Seneca, although, Zeus knows, that man could tell you more than you would wish to know."

"You tell me!" I said eagerly.

He looked around and saw there were only two slaves standing guard at the door, too far away to hear. "Oh my—where to begin? Seneca became known early for his philosophy and his rhetoric, known well enough to run afoul of Caligula."

"Like everyone in the world," I said.

"Caligula didn't care for his writing style. He said it was 'sand without lime'—a lot of nuggets but nothing to bind them together. He was about to have him executed, but, because Seneca had weak lungs, a friend convinced Caligula that he was going to die soon anyway, so why bother?"

"That must be the only time a man could be grateful for weak lungs," I said. We walked over to a bench near a window in my still-new suite of rooms, farther from the guards, and sat down.

"If his lungs were weak, apparently other parts of him were healthy enough," said Anicetus. "A little while later, Messalina accused him of adultery with Livilla, Caligula's sister. Any woman of power was her enemy, as you know full well. She had Livilla, your mother, and Seneca all banished—to different islands. Seneca went to Corsica, where he stayed for seven years. Only when Messalina was dead, and your mother in her place, could Claudius bring him back."

"I've never understood why my mother was included in this trio."

"You are old enough to know all these things now. It was rumored—rumored, mind you, not proven—that Seneca was her lover, too. And that in addition she was plotting against Caligula." He shook his head. "That's all over now. To be forgotten."

As if I could forget such accusations!

"There's another rumor, spread by Seneca's aristocratic enemies, who consider him a venal upstart—that he has made his success by sharing all the appropriate influential couches." He laughed. "When you get a closer look at him, you will understand how preposterous such charges are. Unless . . . there's more to him than we can see, literally."

I wished I could believe that my mother would be dissuaded by a man's looks, but her marriage to Claudius proved the opposite. For myself, I found that beauty of person was necessary for me to be drawn to someone. Did that make me shallow? If so, then most people who have ever been born share this shallowness. That is why our first question usually is, What does he or she look like? It was Helen's beauty that drove thousands to their deaths. If she had been plain, would Menelaus have wanted her back or would he have said, *Good riddance?* And, *Thank you, Paris?*

I looked at Anicetus, the man who had been beside me, steadying me and guiding me, from babyhood on. I would not leave him behind.

"Thank you for this timely education," I said. "May you always speak truth to me."

He reached out and tousled my hair. "May you always be open to receive it." He pulled a few tendrils up. "Too unruly for a princeps. You will have to work to tame it."

I smoothed it down. "I know. It is not obedient but wants to go every which way."

"Like its owner," he said, giving it one last rumple. He stood up; he had heard a sound at the door.

The slaves stood aside as Mother and Seneca entered the room. They were holding hands. Or was she just leading him, as would be perfectly proper?

"Greetings," she said. "I am pleased to find you already in your teaching room, Nero. See what I have made ready?" She pointed to several maps on easels, a round container of scrolls, and a table with wax tablets and styli laid out. I had only vaguely noticed them; the room was so large it swallowed them up.

"Now I do," I said. "And, Seneca, I welcome you and look forward to our lessons." At the dinner I had seen his bald head but not how short he was, nor how thin his legs were, sticking out from under his gown. Oddly enough, his face was fleshy, even though the rest of him wasn't. He did not look like a woman's dream of a lover.

"As do I," he said. He had a slight accent, just barely noticeable.

Mother hardly acknowledged Anicetus, but he made no move to leave. "My son is brilliant, Seneca. You will see. I count on you to polish him, to lead him on higher paths than he has climbed so far"—now she did look at Anicetus—"because there was no one suitable to teach him at that level. However, I did not engage you to teach him philosophy."

Seneca looked startled, then said, "But that is what I have made my name in."

"Yes, but philosophy is of no use to an emperor."

She had actually uttered the word, the forbidden word.

"Or to anyone in a high position near the emperor," she said, quickly catching herself, looking over her shoulder to see if the guards had heard. "Instead, you are to teach him public speaking and political strategy. Practical things, instead of abstracts."

He lifted his chin and looked her in the eyes in a terribly familiar way. "Philosophy is not an abstract; it is a moral guide for how we live our lives. Our philosophy affects our every action. If we believe that it matters how we treat our fellows, then we behave one way; if we do not, then we behave another way."

She smiled and touched her blue silken palla, adjusting the golden pin that held it on her shoulder. "In fact, I see little difference in how people actually behave, depending on their philosophies. I can't tell a Stoic from an Epicurean or a Cynic, by the time it gets to an ordinary man. Take yourself, for example. Does not your Stoic philosophy tell you to be free of material things, that they don't matter? Well, then, how do you explain your five hundred citrus-wood tables?"

"I explain it by assuring you that they don't matter to me!" He laughed. Oh, he knew how to manage her. And how had he learned that so well? *Do not think about it, Nero,* I told myself. *Put it out of your thoughts.* Only later did I realize I had called myself Nero in my own mind for the first time.

She laughed with him, heartily.

"Shall we begin the lessons today?" Seneca asked us.

"Tomorrow," said Mother. "This afternoon we are celebrating. Claudius is speaking to the Senate even now, announcing to them, and securing their approval for it, that he is bestowing the title Augusta on me."

There was a dead silence. Anicetus's mouth made an O. Seneca stared, his pale blue eyes bulging. As for me, my face felt numb.

"What an honor, my lady." Seneca was the first to recover, not surprisingly. "Well deserved, of course, but you join two others of imperishable fame."

He *was* good with words. Yes, he must teach me to be nimble on my feet like this, to always have an arsenal of the right language at hand.

"Livia, wife of Augustus, titled Julia Augusta," he continued smoothly. "And Antonia Augusta. Now a third! But Livia was only made Augusta after her husband's death, and Antonia only received the honor a few months before her death. You are young, receiving the immortal wreath!"

Oh, yes, he was a master. But I was grateful that he filled in the stunned silence of her son and Anicetus.

She noticed. "Does my dear son have nothing to say?"

"It seems I am elevated twice, first to be son of an emperor, and now to be son of an Augusta."

She smiled, but it was no smile. "Ah, the selfishness of youth, thinking only of himself, not of his mother."

"I am in such awe of her new majesty that I sought to shield myself from the direct rays of its brilliance." Seneca almost winced. Not good, then? Too overdone?

"But a son may embrace his mother and say simply and truly, I am so proud!" I hugged her tightly, kissed her cheek. There, was that better?

"Thank you," she said. "Only one thing is lacking today. I wish my father could have known. I wish he could have known." A genuine, not feigned, melancholy tinged her voice.

In all the twists and turns of her life, for all the accommodations she had had to make to survive, the image of Germanicus had remained the one unspotted thing in her esteem, the person she ultimately wanted to please. We all keep one such person—or thing—sacred to us.

There were more stately ceremonies for Mother's elevation, but nothing that I remember very well. Such ceremonies are much the same: the witnesses are of the highest rank; the setting is the most impressive to hand; the pronouncement is read in stentorian tones; afterward there is eating and drinking. In this case, the actual reading was compromised by Claudius's diction, but no matter: the edict was what counted, not the delivery of it.

XXII

I was wary of Seneca, and the first few days I spent in his tutelage were anxious ones for me. He was a famous man, famous in a realm outside the ones I was familiar with—the court and the training ground—and I felt ignorant next to him. He also was Mother's choice, and Mother's creature, just one remove from her herself. But he was a soothing presence, and day by day my little knot of suspicion uncurled.

He was pleased that I could read and speak Greek; Anicetus had given me a good foundation. Although he was to concentrate on teaching me rhetoric—both argument and public declamation—I won his favor when I read his essays and asked him questions about them. There is no man so humble that he does not beam when his work is applauded. Did I do this only to win him to me? Not consciously, but perhaps by instinct. A survivor must have the skill of pleasing others, and the higher one climbs, the more survival skills are needed. Being the emperor's son now made it imperative that I master the utmost of survival skills.

In truth, the parts of his essays "Consolation to Helvia" and "Consolation to Polybius" that interested me were not his Stoical blatherings but what it was like to live in exile.

"Not in exile," he corrected me. "Relegation."

There was a difference?

"Relegation," he said, "means banishment only from one particular place. Exile is not only that, but a loss of civil rights and property and money. So yes, there is a big difference. Like the poet Ovid, I was relegated, not exiled."

"But neither of you could come back to Rome," I said.

He sighed. "Yes, that is true. And I couldn't choose my place of relegation. I was ordered to Corsica."

"You wrote that it was an unpleasant place, bare and thorny, infertile, populated by uncultured people. But Anicetus, who has been there, told me it has a good climate and a lively Roman colony, that it isn't barren at all, but thick with trees."

"Any place is barren when a man is kept a prisoner there."

"Yes, in poetical terms, but in real life, what is the truth about Corsica?"

"Anicetus is right, technically. But the landscape of the mind—"

"The true landscape. What is it like?"

"Much like Rome. It is not far away, after all. It shares the same climate, the same trees, the same crops."

"Where did you live there? How did you live?"

"I lived in a tower."

"All alone?"

He straightened himself on his chair, twitched his robes around his feet. "No, I had my wife and five slaves."

I burst out laughing. "A lonely life of hardship indeed."

"As I said, it is not one's actual situation but one's perception of it." He leaned closer. "The essays were polished writings, meant to make philosophical points about what is important in life. The banishment was merely the background that allowed me to develop those thoughts. I was able to examine how Stoicism could be practiced, to allow me to rise above the situation—or any situation, for that matter. For that is the purpose of Stoicism, to be beyond the reach of fate."

"I don't think it worked, then."

"It is an ideal, probably not attainable in its fullest form."

"But the untruths"—I hesitated to call him an outright liar—"you wrote about Corsica do not make sense." I kept coming back to the facts; they were what was important to me.

"Oh, yes, they do. If I painted a picture of Corsica as a pleasant place, then Claudius would have had no reason to lift my banishment, would he? I write not only for future readers but to influence the present—*my* present."

Now he had admitted the truth. His writings had kept his name alive in Rome, long enough that he could be fetched home in the ripeness of time. They were not a report on Corsica but a plea for recognition.

"Now, young man, if we might turn to the famous declamation of Demosthenes, the Third Philippic—" He deftly steered us away from Corsica and back to the lesson at hand.

To his credit, Seneca became a guide for other aspects of my education. In preparation for the day when I would go through the ritual of assuming the adult toga, he stressed that I must master the long roll of Roman history, and that I must know the sites in Rome relevant to that history. Every stone, every street, told a story, he said. And we would visit them together, and I would learn them.

I shall make sure you are a true son of Rome!" he said, clapping his hands on my shoulders a few weeks later. "Now that it's good weather, we're off to visit the sites. It's always best to see something rather than just hear about it."

It was a glorious spring day, and no cloak was needed. Stepping out of the palace into the warm air, I was enveloped by the luxury of it.

"Now, my young charge, let us look from the heights first." He steered me over to the edge of the Palatine Hill and pointed north. "There's the original Forum, right beneath us. Beyond that are the two new forums—the Forum of Julius Caesar and the Forum of Augustus."

His arm swept over the broad area, still a bit misty; the sun had not reached the lower-lying parts of the city yet.

Just then a puff of breeze scattered petals from nearby blooming trees all over us. Seneca brushed them out of his sparse hair and from the folds of his tunic. I let mine stay; I felt anointed by spring.

"Persephone is back, and the flowers rejoice," I said.

"What nonsense—a silly story if ever there was one." He kept flicking at his tunic. "Now, to the west, is the sacred Capitoline Hill. See the big temple there?"

I could hardly miss it. It gleamed white, already having shed its enveloping fog. "The Temple of Jupiter Capitolinus," I dutifully intoned.

"Where Triumphs conclude, the celebrant dedicates his laurel crown, and the two flawless white oxen are sacrificed."

"I know, I saw Claudius's." I did not want to undercut him, but I already knew these places. Where did he think I had been for twelve years?

"Ah. Yes." He waved his arm once more, then went on with things I already knew. "These areas together—the Palatine Hill we are standing on, the Capitoline Hill, and the Forum in between—are the extent of the original Rome, inside the area called the Pomerium, drawn by Romulus."

"Surely you don't believe Romulus drew a line and created Rome?" I asked.

He sighed. "No, I don't. And I don't believe Romulus and Remus were brought up by a wolf, either. But there are days I wish I did. It's a pretty story."

We descended down the sloping street into the Forum. Seneca was a slow walker, stopping often to catch his breath. "I have weak lungs," he said. "I've been plagued by them all my life. But because of them, I lived in Egypt for a while. Alexandria. Ah, now there's a city! But another time, another time," he muttered, catching himself before he compared the two—to Rome's detriment. "Ah, here we are." It had taken us a long time to make the short walk.

The Forum was relatively quiet; it was still early. Wisps of mist clung to the buildings, filmy as a goddess's gown. Right ahead of us was the Temple of the Divine Julius—a small but tall temple with a columned front porch. Heaps of wilting flowers and wreaths of bay leaves adorned the steps and carpeted the interior, right up to a statue of Caesar with his divine star. They were left from the recent day of mourning for Caesar's assassination. There were also oil lamps flickering amid the offerings, with depictions of Caesar.

We walked circumspectly around it. "The temple is built on the spot where he was cremated, after the funeral speech Marc Antony made that drove the crowd wild," he said.

"The divine Julius," I said. "Do you believe that?"

He looked around to see if anyone might overhear. "That a man can become a god? Or that he *was* a god all along, in mortal disguise? The former, perhaps; the latter, never." We moved back to let two women lay fresh flowers on the steps. "It was almost a hundred years ago," he said, "and people remember. That is one way of being a god, I suppose."

More people were arriving and the small spaces were becoming crowded. "Come," said Seneca. "On to the next forum." On our way we walked past the Curia, its massive doors closed, no Senate in session. And past the splendid gilded pillar that measured all distances from Rome. And past the Rostra, the famous speaking platform adorned with the beaks of captured ships. Then we rounded one building and were within the Forum of Julius Caesar, smaller than the old Forum, but new and symmetrical. At its far end was a high podium temple, its columns sparkling white: the Temple of Venus Genetrix—Venus the Ancestor.

"And here is where Caesar laid the trap that caught him," said Seneca. Before going in, he rested on a stone to catch his breath again. The sun was now well up and warming the grounds. A half-moon was high in the sky, mottled white against blue, a remnant of the night. I was content to wait and watch these things.

He hauled himself up and walked to the steps. Inside it was quite dim. "Close your eyes," he said, "and I will lead you in." I took his dry but warm hand and obeyed. I felt the change in temperature right away as we left the sun. "Now open them."

For a moment I saw nothing. Then, swimming out of the darkness, a golden statue glimmered. She was more than life-sized, posed in a natural stance, with lifelike features. She was wearing what looked like real jewels—pearls in her ears.

"Behold Cleopatra!" he said. "Yes, it is she! He put her statue here, as Venus, in the temple dedicated to his family's descent from the goddess. It was an affront to all propriety. Caesar had now overreached himself—his disdain for public opinion was revealed. And it only got worse from there."

I stared at it. Was this a true likeness? Had her son Alexander Helios stolen quietly in here to look at her over the years?

"Why is it still here?" I asked. After all, Cleopatra had been formally declared the enemy of Rome.

"No one could prove it was Cleopatra. And as time passed and there were no living memories of her, the impetus to remove the statue faded. Augustus was too good a politician to stir up unnecessary controversy."

The dim, cool temple held few people, and it felt good to emerge out into the warmth again. We strolled over to Augustus's Forum, lying adjacent to Caesar's, nudging up against it as his young great-nephew had done in real life. But it was far grander, for it had a massive temple to Mars Ultor—Mars the Avenger—as well as colored marble colonnades on both sides, festooned with Athenian-style caryatids and carved shields. The temple stood on a tall podium, its columns of gleaming white, its pediments ornamented with gods.

In contrast to the almost deserted Caesar temple, this one swarmed with people, mainly youths hurrying up the steps. They were all wearing the white toga of manhood and clutched offerings in their hands.

"I brought you here so you can see what happens when a boy takes the toga virilis," he said. "Two days after the day of mourning for Caesar comes the ceremony of manhood. Roman boys of noble families come here to dedicate themselves to Mars. Afterward the family has a feast."

I watched their eager, fresh faces, glowing with exhilaration as they climbed the steps, the new togas flapping about their legs.

"They are now full Roman citizens," said Seneca. "Adults in the eyes of the law."

We mounted the steps and entered the temple. Throngs of white-clad boys were milling about. In the back was the expected statue of Mars in full battle armor, flanked by Venus on one side and the divine Julius on the other. Arrayed on all sides were Roman standards recovered from enemy hands, crowns, and scepters from bygone Triumphs dedicated to Mars.

"Truly a shrine to war and every tool of it," said Seneca.

"When ages to come look back on Rome, is that what we will be remembered for? War?"

"It seems to be our leading trait."

"I'm not drawn to war," I blurted out. "It doesn't speak to me. It must not speak to you, either. You never served in the army, did you?"

"My lungs—"

"Saved you," I finished for him, although it was rude. "What will save me?"

He looked perturbed. Clearly there was no answer—no ready one, anyway.

"I can't think of anything more unpleasant and boring than marching miles with a pack or setting up a camp," I said.

Seneca laughed. "You would not be doing those things. You would be commanding those who do them."

"Unless I had wings, I would still have to march the miles, even without the gear." I shook my head. "It's not because I can't do those things. I can wrestle, run, and climb with the best of them. But in competition, which has a goal."

"Generals would disagree with you that war does not have a goal."

"The divine Augustus"—I swept my arm across the rows of standards—"was a terrible soldier but he managed to disguise it. He spent the battle of Actium being seasick in his cabin, and he let Antony win the battle of Philippi for him. If only I could be so clever." I kept my voice low.

Leaving the shrine to Mars, we then turned to the shrine to Augustus himself. At the far end of the Forum, in a hall, was a great statue of him. His feet were as long as man's height, and his head reached the high ceiling, as tall as six men standing on one another's shoulders.

His sightless eyes looked down on me. Was that a slight downward turn of his mouth? Was he taking my measure, saying, *Great-great-grandson, what are you made of?*

"You will lay your old boyhood toga at his feet," Seneca said. Bundles of them now lay at those enormous marble feet.

But his voice was faint; Augustus's was louder.

What are you made of? he kept asking.

XXIII

It felt good to leave the worshipful environs of Augustus behind and exit the Forum. Outside, the crowds had increased; it was the busiest time of day now. People were jostling for space to walk, and we had to push our way through. Beggars and vendors assaulted us, pulling on our tunics. A lantern salesman swung his wares in our faces, yapping about how precious they were. A soldier on patrol shooed him away, muttering.

But if I hoped to escape Augustus, I was mistaken. He and his memorials were everywhere, and Seneca was obligated to lead me to them all. Next were the Campus Martius and Augustus's mausoleum, his Altar of Peace, and his Sundial. Sighing, I followed Seneca out of the mob and into the calmer space of the Campus.

The Campus Martius—the Field of Mars—a large area west of the forums and along the Tiber, had traditionally been the place where men practiced military drills and exercised. But it was filling in, and the southern part had many public buildings; the northern part was still fairly empty with open grass fields. So Augustus had chosen that area to build his monuments to himself, to be more visible standing alone in open air.

"Oh my," Seneca said. "The distances seem greater and greater." We trudged along, passing out of the area where Agrippa had built his Pantheon and his artificial lake. There was a straight street between the Pantheon and the mausoleum, bordered on each side by tall trees and a park of open fields. It was entirely refreshing, tranquil, soothing. Spring flowers waved in the fields on either side, little spots of yellow, white, and purple in the green grass.

Off to our right a red granite obelisk beckoned, with an apron of stone pavement around it: the Sundial. As we approached, I saw that the obelisk was casting a shaft of shadow across the pavement, but not a very long one.

"It's noon, so it will be at its shortest," said Seneca, puffing from the walk.

I looked up to the top; it was surmounted by a golden sphere and a spire, making its tip the finger marking the time. My neck strained to bend far enough back to see the top. I would guess it to be as high as ten men, at least.

"Augustus brought it from Egypt," Seneca said. "Another of his spoils." He walked around the pavement, fitted with bronze markers to measure the length of the shadow at different times of the year. "On Augustus's birthday, near the autumn equinox, the shadow reaches almost to the altar table inside the Ara Pacis, the Altar of Peace." He pointed to a low building lying to the east. "The obelisk is dedicated to Apollo, Augustus's divine protector, god of the sun. The shadow will grow longer after the winter solstice, the date that Augustus was conceived, supposedly after his mother's nocturnal encounter with Apollo in his temple. So, this all emphasizes that he was divine."

"A bit heavy-handed," I said. "But the park is lovely."

We walked across the pavement, crossing the various demarcation lines for the seasons and the zodiac. Suddenly we were right before the Altar of Peace. It was a square building with an open portal and an altar inside. Exquisite carvings adorned the marble inside and out. It was surprisingly small, a precious jewel of beauty.

As we entered it, I truly felt a peace descend. Whether the atmosphere inside was sacred, or the carvings depicted such serenity and contentment, I do not know, but the blessing fell over me like a mantle. I felt protected, safe, and held in hands of infinite compassion.

If only I could stay here, I thought. I would never feel pain or fear again.

Seneca stayed quietly in the back, watching me, letting me soak in the balm of this place. Finally he took my hand. "We must complete the journey," he said, leading me outside.

Compared to the holy stillness of the Altar, even the spring park outside seemed garish. We walked silently as I waited for the hush inside me to drain away.

Looming ahead of us was the huge drumlike structure of the Mausoleum of Augustus, surrounded by an arbor and laid out in a symmetrical park. Here he rested, along with the rest of his family. Here it all ended, even for the ruler of the world.

"I saw the procession for the ashes of many," said Seneca. "Not Augustus himself, but Tiberius, Germanicus, and Caligula bringing the ashes of his mother, Agrippina the Elder. It is an honor to lie with the rest of your family in such a place." He pointed toward a white-fenced area to the south. "That is the actual place where Augustus was cremated."

I shuddered, even in the warm air. "Since we cannot enter, let us pay our respects and leave." A sad list of the inhabitants of that gloomy structure was posted near the entrance. Marcellus, Octavia, Augustus, Agrippa, Tiberius's son Drusus, Tiberius himself, Augustus's grandsons Lucius and Gaius, Livia, and the others Seneca had mentioned. A dark parade, into the dark.

The mausoleum lay beside the Tiber, and we climbed down to sit by its banks. I felt as drained as Seneca.

"History is tiring," he said, looking at me with understanding. "The weight of all those other lives can press you down. And those lives were weightier than most." He surprised me by motioning to a vendor on the river path, buying wine and cheese and bread for us. "We the living should picnic by the river in the sunshine, and be thankful." He tore off a piece of bread and handed it to me.

Before us the swollen spring river was flowing swiftly. The scarlet poppies and pale asphodels along the bank swayed bravely in the breeze. *We the living.*

"We have both lost people in our lives," he said. "I lost a son at a very young age and was never given another. And you have lost two fathers. Did you know, Crispus was a good friend of mine? I mourned him on Corsica but could not attend his funeral."

Should I say what I knew? No. It would be dangerous, besides being pointless now. But I was happy to know someone who had been close to him. When the one you love is gone, anyone or anything connected to them makes them live again, in an attenuated way.

"He was good to me," I said. "I will miss him forever."

"The Fates sometimes send us where we are needed," he said. "Where there is lack."

He did not need to say anything more. But I knew what he meant. *Perhaps we can mend one another's lack. You lack a father, I lack a son.*

XXIV

The last halcyon days of my childhood: let me look back on them now. They are made especially precious by being so limited, and so glorious in that I did not know then they were limited.

Why should I? I was twelve years old, a long way even from the toga virilis, a ceremony that was mainly symbolic. Claudius was in good health—well, good health for Claudius was poor health for anyone else, but he had limped along, literally, now for sixty years. Augustus had lived into his midseventies, and Tiberius had been almost eighty. So there was no reason to suppose anything but another decade or two of uneventful life for all of us.

I grew taller and stronger. I learned scholarly lessons from Seneca, worldly ones from Anicetus and Beryllus, athletic ones from Apollonius, and naughty ones from Tigellinus. I avoided Octavia and Britannicus as much as I could, which was not difficult. I saw little of Mother and less of Claudius. In short, I was a denizen of the self-absorbed world of late childhood, before adult responsibilities encroach on freewheeling diversions and passions. I had also begun to play music and had my first lyre lessons. I dashed from the horse stables (my entrée through Tigellinus) to the music room to the gymnasium to the schoolroom. Seneca chided me as an "energetic idler" and a "busy trifler," but I was supremely content.

Of course there were things missing—are not there always? I was alone in a sea of adults. I had no companions, no friends of my own age. I was kept isolated by my high station in life (the emperor's eldest son—no one was higher) and the actual isolation of living in the palace. The boys I knew at the stables and the athletic field would not have been welcomed there, and most of them did not even know my true identity. I had chosen that route in the belief it gave me freedom, but at the same time secrets are isolating in the long run.

Was I lonely? Yes and no. I had never had a friend of my own age, so I could not truly miss what I had never experienced, except as a vague ache. But I was so busy, so challenged and excited by all I was experiencing, I did not brood on what was lacking.

I was paraded out on social occasions and was aware of political tensions between the various advisers in high places, all vying to control Claudius and Mother. But Mother controlled Claudius (who was ever a pliable dupe for his wives) and so it was Mother who was the prize Narcissus, Pallas, and Burrus all tussled for. But no one controlled Mother; they should have known that.

Narcissus was undone when what became known as the "Fucine Lake incident" was blamed on him. Claudius had entrusted him with an ambitious project to drain the Fucine Lake, a malarial lake about sixty miles from Rome. A grand entertainment sea battle was scheduled to be fought on the lake, and then the drainage channels were to be opened and the lake emptied right before the emperor's—and the huge audience's—eyes. However, the first time this was staged, the water failed to drain. The next time, it drained so fast and furiously it nearly drowned the spectators, of which I was one. I had been forced to don military garb and attend the event alongside Claudius and Mother. Wet and sopping, her glorious gold-threaded cloak ruined, Mother used this as a way to ruin Narcissus, saying he had appropriated money meant for the project and thus it was not properly funded and engineered.

True or not, Narcissus was dismissed. Mother had disliked him and seized on this chance to abolish his influence with Claudius. She continued to exercise near-imperial power—visiting public works, receiving foreign envoys, and meddling in financial matters. Her protégé—and some said her lover—the freedman Pallas now rose in power under her aegis. Claudius nodded on, drinking too much at dinners and falling asleep while Mother tightened her grip on national affairs. I fled as much as I could. Cowardly? Selfishly? Naïvely? Perhaps all three.

Twelve is a magical number. There are twelve months in the year, twelve signs of the zodiac, twelve labors of Hercules, twelve Olympian gods, Twelve Tables of Law. And so twelve was the magic year in my life just before I stepped over the threshold into another world.

Just before Saturnalia I turned thirteen. Mother made much of the occasion, reliving the day I was born and all the omens. I had learned to let my mind drift off during one of her recitations while maintaining a look of attention.

". . . and so we will have the ceremony early, by the gracious consent of the emperor," she was saying. Suddenly I heard her.

"What ceremony?"

She was draped over one of the couches in my room, languid after one of those interminable family dinners. Claudius had been carried off in a litter, dozing, to bed. This was happening earlier and earlier. Was it natural, or was Mother plying him with doctored wine? "The toga virilis ceremony," she said. "What did you think it was—an initiation into the Eleusinian Mysteries?"

An initiation she could never undergo, as no murderers were permitted. But Augustus had joined, and he had killed so many people their blood could have coated all the streets of Rome, so how stringent could the rules be?

"Sorry, I wasn't really listening." I sat up. I was exhausted from the boring dinner. Perhaps I should have been carried off in a litter as well.

"I have persuaded Claudius to let you assume the toga early. Three months from now."

"But I am two years underage. One year might not be noticeable, but two . . ."

"You are tall and look older than your age. You will be perfectly presentable."

"What is the point of rushing it?"

She rose and drew her woolen palla around her. It was chilly in the room, and its marble floor did not help. I clapped for someone to bring more coal for the brazier. Only when the slave had come and gone did Mother answer.

"It is important that you be established as an adult as long as possible before Britannicus. This will put you five years ahead of him instead of three. This way you can be given official duties that he is not eligible for."

Official duties! What sort of official duties? They would be tedious. Official duties meant wearing uncomfortable clothes and listening to dull, endless talk about inconsequential subjects.

"It will be for show only," she said. "*I* am the one presiding at official duties these days. I am, after all, the Augusta."

"That title does not bestow an office," I said. "No woman can hold a political office in Rome."

She threw back her head and laughed, her swanlike neck curved sensuously. Her gold necklace rose and fell on her throat, its ornaments tinkling. "That is what you think, child."

"Don't call me a child," I said. "If you think I am a child, then you have no business elevating me to an adult status."

"You will be useful in the position—child. *My* child." She walked toward me, holding out her slender hands. She took my face in them and solemnly kissed each cheek. Her perfume, a heavy lotus scent, rose from her wrists. Her lips lingered on my skin.

Then, abruptly, she turned and walked out.

I sat rubbing my cheeks as warmth spread through them. As she meant me to do.

The ceremony went forward, I the center of it but the still point of the turning wheel, while all spun around me. It was once again March, and now I was to enter the Forum of Augustus along with other candidate boys, all older than me. The day was clear and bracing, the sky a throbbing blue, the brisk wind lifting the veils of mothers watching their sons pass from boyhood to manhood. I mounted the steep steps before the temple, alone, not part of the groups before and behind me. I was, as always, solitary and singled out. As I lifted each foot I was acutely aware that hundreds of eyes were watching me, evaluating how I moved, what my bearing was.

Inside the temple there was only the god Mars to contend with—a far less critical judge than the people of Rome. I looked up at his fierce visage, at all the war standards and trophies, but they failed to stir me. As we came forward one by one, a magistrate and his slave removed our boyhood togas and dressed us in the unblemished white toga of manhood. They folded our old togas each in a neat package and presented them to us, with the admonition to lay aside our childhood and put on the mantle of manhood. To take up the duties of Roman citizenship. To protect the Roman state and found our own families. To serve in whatever capacity Rome might require of us. To live up to the proud example set by our ancestors.

I clutched the bundle of cloth that encapsulated all my years until this day—a small, soft pillow—and turned away to make place for the next candidate. Then on to the hall, where I would leave it at the feet of the Augustus statue. He looked as formidable as ever, as godly and distant as last time. Was it really possible I had the bloodless blood of this creature within me?

"Augustus," I murmured, "if you were ever like me, give me a sign." Nothing happened. But I would be watching for it.

·   ·   ·

For the other boys, the ceremony at the Temple of Mars was the focal point. For me, it was just the beginning. Immediately afterward, I was to march at the head of the Praetorian Guards to the Roman Forum. I carried a heavy shield and led them—hundreds of them—across the way and to the central area near the Rostra. I then mounted the platform, where a party of senators welcomed me and announced that I had been awarded the rank of proconsul, with the powers of a general, outside Rome and made a member of all four of the Roman priesthoods. I then gave my first public speech—written for me by Seneca—thanking the Senate for these honors and announcing a distribution of monetary gifts to the soldiers and citizens in my name. "The largesse of Nero!" bellowed one of the Praetorian prefects.

"The largesse of Nero!" the crowd roared back. "Nero, Nero, Nero!" The voices echoed off the marble buildings surrounding us.

I would be lying if I didn't admit I loved it. It was a drug I never knew I wanted.

In the private celebration later, I was struck by the change in how I was treated. Myths are full of stories of transformations—Daphne into a tree, Callisto into a bear, Actaeon into a stag, Narcissus into a flower—but I witnessed firsthand what it meant to change into another creature. Suddenly I was perceived as an adult, a responsible and influential person, a political presence. It was apparent in every gesture, every word. Only Mother continued to treat me the same way—her wayward boy, in her thrall to command.

More followed swiftly. There were games in the Circus to celebrate my coming of age, and I wore the robes of a general celebrating a Triumph, while Britannicus was in boyhood dress and totally ignored by the crowd. Mother had been right that the contrast between us would be striking, and she meant for us to appear that way in public as often as possible.

That summer Claudius left Rome for three days, to spend some time in the Alban Hills, and appointed me city prefect of Rome. I was to hear law cases!

This was too much! I told Claudius it was not appropriate, but he just said, "It is g-good that you learn. I will instruct th-them not to bring difficult or important c-cases before you, but simple ones."

But they disobeyed, eager to put sensitive cases before me for my judgment. That was due to my new high status—a decision by me would be more prestigious than that of anyone else, even an elder.

I spent hours learning about the legal system and even more hours pondering the cases. To my surprise, I enjoyed studying law. It was a great challenge and an equal satisfaction to apply that knowledge to specific cases. It was also a good feeling to settle something, to find an answer, which did not happen in the rest of my life.

Later I was to have the opportunity to argue about cases being decided. The city of Ilium, ancient Troy, had applied to be exempted from Roman taxes. I gave an oration in Greek supporting its claim, citing the historical link between that city and Rome. The petition was granted, and I like to think I was instrumental in restoring the dignity of this place so dear to me.

XXV

Time flew by, months and months tumbling past in a blur, and one day I came into my room to find a box waiting. Inside were two scrolls, some legal certificates, a gold ring, and a necklace of pearls. I was fumbling through them when Mother appeared.

"What is this?" I knew she was in back of it. I also had a sinking feeling I knew what it was.

She sauntered over to me with the smirk I disliked. The one that said, *The joke is on you.* "It is for your upcoming marriage. Yes, it is time you and Octavia were wed. You are fifteen now, she thirteen. I've taken the auspices, and it shall be in June. You don't look pleased."

"I don't care for her, remember?"

"What has that to do with it?"

"Everything. And when you tricked me into it years ago, you said it would probably never come about."

"I was wrong."

"No, you lied."

She shrugged. "Be that as it may, it was formally sealed, and now the time is at hand."

"And what are these things?" I rattled the box.

Wearing her exasperated frown, she leaned in and picked the scrolls up. "These are the stipulations regarding the marriage, the lineage, your duties, property rights, and so on." She held up the legal certificates.

"These are to be witnessed and deposited in the archives after the ceremony. This ring is what you will give her." She handed it to me. It was heavy, bright gold, and showed two hands clasping. "And this is your gift to her. Pearls from the Red Sea." She waved the necklace about, then slammed the box shut.

She thought she was so clever. But she had overlooked one thing. "You can put those things away. We won't be needing them."

She threw up her hands in aggravation. "Don't be contrary. You are trying my patience."

"Haven't you forgotten?" Now I would deliver the blow. "Octavia is my sister now, and under Roman law a brother can't marry his sister." I crossed my arms and stared at her in triumph.

She smiled her poisonous smile. "Oh, I took care of that. Claudius had her adopted into a compliant patrician family who were only too glad to acquire a royal daughter."

Oh, gods. She had bested me. And all this time I had floated in a false security. "When was this?"

She shrugged. "Oh, a while back."

In secret! "Can't this wait?" My last hope.

"No. It must take place, before things change."

"Change? What things?"

"Things we can't foresee. That is the dangerous game fate plays with us. We must fortify ourselves against disruptive change." Then her voice changed, became soft. "Postponing it won't make it easier; it will make it worse. Why do you find her so repellent?"

I sighed, sat down on the cushioned coach. "Repellent is too strong a word. It's simply that she seems an empty vessel. No spark of life there, nothing I can reach out to. And, perhaps, the feeling that she does not like me, either."

"Have you given her a chance to?"

I shook my head, as if to fling away all extraneous ideas. "Our spirits do not touch one another."

"Bosh. You sound like a schoolgirl. In this marriage only two things need to touch: the first I needn't tell you, the second is the legal boundaries of each family."

I snorted.

She bent down and caressed my cheek, moving her fingers very slowly. I tried not to respond to it. "Remember, we have each other. No one else matters." She kissed my ear, whispered, "No one else." I had a near-overwhelming desire to turn my head just slightly and seek her lips. But it did not overwhelm me. I conquered it.

The upcoming nuptials were formally announced. Now I was publicly trapped. I endured congratulations and smutty, nudging asides from Anicetus and Tigellinus. Particularly Tigellinus.

Since he had been recalled from his exile, Tigellinus had steadily insinuated himself with Mother—who made Claudius revoke the ban on his presence in the palace—climbing ever upward in palace appointments and special duties, always the capable executor of any task, especially the unpleasant. He had won me by taking me into the world of horse breeding and racing. Under his tutelage, I had begun driving, first a two-horse, and now a four-horse, chariot. Next would be learning to race against others. We were looking for a suitable venue, private and safe. Despite Mother's belief that she knew everything, we had kept this hidden from her. So we were allies and, despite our age difference, friends. He understood me, or so I believed.

His was the only teasing I could stomach about the Octavia marriage. One afternoon as we were returning from the stables, he said, "Your little bride grows paler and paler." He was munching hazelnuts, throwing the husks on the ground as we walked. "I would not have thought it possible."

"Yes, she was already a ghost," I said. "Perhaps I'll be lucky and she will disappear."

It was April. There were less than two months left. Rome had just finished celebrating its founding, eight hundred and six years before;

trampled flowers and fruit pits littered the streets. I was supposed to have bodyguards whenever I left the palace, but Tigellinus was the equivalent of three. Strong, quick, and vicious, he was a trained fighter. He had the strapping good looks women loved, with piercing blue eyes that never dropped their gaze in deference to anyone. His high cheekbones and strong jaw made him look noble, even godlike, belying his low background.

He laughed. "You will embrace her and find yourself clasping empty air."

"I wish," I said.

He slowed his steps. "Even if she were lovely, perhaps you would still dread the wedding. People dread a test they dare not take." Before I could question him, he stopped and put his hands on my shoulders, looking at me with that unflinching stare. "Do you know what to do with a woman?"

"She isn't a woman, she's a girl."

"You know exactly what I mean. Answer me."

I could have said, how dare you question me like this? And reminded him of my rank. But as he was one of the few I could be honest with, his question was almost a relief. "Not exactly." Isolated as I was, yet always the center of attention, I had never had the opportunity to learn what other boys my age were indulging in. Maybe he could fix this. He was expert at solving problems.

"Just as I thought. Well, my dear Caesar, there's an easy remedy for this." He turned and gestured in a different direction. "Shall we take care of it?"

I felt my breath draining away. Now?

"It's past the ninth hour; the houses will be opening soon." He turned in the direction of the streets of the common people, right behind the stately Forum of Augustus. As we passed it, I burst into nervous laughter, having to stop and hold my sides.

Tigellinus frowned and looked to see what was unusual in the Forum.

Gasping, I said, "This is—this is—a parody of the tour I took with Seneca, to see all the historic monuments."

"Seneca! Well, Tigellinus will take you to see unforgettable monuments," he promised me. "Much more impressive than all the Augustus memorials." He took my hand and dragged me past the Forum, into the warren of little streets, dark from the shadows of the tall apartment blocks—insulae—on either side. The crowds were pressing, the cooking smells from the little street-level tavernas thick around us, the filth underfoot slippery.

"Not the Rome of marble you've been seeing, eh?" he said. "This is the reality behind it. This is where the real Rome is."

Faces of all nationalities bobbed in the crowd. Dark ones: Nubians, Ethiopians. Fair ones: Germans, Britons. Olive-skinned ones: Arabs, Jews, people of the steppes. Hair straight and curly, black, gray, red, gold. Robes, tunics, turbans, sun hats, helmets, veils. Sometimes there was a flash of gold from a necklace or earrings, startling in the surrounding poverty.

A vendor with sausages stopped us, and Tigellinus bought us each some. "You need your strength!" he said, elbowing me. He gulped his down; I thought of a snake swallowing a mouse. "Look here," he said, indicating everything around us. "This is your Rome. These are your people. When you rule, remember them."

He had said the words that everyone avoided like a rain puddle. *When you rule.*

"Because I can assure you, they will remember you."

Did they recognize me? Was that what he meant? Surely not. They could not have known who I was. Not in this mash.

"Fortified now?" he asked, laughing. "We are almost there."

My throat felt dry and I spit out the rest of the sausage. Hunger had no place in me. We went farther down this street, one of the widest in that area, then turned into a very narrow one with a steep incline. Tigellinus strode to one door halfway up, knocking softly. The door creaked open. A blast of perfume rolled out.

Tigellinus stepped in and motioned me to follow. I had a roiling desire to run the other way. But I entered the house and found myself standing in an atrium flanked with pots of lilies and papyrus. It was nothing like its surroundings; crossing the threshold had taken me into a different world.

A slave girl appeared. "Yes?"

"Is Vorax here?" asked Tigellinus.

"I'll fetch her," she said and disappeared. A few moments later she returned with an Amazon-like creature, taller than Tigellinus, with wavy black hair and eyes rimmed with kohl. Heavy bronze bracelets ringed both her forearms.

"Ah, Tigellinus!" she said. She had an accent of some sort that I couldn't place. "You have been missed!"

He stood in that proud stance, legs apart, shoulders back, that made him so recognizable from a distance. "Duties, duties," he said, spreading his hands as if to say, *What can I do?*

She eyed me. "Brought your young slave with you, eh?"

Tigellinus smiled. "Yes. I thought I would give him a reward for his good service."

I almost choked. But at the same time I was grateful for the disguise.

"And what do you have in mind?" she asked. "Are you being generous today?"

"Indeed." He jiggled his money pouch. "Anything he wants! No expense spared."

"A pleasure to work with such a customer." She smiled and asked the slave to bring her the book. *The book!* The book, duly brought and presented to us, contained drawings of men and women in mind-dizzying varieties of coupling. Some of it was difficult to interpret.

"If there is something you prefer that isn't in the book, we do have girls who specialize in areas we don't illustrate. Just tell us, and it will be available." She smiled sweetly and bent over the book, her breasts wafting the perfume I had smelled.

There was a picture of a woman with long golden hair, almost enveloping her partner, in a graceful pose that looked like a gymnastic exhibition. I pointed at it. I still couldn't get my voice.

Tigellinus shook his head. "Too advanced. I suggest you start with something simple." He turned the pages and found one he liked. "Then afterward, perhaps a surprise from one of the other suggestions." He winked.

Vorax nodded, and the slave beckoned to me, leading me down a hallway with many little doors on each side, with placards illustrating the specialty within. My sandals on the stone sounded unnaturally loud. At the end of the hall, she knocked gently, then pushed the door open. She gestured me inside.

The room was very small, with only a bed, a chair, and a small window that let in the afternoon sun. From outside I could hear the shouts of children, the braying of donkeys. A girl rose from the bed. She looked nothing like the brazen Vorax. She was small and dainty, with clouds of reddish hair pinned up on her head, and a white silky robe. "Welcome," she said, her voice soft. She came over to me and took my head in her hands. "Do I have the honor of being your first?"

It was pointless to lie. So I nodded.

She took my hands and led me to the bed. Gently she eased her robe from her shoulders, then took one of my hands and guided it to her hair. "Pull out the pin," she said. I did, and masses of glorious red hair tumbled down. I put both hands in it, and from then on everything that followed was as lovely and natural to me as that silky hair.

Afterward the slave appeared and led me to another room, a larger one. "You must rest now, and take some refreshment." I was sponged off with perfumed water, given a robe of silk, a cup of sweet wine, all in silence. She lit a small pot of cedar incense and left me, the smoke curling upward. The shades were drawn against the hot afternoon sun, and motes danced in the slanting light. I dozed, still stunned by the initiation in the other room. Time was suspended, as suspended as the motes in the air.

Was it a dream? For I saw, in the swirling light around me, a figure approaching. A woman, older than the one I had just been with. Older! Dressed in a way I knew. She came closer, bent down, caressed my cheek.

"My dearest," she said.

Mother! Her lips were close on my face, her breath warm. She slipped onto the couch with me, embracing me. She slid her arms around me, underneath the robe, peeling it off, and I lay naked beside her. She parted her robe, pressing against me, flesh next to flesh. "I have longed for this," she said. Then she kissed me, the deepest kiss possible, and I pulled her onto me and did what we had long been journeying toward.

On the way home, Tigellinus said, "The first girl specializes in boys who have never . . . But the next was Vorax's idea, really. She said they get many requests for doubles of famous women. Cleopatra, Dido, Messalina. This selection was in poor taste. I apologize."

Had it been deliberate? Did Vorax know very well who I was? Or was Mother an object of lust and fantasy in Rome? Horrible, either way.

"I would have preferred Dido," I sniffed, righteously.

But would I really?

XXVI

The day was almost here. May was an unlucky month for marriages, but June, sacred to Juno, was the most fortuitous—although Juno's marriage to Jupiter was hardly successful. In only nine days I must take Octavia's hand and put the gold ring on her finger.

Mother was as cold-blooded about it as ever, seeming to care only that the legalities were in order. "I was younger than you when I married your father," she said.

"Yes, and you had no choice, either. Tiberius paired you, and there was no argument."

"And had there been, my dearest, there would have been no Nero." She came closer, sliding next to me. I felt myself starting to tremble; her nearness was now tinged with the memory of that afternoon in the brothel. Was it she? No, it couldn't have been, although there were stories about Messalina sneaking out and working in a brothel under the professional name "She-Wolf." But the image, the double at Vorax's establishment, seemed exact, perfect, even to the clothes and perfume and touch. And the knowledge of the acts we had indulged in seared my mind, ever raw and vivid.

"Don't pull away," she said. "I was only trying to tell you how something precious can come of something unwanted. You are the most precious thing in my life." Before I could move, she embraced me and kissed my cheek, lingeringly. Then I did not want to move, no, I did not.

On a hot afternoon I stood with Octavia in a mosaic-decorated room in the palace and we spoke words neither of us wanted to say. She wore the traditional veil of bright saffron; I, a new, blindingly white toga. The windows were open, letting in the sweet early-summer air, with a scent of hay. The families stood watching, along with a very select number of officials and friends: Seneca, Burrus, Pallas, several senators. Anicetus and Beryllus, being freedmen, were deemed unsuitable to attend, even though they were closest to me of anyone, and Tigellinus was ruled equally unwelcome. That was just as well; I could not have endured having him witness my hypocrisy. Or cowardice? Or perhaps, to be kinder to myself, it was an act under compulsion, and only that, not a character flaw.

Afterward there was a small celebration, with wine and music. Poignant lyre music, aching and sweet, made the event even more painful to me, underscoring the gap between what a wedding should be and what this one was.

Bosh. You sound like a schoolgirl! Mother's words rang through my head. Perhaps she was right. But I couldn't help it.

Finally the long day ended: the sun set; the fragrant summer evening began. I was to escort my bride to my rooms, with the procession of well-wishers following us. For ordinary people, the bride was customarily escorted through the streets by torchlight to the groom's house. Since we all lived in the same palace, it was a bit of a farce here. But the torches were duly lit and the musicians accompanied all of us. At the threshold I was supposed to pick her up and carry her in, a remembrance of the Sabine women who were forcibly abducted by the Romans. In this case, it was closer to the truth than usual.

I bent down and picked her up. We turned to look at everyone, then

I stepped over the threshold and the waiting slave closed the door. Outside, a great cheer went up.

The slave scurried around, lighting oil lamps, pouring wine for us, and smoothing the bed. We stood awkwardly waiting for him to be finished. I told him to leave. Then we were alone.

She was looking at the floor, not at me. Her thick, dark lashes made little crescents on her cheeks.

"Please look at me," I said. She raised her eyes. She was paler than ever. "Who do you see?"

"I—I—see Nero, who used to be Lucius, whom I have known all my life. There was never a time I did not know you."

"But who is he to you?"

"He was a cousin, then he became my adopted brother; now he is my husband."

"A raft of relatives all in one." I smiled. But the pleasantry fell short. She gave a weak laugh. I handed her a cup of wine, then took one myself. Perhaps this would help. We both gulped them down.

We must get it over with. It had to be done. I took her hand and led her to the bed. It felt as if I was leading an acquiescent animal to a barn.

She lay down obediently, stiff as an oar. The wine had done no good at all. I knew she was frightened, and I tried to soothe her. I spoke softly, I was careful not to be anything but gentle. But it was nothing like the time at Vorax's; it was utterly devoid of any pleasure at all. Perhaps if I had had no comparison . . . But no, that would have been worse, because then we both would have been fearful and paralyzed into complete inaction.

Summer nights are short, and dawn came very early. I got out of bed and put on a robe while she still slept. The creeping light showed her face, which was pretty enough. She was a good person. There was nothing wrong with her, just nothing right for me. I thanked all the gods that I was a man and would not be bound to her for my one source of pleasure.

She stirred, then sat up and saw me. Instinctively she clutched at the sheets to shield herself.

"Good morning," I said, realizing how trite that sounded but unable to come up with anything else.

"Good morning," she murmured. She scurried out of the bed and looked for her own robe, which she quickly put on. The thick gold ring on her left hand shone in the faint light.

We sat together on the couch. She felt insubstantial next to me, a waif. "I promise to be a good wife," she murmured. She looked up at me, a shy smile on her lips. Her eyes were shining. Perhaps the night had not been so bad for her as it was for me. She entwined her fingers in mine. The ring was cold and hard.

I squeezed her hand, bowed my head, and nodded. But I couldn't say the words I should have replied with. I could not say, *I promise likewise.* I was still young enough to be honest.

XXVII

My married life, such as it was, soon assumed a formal and predictable schedule: dinner with the emperor and family, return to our quarters, and retire to separate bedrooms. I could hear her moving around in her nearby room and chastised myself for my inability to follow her in there. There were a few times when I was able to make myself invite her to my bed, or seek her in hers, but each time was a disappointing failure, and the more failures there were, the less inclined either of us was to repeat it. Every morning we greeted one another politely, perhaps strolled in the gardens together, then separated.

I was curious about what she was truly like, but she was hardly likely to confide in me, nor I in her. Our marriage was doomed by the shadows of our parents: her father was married to my mother, and her mother had tried to kill me. Not promising grounds for love. Oh, I knew tales of the children of enemies becoming lovers, like Jason and Medea, but those usually ended with people killing themselves. So Octavia and I soldiered on, smiling in public, dreaming separate dreams in separate beds by night.

That is not the whole picture, however. My bed at the palace may have been empty, but thanks to Tigellinus I had plenty of company in other beds, even if they were hired ones. The brothels of Rome offered infinite variations and versions of pleasure and I took advantage of most of them. They reassured me that my inability to feel passion for Octavia was specific to her. For I suffered no such shortage of desire for the other women; they were probably relieved that there were more than one of them because I would have worn out my welcome (so to speak) on only one.

Because Rome lured people from all the world, a veritable menu of ladies offered any type I could fancy: strapping Gallic women, delicate blondes from the far north, dusky girls from the Levant, women from the steppes beyond the Caucasus. If I wanted a fragile beauty, she was available. If I preferred a big, domineering one (who might even brandish a whip), she was available, too. What I never asked for again was the second woman at Vorax's. Not because I did not want to but because I feared what I would feel if I did. There were times when it was all I could do not to request her, but two things stopped me. The first, that it would unlock something within myself that I could never cage again. The second, more practical reason was that Vorax would know, and remember, that I myself had requested her this time. I did not want to put such a weapon in anyone's hands, one that could prove so dangerous to me in the future.

"You can trust Vorax," said Tigellinus as we walked back late one afternoon. "You can ask her for anything."

Anything—except that one thing.

"Did you like the Chaldean girl today?"

Vorax had just hired her, a slim, dark-skinned beauty with the longest eyelashes I had ever seen—if they were real. She had whipped me up into multiple passions so that the "short" afternoon visit had lasted several hours. I laughed. "Do you need to ask?"

He gave me a knowing look. "Like most sheltered aristocrats, you crave the foreign, forbidden, and exotic," he said.

"Perhaps." And perhaps that was what was wrong with Octavia, in addition to the other impediments. It was true, I was drawn to people who promised escape, adventure. Like Tigellinus himself. As it was, he functioned as my doorway to it.

A few hours later I was the obedient and dutiful son/husband re-clining on the dining couch at the usual family dinner. I was famished after the exertions of the afternoon so it took no playacting for me to relish the food and down many cups of wine.

Perhaps it was only the contrast, but the group seemed unusually stiff and dull that night. I kept drinking wine to blur the edges. But I could hardly keep up with Claudius, who continually held his cup out for refilling, gulped it down, and requested another round. Mother tried to stop him, but he swatted her restraining hand away. "Leave me 'lone," he mumbled.

"Father, perhaps you should stop," said Britannicus suddenly, his high child's voice sounding shrill. "We want to hear your wise words, so don't go to sleep." But in the last sentence, the voice broke and ended lower.

Mother's face was a sheet of dismay as she heard what I had.

Claudius propped his head on his arm. "'Rhaps you are right, son." He burped. "'Nuff for now, you are r-right." He leaned over and rum-pled Britannicus's hair. "My dear son." He looked around. "So, what sh-shall we—talk about?"

A moment of silence while we all searched for a topic, then Octavia said brightly, "Nero and I would like to redecorate our apartments."

We would?

"Some new mosaics for the atrium—" she continued. But Claudius had already fallen asleep, his head lolling on the armrest, his mouth gaping.

Mother made a cluck-cluck sound. "Too late, my dears. You will have to ask him earlier in the day. But I think I can speak for him and say that of course you may redecorate your apartments. We are pleased at this sign you are so happy together."

Back in our quarters, Octavia did not retire to her rooms but sat in our common room. She motioned to the mosaics on the floor and said, "Do you agree with me?"

I had no argument with a change and said, "Yes. It would be a good idea."

"Perhaps we could visit some workshops together and choose a design. I know you have an interest in art."

"Yes, I do." So she had noticed? "I know more about painting than about mosaics, though."

"We can learn together." She stood up and came over to me. She held out her hands and drew me up. "Oh, Nero, I would like that. For us to have our own project, not a task dictated by our parents." Suddenly she threw her arms around me.

I was so startled I almost fell backward into the chair again. Tentatively I held her. "Yes, that would be welcome." My words sounded stupid and staid. But I had been taken unawares, and every conversation I had ever had with her had been a safe, prescribed one, never spontaneous.

I heard a stifled catch of disappointment from her, then she stood on tiptoe and kissed me. Her lips were cool and soft, but chaste as a sister's—which she always would be to me. "Nero, please," she murmured, taking my hand and turning toward her rooms. Silently she led me into her bedroom, dark and waiting. She sat on the bed. "Hold me," she said. "Hold me." I did, feeling her small body, even the bones in her shoulders, delicate little wings.

"Sometimes I am so afraid," she said. "Of all of them."

I held her closer. "So am I, sometimes." She did not know the half of it. I felt a great surge of protectiveness toward her, truly a helpless victim of her circumstances, which included having to marry me.

Protectiveness, however, is the opposite of desire, and as I held her I felt the bracelet pressing into my forearm: the bracelet that enshrined her mother's attempt on my life, an unbreachable barrier between us. It killed whatever passion was trying, weakly, to emerge for me.

The months passed, nothing changed between us, and Octavia and I had soon been married a year. Summer came again, the noons growing ever hotter, as the sun gathered strength, blazing down upon

Rome. Even on the Palatine, breezes were feeble and the marble halls sweated with humidity, little rivulets running down the walls. Still, life in the palace went on doggedly. Seneca outlined speech material for me to develop; Chaeremon, a tutor from the Mouseion in Alexandria, unrolled the maps of the entire empire, then brought in slaves from different regions to talk about the details of their homelands; my lyre teacher worked with the swollen strings to make melodies of a sort. Octavia busied herself overseeing the new mosaics. Britannicus—who knew where he was or what he was doing? He seemed to have vanished. As for Claudius, there was little for him to do. The empire was remarkably quiet—there were no large-scale rebellions, no major campaigns, even very few foreign embassies seeking audience in Rome. It was a remarkable moment, with the world seemingly holding its breath. Claudius chose to enjoy it by stupefying himself with wine most of the time.

"He is not so insensate as he seems," warned Mother as we strolled together. She had suggested we walk around the Palatine. It was less that she wished to view gardens than that she wanted to escape the listening ears within the palace walls.

"He certainly gives a good imitation of it," I said. Every night he fell asleep (the charitable interpretation) or passed out (the reality).

Far beneath us the Forum was swarming with people. Even in this heat, lawsuits would go on, vendors would sell, messengers would dart about, and the brothels would advertise. We looked down upon it from our rarified perch, Mother fanning herself.

She was, as always, fashionably turned out. While she looked down on the Forum, I studied her profile, her golden earrings swinging against her cheeks. It was rare that I had an opportunity to look at her without her eyes catching me. She was not beautiful but her features were what people called "handsome"—even, strong, and unblemished. Oddly enough, her neck was her best feature—it was long, sweetly curved, and carried her head proudly. Artists do not give enough credit to necks, for our whole impression of someone's bearing rests on the neck. A bowed one, a short one, a fat one, ruins the whole.

Suddenly she turned and caught me. Instead of asking why I was looking, she smiled slyly and cocked her head, her eyes locking on mine. "I am flattered," she said, "that you find me so absorbing."

"Always, Mother," I returned. She had lost the ability to embarrass me; I could answer her on equal ground. "Shall we continue?" I held out my elbow and she looped her hand through.

"I am concerned," she said. Now the real reason for the walk emerged, as I'd known it would. "Claudius frightens me. Lately he has been talking of revising his will. Worse than that, he harps on Britannicus and what a fine young man he is growing up to be. I overheard him saying, 'Soon things will change for you, dear one.' And now that Britannicus's voice has started changing, he doesn't seem like a child any longer. What if Claudius decides to advance him before you? He has never formally designated you as his heir."

An elderly couple approached us, shuffling painfully along. After they were safely past, Mother said, "It is only natural to prefer your own flesh and blood to an adoptee. He is heading in that direction. Every day that Britannicus grows up before his eyes is a day when you diminish."

She was right, of course. I had thought of that myself. But we had done everything possible to put me first, and if nature had overtaken us, there was no remedy. I said as much.

"Do you feel ready to take that place, if it is offered you?"

"I am too young yet," I said. "How could I possibly be emperor? We need more time."

"You are sixteen," she said. "Almost old enough."

I laughed. "Yes, if I were Alexander the Great."

"Perhaps he did not feel ready, either. His father's death was unexpected."

But suspicious. And eerily like my situation. Philip had just taken a young bride and had a new son, whom Alexander's mother feared would supplant her son. His timely assassination pointed to her.

"But not unwelcome, surely," she added.

I did not dare ask her what she was thinking. Kill Britannicus? I did not want to know. Knowing would mean I must either acquiesce to it or try to stop it. If the latter, I would be honest but empty-handed; if the former, a murderer—but an emperor.

"Seneca says there is no one—no one—whose death is not a relief to *someone*," I admitted.

"Wise man," she said. "I knew he was the right tutor for you." She sighed. "The heat is too much for me. I will return to the palace and sit by the shaded fountain. Now that we have decided what to do."

I turned away and continued walking by myself. Now that *she* had decided what to do—oh, gods. I had not agreed, but I had not said no. I had left it all in her hands, as she had managed my entire life up until now, maneuvering and plotting and murdering. Never had I actually asked myself whether I wanted to be emperor. I had assumed when the time came I would know, that I would have a wisdom beyond what I had then, so I needn't think about it. Now I must.

Walking farther down the hill I left the area, skirting the Forum. The heat rose in waves, the damp smells of wilted flowers, overcooked meats, and human sweat smacking me in the face.

The men milling in the area barely looked at me, and when they did, what did they see? A youth with passably pleasing features—not an emperor. An invisible youth, a youth with freedom to pass through them unnoticed. A youth with freedom to go anywhere and leave no trace. If this youth were suddenly transformed into an emperor, his face would be recognizable from one end of the empire to the other, if not in person then on coins.

Did I want to be emperor? Could I be emperor? The questions were not the same.

I stumbled along, only half seeing where I was going. Around the base of the Forum rose the Caelian Hill, the one nearest the Palatine. Its gentle slope beckoned to me, and I began to climb it. In spite of the heat, the olive and cypress trees offered shade, and the walk up was not taxing. There were not many people about, for which I was grateful. Think. I needed to think. *Emperor, emperor, emperor* kept spinning around in my head. The houses on each side were ample, luxurious but not in the manner of mansions, a place where one could be more than comfort-able but not ostentatious. Here lived the magistrates, wealthy merchants, retired generals. One did not need to be emperor to live well. As I was lost in my thoughts, I heard a crowd of people approaching, coming down the street. They were dressed in mourning, and suddenly I realized how familiar this street looked. I had been here before—the ocher walls, the cypress tree—when, when? I kept walking, walking upward toward the direction of the procession. Just as I reached the end, pallbearers emerged from a house, bearing a coffin. The house—the house—yes, Anicetus had taken me here. It was the house of Alexander Helios. I stopped and bowed my head in respect as the coffin passed.

A sign. It was a sign. What could be plainer? How did it happen I was walking here this very day? One era had finally ended. The last of Cleopatra's children had gone. But did I not have Antony's blood? Their story had not ended, no. Or rather, it would begin anew.

I still had the coin he had given me, *her* coin. But his words were what came back to me now, his words I would never forget: *I surrender her and her dreams and ambitions into your safekeeping.*

What would Cleopatra do? Would she hesitate even an instant to become emperor, if fate offered it to her?

XXVIII

Between the first mention of the possibility of the deed and its enacting, I entered into a strange world where everything was suspended, interrupted by brief periods of normal life. I would lie awake possessed by trepidation and suspense, only to awaken to forgetfulness, until the memory rushed on me like a wild beast, tearing at me. I would jump up and make haste to dress, as if daylight and clothes would banish the nightmare.

In the meantime a semblance of normality hung like a pall over us. The family dinners continued. My instructions with Seneca continued. My excursions with Tigellinus continued, although they had lost their flavor for me. My chariot-driving practices continued. The music lessons halted, as I did not want to desecrate the beauty of them with this tainted time.

Mother summoned me for other unpleasant tasks and I dared not disobey. At this point I honestly did not know if she would destroy me as well. Such was my confusion and lack of understanding. I found myself standing before her in her opulent Augusta quarters, a place I had seldom ventured into. The walls glittered with gold inlays, reflected in the black marble floors. She had an unusual number of couches in a variety of styles—ivory legs, carved wooden backs, high ones that required a step stool to mount, low ones where one could faint without much of a fall. It was a long way from her austere hut on Pontia.

"Yes, I enjoy being Augusta," she said, reading my mind. This unnerved me even further. "People say possessions and honor are meaningless. Those are the people without them."

"I can verify that," I said. "My bed here is more comfortable than the one at Aunt Lepida's." But I had slept better there.

She smiled, the curve of her lips animating her entire face. Her eyes shone. "You read my mind," she said, echoing my own thought moments before. "But then, we have always had an extraordinary communication. We barely need words, you and I. We are almost one person."

Then why am I afraid of you? Is it of myself that I am afraid? And why do I dream shameful dreams about you, dreams that haunt me even in daylight, dreams so real I can feel your warm flesh beneath my hands? No, we are separate, as separate as two people can be.

She came over to me, handed me a cup of fresh grape juice. Of course it was in a heavy pure gold vessel. "It is about your aunt Lepida that I want to speak."

I felt relief flooding me. It wasn't Britannicus; it wasn't Claudius or Octavia. "What about her?"

"I need you to testify against her in a trial I am bringing against her."

"A trial! Whatever for?"

She turned away in that graceful way she had, swishing her gown out to one side, then turning to look at me over her shoulder. "She is dangerous. She is plotting against me, and Claudius. She has never forgiven him for executing her daughter and husband. She must be stopped."

I had long wondered why she had not turned on Claudius, even though Messalina had deserved her fate. A daughter is always innocent in a mother's eyes.

I almost laughed, though, at Mother pretending to be Claudius's fierce protector. Perhaps she didn't want anyone to have the honor of murdering him but herself.

"How do you know this?"

"There is nothing that happens that I don't know about." She looked at me tellingly. "You needn't bother with the details. But they will call you as a witness."

"What are the charges?" I would not lie. I would not! And how could I be a witness to anything in her house when I had left it over a decade before?

"Using magic," she said. It was a capital crime. "I know you saw it when you were there."

A sickening remembrance raced through me . . . the session with the magus, when they tried to infuse a dream into me that would beam itself to Claudius and save Silanus.

"We have the magus. He has confessed. All you need to do is confirm what happened."

But it was innocent. Lepida was only trying to save her honest husband, who had acted honorably in rejecting Messalina's vile approaches, and now this was her reward.

"Even if it was true, it has nothing to do with plotting against anyone now."

"I don't care what's true; I care only for what can be made to look true. The fact that she once practiced magic is enough."

"You are monstrous." There, I had said it. "I won't do it."

Her eyes narrowed. "Oh, yes, you will. If you don't, I will ruin you."

"That would hurt you far more than me, Augusta. All you have worked for all these years, destroyed?"

"I have other arrows in my quiver," she said. "Do you think you are the only one?"

"I am your only son, that much I know."

"In nature, yes, but the law is not nature. Now, let us not fence and quibble. You will witness against Lepida, and you need speak only the truth. The truth will condemn her. I am not asking you to lie, only to tell the truth. Why are you balking at that?"

"She was kind to me. I have no wish to cause her any sorrow."

"So you side with someone who is plotting against me?"

"So far you have given me no evidence that she is plotting against you, only that you claim she is. You will have to do better than that."

"I don't have to do anything. You are not the judge, only a witness."

Now she turned wheedling. "Come, come, be reasonable. We must elim-inate all enemies. What was it Augustus was told, to justify his killing Caesar's son by Cleopatra? 'It is not good to have too many Caesars.'"

"Hardly the same situation."

"My, what a stubborn lad you are. So argumentative."

"A novelty for you, I am sure. No one else would dare."

"A novelty I only applaud coming from my son. It means—it means—that when you take power, no one can sway you. You are your own man."

And in mentioning that, she cinched her case. I would have to testify; she had dangled what we both knew was the ultimate end of it all.

Still, I found it anguishing to testify; I hated every moment of it. Afterward I went back to my room and wept.

Lepida was found guilty and executed. On the day she died, I fasted and asked her forgiveness.

For a great while after that—or so it seemed, for time had taken on phantasmagoric aspects for me—nothing happened. Gradually my apprehensions subsided. Perhaps it had all been talk on Mother's part, like her threat to ruin me, to destroy her handiwork. The weather turned; autumn arrived. Somehow that convinced me that our talk in the searing summer heat had not been real, as if one season canceled out what happened in a previous one. Perhaps I myself believed in magic—that cool air could erase what had come before.

Then I saw her. Hurrying out of the Augusta's apartments, her head covered by a shawl but her face visible. Locusta. Then I knew. I knew the instrument she had chosen, the means she would use.

XXIX

LOCUSTA

I stood stock-still. There he was, staring at me. Agrippina had assured me he never came to this section of the palace. But now he was here, blocking my path.

I had not seen him in seven years, but I would recognize him anywhere. He had distinctive eyes, blue-gray, that seemed to see right through a person. He was almost a man now, grown tall, with broad shoulders and strong legs. The timorous child was no more. There was no escape; I would have to face him.

"It is, I believe, the prince Nero," I said. I smiled. Perhaps he did not remember me.

"It is, I believe, the poisoner Locusta," he replied. His voice was an adult's, cold and deep.

I was undone. Agrippina had miscalculated. I thought, fleetingly, of pretending I was someone else, but he was too intelligent for that ploy. I would have to honor that, meet intelligence with the respect it deserved. "Yes," I admitted. "That has been my calling. But I have paid for it. I have spent the past few years in prison."

"How did you get out?" he asked warily.

"Your mother sent for me."

"Of course." He motioned to me. "Let us find a place where we can talk." He nodded toward the Augusta's apartments. "Away from here."

That was fine with me. If Agrippina saw what had happened, she would have blamed me for blundering, not herself for making a mistake.

He led us to a bench on the far side of the palace gardens. There were only a few gardeners about, clipping and pruning. We made sure to sit far from them. A fountain splashed noisily nearby, masking our conversation.

"You killed my stepfather," he said. His tone was one I hope never to hear again from another human being—hard, pitiless like the gods. "You pretended to comfort me, all the while taking him from me."

"I was hired to do so," I said. "I had no choice in the matter."

"You could have refused the assignment."

"A tradesman cannot refuse assignments."

"And now you are here to take someone else from me. Who?"

"I don't know."

"What do you mean? How can you not know?"

"I mean, the poison is generic. It can be used on anyone. She did not tell me who. Perhaps she felt it was safer that way."

"Can't you force her to tell you? Ask for particulars so you can tailor the potion?"

"Have you ever tried to force the Augusta to do anything? It is impossible for someone like me. And my, you seem to be knowledgeable about the way poisons work yourself."

"Mother takes antidotes, that I know. That way she feels she is protected."

"Perhaps everyone should." I laughed. "But I will tell you a secret. They don't work. People imagine they do, it gives them security, but they are living in a fool's paradise. They are easier to poison because their guard is down."

For some reason this softened him, made him smile. A funny little secret smile. "What does it feel like, having power over life and death? Knowing you can erase someone's future with one swallow? How do you feel when you look at us? Amused? Sorrowful?"

I looked him straight in the eyes. Oh, those eyes, penetrating, knowing. "When you are emperor, you will know how it feels."

XXX

NERO

I was shaking. The encounter was traumatic, blending the past—the aching loss of Crispus—with the present and its swirling fears. The proof was Locusta here: Something was going to happen. Someone was going to die. Soon.

Or, I assumed soon. Perhaps Mother would keep the poison for future use. How long did it retain its potency? I should have asked. Oh, what thoughts were these? How much had she concocted? Enough for several people? Who was the intended victim? Could it be, might it be possible, that I was the target, and Mother's threat to me was no idle one?

No, no, I reassured myself. The person must be Britannicus. That made the most sense. Claudius she would leave alone; he was harmless enough now, and the older I was before he passed away, the better a ruler I would be. With no Britannicus, there was no one for him to prefer before me. Yes, it must be Britannicus.

It caused me to look at him with new eyes. He had had a miserable life so far. To be Messalina's child was bad enough. And who knew if Claudius was really his father? It could have been that actor she'd slept with, or any number of men. Perhaps that was why Claudius had adopted me, since he could not be sure Britannicus was even his son. He was seven when his mother was executed. Then I came along, older and taking the center stage from him. Besides that, he was sickly, prone to bouts of what may have been epilepsy. That was the surest proof he was Claudius's true son, for Claudius had so many infirmities.

But his very misfortunes made him dangerous, for a person with a grudge can be set on revenge. He still insisted on calling me Lucius, to emphasize that he did not recognize my place in his family. When he was declared an adult—he was still six months away from his fourteenth birthday—who knew what he might do?

Yes, it must be Britannicus Mother would strike at, as a preventive measure.

There was no point in warning him. There were already professional tasters to protect him, but I assumed Mother and Locusta had already thought of that. All I could do was be watchful and hope I could actually intercept some other measure, such as Mother handing him a tainted tidbit in a setting where no tasters were about. I did not want him to die; it was the ultimate cheat in a life already cheated of so much.

September passed with nothing untoward, but I could not relax my vigilance. I would not be soothed, beguiled. The warm, somnolent days of October fell over Rome, turning everything golden. Fat leaves swirled down, spiraling like benevolent spirits hovering over us. Octavia was particularly pleased that the autumnal mosaic she had selected was finally finished, just in time for the season.

"Don't you think her face is lovely?" she asked me as we stood over it.

The face had extraordinary beauty, as if the passing of a season, of completion, was to be embraced, not mourned.

"Yes," I agreed. "You have done well. Her face looks familiar, but not quite."

"That is because you have seen it," she said. "My attendant served as a model."

"Indeed? I don't remember ever seeing her."

"That is because you so seldom come to my apartments." She said it matter-of-factly, not accusingly. Our lives were parallel, running on different roads.

I stared at the face, perfect in its ripeness. "She seems the very goddess of autumn."

"I don't think you believe me," she said. "Well, I'll call her and you can see for yourself."

"Oh, you needn't—" I was in a hurry to get to other business. I had only stopped to visit her to be polite. But she clapped her hands and bade the slave bring Acte quickly.

"I won't delay you," she said apologetically. Her whole relationship with me was based on apology, it seemed. "Oh, here you are!"

The woman in the mosaic, living, breathing, moving, came into the room. Perhaps it was that aspect that struck me dumb, a work of art brought to life, even though of course it was the other way around. But I had seen the art first, so to me it was the original.

"Acte, my husband so admired the mosaic he could not believe it was modeled on a living person. So I wanted to prove it."

"It is true," I said. "I should have known no artist could have invented you."

The woman smiled without a trace of a simper. She bowed her head. "It was my honor to do it. I wanted the mosaic to be exactly what you and my mistress wanted."

Her hair was dark, her eyes warm and inviting to conversation.

"'Acte'? Are you Greek?"

"Yes. My family is from Lycia."

"Her father was captured by a Roman garrison commander, executed, and his whole family forced into slavery," said Octavia. "They were of noble standing in their homeland but put into chains because they resisted becoming a Roman province!"

Acte did not comment or attempt to excuse her origins.

"It is a long way from chains to a princess's quarters," I said, hoping to prompt her. I wanted to know all about her. I wanted to stand there as long as possible, looking at her.

"I am a freedwoman now," she said. "I am here out of choice. I served with the foreign-born household staff of Claudius and, when she married, the lady Octavia chose to take me with her." Her voice was as rich and assured as her bearing promised. "My Roman name is Claudia Acte, as I was freed by that household."

I felt as I imagined Hades must have when he saw Persephone gathering her flowers in the field; I wanted to abduct her, carry her away, spend hours finding out all about Acte, the Greek from Lycia. Instead I just nodded and said, "Thank you, Octavia, for showing me the inspiration for the mosaic." I looked at Acte. "Every time I see it I will bring your face back into my imagination." Then, abruptly, I turned and left.

Even Acte and the thought of her (in my bed? walking beside me in the fields? lying on the banks of a stream with me, watching the birds soar?) could not banish the gnawing anxiety within me. I would jump every time there was a loud noise, watch suspiciously if any unknown person was seen in a palace passageway. Yet I never discerned where the danger would strike, or how near it was.

The annual observance of the divinities Fides *et* Honos—Faith and Honor—was upcoming, and Claudius decided to have a banquet to celebrate these quaint virtues, sorely lacking in his own household. There were entertainments—acrobats, dancers, poetry recitations—that lasted long enough that by the time we were called to dinner our appetites were keen.

What a jolly gathering. Mother was next to Claudius on the left couch, and I was next to her. The middle couch had a familiar-looking stocky fellow in the place of honor, with Britannicus next to him and Octavia at the end. Directly across from me was the couch with Seneca and two men I didn't recognize. At least this promised novelty in conversation—three people I wasn't familiar with, a rarity at an official gathering. Behind us, a second arrangement held another three couches with more people I didn't know.

Claudius flourished his goblet and gave a confused speech about the history of faith and honor in Rome. He was sober at this point. Mother also welcomed everyone and spoke effusively of the nobility of the Romans. I knew she would manage to slip in Germanicus's name somehow, and she did. She announced that she had just renamed the fortress on the Rhine where she was born Colonia Agrippinensis. "I was born when my noble father, Germanicus, commanded the legions there," she said. "It will be a colony where retired soldiers will settle."

Let no occasion pass without a bow to Germanicus. I held out my cup for more wine.

"Another first for the Augusta," said Seneca, across the way. "A colony named for a woman!" He lifted his cup.

The man at the end of his couch chimed in. "About time! I say, who's next?" He had the broad face and ready smile of someone who always brought the wineskins to the party.

"Serenus," said Mother, "who would you nominate? One of the damsels you have rescued from a fire?" In so doing, she put him in his place. He was commander of the watch—chief of the city fire brigades, the Vigiles Urbani—I found out later.

"My cousin would have many to nominate, then," said Seneca smoothly. "He is a favorite with the ladies."

"Indeed," piped up the man in between them, a foppish-looking fellow with a disarming grin. "I know, I've been on rounds with him."

"That lasted well past the time the fires were put out, eh, Otho?" said Serenus, nudging him. Otho giggled. Was that a wig he was wearing?

"Days and nights mix all together with him," said Otho.

Mother put a stop to this frippery by saying, "Now, here's a true soldier and protector of Rome," indicating the stocky man with the short choppy hair in the guest of honor place. "Sextus Afranius Burrus, who has just been appointed head of the Praetorians." The man nodded curtly.

"I thought there were supposed to always be two heads of the Praetorians," said Britannicus. His voice had completely changed by now. "What happened to Rufrius Crispinus and Lusius Geta?"

"It's better security to have it all in the hands of one person," said Mother airily. "Burrus is well qualified. He's served bravely in the army—injuring his hand in the process—as well as a financial agent to myself and the emperor." *Don't argue,* her mien announced. Britannicus glowered and looked away.

"I will always make the protection of the imperial family, and Rome, my highest priority," Burrus said. For some reason I believed him. Could it be that he was actually honest? He nodded to the company, and we all drank to him.

Claudius said nothing; he was unashamed that his wife made all the political appointments and openly admitted it. But what was that, next to the fact that he allowed her to receive foreign ambassadors on a dais next to his, as if she were an equal ruler? I glanced over at him. He was beginning to look drunk already.

The long parade of courses and food commenced. Pigs' teats stuffed with sea urchins. Herons' tongues in honey sauce. Moray eels drowned in hot sauce. In between, oceans of wine.

Claudius was nodding. Then a platter of stuffed mushrooms was proffered. The odor was tantalizing. Mother extended a long, thin blade and speared one for herself, munching it noisily. I started to reach for one myself, but she forestalled me, selecting one from the edge of the platter and feeding it to me; I sucked it off the end of her knife, succulent in all its juices. It was oddly erotic; she looked at me deeply, holding my eyes with hers. Then she turned and speared another one from the middle of the platter, offering it to Claudius. He opened his mouth like a great fish and took it in. In a few moments his head drooped and he fell asleep. No one noticed at first, it was such a common occurrence. But when he could not be roused, Mother ordered a litter to be brought and for him to be taken to his room. She assured the guests that there was nothing amiss. "Alas, the emperor often drinks too much at dinner," she said. "But he would be disappointed if tomorrow he learned that his sleepiness had spoiled the banquet. Stay, stay, drink and enjoy yourselves."

She slid her hand across my back, caressing me. I knew then that there would be no tomorrow for Claudius. *It* had come, the danger I had watched for, right under my nose, and I had missed it. Then suddenly I wondered what was in the mushroom she had fed me. Moments passed, and nothing happened. My stomach felt the same. At least so far. But she had had the power to kill me then and there and chose, for now, to spare me. That was what her caress had said. *I could have, but I did not. See how I love you?* Or perhaps it was only to allay suspicion. It would have been too obvious if both of us had died the same night. Lurching, my legs shaking, I got up from the couch and left the room.

I did not sleep—how could I? Instead I sat in my tunic, perched on the side of my couch, watching the flames flickering in the oil lamps. Dancing, jumping, swaying, throwing shadows on the walls. Outside, the winds of autumn blew leaves against the windows, making a crackling sound. The wine wore off and the naked truth stood before me, too large to comprehend. I stood on a precipice, looking down into an abyss—the abyss of the future. Dark, dark, no bottom in sight.

Gradually the darkness faded and the sky grew gray; the light from the lamps faltered and sputtered out. Mother stole into the room, a ghostly figure who slid next to me. She put her arms around me and rested her head on my shoulder. The feel of her was comforting, for at that moment I was a child again, a lost child adrift on a perilous sea.

"You are shaking," she said. She held me tighter. "Do not be afraid. This is what you were born for. The moment that has waited for you."

"Claudius is dead?" I asked.

"Yes. Just now. It took several hours." So she openly admitted it. "He didn't suffer. In fact, he never woke up. It was like every other evening."

"Except that it ended." I drew back. "How did you accomplish it? The tasters had tested the platter, I assume."

"Only one mushroom was poisoned," she said, "and only I knew which one. I knew they would test an outer one; they always do.

Predictability makes any system easy to evade—a guard who always passes at a certain hour, for example."

So her aim had not been Britannicus after all. I had been looking in the wrong direction.

"Now listen," she said. "Here is what will happen. We will give out the news that the emperor is ill. We will seal the palace shut and let no one in or out. Burrus—why do you think I appointed him?—will summon the Praetorians. The Senate will pray for the emperor's recovery; we will have the acrobats from last night perform in his chamber to entertain him. At noon, the time the astrologers have told me is the fortunate hour, you will step forth out of the palace gates and be announced as emperor. The Praetorians will cheer and march you right away to their barracks, where they will salute and proclaim you emperor. You will give a speech and distribute money. Then you will go to the Senate house and have them formally recognize you as emperor. You will give this speech"—she thrust a scroll into my hands—"prepared for you by Seneca. We want no nonsense of the delay that kept Caligula and Claudius in limbo before they could assume the office."

I toyed with the scroll. So Seneca was in on it, too? How many people were party to this plot?

Once again she read my mind. "I learned from the mess with Caligula—that botched assassination. I knew I should manage it myself. Conspirators are a nuisance. But it's been obvious you would succeed Claudius. Seneca merely prepared a speech to be used anytime."

She was lying, of course, but doing it to assure my cooperation and assuage my conscience.

"Now make yourself ready, my son. My son the emperor." She stood, bent down, and kissed my cheek, then held my head against her, cradling me. "The youngest emperor there ever has been, you are. Even Alexander and Cleopatra were older. But you will eclipse them both; your name will be legendary. So do not fear."

Light was stealing into the room by the time she left. It was true morning. Morning of the first day I was emperor.

Emperor. I could barely comprehend it; my head swam from the lack of sleep and the emotions. They say that a dying man sees his whole life pass before his eyes, quick as a flash. I was dying, dying to my old life and my old self, and it was true, a pageant passed before my eyes: the boats of Caligula, the olive harvest at Aunt Lepida's house, the house of Alexander Helios, the sands of the practice arena, the oracle at Antium, the Troy game. Sixteen years of life. Sixteen years that were hardly adequate preparation for what lay before me.

I stood up. Is anyone ever ready, ever prepared, enough?

XXXI

The palace was quiet, as if it lay under a spell. I stole down corridors, devoid of the usual bustle and company. I had dressed in a clean tunic and under my arm I carried my finest toga, which I must appear in when I first stepped out of the palace. It would be the first glimpse the crowd would have of their new emperor, and may all the gods let me look like one.

Within Claudius's quarters, another spell was working. The dead emperor was propped up in bed, resting against pillows, while the troop of acrobats performed their antics to amuse him. Either their eyesight was bad (doubtful) or they had been well paid (more likely) not to notice that the emperor's expression never changed.

I made my way over to him, bending close. In that instant I comprehended the enormity of death, how utterly different it was from life. The face was the same, the expression one I had seen many times, but the form was as remote from life as a statue is. With no one looking, I slipped a coin for the Ferryman into his cold mouth.

"Farewell, my father," I whispered. He had been kindly to me. I pressed the little ring he had given me long before against his arm. "Safe journey, dear friend. I thank you for your protection all my years."

"Sssh, he is resting." Mother appeared by my shoulder.

In one corner, Britannicus and Octavia clutched one another, weeping. Did they know, or were they blind, too?

"I should not have argued with him," blubbered Britannicus. "How did I know it was the last time we would speak?" So he knew.

"No matter when or how we part in life," Mother said, "we always feel that way." She clasped him to her bosom. "Oh, you are the very image of him, all I have left of him now!"

There was a clamor outside the door, and Britannicus turned toward it, but Mother clung to him, preventing him from moving. The last thing she wanted was for anyone outside to see him at this time. She managed to keep both Octavia and Britannicus effectively detained inside, shoving them into the keeping of one of the chamber attendants.

While the acrobats were performing their finale, Mother told me, "Put on your toga; the hour is here." I did so, and before Britannicus or Octavia could see us at the far end of the room, she threw open the doors and quickly closed and locked them behind us. "Outside, quickly!" We walked through the corridors and out to the palace steps, where a vast crowd had gathered, ringed by the Praetorians.

The sun was at its height, the auspicious hour predicted. Bright sunshine poured down, anointing my head. I stood and surveyed the people stretching out as far as I could see.

Burrus, impressive in uniform, signaled for the trumpets. The rich sound rang out, echoing from the surrounding buildings. "Emperor Claudius is dead. Behold your new ruler, Emperor Nero." There was a moment of stunned silence. Where is Britannicus? they were wondering. Then a roar of approval, of welcome.

It was a sound I was never to forget, as sweet as any notes from a lyre, and more eternal.

Everything happened as Mother had planned. I was carried in a litter through the streets of Rome to the Praetorian barracks; as our journey progressed and the news spread, more and more people came out, and the crowds choked the streets. "Nero! Nero!" they cried. I reached out from the litter and clasped their hands as I passed. They threw flowers in. It was Fontinalia, the Festival of the Fountains, and every fountain in Rome was draped with garlands. The waters gurgled and sang as I passed, and did not begrudge me the flowers the people robbed them of.

The twelve thousand soldiers at the barracks formally proclaimed me emperor, and I announced the monetary gifts they would receive—the equivalent of twenty years' salary for each man. Just so is the price of the emperorship.

I was then taken to the Curia in the Forum, where the senators were waiting, rows of solemn faces. It was late afternoon by then and the sun's rays were slanting, bathing everything in gold. Also as Mother had planned, the swiftness of the events and the wholehearted endorsement of the Praetorians had squashed any possibility of the Senate nominating a candidate of their own. Standing before them, I read the speech Seneca had written; it was, of course, perfect and reverential, and it involved many promises of my future rule. As I finished, the senators proclaimed it was the speech of a god, and that it should be inscribed on a silver tablet and read every time a new consul took office. Just so is the transition from citizen to supreme ruler—my words (not even my own) were now divine.

They heaped many titles on me, but I refused the most unwarranted: Pater Patriae, Father of His Country. Let me earn it first, I told them.

Back in the palace, Claudius's body had been removed. I was to move into the emperor's quarters but only after the funeral. For now, I would remain in my old rooms. I sought them gladly. There had been enough change today. I watched the stars come out, one by one, ending this unique day. The sky grew darker until it was full night. The oil lamps were lighted again, making a full circle of time.

Mother stole in and stood beside me. Hand in hand, silently, we stood before the night sky, no words necessary, no words adequate. After a time she quietly left the room, depositing a scroll on my table. The door closed softly.

I slumped down on a stool near it. Should I even open it? Should I save it until this exhaustion passed? For I was beyond exhaustion. No, whatever was in it belonged to the memory of this day, made sacred by it. I unrolled the scroll and read, spelled out in order, the offices that I now held, the extent of my power.

Commander in Chief of the Army: absolute control of all legions throughout the world on land and sea. Twice a year they would all pledge allegiance to me. I had the power to declare war and conclude peace.

Supreme Governor of All Provinces: throughout the empire.

Tribune of the People: I could veto any measure the Senate enacted.

Pontifex Maximus: head priest of the Roman religion.

Augustus: the head of state; anything against me was lèse-majesté, treason.

Oh, to put such power in one person's hands—mine. I was stunned, distrustful of myself. I rolled up the scroll. I must never forget this first feeling of trepidation, and make sure I never betrayed this trust.

There was a soft knock at the door. A guard stepped in. "Imperator, what is the watchword for tonight?"

"Optima Mater—the Best of Mothers."

Thus the day ended, as even the most golden extraordinary days must, and I slept at last.

XXXII

The next day is a blur in my mind, as slowly, like a silk square drifting to earth, the unreality of the time preceding settled into the worldly time before me. There were a thousand practical matters to be attended to. Claudius's state funeral. Congratulations and recognition from all quarters. The move into Claudius's palace quarters. The acquisition of the imperial signet. The assumption of all my titles and prerogatives.

Unlike foreign realms, which have kings, Rome has no coronation ceremony. There is no special moment, no anointing, no diadem, no crown, no one gesture or object to demarcate the moment I passed from citizen to supreme ruler, which is why it all melds together in my memory. But I felt different; something infused me that had not been there before.

Others saw it, felt it. I sensed an awe, a hesitation in those I had always been carelessly casual with. Even Seneca was diffident, approaching me with a slight hesitation.

"Come now," I said. "Please do not treat me differently. I am still the same person."

He shook his head, almost pityingly. "No, my lord, you are not." That was when I knew. No one could be honest or open with me ever again. I had entered an unknown country, where I would always be traveling alone.

•   •   •

There was only one person who did not understand this: Mother. When she looked at me she did not see the emperor but the same boy who would be—or should be—obedient to her. She had made me emperor not so I could be one, but so she could be empress behind my facade.

I had not assumed the office for a week when I came upon her ordering a statue—a statue of her crowning me!

"It is not for Rome," she said, "but for the provinces. Don't you like the design?"

It showed me, in military garb, standing to her right, while she leaned over and officiously bestowed a laurel crown on my head. She was taller than me in this depiction, altogether more stately, while I looked pouty and disaffected.

"No, I don't," I said. "And you have no business ordering such things, let alone installing them."

"All right, then, I'll have the artist make changes. What would you like?"

"That you scrap the whole thing," I said.

"I agree, it's wrong, I'm not taller than you. I'll make sure it's corrected."

"There'll be no statue!"

"Oh my, now you seem as petulant as the statue itself. Perhaps it's realistic after all." She rose and stroked my cheek. "Let's not quarrel. Forget the statue."

But she didn't forget it, I discovered later. She ordered it and had it shipped to Aphrodisias, where it was set up in the imperial cult temple. More ominously, using her authority as Augusta, she ordered new official gold and silver coins, coins that proclaimed all over the empire, in the code of coinage, that she was the true ruler. The obverse—the important side—showed our profiles facing one another, equal size, with her titles circling us, while my titles were relegated to the back. Furthermore, her titles were listed in the grammatical case of a ruler, whereas mine were in the case of a mere dedication. Subtle differences but all-important.

I flew into a rage when Tigellinus brought me one of them. The effrontery! I closed my fist over the offending coin and took several breaths to try to control myself. "Thank you," I finally said. "You are a loyal supporter."

He merely inclined his head. "I am only doing my job."

"Who does she think she is?" I burst out, then laughed at how dumb that sounded. She was my mother, obviously.

"She thinks she is still empress," said Tigellinus.

"What do other people think?"

Now he looked embarrassed. If it had not been unlikely for the burly reprobate, I would have sworn he blushed slightly. "That she controls you by an incestuous relationship."

"Lies!" But were they entirely? What is real, what really happens or what happens only in our minds? Perhaps both?

"I would suggest that you stop traveling in the same litter, then."

"What do you mean?" We very rarely did.

"They say it's obvious what's been going on when you emerge from the litter, because your clothes are all stained."

"How absolutely absurd!" I bellowed. "Why, when I have an entire palace and private quarters, would we resort to a litter in public?"

"Gossip is not logical, Caesar. Of course it is absurd. But colorful, you must admit." He permitted himself a laugh. I joined him.

"No more litters, then. But they will just invent new settings, I am sure. And this coin does not help! No, it confirms the idea that she rules me!" Back to the coin.

"Then order the mint to stop producing them," he said.

Yes. That was obvious.

* * *

I had the mint cease production of them and start making a new coin to replace them—a coin that had both our profiles, but not facing one another. Hers was behind mine, just an outline. My titles were changed to nominative and put on the obverse, while hers, now dedicatory, were banished to the back side. If she noticed, she never mentioned it. But of course she noticed.

Nothing deterred her. She wanted Senate meetings to be held on the Palatine, so she could eavesdrop from behind a thick curtain and listen to the deliberations secretly, since women were not allowed in the Curia itself. During Claudius's reign she had received embassies and envoys with him, on a separate dais. In mine she once attempted, when ambassadors from Armenia came, to mount the dais and actually sit beside me.

I saw her marching down the aisle, making for the dais. Seneca, who was standing at my side, muttered, "No, no! Stop her. Get down from the dais, greet her, and lead her away." I stood up and left the dais just in time, for she was almost to the foot of it. I halted her, took her hand, and said, "Welcome, Mother." Then I steered her to a seat in the audience. I could tell by the rigidity of her body that she was furious. But she dared not resist.

She also tried to stock my quarters with military commemorations, busts of generals, ceremonial swords, war memoirs (including two copies of Caesar's *Gallic Wars*), and the like. It was telling that the offensive Aphrodisias statue showed me dressed for war. I ordered them all out and replaced them with Greek statues of athletes. To counteract this, she presented me with a bust of Germanicus for my birthday, saying it was a treasured family heirloom.

Even though I evaded a military uniform, I had to wear a toga more than I ever had before, for a multitude of public appearances. For my first formal meeting with the Senate, in which I would outline my policies, I must be especially well attired. My hair must be tamed; it was curly and unruly and had a mind of its own. The stylish austere Augustan look, with stick-straight hair combed forward, was a challenge for me to meet. My barber fussed and fussed with it, plastering it down with water. When it was wet, it was a docile light brown and flat, but once it dried it was blond—and wavy—again.

Nonetheless, curly hair or no, I stood before the Senate to address them for the first time since they had confirmed me as emperor. The Curia was packed; there were technically about six hundred senators, but usually no more than one or two hundred met. This time, curiosity about the young emperor had brought them all out, and there was standing room only. I was aware of hundreds of eyes staring at me, trying to take my measure. Even from the shadows in the back, eyes gleamed.

I began by thanking them for all their benefactions and courtesies. I praised their history and gave their exalted status its due. I then told them what they already knew—that the empire was in good state, peaceful, prosperous, and a joy to administer.

"I am fortunate to have good advisers"—I nodded to Seneca and Burrus, sitting in the front row, and to the Consilium, the imperial council of twenty or thirty senators and other reliable men I had singled out—"and the examples of wise rulers I can follow. But most fortunate of all for you, I bring with me no feuds, civil wars, or family quarrels that hang over me. So everything is new with me, no carryovers from the past."

I did want everything to begin anew. The past was sordid, a tissue of treacheries and lies, even if they had brought me to stand where I did today. But the faces looking back at me were carefully blank.

"I renounce proceedings that have been questionable. I will not judge cases secretly. I will not allow bribery and favoritism. I will keep personal and state business separate. I will oversee the legions and make sure all is in order. And, most important, the Senate will retain its ancient functions."

At the last pronouncement, the senators leapt to their feet and cheered.

Back in my office—part of the imperial apartments—I relaxed, toga thrown over a stool, feet up. "How did I do?" I asked Seneca.

"Very well, I think," he said. "They seemed to believe you."

"I was speaking the truth," I said. "Why shouldn't they?"

"With all due respect, they have heard promises from many emperors, and may be forgiven for waiting to see if the words come true."

I shrugged. Let them see. They would come true.

A nd what I'd said about the empire was correct. We were in a period of peace. With Claudius's conquest of Britain, our territory stretched twelve hundred miles long, from Britain to Mauretania, and twenty-five hundred miles wide, from Spain to Cappadocia. There were thirty-three provinces, all obedient and sending tribute or goods to Rome. From Alexandria came the big grain vessels that supplied our bread; from Cyprus, copper; from Greece, artworks; from Spain, horses, just as a sample. The armies, having no battles to fight, busied themselves transforming their territory into Romanized areas—building roads, bridges, and aqueducts, forums and temples.

"It is running so well even you can't destroy it," said Mother. She said it offhandedly, making it sound lighthearted, a joke.

For some reason, this insult—the sort she routinely threw out—was too much.

"Never speak to me this way again," I said. "I am the *emperor*."

She just stared at me. "And you must never forget who made you so."

"I think, Mother, it is time *you* forgot it. It is done, and how it was done is past."

"What is done can be undone. You must never forget *that*."

It was a bluff on her part. It had to be. For what could she do to undo what had been done?

✦ ✦ ✦

For official functions, Octavia appeared with me. She kept her old quarters, declining to move into the vacated imperial ones.

"I am settled here," she said. "And you know, I am so fond of my new mosaics."

She smiled timidly. I pretended to believe her, knowing all the while that she simply did not want to live near me. The marriage was a pretense, but an amiable one. Such marriages survive only on polite evasions and courtesies.

XXXIII

Saturnalia, and my birthday. As I have already noted, Mother celebrated by presenting me with the Germanicus bust. I celebrated by having a private banquet with guests limited only to those I really wanted. That was my gift to myself. The only obligatory guests, lest otherwise it give scandal, were Octavia and Britannicus. For the rest, I would have only jolly companions and amusement. I had been confined and isolated too long. Now I would have friends, at long last.

There was a man I had wanted to know better, Gaius Petronius Arbiter, a smooth, dark character ten years my senior. There was Annaeus Serenus, the fire brigade man. There was Claudius Senecio, a man Seneca had said was "steeped in luxury and vice." That alone made me curious, and besides, he had a winning smile. There was Marcus Otho, the little man I had seen at Claudius's banquet, suspected of wearing a wig. Tonight, at Saturnalia, everyone would be wearing wigs, or worse. I myself put on the garments of a charioteer—the Greens, of course.

There were others that I won't recount here; more of them later. Out in the streets, slaves were dressed as masters, masters as slaves or athletes or actors or dancers. Respectability was thrown aside, rules suspended, everyone in theory equal. License in all things prevailed. It was my favorite holiday, and I would celebrate it for the first time as emperor by doing as I pleased in the guest list.

Octavia hugged the wall, as if she wanted to melt into it and disappear. She was costumed as a Vestal. How appropriate, I thought. Beside her was the lovely woman model for the autumn mosaic. I went over to them, welcoming them.

"My dear, you look lovely," I said, complimenting Octavia. "But not transgressive enough. Tonight all decorum is thrown to the wind." I turned to her companion, the person I really wanted to talk to. She was magnificent in a Greek gown, her head crowned with wild ivy. Before I could ask, she said, "Sappho. Tonight I am Sappho."

"Now, that *is* transgressive," I said. I then reeled off one of my favorite quotes from Sappho: "'For the Graces prefer those who are wearing flowers, and turn away from those uncrowned.'" I reached out and touched her ivy crown. "We must wait for the season."

She countered with "'You, be my friend'" from "Glittering-Minded deathless Aphrodite" in perfect Greek. But then, of course, she *was* Greek.

Should I answer? The lines just before it were "Come to me now, then, free me from aching care, and win me all my heart longs to win." No, that was too provocative. And had she silently meant them for me, knowing I would be familiar with them? Octavia was staring at us, so I just nodded and moved on.

Petronius was lounging on a couch, entertaining those around him. He was dressed as a shepherd, with a crook shaped like Priapus and his outsized phallus. "I say, those who claim purity are hypocrites. What is it that the Hebrew prophet says? 'Our righteousness is as filthy rags'?"

"When did you start reading the Hebrew prophets?" asked Otho. Indeed he did have on a wig, an orange one tonight.

"Petronius reads everything," said Serenus, caressing the lewd carved head of the staff. "The better to know all the dirty parts."

Petronius raised his cup. "I acknowledge your salute," he said, sipping the wine slowly.

Serenus threw back his glass and gulped.

"Manners, manners," chided Petronius. "You are in the company of the emperor. Show respect. And, even if you were with a slave, never bolt your wine. It isn't seemly." He dabbed his lips with his personal napkin fastidiously.

"Tonight I am a charioteer," I said. "You can say anything in front of me."

Petronius raised one shapely eyebrow. "You may regret that."

It was only then that I spotted Britannicus, seated in a corner, arms crossed, staring down at the floor. He wore no costume at all, no adornments, just a plain tunic. I had hardly seen him in the weeks since Claudius died. He had been at the funeral and after that disappeared. I went over to him, motioning for a server to bring him some wine. He gruffly shook his head.

"No wine tonight? You indeed want to turn things upside down."

"I do not care for the type you are offering," he said. He glared at me as if I were a brigand. "No wonder you are dressed as a charioteer, since that is what you really want to be."

"We are what we are. In any case, there is plenty of other food and drink," I said.

"I'm not hungry," he said.

"Suit yourself." I gave up and went back to Petronius, who was holding forth on Ovid and his writings. He looked up at me lazily and said, "Birthday Man! Does anyone know a poem about a seventeen-year-old emperor? No? There haven't been any, that's why. What about a seventeen-year-old, period?"

"If you don't know it, Petronius, no one does!" Otho cocked his head. The wig moved.

After the banquet, in the early hours of the morning, we played games of forfeit and fortune. We took turns leading the games, drinking with each forfeit, so that by the time I had my turn directing, the room was spinning. I was to appoint someone to do something they probably didn't want to do. Britannicus had been ignored all evening, but now I would single him out. Perhaps it would make him feel more welcome. After all, he was younger than everyone else, still not eligible for the toga virilis, although he would be soon.

"Britannicus," I said, pointing at him, "I command you to entertain us with a song."

He rose, probably the only sober person in the room. He took his place in the middle of the space, then burst out into song with a surprisingly loud and practiced voice. He turned as he sang, directing his words to everyone present. Drunk as I was, I knew the song. It was from *Andromache*, a lament for a lost throne, stolen from its rightful owner.

Without father, without home,
Without inheritance,
All taken, all stolen,
All gone,
All hope flown.
Return it to me, O ye gods!

He then stopped in front of me and said, "Felicitations on your birthday, Lucius Domitius Ahenobarbus." Then he turned his back on me and left the room.

A stunned silence fell over the entire company, until Petronius drawled, "I told you you'd regret it."

It was Britannicus who would regret it! Oh, yes, I lost all sympathy for him, insulting me in front of my guests, on my birthday celebration. My birth name was nothing to be ashamed of, but by this he had openly refused to recognize my adoption as a Claudian and as emperor, announcing publicly that he was making that claim for himself. Although the gathering was a private one, there is nothing private at court or in Rome, and by the next morning everyone would know about it.

And sure enough, Mother knew by noon; she pushed her way into my quarters where I was working on dispatches from the Armenians and stood, smirking. I waited for her to speak, to see what direction her tirade would take.

"I suppose you stood there like an ox while he held forth," she said. "You were never quick on your feet."

"It was beneath my dignity to respond," I said.

"A high-minded excuse." She lifted her chin and looked at me with narrowed eyes.

"What if it is? Better to be silent than to blurt out foolish words."

"I am beginning to agree with Britannicus, and others. It was a mistake to make you emperor. I have had doubts for some time."

Her doubts had started within a month of my accession, when I made it clear that she was not to rule alongside me. I said as much. "I suppose you think Britannicus could be more easily managed," I said. "But perhaps he would have a nasty surprise for you, too." I moved closer to her, crowding her back against a table. Still she refused to give ground, until I was almost pressing against her. "Here's a secret, Mother," I hissed in her ear. "No one, not even a child, likes to be ruled by anyone else, dictated to, controlled. Britannicus has shown that he is hardly the docile lamb you would require."

Now she moved back. "He at least is loyal."

"To his dead father? It is easy to be loyal to the dead; they make no demands. If by that you mean I am not loyal to you, that is not true. To be loyal does not mean to acquiesce in everything that person might want, especially if it is harmful."

"As if I would ever want anything harmful for you," she said, her voice sad. But she could summon any emotion she wanted to color her speech. It was no longer effective with me.

"It takes great wisdom to know what may be harmful in the long run," I said.

She laughed. "And you have that? You, who spend your time on poetry and cithara lessons?" She had spotted my new cithara, just delivered from a master artisan, lying on a table. I had progressed beyond the lyre now, and Terpnus was to start instructing me in a few days.

"This is ruining you!" She raised her foot and kicked the instrument off the stand; it flew through the air and landed with a thud on the marble floor, shattering.

This was sacrilege! I knelt and gathered up the pieces. The fine wood, the carvings, the workmanship destroyed. "You understand nothing, nothing of me." I rose, the pieces cradled in my arms.

"I understand enough to know that I never should have made you emperor." She turned and left the room.

I half expected an apology from Britannicus sometime that day, but nothing came. Only Mother and her attack on me and her veiled threats. I remembered her saying earlier, *What is done can be undone.* Would she go to him, team up with him to unseat me? It seemed unnatural. I was her son, after all. But Mother had never balked at what was unnatural. Perhaps I could mollify her by some token, something significant. I called for the wardrobe mistress and asked for an inventory of the imperial gowns. There was a full treasury of them, and I selected a ruby- and pearl-encrusted robe to be sent to her, with fulsome expressions of my appreciation of her.

I tried to put it all out of my mind and concentrate on matters of state. There were appointments to be made for governors of the provinces of Cilicia, Portugal, and Syria. Syria was always a particularly delicate assignment. There were also gaps in the military commands, positions that needed to be filled. The main Roman fleet was at Misenum, near Naples, and its present high commander was retiring. I would have to find a replacement, someone I could trust utterly. I wanted to create an elite navy, a military arm to counter the power of the Praetorians. Claudius's new harbor at Ostia was functioning well, able to handle three hundred ships, but how much better it would be if the ships could sail directly into it from the Naples area, avoiding the disastrous storms of the open sea, possibly through Lake Avernus, using a canal? Would such a canal be possible? I wanted to consult with engineers about this. It would be quite long—some hundred and twenty miles—but Roman roads and aqueducts and artificial harbors had proved we could accomplish astounding engineering feats. For the people of Rome, I also wanted to improve the provision markets and drew up plans for a new domed one, the Macellum Magnum, at the top of the Caelian Hill, as well as public baths and an attached exercise complex in the Campus Martius. In addition, I would build a wooden amphitheater nearby, for a better games venue. In the new year I would be consul and would work with the Senate on all these ventures, or at least with the Consilium.

So my days were busy with these governing matters, and my evenings were for theater, dance, and composing poetry and music. And, of course, there were the parties of Petronius and Otho that lasted until the darkness of night was just shifting toward dawn.

At length, after much thought, I decided on the new commander of the fleet. He was clever, utterly loyal to me, experienced, and resourceful. He also deserved a token of my esteem for him and my gratitude for his years of service and companionship to me. But before I could send for him, he came to me, proving our reciprocal friendship once more.

Anicetus had standing access to the imperial quarters, but he seldom invoked it. In fact, I had seen little of him since my accession, so I was particularly happy when he was announced. He strode into the room, and before he could bow, I took his hands.

"Dear friend," I said, "as always, we think alike. For I was going to send for you. You have forestalled me."

"I hope, Caesar, that you were sending for me for a happy matter," he said.

"Yes, indeed it is. I have an appointment for you. A promotion, of sorts."

"If it takes me away from you, I am not sure I would call it a promotion."

I tapped his arm playfully. "You flatter skillfully, as always. But this appointment you should not spurn. I want you to be admiral in command of the fleet at Misenum."

His broad face showed shock. Like all truly loyal people, he had not named stations and positions for himself in his mind, so his surprise was genuine. "I will, of course, accept. As you know, I had a great deal of sailing experience in Greece, in my other life. So I feel at home on the sea."

"I am not sure how much time you will actually be at sea," I confessed. "It is more of a strategic position."

"Yes, but I understand the sea, ships, and sailors."

"Who better to command them, then?" I clasped his elbows. "Then it is done. Congratulations, Admiral." I clapped for a servant to bring us wine and dainties. I waved him over to a couch where we could talk. "Now, you must tell me all your news."

He took a deep breath. Before he could say anything, the server appeared with the tray of refreshments. We helped ourselves, then I asked that he withdraw and leave us alone. It was so good to see Anicetus again. We spoke of many things, as we had always done. I told him of seeing the funeral procession of Alexander Helios, and of the thoughts that had gone through my head. "I vowed to always remember what he told me about looking to the future," I said.

"Agrippina Augusta," a voice announced from the entrance doors. Before I could say, *Send her away, I'll see her another time,* she was on the threshold.

She walked in, all swirls and imperiousness, flicking a fan—utterly useless in the January cold, an affectation if ever there was one. Her eager expression turned sour when she saw Anicetus with me.

"Oh my, are you still seeing him?" she said. "This relic of your childhood before you had a proper tutor?"

The brazier nearby glowed with its heated coals, but it was not the coals that made my cheeks burn. I stood and said, "You are speaking of the new admiral of the fleet," I said. "My trusted commander and friend, Anicetus of Greece."

Her mouth twisted in disdain. "You have made a freedman an admiral?"

"I am sure he will prove a good admiral."

"I am sure this proves you are an incompetent emperor," she said. "Unfit to rule!"

I turned to Anicetus with a smile. "It's a wise father who knows his own son, they say. And an unwise mother who does not know hers."

Instead of answering me, she hissed at Anicetus, "Greek slave who does not know his place!" Then to me: "You will lose the empire!" She turned her back and walked out, as quickly as she had come.

I sipped my wine and tried not to be unsettled by this. "I apologize for her insult," I said. "It is best to ignore her." Apparently my gift of the gem-laden gown had gone unappreciated. Her tantrums had lost their effectiveness and now merely wearied me. "Please, pretend she did not intrude."

He ran his hands through his hair, still thick though with strands of gray. "It is she I came to speak to you about." He sighed. "I would not, until I was sure of it. But you should know. She has been currying favor with Britannicus, seeking him out in his rooms, telling him that his rightful place was stolen from him and that she can and will restore it to him. I am not sure of what means she will use." He hung his head as if he was the instigator of it rather than the reporter. "I have my informers, but they cannot be present everywhere. I would just say—be wary at mealtimes. Or even—now." He cast a glance over at the platter of apples, figs, and nuts. "I wish I had spoken first, before she came in, lest you think I am just saying this to get revenge for her insult to me just now. But I swear, this is the matter I came to tell you."

"I believe you," I said. "I would trust you with my life."

"It would seem that is what you are doing just now."

"Thank all the gods for you, Anicetus." I clasped him to me.

"Be watchful, dear friend. Be very watchful."

XXXIV

I was working late, guardedly, in my quarters. I had withdrawn into them early to try to address legal questions that were awaiting my decision. But I found it hard to care whether this senator received his income from his grain ships or whether that magistrate in Campania had his adoption by his aristocratic neighbor approved.

It was a bitterly cold night. I had two braziers filled and glowing, and still the cold crept through my feet and slowly up my legs. My fingers were so chilled I found it hard to hold the papers.

I stood up and went to the window. Outside, the bare branches of the trees made stark shadows on the ground, beneath a white full moon. Far below, the Forum slept in the moonlight, quiet at last. The tall columns of the Temple of Castor stood serene, eternal. Truly Rome was a glorious city. As always when I saw her spread out like this, in all her beauty, my pride swelled and I wanted to embrace her.

I was her caretaker, her protector. But what did I want for Rome? Greatness, of course. But what sort of greatness? She had been placed in my hands, but as I now knew, only provisionally. She might be taken away at any moment.

What made an empire great? Our earlier leaders had an answer, the same answer going back to the Babylonians, the Assyrians, the Egyptians: territory. Conquests. But we had done that. That phase was over, and we must build a new one, perhaps one the world had never seen before.

But such lofty thoughts were not to be pursued tonight, when the magistrate and his adoption were calling, and my hands numb. I must finish with this and go to bed.

I moved the oil lamp closer to the papers and sat back down. Slowly, very slowly, I became aware that there was someone else in the room. I stiffened and stood up, pulling out the dagger I now kept on my person at all times.

The room was quiet; I saw nothing, but the corners were dark and impenetrable. There were guards but they were some distance away, beyond the closed door and down the hallway.

The door. The door was locked. How could there be anyone else in here? The balcony? I turned slowly, my eyes seeking any sign of movement, my ears straining to hear breathing. Yes, it was coming from that far corner, behind the curtain. I rushed over to it, dagger pointed at it, when with a rustle the curtain parted and someone small stepped out.

"Please!" a voice said. "Quiet. They must not hear!"

Now she moved into the faint light and I saw who it was.

"Acte?" I whispered.

"Yes, it is I." She threw her arms around me and buried her face against my chest. I dropped the dagger. "I can't bear it. I can't bear it. I had to warn you."

Gently I untwined her arms. "Warn me of what? And how did you get in here?"

"I have lived in the palace for many years," she said. "I was in the imperial apartments of Claudius before I moved to the lady Octavia's establishment. I know all the secret passageways and connections."

We moved from the shadows of the curtains, nearer to the oil lamps. I stroked her shoulder. "Now, tell me what you have come to tell me."

She took a deep breath. Oh, by Zeus, she was fair in the lamplight. "I am betraying my friends—for they are friends and I am part of their household, not a servant. But I have heard too much and I hate what I have heard."

"What is it?" Out with it, whatever it was.

"They are going to kill you. At the banquet next week just before Britannicus comes of age."

"Who is 'they'?" Oh, let it not be my wife or my mother.

"Britannicus. Octavia. Agrippina. The plan is that you will die that night, the next day Britannicus is of age, your mother takes him to the Praetorians as the rightful successor, and they proclaim him emperor."

"And what happens to me?" How calmly I asked that, as if it was only a matter of curiosity for me.

"You will be hastily cremated that very night. They are already—already gathering the wood for it. It's being constructed behind a fence, so no one will see it until the night."

Cremated. They were already building my bier!

"I've heard them laughing and talking about it, about you—it's obscene—they are evil. Especially Britannicus. He said he wanted your head cut off and brought to him."

And what of Octavia, my wife? I thought she was fond of me at least, respected me at least.

"Octavia was reluctant at first," said Acte, answering my unspoken question. "But in the end, she was won over by the effusive flattery of Agrippina and the resentments of her brother, who feels he was cheated."

"I see." It took all my self-control to say only those two words.

"Octavia was vulnerable to the attentions of Agrippina because she has been overlooked her whole life, and suddenly the light was shining on her and she was won over. She is as always a pawn."

"Why have you come to me? Why did you not just sit back and let things unfold? Your lot is with them."

"I choose my own lot," she said. "My lot is now with you."

"Why?"

She smiled, a hesitant smile that was tentative, nervous. "Because I wish to be. Because I admire you—and because I want you."

And as quickly as that, we passed from acquaintances to lovers.

I held her to me. "I have wanted you ever since I saw you beside the mosaic," I whispered. "But that was for your beauty. Now added to that is courage, which is much rarer and more to be prized."

We retreated to the room adjacent to the workroom, where my bed was. Several small oil lamps were flickering on their stands. It was very cold in the room; only one brazier gave off a feeble glow. But I no longer noticed the cold; the warmth of her body, the heat that grew as we held one another, dispelled any chill. She was everything I had ever wished to hold, and her glorious hair, spread out all around her, slid under my hands and I buried my face in it. Between her breasts there was the smell of cypress, a faint scent just barely there. The danger all around us only fueled the desire and the urgency, made it seem more reckless and desperate.

Our first coupling was fierce and heated. Afterward, lying under the sheet, she laid her head on my shoulder, running her slender fingers up and down my arms. "I have known you ever since you came to the palace, have watched you grow to manhood. I have known you, but you have not known me."

"I have seen you without knowing you." I sighed. "Perhaps in my dreams I have known you, without truly knowing your form or face." I held her closer. "But now I know both."

We moved closer together, neither wanting to say the words *Do I have you now? Or is this just for tonight, just because of the danger?*

Now we made love languidly, joyfully. The brazier burned out, and the cold tightened its grip on the room, but we paid it no heed. The moment felt eternal, sacred, protected.

The oil lamps were spent, and a faint light was spreading along the eastern rim of the horizon when she woke me, caressing my shoulder and whispering, "I must go. I must not be seen here."

Before I could protest, she was out of bed and leaning over me. "No one must know."

My mind, still fogged, did not forget the important question. "About tonight? Or about nights to come?"

"Both," she said, kissing my cheek. Then she was gone, stealing away in the early dawn.

XXXV

ACTE

I was safely back in my rooms. No one was stirring yet. Octavia was a late sleeper, and Britannicus likewise. Oh, I had done it. I had done it; I had saved him. For I had no doubt that he would now take measures to protect himself. What would befall the others I could not know, nor could I take responsibility for it.

Quickly I undressed and sought my own bed, so I could seem to have spent the whole night there. As soon as I lay beneath the sheet, a warmth and blush spread over me as I remembered details of our night. The first time, he had made ferocious love; the second revealed he knew considerable about the arts and refinements of love; the third . . . acute, aching desire characterized that one.

I smiled. I had indeed watched him grow up, but from my first glimpse of him I knew he would grow into a man to be reckoned with. I had first seen him at the palace celebration of the marriage of his mother to Claudius, when he was eleven, and I was seventeen. I had spoken to him in the crowd, but he would not remember that. I think his greatest appeal was his fresh-faced youth, so shining and clean. He never lost that.

When I met him again, grown to manhood, and Octavia presented me as the model of the mosaic, I suddenly wanted him. The force of that desire took me by surprise and had no excuse. He was her husband, and I have never been a thief. So I watched him from afar and left it at that. But after what I heard tonight in her chambers I could do nothing other than what I did. I did not plan to go to his bed—wanting is not the same as planning.

He had lovely hair, blond and thick, and tonight it had smelled of smoke, smoke from the brazier, a woody, heady scent.

I loved him until the day he died, and I shall love him until the day I die.

XXXVI

NERO

I never slept after she left. I lay in bed, watching the room grow lighter as the late-winter sun finally rose above the horizon. The faint scent of her was all there was to prove that the hours had not been a dream. I had spoken true when I said I might have dreamed of her, just not by name. She had long been in my consciousness, swaying gently in secret regions of my mind, an unseen presence.

The scent of her, and the dagger lying where I had dropped it . . . that was what remained of the night. I wanted to believe her, but such heinous accusations had to be confirmed. What had she said about the bier? That it was concealed behind a fence. It could only be in the Campus Martius, for that was tradition. Surely they would not rob me of the honor of a traditional funeral.

Funeral. One was being readied for me.

I hastily dressed, putting on old clothes and a dark wig, and told my attendants that I was going to inspect the grounds for my new baths in the Campus Martius but did not want the builders to know I was there. They could follow me, but not closely.

Once I knew what to look for, it was easy to find. Had I not known, I could have passed it by as others around me were doing. There was a tall fence of fresh-cut wood, a sheen of frost on it in this early morning. I peered through a chink and saw the workmen heaving logs onto a structure that was unmistakable in its geometry. A square of big logs formed the base, and arranged neatly on top of that were ever-decreasing levels of wood, climbing up almost to the top of the tall fence. A cremation tower. Atop it would go the litter with someone on it.

I did not try to enter. They must not know I had seen, and knew.

It is not every day that one beholds one's funeral pyre, especially if one is feeling healthy. How did they plan to do it? An assassin with a dagger, like the thugs Messalina had sent against me as a child? Or would they surround me and strike me down like they did with Caligula? They would have to corrupt the Praetorians first, and there was no evidence they had unkind feelings or complaints toward me. Probably that would not be the way.

An accident? A fall from the palace roof or balcony? A horse that bolts? But they had only a few days to execute the plan, and this was not the season for riding, nor of seeking the palace rooftop.

There was only one sure way, one way that I knew Mother favored.

Therefore I was not in the least surprised to see Locusta near the apartments of Britannicus. In fact, I had waited for her there, sitting quietly on a bench hidden behind a marble urn.

XXXVII

LOCUSTA

We meet again." The voice came out of nowhere, and then he materialized. Nero, suddenly in front of me. He blocked my way.

"Indeed," was all I could say. My heart was racing. This was as bad as it could be.

"I thought you were in prison," he said. I could not read his face. It seemed to have a blank expression.

"I have been released," I said, "through the kindness of your mother."

Now he laughed, a bitter laugh. "Beware the kindness of my mother. You have been sent for, that is what you mean. She has a task for you. After that task you will be returned to prison, as you were the last time."

I stood silently. Whatever I said would be a trap for me.

"My mother is persuasive, and of course she is a longtime client. But a—what did you call yourself once? tradesman?—a tradesman must always seek new clients. So I am prepared to outbid her."

"What are your terms?" I asked. I might as well be blunt with him, as he was with me. And I was ready—no, eager—to switch sides, because the thought of harming him weighed heavily with me. From the first time I had seen him, even as a child, we had developed a strange, strong bond.

"Turn your wares on the employer rather than the intended, and the intended—that is, I—will reward you beyond what you dream." He paused. "Never to go to prison again. Much gold, in jewelry and in ingots. And I will arrange for you to have your own academy where you can train others. After all, you are a master, and you should pass on your skills and knowledge to others. There will always be a demand for them."

My own academy! To openly teach my arts, but no longer have to practice them and be caught in the web of murderers, pursued by fear? To never see the walls of a prison again. And to spare the life of this extraordinary youth.

"It is a bargain," I said.

"I thought it might be." Oh, why didn't he smile? His face was still a tight mask. "Now, let us withdraw to a private place where we can talk."

He wished to know the details, but I told him it was a professional secret and that he must respect that. He asked how I would evade the tasters, and again I demurred, pleading professional courtesy. He was uneasy and I knew he would eat absolutely nothing. There was truly no reason he should trust me and I did not attempt to assuage his suspicion. After all, too many people have died of overtrusting and very few of overcaution.

He needn't have worried about the tasters. Of course there would be tasters; amateurs are stopped by tasters, but I would not be. I had a foolproof two-step plan. The poison would be in the water used to cool the wine, which would already have been tested by the taster, then intentionally heated too hot for Britannicus's taste.

Britannicus was a nasty sort and I felt no sorrow for him ending up on the bier he had planned for another. Such justice rarely happens, and I was honored to be its instrument.

XXXVIII

NERO

When the sun set that day, a bloody circle embedded in a red-streaked sky that looked like an inflamed wound, I wondered if anyone would consider it a portent. I was thankful that it wasn't mine.

Yes, they had meant it to be my last night on earth, my last sunset. The pyre must be finished now, awaiting its victim. I shuddered and turned away, asking a slave to draw the curtain and veil that sky.

They set a supper before me, and I asked to be alone. The platter held cold meat, dried figs, cheese, and bread, but I wouldn't touch any of this. I would dispose of it by dropping it over the balcony, leaving only a few crumbs on my plate, attesting to a hearty appetite. All must seem normal, and I, unsuspecting.

When it was still early I retreated to my inner chamber and attempted to read, but the words were meaningless and unintelligible. Even poetry, usually the most accessible to me, was out of reach. I put Catullus down and stared out in space, my eyes almost unseeing. There was a roar in my head, a steady swell that drowned out all coherent thought. Instead, images and feelings raced across my mind, twisting and fading. Oddly enough, they were of people I had never actually seen—Julius Caesar, Hannibal, Ptolemy, my grandmother Antonia. Perhaps when we come close to death we are visited by people already dead, expecting to welcome us. Last of all came Augustus, and unlike the others, he did not fade and recede but came right up to me, his face only a handsbreadth away. He turned and whispered in my ear, "It is not good to have too many Caesars." Then he nodded and vanished.

Augustus had known that, and now, to my sorrow, I knew it, too.

So I was following in his footsteps, in the footsteps of all those before me who had found it prudent to prune the ancestral bush and eliminate the other branches. It was not what I had thought myself to be. I was not one of *them*. But it seemed that, after all, I was.

I sought my bed. Only sleep could vanquish these torturous thoughts and images. If sleep would come . . . oh, let sleep come. I dared not take a draft because it might leave me drugged the next day, when I needed to be utterly alert and in command of all my senses.

Waves of guilt washed over me as I lay there. But finally I got hold of myself and asked, Which would you rather be? A guilt-ridden survivor or a dead innocent? There is no other choice.

The banquet was ready, spread sumptuously in the large chamber reserved for such feasts. There were several couch arrangements of nine people, and in the center, a large table where imperial children and sons and daughters of aristocrats dined. This would be the last time Britannicus would sit at the "children's table" and it was this occasion being celebrated, as the next day he would be fourteen. It was, in actuality, the last time he would sit at any table, as only Locusta and I knew.

An array of high-ranking guests were assembled: the imperial family, of course, but senators, court officials, and friends as well. They included Burrus, Seneca and his protégé Serenus, and Vitellius—that stout buzzard from back in Tiberius's reign. Britannicus had gathered together a number of his friends, including Lucan, Seneca's nephew; Titus, his schoolmate and General Vespasian's son; and a coterie of sympathizers.

Mother glided up to me, wearing the pearl- and ruby-encrusted gown. Her manner was entirely natural, not that of a mother who would not see her son alive again after this night. What a family of actors we were. Is it any wonder that I later stepped over the line and turned professional?

"I see you are wearing my gift," I said.

She shrugged dismissively. "A gift? All the imperial wardrobe was mine. You merely gave me something I already owned."

Why argue with her? I held the power now and need not waste my energy trying to convince her of anything or win an argument. "I am sorry you see it that way, Mother," was all I said.

Musicians sat discreetly in the back, playing the lyre, the flute, and the harp, soft melodies that blended into the background. Slaves sprayed scent around the room, attar of rose and lily. The wine was served in tall stemmed silver goblets, the finest from Albano, aged nine years, its distinctive trademarked amphoras lined up against the wall to assure the guests the supply was practically unlimited.

Britannicus was holding forth with his friends, being feted and flattered. Titus, a stocky, bull-necked boy, looked every inch a general's son. Lucan, a more delicate-featured lad, was animated and flushed.

As the time came for us to take our places, it fell to me to say a few words. His mother and father were dead and there was no one to speak for him. So I welcomed the company and congratulated Britannicus. At that point Lucan asked if he could read a poem he had written for the upcoming birthday and proceeded to do so. It was surprisingly good. Then—I do not know what overcame me—I suddenly said that I was so happy to welcome my brother into his adulthood, as I would rely on his help in carrying the burdens of empire. It was perverse of me, but it just came out. I knew people would remember it the next day, while right now it would reassure Britannicus that I was ignorant of what was slated to happen. Satisfied, I took my place on the imperial couch and was joined by Mother, Octavia, Seneca, Burrus, and four senators.

I looked around the room. Tasters were stationed behind every couch, spearing food on the passing platters, sipping wine from slender pitchers. A huge platter of mushrooms was put before me and a taster dutifully took one from the edge, chewed it, waited a moment, then nodded. I took some but of course would not eat any. Britannicus glanced at me from time to time to see if I was eating. Mother, too, leaned over to glance at my plate.

I was still in ignorance about how Locusta would keep her commitment. The tasters were vigilant tonight. Could it be a poisoned cushion or a poisoned napkin? Perhaps it was not what we would eat but what we would handle or sit on. Or perhaps it was in the perfume being sprayed, lethal to breathe? Or in the smoke from the braziers? If in the air, it would be general, not specific. My chest started to feel tight.

Britannicus stood and held his goblet aloft. "I must say something. My dear friends, who have surrounded me with care, my dearest sister, Octavia, this is your night as much as mine. Be with me on the onward journey." He raised his goblet, then sat back down. Everyone drank.

An instant later he jerked up, convulsed, and fell rigid onto the floor. His limbs twitched and his head rolled, then his eyes closed and everything went limp. In falling, he had swept the platters off the table and now they clanged around him, their food everywhere.

Everyone sat frozen like statues, then a number of the guests scrambled off the couches and ran for the doors. At Britannicus's table, Titus grimaced and grabbed for his throat. On our couch, Octavia was speechless and wide-eyed.

It was up to me to lead the way. I leaned back and said, "It is of no concern. This happens to him often, as it does to epileptics. He has suffered from this since childhood. He will recover consciousness soon. He must be taken to his chamber." I motioned to a petrified slave and told him to get a litter. Two slaves soon loaded the flaccid Britannicus onto it and out of the room.

As if a spell had been lifted, the company went back to eating, playing their parts. But Mother turned to look at me, terrified. Her eyes told me everything. Is there anything more frightening than realizing your enemy has outsmarted you and has you at his mercy? Especially if you pride yourself in always having the upper hand?

"A pity," I said. "His birthday dinner is spoiled. But he had some lovely poems first." I patted her hand.

Later that night the physician told me that Britannicus had died. "He was dead before he finished falling," he said. "There was no hope of reviving him."

"A life cut short. A tragedy when that happens."

I gave orders that he should be cremated that night. "It is an old custom that untimely deaths are not publicly celebrated, forgoing processions and eulogies, lest it is too disheartening." Then, as if I had just thought of it, I added, "You may use a cremation tower already prepared in the Campus Martius that I recently saw, not far from the river. I am sure whoever it was erected for will not begrudge its use for this tragedy in the imperial household."

It was over. I had prevailed. But now I had joined their ranks—the ranks of imperial murderers, stretching in a long line behind me. I flung off the robe I had worn. I would order it destroyed. I took off the snake bracelet. It had done its job, protected me. Perhaps Mother regretted having me wear it.

Oh, I was weary. Weary, weary, heartsick. I flung myself onto the couch and lay staring up at the ceiling. I did not sleep but wandered in a field of dreams and phantoms. Hours must have passed. Then beside me, Acte touched my shoulder.

I jolted full awake, heart pounding.

She was silent and embraced me. I held her. We lay side by side the rest of the night, in one another's arms, no word spoken.

XXXIX

The sun rose upon a world without Britannicus. Everyone by now knew that. I must make an official appearance, issue a statement. Looking over the balcony, I could see restless crowds in the Forum below, milling about. I could not see the Campus Martius from that angle, but the smoke from the cremation would have dissipated by now.

I called for the Senate to meet and duly went to the Curia that afternoon. It had to be done. In the winter gloom, faces just as gloomy stared back as I stood in the middle of the room and pronounced the sad news that the young prince Britannicus had been taken from us. He had the falling sickness, the affliction of great men like Caesar. I was all alone now to carry the burden of the empire that I had planned to share with him. My hopes were now centered only on Rome, and they, the Senate and people of Rome, must make up for my loss by giving me greater support, as the only surviving member of my family, exalted now by destiny.

I was daring the gods to strike me down by uttering such words, but it was a chance I had to take. Better the gods than other men.

They all applauded me and swore to give me all I needed, to stint me nothing for the glory of Rome.

On a day torn by winter storms and peals of thunder, Britannicus's ashes were deposited in the Mausoleum of Augustus. The funeral procession was lashed with sleet and rain and was a dismal affair. I did not attend.

The Senate was taken care of. The interment was over. But those were public events. Now came the difficult scrutiny of those close to me, the circle I relied on and who must acquit me if I were to stay in power. I particularly dreaded having to convince Seneca and Burrus of my innocence.

The day after I had addressed the Senate, I called them both to me, to as private a room as I could find. (Nothing is truly private in the palace.) The greetings over, the refreshments offered and refused, all shields between us gone, I began. *Admit no guilt* was the maxim in legal cases and I must follow it here, not incriminate myself. It did not help that they were both staring at me with solemn faces, arms crossed.

"This turn of events is tragic," I said, "especially for my wife, who has now lost every member of her family."

Still they stared and said nothing.

"Yet, we must go on. The emperor cannot be prevented from carrying on the business of the empire, or it will be a double loss."

"It will be difficult, bowed as you are by grief." Burrus spoke in his rough voice. The soldier in him usually said everything plainly, without a nuance of irony, which made his words all the more stinging now that he employed uncharacteristic sarcasm.

"We must carry on," I said.

"Indeed," said Seneca. "That is the way of the world."

It was too good to be true. They, my mentors and moral guides, were looking the other way. "It is a custom to distribute gifts in the name of the deceased," I said. "As Britannicus has no heirs, his estate descends to me. In his honor, I wish to present you with some of his valued property in Rome."

Burrus nodded, and Seneca, the moral philosopher, said, "Thank you." Thus they allowed themselves to become beneficiaries and accessories of the crime. I had not convinced them, but I had bought them.

· · ·

Later that year Seneca soothed his conscience by writing a long-winded essay addressed to me entitled "On Mercy." In it he extolled my natural clemency and said I was a model of mercy that everyone could follow. What he meant was, *You got away with it once, but don't try it again.*

I honestly tried to concentrate on my political tasks, hoping that the demanding details of each project or problem would absorb me and help me forget the choppy seas I had just sailed over to safety. I embraced my Augustus side, even praying before his shrine. I knew now that he understood me because he, too, had had to make wrenching decisions and had killed a great many men before he could pose as the peacemaker. *It is not good to have too many Caesars.*

When spring came, after those dark weeks of winter, it was time for me to participate in an old imperial ritual at Augustus's house. Back in his reign, an eagle had dropped a chick holding a laurel sprig in its beak in Livia's lap. She raised the chick and soon there were a flock of them. She planted the laurel sprig and a tree grew. After that, every new emperor took a sprig from it and planted his own tree. While he reigned, these laurel leaves were used in his ceremonial wreaths; and when that emperor died, his laurel tree withered.

The winds were warm at last, the true breath of spring. All around us on the Palatine the grass was thickening, turning rich green. The branches of the fast-leafing trees swayed like young girls, supple and quivering. A company of magistrates stood waiting, including priests from the *sodales Augustales,* for this was a sacred rite. I could see the remains of the deceased emperors' trees—Augustus's was a blackened short stump, Tiberius's likewise, Caligula's taller and less decayed, and Claudius's still had branches but the leaves on them were gone, and nothing was budding this spring, or ever would again. Behind them was the huge flourishing laurel from the original shoot. A priest solemnly cut a shoot from one of its lower branches with a silver knife and held it, waiting.

Mother, as a direct descendant of Augustus, the only one residing in Rome aside from me, had to hand me the laurel twig and speak the formulaic words of the ritual. She and I had not met since the night of the banquet, but I could still read in her eyes her incredulity and fear at what I had done.

Dressed in white robes, with pearls in her hair, she stepped forward and handed me the bushy twig, saying, "In the name of the god Augustus, I bid you take this cutting from the tree of his ancestral house, plant it, and flourish as emperor."

I took it, my eyes holding hers for a moment too long. Neither of us would look away, neither of us drop them in deference. Then I turned to the spot where the priest was waiting, with his sacred vessel to water the new-planted shoot, while I would use a silver spade to dig a little hole for it. It went into the ground and I spoke directly to Augustus, again with a formula.

"Great god and father Augustus, look on this planting with favor. Raise it up to be a great crowned tree, and let me wear its laurel with honor for the empire."

The little thing looked so small and vulnerable, with such a precarious hold on life. The gods would have to protect it. They had done so for me thus far.

The next duty before me was to visit the Praetorian camp in the northeast corner of Rome. Burrus, their commander, urged me to do so.

"They need to see you again," he said. "You have not visited them since the day they proclaimed you emperor in October." He held up his hands. "I know you gave them a hefty subsidy, but there is no substitute for visiting them in person."

If he expected an argument from me, he was disappointed. Upon their loyalty my safety and continued rule depended, and I knew it. They were my greatest security and also my greatest danger, if they turned against me.

The gruff commander and I rode out on a glorious spring day, skirting the Circus Maximus and its crowds, around the Caelian Hill where my new produce market was already under construction, then across the base of the Oppian Hill, a refreshing green spot on a gentle rise. Already the air was healthier here and I thought what a fine location this would be for a villa. Next we passed the border of the Gardens of Maecenas, magnificent grounds that were imperial property. By this time the word was out that I was riding through the city, and throngs came out and cheered. A sea of faces, of so many races and countries—for Rome is the center of all things—smiled at me, more warming than any sun could be to me.

"Nero! Nero!" they cried.

"I love you, my people!" I called back, and it was true. I loved them because they first loved me, and without reserve, something I had never experienced. Oh, the love of a crowd is a heady, intoxicating, overwhelming thing, and I drank it in, I swam in it.

On rising ground outside the city, we approached the high walls of the massive square fortress and the doors were opened and trumpets sounded the arrival of the emperor and their commander. We rode into the wide thoroughfare inside and were welcomed by the next in command. I was led past the rows of barracks on each side, to the tribunal with its shrine for the standards of the empire, and its adjacent shrine to Mars. The troops—thousands of them in their gleaming military dress of leather and brass—gathered at the foot of the tribunal to hear me speak.

I said little besides the obvious: that I was proud to be their commander in chief, grateful for their loyalty and support, and devoted to the safety of the empire, as they were. I would never endanger it or sacrifice its security, and I relied on them to guarantee my promises. I admired them and trusted them.

The sea of faces that looked at me here were different from the crowds on the road. These were men in the prime of life, healthy and strong, no weakness among them. They were recruited mainly from the home territories, not the provinces—Roman to the core.

My ancestors had led such men on the battlefield but I was thankful I did not have to. I did not question the fact that the empire rested on the backs of soldiers and would collapse without them, but I did not want that life for myself. There must be another way to be a great man, to become legendary, without being a military leader. After all, my ancestor Aeneas did not die fighting in the Trojan conflagration but fled to found a new city, Rome itself. My empire now had a hundred million subjects and I wanted to do glorious deeds for them, but not in combat.

The empire and its provinces were quiet. Except for the twelve cohorts in the Praetorian camp, most of the twenty-five legions and three hundred thousand soldiers were stationed on the borders of the empire, to protect against outsiders rather than insiders. From the provinces goods poured in, most important of all the grain from Africa, especially Egypt. When Egypt fell to Rome eighty years before, our grain supply was guaranteed. We needed seven million bushels a year and Egypt could supply a quarter of that. We had long since lost the capability of feeding our huge urban population from local supply. Now there was free or subsidized grain for the poor, about a fifth of the city population. It is distributed near the Circus Maximus. Being able to facilitate the grain supply is vital to an emperor and woe to one who cannot. Riots and attacks would start, and who knew where they might end? I had to make sure that never happened.

Well aware of my administrative duties, I met with my chief councilors on a regular basis. They were, of course, Burrus and Seneca, but they did not carry all the responsibilities. I had the Consilium, with its selected senators and other trusted advisers I consulted on legal and judicial matters, as there were many such I must judge. I preferred to have all arguments written out and delivered to me privately, rather than argued in public as was done in Claudius's reign. Then I would study them and render judgments likewise in writing. This system prevented oratorical flourishes from swaying the decision.

The Consilium also addressed general business, such as public order, forgery, and sponsorship of gladiatorial games in the provinces.

For administrative help I had several appointments. Aristocrats did not deign to take what they deemed subservient positions and so these were filled by capable freedmen, mainly Greeks. My secretary for Greek letters was my former tutor Beryllus, and I had another for Latin letters. Only governors of provinces were allowed to write me directly, and my secretaries dealt with those letters, a weighty responsibility. Below them was the minister of notes. Notes were lesser communications than letters, usually appeals from Greek communities. I had appointed Doryphorus, a handsome and ingratiating man from Kos, to handle this duty. My minister of accounts and revenues was Phaon, another Greek freedman who was extremely capable as well as resourceful. Since the post required him to manage the empire's accounts and the disposition of its revenues, he had better be. I had Epaphroditus, another freedman, as my secretary for petitions. As you can imagine, there were a lot of them.

Meetings with my secretaries were relaxed and pleasant affairs, with joking and camaraderie; meetings with the Consilium, no such atmosphere.

These meetings, along with consultations, took a great deal of time, but I did not want to stint them. However, I rewarded myself by going back to my cithara lessons and by studying poetry and writing verse myself afterward. Gradually I gathered a group of young and promising poets and writers around me, inviting them to the palace for gatherings where we would read one another's compositions, recite, and drink the finest wine.

I seldom saw Octavia, and then only at formal occasions. She did her best never to look at me, for when she did, her eyes were full of hate. Not that she minded my seeing that, but others would. Acte had left her quarters entirely and so I no longer heard what was being fomented there, although there were reports that Mother was still fawning on Octavia.

Acte, being free to live wherever she chose, had moved to another wing of the palace and, under cover of other interests and demands, had drifted away from Octavia. She did it gradually so as not to attract attention. Our liaison was still secret, but it could not go on this way much longer.

Why did it matter if it were known? Did not emperors have mistresses and lovers galore? The reason had to do with us, not with custom. She was too precious to me to expose to gossip and cruel comments. I had always had a proclivity for privacy and secrecy, believing it protected whatever I loved or valued. And I loved and valued her more deeply than any person I had ever known. In some ways, being with her gave me the same joy art did, a freedom and endless horizon, bounded only by my own limitations, a place where I could be myself and more than myself.

XL

My baths were rising on the Campus Martius, and the gymnasium next to it. They were situated near Agrippa's but would be much more modern. I had hired builders and designers to carry out my idea of a bath as grand as a palace.

"Why should it not be?" I had asked. "Soaring vaults, fine mosaics, a symmetry in the halls. And in the name of Zeus, truly hot water!" So often the waters that were artificially heated, as opposed to those in natural springs, were not hot enough. The designers obeyed me so well that my baths became notorious for their high temperature!

The covered gymnasium next to the baths also had a long, rectangular, open-air yard for exercising, surrounded by colonnades and benches. There would be a library attached to it, and niches would hold artworks. The body and the mind, working together—the gymnasium would honor that ideal. I hoped in this way to introduce Greek custom to the Romans. Perhaps its being next to the baths would lure them in.

On the other side of the baths the wooden amphitheater was being constructed. It was to be larger than the stone one Statilius Taurus had erected and better made, to hold more people and give better views of the exhibitions. Mine was wooden so it could be quickly built. An enormous larch tree, about to be cut into timber for it, was now on display, drawing crowds to see the largest tree ever exhibited in Rome. In my dislike of brutal gladiatorial games I had forbidden anyone to be killed. (Is it not a fine thing to be emperor and outlaw that which displeases?) Instead there would be exhibitions of skill. I hoped the audience would not find them boring without the bloodshed. But people must be trained to acquire new tastes.

The first anniversary of my accession came around and was duly celebrated with processions and festivities. I hoped the amphitheater would be ready by the following year and I could present a spectacle for the people. For now we must be content with the more restrained demonstrations.

"What was good enough for Augustus should be good enough for Nero," said Acte, teasing me with a fan from the streets with "Nero the Great" painted on it, along with a sketch of me in a chariot. "Why the need for excess?"

I took it from her and examined it. "A genuine tribute," I said. "I did not pay anyone to do this, I promise."

"Indeed, it is the sort of compliment you cannot buy. But about the excess—"

"Excess makes a statement."

"Yes, a very loud and vulgar one."

"It depends on what sort of excess it is." I grabbed her and kissed her. "This sort of excess I haven't heard you complain about." I took her hand and pulled her toward the bedroom.

It was noontime but time did not matter. (Is it not a fine thing to be emperor and have the clock at your command?) Daytime lovemaking had its own charms; namely, that I could see her so well, could look into her eyes and drown in them. I could see the sheen of the lotion she smoothed on her skin, could see the little scar across her cheek that she had had since a childhood accident. An imperfection that made her perfect. The eyes dominated daytime lovemaking, whereas touch and taste were masters of lovemaking in the dark. It was a palette of pleasure, day or night, no matter which senses were in play.

In October, the days were cool, but by the time we lay side by side under the wrinkled and twisted sheet, we were covered in sweat. Sweet sweat, the kind bestowed by the gods.

She moved closer to me and laid her head on my chest, as she often did. She gave a great sigh.

"What is it?" I ran my hand over her shining hair.

She sat up, propping herself up on one elbow. "This is not enough," she said sadly.

"I didn't please you?"

"Yes, you did. Too much. That is why I say it is not enough."

"I don't understand."

"I love our private times together. But oh! I wish I could be with you beyond the secrecy of this chamber."

"So do I. But we are bound by restrictions in every direction. This is our only safe place."

She lifted her chin, in that way I loved. It made her look like a noble warrior. "I have been thinking. And thinking. Because there must be a way around this. And last night, after you departed to see your friends, I thought, why not pose as a mistress of one of them? They can serve as a shield for us. I can pretend to be the mistress of Senecio, or Otho. They can see me openly, all the while acting as a disguise for us."

"I don't like it." It brought others into our secret world, and what if they formed a bond with each other?

"Don't you trust me?"

"Yes, of course I do." But they did not come with my restrictions, and that in itself might prove attractive.

"Do you not trust them, then?"

"Normally, yes. But you are not a normal temptation."

"I make my own choices. It does not matter to me whether they are tempted by me or not." She took my face in her hands. "When will you believe that I love you, and nothing will change that?"

But nothing had been certain or unchangeable in my life so far. Even my own mother had tried to kill me.

"I believe you." Now I would see. Perhaps my dreary history of betrayals would be rewritten.

✦   ✦   ✦

My life by day would have passed muster even with Augustus. His patron god, Apollo, drove the chariot of the sun and was bathed in its rays, giving glory to what happened in the sunlight. But, as twilight came, I, like the crepuscular animals who became active then, felt a change come over me, an inward shift from things that must be done to things I wanted to do. Twilight was the time of my cithara lesson, an hour hushed and suitable for the poignant sweet notes of that instrument. I had mastered basic plucking from the front with my right hand and was now training to use my left fingers at the same time from behind, a challenging advance in skill and one that would put me far beyond amateurism. Twilight was the time the poets and artists gathered with me in the palace. With all the night before us, we could take our time discussing our compositions, reciting them, and then critiquing them. I urged everyone to speak freely and not hold back their true opinions. Sometimes we composed short poems or essays while we were there.

By the time our gathering was over, true night had come. After that another sort of gathering took place—a drinking party and philosophical salon—with different guests. At this one, where bawdy talk and excessive wine consumption reigned, the poetry was not so delicate. By the time I was there, and had imbibed enough wine, I felt completely transported, having shucked the Nero of daytime and emerged as the Nero of night. No toga, no protocol, no duties. I was not even the leader of this group—it was Petronius, with his saturnine elegance and ennui. He was the master of sophisticated debauchery and sardonic remarks. Around him were the smart young set of aristocrats—Otho, Serenus, Senecio, and others I came to know only too well.

One evening after we had finished arguing about the merits of Catullus's attitude toward wine (was he serious in saying it was "the blood of Bacchus"?) and everyone was too drunk to remember what was decided, Serenus said, "And what about that old Seneca? How did you like being lectured in public in that 'On Mercy' essay?" He stretched out on the pillows on the floor—we had long since slipped off the couches—and laughed.

"I thought it was comical," said Senecio, his dark eyes narrowing. He always had a shifty look anyway. "He couldn't have been serious."

"Oh, he was serious," said Petronius. He leaned over and took a handful of grapes, which he dropped one by one into his mouth before continuing. I could hear each of them burst against his palate. "He means to rule, to be at least Aristotle to your Alexander. The great philosopher guiding the innocent young emperor."

Otho snorted. "Innocent?"

They knew. They all knew. Probably everyone in Rome knew. Well, what of it? But I would answer the first question, not the last. "I didn't like it. I don't care to be scolded and lectured to."

Serenus rolled across three cushions and came to rest on his back. "Why do you obey them? You are the emperor, not them."

Them. All of them? Seneca, Burrus, and Mother? The Senate?

Suddenly I remembered what Acte had said. "I don't obey everyone. In fact, there is something I'd like you to oblige me with . . ." And I explained about Acte and asked if one of them would pretend to be her lover. "I want to give her gifts but I cannot do so without attracting . . . attention." I did not need to specify whose attention. "I also cannot leave the palace with her. But if one of you would act the part of her paramour, you could be a cover for us."

They eagerly agreed and began to outbid one another for the honor. Only Petronius held back, saying, "She must be a treasure to have so captivated you, and I cannot trust myself around her." Serenus won the contest to be my accomplice, and I clapped him on his broad shoulder and said, "You can begin right away!" Oh, the promise of being free of the restraints we were under.

Petronius stood up and held his goblet aloft. "I say, Nero has proved himself one of us. So shall we invite him to join us in our nocturnal ramblings?"

The company all nodded, their faces only half-lit by the dim lights in the room, so I could not read their true expressions.

"You see," said Petronius in his deep, rumbling voice, "we play Saturnalia all year long." He arched an eyebrow. "We disguise ourselves as slaves, vagabonds, and ruffians and roam the streets of Rome. And do more than roam. Are you willing?"

This was truly to embrace the night. But a part of me craved it. "Yes," I said.

The night crawls, as they called them, took place during the dark of the moon. Some twenty of us met at the Milvian Bridge on the Via Flaminia north of the Campus Martius, heavily disguised in cloaks, torn tunics, and wigs. We had torches and carried clubs, but no knives or swords.

"The night is ours!" said Senecio, waving his club. "Onward, men!"

The streets closer in to the city were narrow and there were usually only a few people still out. Most of them carried lanterns and were protected by a slave; they darted into an alley or doorway when they saw us coming. Only large parties did not shirk or flee; those we harassed and frightened, chasing them down the ill-lit streets, yelling and waving our torches. If a tavern was still open, we burst in, terrifying the patrons, and demanded free drinks. For me, who had always been so circumspect, seeing the expressions on the faces was the most rewarding part of my misbehavior. I often left a bag of money behind on a stool but was careful not to let my companions see. We also broke into closed shops and helped ourselves to their goods. Somehow the paltry wares, not anything we would normally want, seemed enticing if they were stolen. Again, I tried to surreptitiously leave behind money, not in any bag that could be linked to the palace.

What I liked best were the times we split into smaller groups and, rather than rampaging, infiltrated taverns and sat drinking with the other patrons, spying on them and prompting them to reveal their opinions. Then I could ask questions about the new emperor and what they thought of him.

In one tavern, a group of five men were at my table, already quite drunk. They took eagerly to the question. The first man, as rotund as a pregnant cat, belched and scratched his stomach. "He's all right. So far, at least. He's generous at the games."

"I heard he gave away tokens and prizes for horses, gems, and wine at the Circus. Let him keep it up, I say," said a man with a mass of bright red hair.

"They say he likes to drive chariots. Maybe soon he'll race at the Circus. Wouldn't that be a sight? They also say he exercises out in the open, so if you want to see your emperor with nothing but a loincloth, hurry down to the Campus Martius." A thin, dark-skinned man offered this. This was not strictly true, but I did not correct him.

"I heard he likes to write poetry," said another.

"Is it any good?" said the red-haired man.

"Who knows? If the emperor writes poetry, is there anyone to tell him it's bad?" answered the fat man.

So this random group judged me on what gifts I might provide them with. (Which is the way most people judge people in their lives.) They mentioned my interests. (At least they had noticed.) Then they touched on the tender question that would always plague me: how can an emperor ever be fairly judged if he competes in the arts? (They identified this quandary so quickly and succinctly.) The wisdom of the common people was not just a saying, then.

In the dark of the moon in autumn, the temperature was low enough for us to tolerate being swathed in our disguises—we had sweltered in summer.

"We've proved our resolution," said Otho. "Now we can carouse and waylay to our heart's content in comfort." He was wrapped in a ragged cloak and wore a mask. His bandy little legs stuck out below the hem.

We were by the Fabricius Bridge, near the Theater of Marcellus and the Portico of Octavia. With no moonlight, only torches here and there illuminated the statues by great Greek sculptors in the niches between pillars in the portico. By day people strolled and rested here, but by night the niches provided a hiding place for robbers. The rounded edifice of the Theater of Marcellus likewise held statues—gods and goddesses and emperors. I suddenly wondered why all the statues of emperors were so small. We needed a colossus. Why should tiny Rhodes have one and Rome not? We should erect one large enough to displace the Rhodian one from the seven wonders of the world list.

The theater was just letting out, and patrons were streaming from the various exits. They were met by their waiting slaves, holding torches and lanterns to see them safely home.

A large group emerged and turned south, heading for the Aventine Hill.

"Those are ours, boys!" said Serenus. We followed them. At first there were many people about, but the farther we got from the theater, the thinner the crowd, and we were conspicuously following the group. Sound died away and our footsteps rang out loudly. The group walked faster, and so did we.

There were women in the group, and their men tried to hurry them on. Some broke into a trot and others started running. Petronius gave a whoop of delight and started to sprint, and so did the rest of us. We caught them easily, then they stood their ground and yelled, "Keep away! Keep away!" But Serenus and Senecio took that as a challenge and charged at them, knocking one old man over and trampling one of the women. Otho hit one man over the head and stout old Vitellius pummeled him with his fists. He went down in a heap. Suddenly a tall, strong man was attacking me, hitting me in the face with his fists, then smashing me over the head with a club. I smashed him back, sending him reeling. As he fell backward I recognized him—it was Julius Montanus, a new senator. I was horrified. I was even more horrified when he struggled to his feet, wiped his bleeding nose, and bowed. "Forgive me, Caesar. I did not recognize you."

Did the man have no sense? "It were better you did not admit that you did," I said.

"But—but—" He floundered.

"Go home, all of you," I said. I meant us as well as them.

He had given me such bruises and a black eye that I had to stay in my apartments for several days. The thrill of pretending to be a robber or thug had worn off and I could see how pointless and dangerous it was. The only purpose of it was for me to assume another identity, at least briefly, but it was a foolish identity to take. No, I must be myself from now on, always myself, even if the real me displeased or shocked people. I wished I could still sneak out under cover and hear what the people were saying and thinking, but now it was impossible.

The incident was not over. I received word that Senator Montanus had committed suicide because of his shame at having attacked the emperor. Oh, why had he revealed that he knew me? And why, even after he had, did he not realize I did not hold it against him? Should I have specifically said, *I forgive you?*

As if this had not been enough, once the word was out that the emperor prowled the streets in disguise, gangs of pseudo-Neros took to the streets, causing genuine havoc, even murdering people. I had to put all this down, and sadly see that avenue of escape from my daytime self closed off.

If that avenue closed, I would find another. I told Acte that we were going to inspect the site where I would build a new villa, about fifty miles east of Rome, in the mountains just below the river Anio. We would go openly together, but once there we would have privacy. "I intend to create a world of my own there," I said.

XLI

We stood on the rough terrain of the Apenninus Mountains, looking at the rushing Anio before us. A brisk breeze rustled through the pines and carried with it the scent of resin. Up here everything seemed cleaner and clearer. Yes, this was the place where I would construct my villa.

Acte stood beside me. She reached out and smoothed my wind-mussed hair. "Already you sound more rested," she said.

I was. The bruises on my face had faded and I could be seen in public again. "Come, let's explore." I took her hand and together we clambered over the rocks and uneven ground. Below us a lush valley opened up, green and cool.

"The villa should cling to the cliffs of the valley, seeming suspended," I said, seeing it in my mind. "And . . ." All that water rushing by seemed a waste. "We will dam the river and make three small pleasure lakes out of it. Then situate the villa below them. We can name it Sublaqueum—Under the Lakes."

My architects, scrambling along behind us, caught up. "Yes, Caesar," they said. "You have the eye of an architect."

"Is this possible to build?" I asked.

Severus, the older one, hedged. "We can try."

Celer, the younger, said, "Yes, we can."

"How soon?" I asked.

"First the damming. That must wait until early spring. Then the lakes must fill—although that should not take long," said Severus. "During the winter we can draw up plans. What size building did you have in mind?"

"I don't want one building. I want several smaller ones, all linked by walks and canals."

Celer raised his eyebrows. "The other villas nearby, like Claudius's, have conventional layouts."

"I don't care what Claudius built. In fact, whatever he built, I want the opposite!"

Severus nodded. "With the uneven terrain, a series of smaller buildings would be better. You see, we are right—you do have the eye of an architect!"

"He has the eye of an artist," said Acte.

That night we lay in a tentlike structure, hastily erected for our visit. Our bed was pine boughs overspread with rich eastern textiles. Covered lanterns hung from the tent poles and sat on the ground. Our food was a picnic—wine, bread, dried fruit, cheese. We ate on our bed, leaning on our elbows, as if we were at a proper banquet. Every time we moved, the heady fresh scent of the pine branches beneath was released. Outside, the wind whistled, and we could hear the rush and tumble of the Anio waters.

"You are a genius to have thought of this," she said.

"Not a genius," I said. "But my choice was lucky. The site is even better than I had imagined. With the new lakes, we can have a seaside villa high in the mountains—an engineering marvel."

She lay back, putting her arms behind her, looking up. "This reminds me of my homeland. Lycia is mountainous, much like this."

Her homeland. It was so easy for me to forget that she had once been a slave, as she was so refined, elegant, and well educated. "Does it pain you to remember?" I asked. "Do you want to go back?"

"No," she said. "I am free and could return anytime I liked. But once I was there, that would be painful."

"I could go with you!" Before she could protest, I said, "I want to travel. There is so much in the world I want to see."

She smiled. "You are kind, but I do not care to go back."

"Tell me of your life there." I knew nothing of it, nothing of how she had lived before she came to Rome.

"I can tell you only of the first twelve years, and that means you will hear only what a child remembers. My family were of the aristocracy there, but those were the very ones enslaved, punished by the Romans for protesting Claudius's suppression of the Lycian League and annexation into a Roman province. My father fought against the agents sent to implement this; he was executed."

I took her hand and held it. "And your mother? Your brothers and sisters?"

"My mother became a slave in the household of the new governor of the province. She died not long after, I found out—possibly by her own hand. I had no brothers or sisters. I was sold and sent to Rome, luckily to the imperial household."

What could I say? That it was undeserved? That Rome was cruel? But that was how the empire operated—suppress, crush, expand. "I am grieved to hear of it," I said. "I can only say that the gods brought you to Rome—and to me."

"I suppose they did. If you believe they look out for us at all." She turned and looked at me. The lantern just behind me illuminated her face. "Let me tell you a little of Lycia. You would feel at home there. It is a Greek land, thoroughly Greek. We are even mentioned in Homer, as an ally of Troy."

"Troy! You supported Troy, even though you were Greek?"

"Well, so they say. And Sarpedon, Zeus's own son, was from Lycia."

"So the women of Lycia were always fair?" I asked. "Fair enough for the gods?"

She laughed. "Zeus was not particular. But yes, a Lycian woman caught his eye. I have always liked that part of *The Iliad* where Zeus wants to bring Sarpedon back to life and Hera says, 'Well, if you must, but realize that you are setting a precedent and soon all the sons of gods by mortal women will want to be brought back to life!' There were a great many of them. Half the armies were the sons of gods." She sighed. "Later his body was brought back to Lycia by Sleep and Death. I've seen the tomb."

I rolled over and embraced her. The feel of her in my arms, with the sweet-smelling pine beneath us, seemed worthy of any god. I wished to possess her in every way, to make her mine forever, not just at this moment. Our clothes were flung off and we pressed against one another, warm flesh to flesh. "Do you remember the night we spoke of Sappho together?" I whispered. "I wanted to say the rest of the words but I could not, not there. So I say it now: 'Come to me now, then, free me from aching care, and win me all my heart longs to win.'"

"I am here," she said. "Here and ready to free you."

The lanterns had almost burned out; they were flickering and guttering. We had given ourselves to one another time and again. It must be almost dawn.

"I want to marry you," I said.

Drowsily she laughed.

"I mean it."

Again she laughed.

"I am serious."

Now she opened her eyes, startled. "Do not say such things. Do not tease me. I cannot bear it."

"I am not teasing. I want to marry you."

"You are already married."

"It is no marriage! You know that. I was forced into it. She hates me. I never see her."

"She is the emperor's daughter. She cannot be set aside."

"That emperor is dead."

"But his daughter is not, and cannot be dishonored."

"I cannot go through the rest of my life yoked to someone who hates me, when I love someone else."

"You will not be the first."

"Then let me be the last!" I grabbed her shoulders. "Oh, let me be happy! You said you would free me from aching care. Now keep your word!"

She sat up, fully awake now. "It is not that simple. You cannot marry a former slave."

"But you come from noble stock. And if that is not enough, you are probably linked to royal houses in Lycia and nearby provinces. We'll find a pedigree for you."

"A bogus one," she said. She leaned over on her elbow and held out her hand, stroked my face. "Not a worthy wife for an emperor who has the blood of the Caesars."

"I *am* the emperor! I decide who is worthy!"

"Oh, my dear Nero. That is what I love about you—well, one thing. You are so innocent."

But it was she who was innocent. The fact was, the emperor had infinite power. I was only just grasping this, grasping the extent of it.

XLII

Seneca and Burrus were not pleased with my plans for my new villa. Truth be told, they were not pleased with much of what I was doing or proposed to do.

The third anniversary of my accession was coming up and the amphitheater at last was ready for the delayed celebrations, as the theater had taken longer to build than expected. But no matter. There would be games all day, wild-beast hunts, and bounty for the common people—grain, silver, birds.

I would drive a chariot out into the arena and from there throw out the tokens to the crowd.

"Ill-advised," said Seneca. We were meeting in a secluded room of the palace, with windows that gave out onto the landscape of the Palatine. The gardens were still blooming, but the winds of autumn would soon strip them. "The chariot—not proper for you. And the largesse—impractical. If you start doing that, people will expect it every time. Your treasury is not unlimited."

"The Senate will not approve," said Burrus.

I looked at both of them. Seneca was getting stooped and Burrus had worry lines all over his leathery face. Old men. Old men who could not understand what glory and freedom meant.

"And this villa you mean to build—why do you need it?" Burrus went on. "It's ruinously expensive, what with the dams and the engineering."

"I do need it," I said.

"What you mean is, you want it," said Seneca. He almost wagged his finger.

"Yes, that is what I mean. I want it, and I shall have it."

"The Consilium will not be pleased. They may refuse the funds."

I laughed. "The Consilium has no power over the finances. All they can do is advise. The minister of accounts and revenues, my friend Phaon, will approve. Not that he has the power, either, to deny me."

Burrus and Seneca exchanged meaningful looks. "Your attitude is unfortunate. Be careful of proceeding without caution or advice."

"I will," I said.

"You have surrounded yourself with freedmen, who will always be subservient to you. It may be difficult to get unbiased advice from them," said Seneca.

"Such as you give?" I asked. "You are representative of your class, the senatorial one, as much as they are of theirs. If the mighty senatorial class were willing to serve as advisers and ministers they would not be shut out of decisions. But since they persist in thinking the only honorable sources of wealth and power are land and the army, not trade or finance, they have sabotaged themselves and handed the power over to lower classes."

Seneca winced. "You are quite a champion of the lower classes, it seems."

"They aren't hypocrites," I said.

"But they are just as self-seeking," said Burrus. "Aspiring to positions above their station."

"Insinuating themselves in the affections of gullible people," chimed in Seneca.

He meant Acte. I sat silently, waiting for them to say the words. The quiet stretched on, filling the space.

Finally Seneca said, "It has come to our ears that you have taken up with a slave girl."

Burrus cleared his throat. "A freedwoman, rather."

I let the silence draw out a bit longer. They began to wiggle and fidget. "Yes, and I mean to marry her."

Now they almost fell off their stools. Seneca blanched and gasped for words, his mouth moving like a fish's. To his credit, he found them. "We have heard good things about her. Not only is she beautiful, she has a fine character. But to marry her, no, you cannot consider it."

"I have already considered it and have made up my mind."

"Does anyone else know about this?" Burrus spoke.

"It is between us for now," I admitted.

"It must stay that way," said Seneca. "And you must abandon the idea. Oh, in many ways she is ideal. It is better that you not meddle with aristocratic women or—gods forbid!—debauch the wives of senators, like Caligula did."

"Your marriage is unfulfilling," said Burrus. "We understand that. You need another outlet, and as Seneca says, not with highborn women. But marry her? No."

The words of Serenus floated through my mind. *Why do you obey them? You are the emperor, not them.*

"I shall do as I please. I deserve to be happy!"

"Does anyone deserve to be happy?" asked Seneca. "And what is happiness?"

"I don't need a philosophical discussion of happiness, Seneca. I know what happiness is, and I want it."

"There are no happy lives," said Burrus. "Only happy moments." The old soldier at least had common sense.

"Then I want the maximum of happy moments," I said. My music gave me happiness, my poetry, watching drama, driving chariots. What was happiness, indeed, but defining what makes one happy and resolving to do more of it? In reverse, defining what makes one unhappy and resolving to do less of it.

"Does roaming the streets with a lot of ruffians give you happiness?" barked Seneca. "Shocking behavior, most unworthy of you."

"What is worthy and what is not? I used the opportunity to hear, firsthand, what my people were saying and learn what they were thinking—unfiltered by anyone else's interpretation. Oh, it made my ears burn sometimes. But better to know. But I can't do that anymore. It got out of hand."

"It certainly did!" Burrus crossed his arms. "It had to stop."

"And it has," I said. "But the villa and the celebrations and Acte have not, and will not."

They attacked me for public actions, and Mother did for private ones. I had seen little of Mother since she had tried to kill me (how casually I say this, which proves that the most twisted and dangerous situations can come to seem normal) and failed. I avoided her as much as possible, which was easy to do. Her apartments were on the far side of the palace, and she was not admitted to Consilium meetings or private ones with my secretaries. I made sure my quarters were well guarded at all times and kept a dagger near me day and night. I hired extra tasters. I knew Locusta would not turn against me, but there were plenty of other poisoners for hire and Mother could find them. I had informers who kept me abreast of her doings. There were hints of other plots and she was still championing Octavia, to what end I could not discern.

So I was startled and taken aback when one chilly day she was announced at my quarters. I composed myself and rose to meet her. I removed my cithara from its resting place and out of her sight. I would not have this one destroyed. Nor anything else, for that matter.

She emerged from the hallway into the receiving room as if she owned it—which, at one time, she had. She looked much the same, lovely as always—although she was showing slight signs of aging around her eyes and mouth. She was only forty-one, which I found hard to remember. She seemed ageless, present since mythological times. But she was still within childbearing age, as Tigellinus had ominously warned me; if she should find a man of appropriate lineage—preferably one descended from Augustus himself—to take up with, she could produce another Augustan heir.

I rose to meet her. "Mother," I said, going to her, taking her hands, leaning to kiss her cheek. She smelled of roses.

"Emperor," she said, bowing. She looked around the room. "You have changed things."

The outer receiving rooms had been stripped of their austere busts and uncomfortable bronze benches, replaced with Greek statues and padded couches.

"Yes, they are all originals," I said, pointing to one by Phidias. "My agent got it in Olympia." I could see her looking for the bust of Germanicus, now retired to a workroom no one frequented. "I find artwork helps me to concentrate."

She smiled. "Dear son, it has been so long!" When she smiled she was most entrancing—and dangerous.

"What can I do for you, Mother?" I ushered her to one of the couches and clapped for a slave to bring us refreshments.

She sank down, tucking her sandaled feet under her voluminous gown. She sat regally, upright, not sinking back into the cushions. "Does a mother need a reason to see her son?"

"Most do not, but this one does." I smiled.

"Oh, how did I raise such an unnatural son?" Sadness chased across her face.

"Perhaps by being unnatural yourself," I said. "It is my heritage, dear Mother. Now, as I asked, what may I do for you?"

She smiled again and touched her hair, carefully dressed in braids, ornamented with pearls. "I wanted to see you, see you ensconced in your imperial quarters—quarters that I know so well—and know you as emperor."

Just then the slave came with the tray of drinks and tidbits. It was first offered to Mother. She took a goblet and picked up a piece of dried fruit. She held the goblet to her lips.

"You may drink," I said. "It is safe."

She smiled, the smile of a cobra, tilted the cup back, and drank. Her sensuously curved neck moved as the liquid descended. The neck . . . yes, Tigellinus was right. She could still command lust and desire, and she might use it.

"Well, now you see me as emperor." I stood up and turned slowly around. I was wearing one of my best tunics, decorated with gold threads and stars. "Soon you can see me publicly at the anniversary celebrations of my accession. They will be spectacular."

"I had heard you had taken to wearing tunics instead of togas," she said, ignoring what I had said. "It isn't seemly."

"They are comfortable," I said.

"People won't respect you," she said. "You must dress as emperor, not a libertine."

"Emperors and libertines are synonymous," I said. "Mother, why are we talking about my clothes? Surely you did not come for that."

"At least you are still wearing togas for ceremonial occasions."

"Enough about the togas!" I yelled. She had done it again, made me lose my temper. "Now, what do you want?"

She rose, put down her goblet. "Since you won't be civil or polite, neither will I. I've come about that Greek slut you have taken up with."

For an instant I did not connect that with Acte, not at all. "I haven't taken up with any Greek sluts," I said.

"Yes, you have. Do you think that ruse of having Serenus pretend she is with him has fooled anyone?"

"You mean Acte," I said. "Claudia Acte. She is not a Greek slut."

"She's a slave."

"She was once a slave, true. Her family had the misfortune to oppose Rome in its greed to annex her country. But she is free now, educated, honorable in every respect."

"Honorable! Ha!"

"You are speaking of my future wife," I said.

No sculptor, no, not even Polyclitus or Kresilas, could have captured the expression of shock and horror on her face. For once she, the mistress of retorts and snipes, was speechless. Finally she choked out, "No!"

"Yes," I said. "I have found the person who makes me happy, and I mean to make her my official wife."

"What of Octavia?"

"I will divorce her. She will be glad to be free of me—although probably not of the status of being the emperor's wife."

"You can't do this," she said.

"Yes, I can and I will."

"You have taken leave of your senses!"

"No, I have come to my senses," I said. "I know now that I am emperor, and what that means. So, if this is all you have come to say, I bid you good day, Mother."

I clapped for an attendant, who appeared instantly. "My mother is leaving," I said. "Please escort her out as befits her station."

She glared at me, then drew herself up. "As you please," she said. "And we shall see."

XLIII

The day was here at last—the grand celebrations of the day I had come to the throne. The wooden amphitheater, the first of the complex that would include the baths and the gymnasium, was finished, and it would be inaugurated with spectacular exhibitions. For days Rome had been readying herself, and on the morning of October thirteenth crowds had been waiting since midnight.

I, too, had been sleepless since then. The day itself was sacred to me. I had not forgotten a single instant of that very long day that preceded it. Three years had brought profound changes to me, and now I was emperor in fact as well as in name, regardless of whether I was wearing a tunic or a toga. I could be naked and still be emperor.

Today I would wear a purple cloak such as triumvirs wore, with a sun-ray crown, as Apollo's chosen, when I drove my chariot. Yes, I would drive that chariot out into the arena, publicly.

The sun rose on a perfect day. Thank you, Apollo.

The stands were full; as far as the eye could see, crowds squeezed into the space, and still more were coming. The faces looked as numerous to me as the stars. Those unable to get a place thronged the outside, and as I drove through them, they swarmed my chariot.

"Nero! Nero!" they cried. They waved branches and banners and screamed.

Why should they be excluded from the rewards? Did not Apollo send his rays upon all? I reached down into the pouch with the tokens I was to throw out into the crowd inside. I tossed a handful out, and they scrambled for them.

"Report to the arena office to claim your prizes," I said.

"Glorious emperor!" they cried.

When they turned in their tokens, they would be astounded: gold, jewels, even houses were awarded. I wished I could see their faces.

Driving out into the arena, with its blue awning spangled with stars, I circled once around, slowly, to the calls and cheers, then drew up the horses. A herald sounded the straight trumpet and proclaimed a celebration for the beneficence of the gods in bringing the emperor Nero to the people of Rome.

"For they have blessed us, have looked kindly on us, and for this we give them deepest thanks."

Although the arena was large and my words would not carry to all, I cried, "It is I who am blessed, to have such people to rule!" I then drove around the periphery again, throwing out the tokens until the bag was empty. "All I ask is, wait until the games are over before claiming your prizes. For you will not want to miss the exhibitions."

There were wild-beast hunts—men versus animals. They were imported from all over the empire—leopards, ostriches, lions, and bears, as well as more common animals like deer and gazelles. Next were fights between animals—bulls against elephants, rhinoceroses against crocodiles, bears against lions.

Then came the human fights, many gladiatorial contests, with all twelve types of gladiators represented. But, unlike in other contests, no one would die. There were a number of innovations, such as the *dimachaerus*, the two-sword man, and the *laquearius*, with a lasso, as well as the common *mirmillo*, *retiarius*, and Thracian-style fighters.

Last was my favorite, a new presentation: reenactments of mythological scenes, complete with scenery and costumes. There was Hercules in his flaming shirt (he was wearing a fireproof vest underneath); and Orpheus and Eurydice with her poisonous snake (a harmless one).

As I watched them, I suddenly thought how becoming a mythological character was the ultimate in freedom, at least for those moments. When Icarus put on his wings, did the actor himself disappear, if only for a brief instant? Did the actor truly become Hercules, leave himself behind? This was a step beyond where drunkenness could take one, where dreaming left off and turned to flesh. I envied them.

The celebrations over, Rome was quiet, anticipating winter. The weather had waited to turn cold until after the games (thank you again, Apollo). The trees lost their leaves, swirling vortexes of them flying overhead. Darker clouds chased one another quickly through the sky, the wind whistling.

The meeting with Mother had disturbed me. I had consigned her to the past after the Britannicus episode, almost as if she had died along with him. But she was still very much of the present. My mother . . . But I had had a father, too, although I did not remember him. The adoption by Claudius had not erased the fact that I had a genuine father. I determined to visit his grave, ashamed that I had not done it earlier. Just because he did not exist for Mother did not mean he did not exist.

The Domitian family tomb lay on the outskirts of the city, in gardens at the top of the Pincian Hill. It was a long ride out along the Via Flaminia, past the Ara Pacis and the Sundial, then past the mausoleum. Finally I was at the foot of the hill, planted thick with plane trees and cypress. It was a beautiful spot, even in this autumnal time of year.

The tomb at the summit was constructed of white marble, with a balustrade guarding the outside, and there were markers for not only my father but my great-great-grandfather, Lucius, a consul; my great-grandfather, another Gnaeus, also consul, who had served with Antony but defected to Augustus; and my grandfather, Lucius. On his marker it recorded that, in addition to being consul, he had been a famous charioteer in his youth. I smiled when I read the list of his feats on the racetrack.

Ah, I got it from you, I thought.

Then there was my father's marker and tomb. I stood before it, wishing I could remember him, anything about him, even the sound of one sentence he had spoken. But he was lost to me, except in imagination and an act of will.

The wives were all there, too, their names marked and their ages.

"I will decree that your birthday is honored," I promised Father. "I will propose it, and the Senate will approve it. There is no question of that."

I owed this to him, and I would see it done.

XLIV

The sparkle off the water was so scintillating it made me shade my eyes. The Bay of Naples spread out before me, the day was clear and I could see all the way to Vesuvius. Naples, that Greek-inclined city, was spread out to the left of the mountain. Lake Lucrine, a shallow lake near it connected to the sea by a canal, was the historic site where Agrippa had trained the navy for the battle of Actium against Antony. Today the Roman fleet was based nearby. I was visiting Otho's villa at Baiae. Unlike my secluded one at Sublaqueum—which I had indeed built—this villa was in a holiday resort. On all sides of the peninsula, villas of the wealthy crowded up against one another, Rome transported to the seashore. Even Seneca had a place here (although he complained about the noise and immoral goings-on, calling it "the inn of all vices"), where Julius Caesar's father-in-law Calpurnius had set the standard for luxury more than a hundred years before. Otho came from an old aristocratic family and the villa had been theirs for a long time.

What was there to do in Baiae? Indulge oneself, that was all. The hot springs gave us baths; the bay gave us sailing; the villas delighted us with views and feasts. After dark, lighted pleasure vessels plied the waters, music trailing in their wakes.

I had brought Acte with me, for here I did not have to pretend she was with anyone else. Otho was preparing to marry and made much of this being his last season as a bachelor. That did not stop him from having a woman with him now.

"I shall be that sad specimen, that butt of comedies, a husband," he said, waving his goblet around.

"Husbands are only the butt of comedies if they are cuckolded," I said. "And surely you won't be. Who is this woman who has snared the elusive Otho?"

For although he was short, bowlegged, and bald, necessitating the wig, his wealth, wit, and lineage made him a desirable match. Oddly enough, he was vain about his looks, softening his beard with moistened bread crumbs and having his body hair plucked.

His cynical expression melted away, replaced by a dreamy look. "Oh, she's a goddess."

He wasn't joking. He was truly smitten. I was taken aback. "Who is this goddess?"

"Her family is from Pompeii. That is how I met her, when I was visiting there. We will have to go over there—I want to show you the frescoes—"

"You still haven't told me her name. I know about Pompeii; I want to know more about this woman."

"Her name is Poppaea," he said. "You may have heard of her mother—she was Poppaea also, reputed the most beautiful woman in Rome—but I tell you, her daughter eclipses her."

"Poppaea—Poppaea—" I was good with names, and I knew I had heard of her, but where?

"She is the wife of Rufrius Crispinus," said Acte.

"Was the wife," said Otho. "They are divorced."

"She must be a goddess, for you to be content to be second and not first."

"You know the saying: better to be someone's last love than their first," he said. "Besides, everyone is divorced. General Corbulo's mother was married six times!" Dinner was announced, and the guests began to stream into the huge dining room. Before we took our places, slaves knelt before us and drenched our feet in costly perfume. Otho winked. "I say, extravagance should always be in the grand manner." He then daintily tiptoed to his place at the dinner, perfume dripping from his feet.

One of the other guests was Gaius Calpurnius Piso, who also had a villa in the area. He was distantly related to Julius Caesar's wife's family and had had an unfortunate run-in with Caligula. As astonishing as it may sound, Caligula wanted Piso's wife, forced her to leave him, then accused Piso of adultery with her and banished him! For that alone I felt a kinship with him—torment at the hands of Caligula. But more than that, he performed dramatic roles onstage, sang, and wrote poetry. I was most anxious to talk to him. I had no trouble identifying him—he was very handsome, with the sort of looks that put others at ease rather than exciting envy.

In one way I was the eager seeker after a more experienced person, but he instantly almost prostrated himself before me, and once again I was all too aware that even when I forgot I was emperor, everyone else remembered.

"I have long wished to talk to you," I said after dinner. "I believe we have much in common."

He smiled, a winning, open smile. "And what might that be?"

"I, too, am interested in the arts. I do not go so far as to claim to be an artist, but I am drawn to it. And to music and acting. Tell me—where do you perform?"

"In private homes and on private stages," he said. "There are many opportunities."

"Have you never thought of performing publicly?"

He threw his head back and laughed. "No! I would not dare."

"Why not?"

He looked at me pityingly, as if thinking, *What a fool.* Then he straightened his expression. "It would give great scandal. Someone of my station could not appear onstage."

"Why not?" I was persistent.

"Because actors, singers, and dancers are of the lower classes."

"Yet we admire their talent and make many of them wealthy."

"That is true. But class is more than money. It is lineage and position." He began to look uncomfortable.

"Ah, but everyone's family honor begins somewhere back in humble origins. That is, if we are not the result of Zeus's roving eye, giving us divine lineage, and there are few of those about these days."

Now he did look uncomfortable. "Yes, yes, I see." He was remembering that the emperor was said to have a fondness for the common people, or, as Piso would call them, the riffraff.

"I would sponsor you to go on the public stage," I said.

"Perhaps, perhaps. Thank you for your generosity." Then he sidled away. I almost laughed. He was too conscious of his station in life to be a true artist.

That night, as I lay on the bed in the echoingly large room, I heard the tinkling sound of music carrying across the water. A clean, fresh breeze came from the open balcony that overlooked the bay.

Piso . . . Otho . . . Otho's future wife . . . I tried to imagine what she must be like to have elicited such a response from him. Rufrius . . . Suddenly I remembered. I had seen her. I was only a boy, out with Crispus, that day he took me to the races. That woman who squeezed in beside me . . . married to the old Praetorian . . . O gods of Olympus, she belonged with them there! If she was mortal, she had sipped the ambrosia of the gods and become one of them. The woman who had enabled me to envision Helen of Troy. A woman . . . some years older than me . . . how old would she be now? I fell asleep trying to deduce that.

I visited the fleet at Misenum, the cape at the tip of the peninsula, with its inner and outer harbors. Anicetus had been commander of the fleet for some time now. Seeing him again was a great joy to me.

"Dear friend," I said. "I miss you at Rome horribly, but I know it is best you are here. I do not lose a moment's sleep worrying about the fleet."

He put his hands on my shoulders, looked deep into my eyes. "I miss you, too. I think of you often, hoping that you are protected and safe."

"I am," I said. "You need not worry."

In only a few moments, it was as if we had never been parted. He gave me a report on the fleet and some activities he had not put into writing. New trading links were being formed with India; he said we might consider moving some of the fleet to the Red Sea to be better positioned for the journeys there around the monsoon season. He also mentioned that the water level in the bay had changed a bit, and there had been small tremors in the area, but nothing to cause alarm.

"Stay with us tonight. We will put on a show you'll enjoy."

He was as good as his word. The sailors staged a mock sea battle on the bay, better than any I had ever seen in the confined spaces of flooded amphitheaters. Three ships fought and grappled with one another, then one dramatically sank, all hands aboard, sliding into the water so quickly people did not have a chance to jump.

"The boat was specially constructed to fall apart," he said. "But it looked real, didn't it?"

It certainly had. I shook my head. "What ingenuity."

The combatants were swimming back toward shore. Of course, they were all trained and knew what to expect.

"Don't worry, no one drowned," he said. "You appreciate illusion and reality, yes?"

XLV

Months passed, and I quietly moved forward my plan to have Acte declared of royal descent. I consulted with a specialist in the lineages of the royal houses of that part of the world. There were many small realms there—or had been, before Rome swallowed them up—and among so many, she must surely be connected to one. At length he drew up an impressive-looking chart, tracing her back to Attalus I of Pergamum. I presented it to a group of senators, asking them to ratify it. They did. Happiness was within my grasp now. Acte was not so sure and cautioned me not to expect so much.

"There are still many hurdles ahead," she said. "No imperial decree can change people's hearts and I would do nothing to harm your position. You are very popular now, but it does not take much to change people's minds. People are fickle. They almost look for faults and are gleeful when they find one."

My love for her had grown, not diminished. "They can look and look and they'll find no fault in you."

"I don't care if they find fault with me, but if they find fault with you because of me, that is what I fear."

"Nonsense!" I sounded more sure of that than I felt.

. . .

After her attempts to dislodge Acte failed (threats, and even having some people beaten), Mother disappeared from the palace. I was told that she was at the villa at Antium; I certainly did not miss her. It was a soothing relief to have her gone. For her to be nowhere in sight. Or even out of sight, but lurking nearby.

So imagine my wariness when a letter was delivered to my quarters— from her. I opened the familiar seal with trepidation.

My dearest son,

In my time of retreat at the villa, I have come to understand my mistake, and I beg your forgiveness. I was wrong to oppose your love for Claudia Acte. It is hard for a mother to admit to herself that she has been displaced in the life and heart of her child, but such is the course of nature and it is futile to rail against it. Please accept my deepest apology. I am returning to Rome and when I am there I will have something to present to you.

Your loving Mother

I was stunned. But immediately the saying *Beware of the Greeks bearing gifts* flitted through my mind. A gift from Mother, even though she wasn't Greek, was never something of unequivocal good.

True to her word, as soon as she returned to Rome I received an invitation to come to her apartments. I made sure I did not wear a toga.

She greeted me effusively, warmly. She stood on tiptoe to kiss my cheek and did not mention the tunic. She ushered me into the first room and showed me some new bronzes she had just obtained from Corinth. "These are all yours," she said. "But, come, see the rest."

She led me back into the deepest part of the apartments, the most private. At the very end was a room darkened with draperies, hung with expensive tapestries. It took a while for my eyes to adjust. When they did, before me was an enormous flat wide bed that looked as big as Lake Lucrine. Heaped upon it were pillows with silken covers, furs, and scarves. To each side were huge lampstands shaped like trees.

"This is what they have in the east," she said. "I have made much study of it."

What was this all about? I just stared at it.

"It is for you and Acte. She is from Lycia; this will make her feel at home."

"What?"

"You can bring her here—have absolute privacy—and I have stocked it with every luxury—"

"Are you mad?" I cried. "What has possessed you? Why would we come here?"

"I am trying to show you that I am in favor of your—your—"

"You can't even think of the word, can you? You don't even know what to call her! And the thought that I'd bring her here, under your roof—" I turned on my heel and marched out, down the long hallway, back out into the light. She *had* gone mad!

She ran after me, her fine little slippers making *slap-slap* noises on the marble. She grabbed at my arm, but I flung her off like an annoying insect crawling on me.

I reached the outer receiving room. She was still on my heels, clutching for me. Behind me she gasped, "Please, do not run away. Please stay. I am sorry if I offended you. I—I—do not know how to please you. I was trying. I was wrong."

With a great sigh I stopped and turned around slowly. There she was, abject and almost cringing. "Yes, you have offended me. Deeply. And I think you may have lost your mind, frankly."

She bowed her head. "Please. Let us end our estrangement. I cannot bear it. I will do anything."

"Anything, apparently, but behave in a normal fashion."

"I admit it. I have been wrong. I will admit anything if you will just smile and say you forgive me and that we are close again."

I felt like an animal in the tightening coils of a snake. "I must go!" I said.

"Please, at least drink something with me in amity. Do not sever us from one another. It must not end like this." She went over to a tray laden with drinking cups and wine bottles. She started to pour something, and I laughed.

"No, Mother, I must decline to drink anything you offer. You can understand why."

"But to seal our peace with one another, we must partake of something. I know." She clapped for a slave, and when she entered, Mother said, "Bring me a bowl of the snow."

In a few moments she brought a bowl with packed snow. "Kept in our icehouse. All the way from the mountains of Gaul." She scooped two portions out and put them in two goblets. "Surely you can trust snow," she said. She held her goblet over the flame of a lamp and soon the snow melted. I did likewise.

We stood looking at one another. With all my being I wished that all that had happened in our years together could vanish and we could start again. But what I was really wishing for was that she be other than she was. And that was as impossible as for me to be someone other than I was.

The snow had a flavor different from plain water; freezing and thawing lent it a different taste. We held our goblets up and touched them, briefly.

Slowly—or was it quickly?—the room took on different properties. Slowly—or was it quickly?—I was floating somewhere, high above the colored floor marbles, which I could see clearly beneath me. My arms grew long, then shortened. An exaltation seized me, a burning in my soul. Suddenly I was in that huge bed—no, *we* were in it, tumbling against one another, falling into another world, a deep pit where we landed, clinging to one another. Was this what had lain hidden inside me, now released? Or just madness, a nightmare?

◆   ◆   ◆

The drug took a long time to wear off. I found myself naked on the big bed, shivering because I was cold. Gradually I regained control of my limbs, my mind. Mother was curled up beside me, a smile on her face, also naked.

She reached out and touched my cheek. "Now you are mine," she murmured. "Forever."

I jumped up, repulsed. "Oh, gods!" I felt frantically for my clothes, grabbing them, pulling the tunic over my head, running away without my sandals or outer cloak. I fled as if the lord of the underworld was after me.

Once out of her apartments—luckily it was late; there was no one about, except the usual guards—I stopped to catch my breath. I felt sick. Defiled. I was afraid I would vomit on the fine polished tiles, imported from who knew where.

My mother had drugged me and seduced me. She had planned it all along. Did she want to turn me into Oedipus? Bind me to her in perversion? I shook with horror and disgust.

I couldn't go back to the imperial apartments, could not go back to Acte in this state. I had to wash off the filth, the degradation. I had to be cleansed. There was only one place. Sublaqueum.

Fleeing through the night on a swift horse, with only one attendant, I reached the villa late the next night. I did not stop to rest, did not eat, and changed horses along the way. At last I stood before the largest of the three lakes, high on the mountain, the lakes I had created. There was a half-moon, rising late over the smooth-surfaced water, reflective as polished silver. I plunged in, relishing the chill, the astringent sting against my skin, that would purify me and make me whole again.

She had had the snow laced with the drug, prepared and waiting. Should I be thankful it was only a temporary effect, one that robbed me of myself but not of my life? The obscenity of it, the taint—could I ever be cleansed of it? I dove down into the dark depths of the water. Wash it away, wash it away, I prayed. But how to scrub the stain out of my mind?

At last, tired and spent, I climbed out of the lake. I did feel purified, made new. I stared back out over the water, still rippling from my movement through it. It held a mystery, but its power had restored me, expunged the evil.

XLVI

I returned to Rome, vowing never to reveal what had happened with Mother. For the first time, I could not be honest with Acte. I merely said, since she knew about the letter from Mother, that she had softened in her attitude and would stand aside from hindering us. I was likewise vague about why I had suddenly gone to Sublaqueum without her in such unannounced haste. I mumbled something about receiving urgent word that the dams were leaking. I could tell she did not believe me and knew there was another reason. But whatever she imagined it was, nothing could come close to the horror of the real reason. And that she must never know.

Mother had abruptly departed from the palace and retreated back to Antium. Now what would she do? What would be her next move? Having failed to ensnare me, having driven me away, would she now openly become my enemy? She still had resources, loyalties with the Praetorians and senators she had given lavish gifts and bribes to. Most members of her household were fiercely loyal and it was difficult for me to find any informer in their midst, so she had a protective shield around her.

Now Tigellinus's words about her finding a new husband, about still being of childbearing age, came to haunt me. Might she do that—marry herself to someone who could plausibly stake a claim to the throne and challenge mine? Or . . . oh, the dark thought of it, too terrible, too abhorrent to contemplate . . . what if we had conceived a child from that drugged night? I would be living in an Oedipal nightmare, stepping directly into what had been only a myth. I could not even say "the gods would never be so cruel," because they delighted in being just that cruel.

While I waited, half expecting this to come true, I was suspended in a strange world, almost as disorienting as the drug itself. But as time passed and nothing was heard, or even rumored, of this, my fears ebbed away.

In my meetings with Seneca and Burrus, they seemed suddenly alarmed about Mother, but for normal political reasons.

"There's been a report that she is plotting again," said Burrus. "This time to marry Rubellius Plautus."

He had almost—not quite—as much of an imperial bloodline as I did! Descended from both Augustus's sister, Octavia, and from Tiberius, he was only four years older than me, and twenty years younger than Mother! But Mother had proved she would take on all ages, from elderly Claudius to . . . no, I would not think of it!

"There are also credible reports that she is instigating him to a rebellion against you—once they are married."

Was there no end to her provocations? Would there never be peace, as long as she walked the earth? "I will dismiss her German bodyguards and the military escorts she has been given as a courtesy and order her to vacate Antium and move to the home of the late lady Antonia." Where I could keep better watch on her.

I must leave this worry behind. My baths and gymnasium were just finished, and with great fanfare I was to declare them open and dedicate them. They had been years in the building, but now they rose, magnificent and shining, over the Campus Martius. The baths put temples to shame in grandeur, and the artworks surrounding the perimeters of the exercise yard made a visit there for that reason alone worthwhile. I invited the entire Senate to the opening and gifted each

man with an aryballos juglet of finest olive oil, to be used in athletic
exercises as they did in Greece.

"For I wish everyone to feel that he has been personally invited to
the baths by me. They are yours!" I passed my arm over the senators.
Behind them was a vast crowd of other Romans. "And for all of you!"
The plebians cheered so loudly my ears rang.

But somewhere on my way from the Palatine to the Campus I had
decided to put an end to Mother. When I started the short trip I had
had no idea of it; when I arrived it was a resolution. How it had come
to me in complete conviction en route I do not know. But it had. I could
no longer live with the provisional nature of my emperorship, under the
cloud of a woman who had clearly lost her mind and could have the
power to destroy me. So I barely heard the cheers, and the faces looking
back at me, smiling, were like faded ghosts to my great purpose.

That night, alone in my withdrawing room, I pondered it. No longer
did I have the nervous feeling that something was about to happen,
might happen, could conceivably happen. Now all uncertainty was swept
away, and the sword of Damocles that had been hanging over me all my
life would be sheathed.

But how and when to do it? It was true, the list of her crimes would
certainly convict her in a court—all her secret murders, revealed, alone
would damn her—but that was not the way. It must be swift, sure, and
secret. And, ideally, painless. I had no wish for her to suffer. That let
out assassination—it relied on too many other people, as Mother herself
had recognized when she did away with Claudius. No poison—too
obvious, and she would be guarding against it. An accident? Now there
were possibilities. Something falling on her? Too uncertain. A fire? Too
horrible. A fall? Again, too uncertain. Drowning? My recent swim at
Sublaqueum came to mind. Water was soothing, embracing. They said
drowning was the least painful death. But deaths in swimming pools
were too obvious, and she did not swim in the ocean.

But if she were out on the ocean . . . Something was coming to me . . . a picture in my mind . . . I had seen something recently . . . the collapsing boat in the staged sea battle at Misenum!

Yes . . . an accident at sea, far from land. It happened all the time. Seafaring was dangerous; a large portion of ships sailing from anywhere went down. Recently a shipment of Greek bronzes and marbles, secured by my agents and bound for Rome, had foundered off the coast of the Peloponnese and the treasures were lost. Such losses were routine.

After the tragic accident, I could mourn for her and erect a temple in her memory. And before that, we could be reconciled. I could send her on her way with happy feelings on both sides. I could assure that her last day on earth was a joyous one—how many people have that blessing? Most deaths are preceded by wretched days leading up to them.

It had to be. It was the best I could manage, under the circumstances.

Now that I had decided, I was anxious to move ahead, before I could falter. I sent for Anicetus. For he was vital to my plan.

Secluded in my most private room, he and I looked at one another across the little table where the oil lamp burned, its flame flickering. In the uneven light, sometimes his eyes were illuminated, sometimes not. But I knew him well enough to read his expression even in the uneven light. No hint of condemnation showed on it. Quite the opposite.

"It has to be," he said. "As you know. And I agree entirely with your selection of method. I can have the ship ready in time for next spring's Festival of Minerva at Baiae. You have attended that before, have you not? It's very popular, and if you are there with a contingent of friends, what more natural than that you invite her to join you?"

At this point nothing was natural between Mother and me. But I had time. Time to affect a reconciliation. Time to make a grand gesture of appeasement.

"Build the ship to be beautiful. Spare no expense on ornamentation," I ordered him.

"But if it is just to go to the bottom of the sea—"

"It is to be a gift. An extravagant gift. And thus it must look the part. She must be eager to board it, be proud to sail in it to her villa."

"I see. I will have it done." He nodded smartly.

I was overcome. I rose and embraced him. My oldest, firmest friend. My right hand.

From somewhere came the fragment of a poetic line I had heard once, from someone in my writers' group who knew Hebrew writings. *If I forget thee, O Jerusalem, let my right hand forget her cunning.* Anicetus was my right hand, and in his knowledge of boats and the sea lay the cunning.

XLVII

Bad weather descended on Rome as the year turned. Saturnalia came and went; so did my twenty-first birthday. There were celebrations, but I paid them little heed. At New Year's I wore a white and gold robe and accepted the renewal of all the legions' allegiance throughout the empire, standing before the troops of the Praetorians. On January third I stood at the Forum Rostra with Octavia by my side to accept vows for the welfare of our divine essence, our *genius*. We did not look at one another but stared straight out, looking toward the Temple of the Divine Julius and the Augustus Triumphal triple arch beside it, sparkling with a layer of frost.

The sea was still choppy, too dangerous to sail. Usually the Festival of Minerva marked the beginning of the safe sailing season. Oh, would it ever come? I remembered that Agrippa had taken Antony completely by surprise—and ultimately to defeat—by crossing over into Greece when it was deemed too early. He landed and that was that. On such gambles are empires built.

I had to grit my teeth and pay courtesy calls to Mother, now settled (by my orders) in her paternal grandmother's home on the Pincian Hill. The sudden move there, and the loss of her prestigious guards, signaled to all Rome that her power was waning, and her erstwhile supporters and sycophants peeled away like skin from an overripe fruit.

When I went, I took along an escort of staff officers and did not linger. But I gradually increased the time I spent there, and modified my demeanor to be warmer, all to build up to the invitation to Baiae. She must think that I had softened, forgiven her for the heinous act she had visited on me—or better yet, forgotten it, the drug having erased it from my mind. But no, it was burned there for eternity.

At last, after several of these visits, I accepted her usual offer to sit with her and talk and dismissed my accompanying officers. I sank down onto a padded couch and even put my feet up on a footstool. She did not offer refreshments lest they be declined. She took a seat near—but not too near. She sat demurely, her hands folded in her lap. She was modestly dressed in a gown of pale blue, the color of the sky at daybreak. It flattered her complexion and her rich brown hair. I found it hard to look at her.

We spoke of nothing—the weather, that perennially safe subject; gardens, another safe subject; upcoming holidays. Here was my opening. Perfect.

"Mother," I said, leaning forward in what I hoped simulated friendly ease, "I long for the end of winter and am looking forward to celebrating the Festival of Minerva at Baiae. It promises to be particularly festive this year. Oh, it will be so good to cast winter aside at last!"

She made a sour face. "Too much noise and merrymakers at Baiae then. I gave up on that holiday long ago."

Not the response I needed. "You do not plan to go, then? A pity. I was hoping I would see you there." The promise of a reunion was thus dangled.

Her whole expression changed. "I do have my villa there—on the shore of Lake Lucrine. I could have it readied, if you thought . . ."

"That's a piece from where mine is but not inconvenient," I mused. "Your area is quieter, and you would be spared much of the noise and crowds."

"True, true . . ." She was thinking.

"I will give a lavish banquet for all my friends the night before the ceremonies for Minerva," I said. "If you were there you would be the guest of honor." Take the bait, I thought. Take it!

But she shook her head. "Perhaps it is best if I am not present," she said. "I do not wish to interfere. I know I am hardly beloved by many of your friends." She shook her head meekly. "I do not want to spoil your banquet."

"Spoil it? Oh, no. You would be the crowning of it." I got up, crossed over to her. "You would be welcomed. Our estrangement causes people unease."

"I don't care about other people—it causes *me* sorrow and grief."

"Then, Mother, say you will come." I forced myself to take her hands and draw her to her feet. "For me."

Her cooperation now secured, I must broach the subject of the gift boat. But not too early. It must be bestowed nearer the time, as our guarded behavior thawed and it would not seem out of place for me to proffer such a gift.

I told Acte that I was planning to return to Baiae for the festival. To my surprise she did not want to go, and for many of the same reasons as Mother. Too many crowds, too much noise. And she felt out of place with my friends. I would be too taken up with them, there would be interminable banquets and entertainments, and she would see little of me. And she was skeptical of my "reunion" with Mother, although I assured her I had decided it was best to appear at peace in public.

But since the happening that had sundered my ability to be truthful with her, the separation kept growing. If I could not tell her about what had happened in the palace, I could certainly not tell her what I had re-solved to do at Baiae. I felt now that I was three people, not two. I had grown accustomed to there being two Neros—the Augustan one of public duties and Roman virtue, and the Apollonian one of music, art, and poetry. But three? I was afraid I would break apart like the boat Anicetus was constructing. Acte loved the first two Neros but would not love the third, dark one that was emerging. I was not sure I loved him, either, but I had no choice but to claim him as part of myself, whereas she could walk away.

"Acte, please come," I urged her. "I really wish you to be with me this time."

She just smiled. "I'd rather not. It's just another festival, another banquet. I'll be waiting when you return, and you can tell me all the details. And then I will have you all to myself."

All three Neros; you will have all three to yourself, I thought. The third will come of age while we are apart.

Oh, Acte.

My refuge with her gone, I escaped more and more into music and poetry. They were a bright, clean, shining world that welcomed me and strengthened the best in me, and where I wished I could stay forever.

XLVIII

As the earth warmed and winter receded, I now wished there was a way to retard its inexorable, deadly creep toward spring. Every day closer to the festival increased the dread in my heart. By the time the ides of March arrived, I was scarcely sleeping.

I had made a quick trip to Misenum and conferred with Anicetus, who assured me the ship was receiving the finishing touches and that a corps of trusted sailors were being trained in "the naval exercise," as he called it. "Put your mind at ease," he said. "It is all as you ordered."

My mind at ease. Nothing was more impossible. But I thanked him and asked only where it would be docked and when I might present it to her.

"Her villa is on the shores of Lake Lucrine, isn't it? Yours is at Baiae, and farther down, close to Misenum, are other villas. I think you should have the banquet at someone's villa there. I can have the ship docked there, you can present it to her upon arrival, and after the banquet she can be conveyed back to Lake Lucrine aboard it."

"I don't like having to entertain at someone else's villa," I said. "Why not mine at Baiae?" I hated to involve anyone else.

"The distance is greater between Misenum and Lucrine," he said. "It will give the crew a chance to take the ship farther out."

"I see." I would have to ask Piso or Otho to host the banquet, then, in my name. What excuse would I give? With those two pleasure lovers, I hardly needed an excuse. They were always ready to entertain.

"She will arrive by sea in a boat of her own," Anicetus reminded me. "She was accustomed, when she was empress, to having the imperial fleet at her disposal for journeying. Now you must convince her to abandon her own ship and take your gift one."

So many things to manage. So many people to convince of this or that. And all the time my heart was thundering and I could hardly think. "I will."

The bay was ready for its five-day celebration. Banners fluttered from trees; scores of boats with colored sails rocked in the water. Some were draped with garlands of new spring flowers, and raucous laughter pealed from their decks. Meanwhile in port amphoras of wine were being unloaded to satisfy the thirst of the holiday, along with barrels of fresh oysters and mussels. Crowds were heading for the thermal baths, where they would soak by day to recover from their overindulgence at night. As for Minerva herself, the ceremonies to honor her were lost in the circus of eating, drinking, sailing, fishing, singing, dancing, and adultery. Supposedly this festival was in honor of reopening the naval sailing season, and a nod to her status as the goddess of controlled warfare. This new sailing season would be remembered forever, and not because of Minerva or controlled warfare.

I stood on the dock watching Mother's ship approach. I was trembling so visibly that Anicetus took my arm to steady me and said, "Take hold of yourself. Hold fast to your purpose."

A loud clunk sounded as the ship bumped the wooden dock and shuddered to a halt. Sailors jumped off and quickly tied it up. A gangplank was thrown out, and Mother stood at its head, searching the dock. A light breeze stirred her gown, lifting it in an airy train behind her. It pressed the silk against her body, outlining her curves and strong stature. She saw us and descended the sloping plank.

"Mother." I opened my arms in a gesture of welcome and leaned forward to kiss her cheek. "Welcome."

She looked around. "The admiral is here, I see." She spoke to Anicetus.

"It is my honor, Augusta," he said, stepping back into the background and leaving me on my own.

"I suppose he has become accustomed to his high status," she sniffed. "Freedmen do that."

Ignoring her predictable snipe, I smiled and said, "I am so pleased you have come!" I turned to the harbor and gestured toward all the boats bobbing on the water. "All of the bay rejoices that you are here." Then, slowly, I moved my arm to indicate the gift boat.

"Oh, that is magnificent. And it looks brand-new. The gold is gleaming on it," she said. "Whose is it?"

"Yours," I said. "It is my welcome gift to you."

Instead of smiling or clapping her hands in delight, she looked puzzled. "For me?"

"Yes, dear Mother. With all my love." Getting those words out was as difficult as swallowing a rabbit whole with all its fur. But I did it.

Still she looked puzzled. "It is lovely. But I already have a boat. What in the world would I do with two here?"

"Ah—you can leave one here and take the other back to Antium."

We walked closer to it and she took in the gilded carvings and the polished bronze oarlocks. "I had it outfitted with every luxury befitting your tastes," I assured her.

"Thank you, dear son. But it may be too much for me." She turned and seemed to lose interest in the boat. "I shall rest up for the banquet tonight. I assume Otho has a room for me to dress for the evening in?"

"Oh, yes." I pointed to his villa, perched on a hill overlooking the water. "You will find everything at your disposal."

A slight frown crossed her face, more puzzlement. "Why did you decide to entertain in his villa rather than yours at Baiae?"

"Oh, for variety. One gets jaded always at the same place."

That seemed to satisfy her curiosity, and she and her party set out for Otho's. As soon as she was out of sight I reunited with Anicetus. "She suspects something," I said. "She hesitates about the boat. What if she doesn't get on it?"

He looked at me in the way he used to when he was explaining a Greek passage I was having trouble translating. "You must make sure she does."

Yes. That was my part. I must think of every objection she might make, ready to counter each one.

The sun slid slowly beneath the waters of the bay, unusually serene now. The breeze that had ruffled Mother's gown was gone and the air was still. Pink-gold streaks surrounded the sun as it disappeared, illuminating the clouds from within, making them glow.

I attired myself in a green silk tunic, whisper thin and fine. As beautiful as it was, I knew I would never want to look on it again. I stood still in the sumptuous chamber Otho had lent me, closing my eyes and willing myself to be calm. Then I stepped out and made my way to the enormous vaulted hall where the night's festivities would be held. It overlooked the bay, its wide windows embracing the entire sweep of it. Across the water I could see the lights of Pompeii, little pricks of yellow from the torches. Nearer us, lanterns from the hundreds of pleasure boats twinkled, reflecting in the water.

Otho appeared, the eager host. "You are early!" he said. "I am so honored you would allow me to host an imperial banquet." He plopped a wreath of roses, violets, myrtle, and ivy on my head. "The emperor is crowned; the festivities are officially open!" He put one on his own head as well. There were stacks of them on a stand, awaiting the guests. Slaves were scurrying about with baskets of rose petals, scattering them underfoot.

"From Alexandria," he said. "It's too early for them here."

"Oh, roses!" Petronius had appeared, seemingly out of nowhere. "That is so passé!" He helped himself to a wreath. "Didn't Antony do that at his banquets? And how many years ago was that?"

"He was already in Alexandria, so it was easy for him."

"Whereas you must spend a fortune having them imported," said Petronius. "How profligate."

"Profligacy has its merits," said Otho. Just then more slaves appeared, bearing slender alabaster jars of perfume. He ordered them put on a table nearby, but one was emptied out on our feet. It smelled of narcissus. Otho sniffed it and pronounced, "From the forests of Germany."

"Yes, we Romans comb the world for luxuries," said a familiar voice. Seneca's. I was genuinely glad to see him.

"So you are here!" I said. *Keep me from doing this unspeakable deed,* I wanted to beg him. *Save me from myself.* But instead all I said was, "I am glad."

"He still calls Baiae 'the vortex of luxury,'" said Burrus, standing beside him.

Seneca looked around, enjoying his distaste of the tasteless display of wealth. "I came to inspect the perfect example of it," he said, as Otho rushed up and put wreaths on their heads.

"I expect an essay about this!" he said gleefully.

"I have already written it," said Seneca.

Now more people were pouring into the room. I saw Piso in a crowd of guests: senators and officials, all having shed their gravitas and ready to frolic. There was not a toga in sight.

Musicians entered in the back and began playing—lyres and flutes. They were not particularly skilled, but with all the noise no one would hear them properly in any case, and an artist like Terpnus would have been wasted—and insulted—in such a venue.

Veiled women sat at booths along the walls—fortune-tellers. People lined up to have their futures told.

"I hired them from Cumae, which isn't far," said Otho.

"They are all charlatans," said Seneca. "Just because they come from Cumae does not make them true sibyls."

"Perhaps it rubs off on them!" said Petronius.

Genuine or not, I would not dare consult one now. I touched the gold bracelet I had worn especially for this occasion. Would it protect me or would it protect Mother? It would have to choose. How ridiculous. As if an object could choose. Nero, take hold of yourself!

Beautiful women glided through the crowd, their hair piled high, adorned with pearls and jewels beneath the floral crowns. Were they wives, daughters, courtesans, or some of each? But my ordinary appreciation for such creatures had fled; in fact, my apprehension this evening had killed every appetite I had ever had.

Just as I was thinking this, however, a woman of such sublime beauty floated past that I gaped. It was—it had to be—Otho's new wife, Poppaea. I blinked, and when I looked again, he was leading her over to me.

"May I present my wife, Poppaea Sabina, my dear emperor?"

She knelt, then rose with a fluid motion.

"You are blessed, Otho," I said. "And I congratulate you on your good fortune."

Poppaea was looking straight at me, not dropping her eyes in deference as was usual. They were of an amber color. In fact, all her being was tinged with amber, and her hair had all the shades of the most costly amber—tawny, gold, honey, bronze, hazel, tortoiseshell—for amber is not one color but many. I had never seen such richness of color, so vibrant it made all others look faded.

"I am honored," she said. Her voice was as rich and promissory as her looks. "*We* are honored that you would choose our villa to host not only yourself but your mother."

Mother. She had not yet appeared. Was something wrong? Had she been told about the boat? Her spies were everywhere, and the necessity of the trained crew made too many people knowledgeable about the plot. "You are the true hosts," I said. "And the Augusta and I are grateful." But where was the Augusta?

The food service was about to begin; Otho had announced his welcome to the guests, and I had spoken to them as well. Slaves were carrying in platters with artfully arranged dainties that would begin the banquet. The place for Mother on the dining couch remained empty. I leaned on mine, willing her to appear. Would she have to be sent for?

The platter of snails, oysters, and sea urchins was set before us. We must begin. Just then there was a stirring in the back of the hall, and Mother entered. Relief flooded me, followed by fear. It would happen. The hope of it not happening was gone. I was not to be spared. Neither was she.

She strode through the room like Athena, lesser mortals cast aside. She approached the head couch, seeking her rightful place.

"Good evening," she said. Otho enthusiastically welcomed her and bade her take her place.

"We are just beginning," he said. "You have before you the offerings of Neptune." He indicated the platter.

She stretched out on the couch, leaning on her elbow. She was facing me, her eyes searching mine.

At that moment Petronius stood up and was announced as "the Umpire of Drinking." "I will decide how much wine we shall imbibe and what proportion of water will be mixed with it." He swirled his hands around and pointed to a giant amphora. "Setine!" he said. He walked to another amphora and cried, "Falernian!" Then to yet another, announcing, "Massic! My preference is for Setine. Shall we begin with that? Can we finish all three by the end of the evening? And rest assured, our host the emperor has many more at the ready, so drink your fill. And I decree—half water and half wine." There were groans. "Very well, one third water and two thirds wine. Servers, pour!"

Mother took her cup and looked into its depths. "I throw caution to the winds," she said, taking a sip.

"All that is past," I said, tilting the cup to my lips.

Oh, she was fair that night. Lovely in the way only autumnal beauty can be. She was charming, lighthearted, making clever conversation with everyone surrounding her. When the formal part of the banquet was over, she exchanged places with Piso to be beside me. All around us the guests were halfway to being drunk, in that delightful state where desires are heightened and cares fade to shadows. But I had not drunk much, and neither had she. We looked at one another with clear eyes.

There was an intimacy between us, not as one normally means the word, but something deeper than that. She leaned her head on my shoulder, as if she was weary and finally putting down her burden. As if all guards were dropped between us. As they were, since this was our last time together.

"You have made me very happy," she murmured. "More than I can say."

So that was my gift to her. Her last day was happy, all that she could wish.

Now we both drank, free to let go. I cherished her in those moments, and she did me.

The evening ended. Girls from Spain had performed posture dances. Acrobats had entertained. Players had wagered sums on dicing. Petronius and his cronies had departed for a private evening of sex games. The floor was littered with food scraps, crushed rose petals, and trampled floral crowns. Pools of spilled wine seeped into the stone. Mother and I stood up, shakily.

"Thank you," she said quietly.

Should I say, *Stay here—spend the night here—do not go back to Lucrine?* But it was too late. The thing had taken on a life of its own, hurtling toward its destination.

"Let me come with you to your boat," I said.

"Boat?" She seemed to have forgotten it. "I will return to Lucrine by litter, I think."

"It is too far, and the litter bearers will stumble in the dark," I said. "The boat is faster and safer. Come."

Our guards escorted us down to the dock. She stood looking at her two boats and started to enter her own. But the crew was not there.

"Look, your new one is ready to leave this very moment!" I said. Anicetus had made sure the sailors had remained onboard. "And if you don't choose this one, I shall take it amiss, think you have spurned my gift."

She clasped me to her. "This is your gift. To let me embrace you again."

I embraced her back, tortured by what I knew. "Gladly given," I said. I kissed her.

She took my hand, then touched my arm. She felt the bracelet, caressed it, turning it. "This has kept you safe," she said. "Safe, safe, and I rejoice."

I let her go, and she mounted the gangplank. She turned for an instant and looked at me; she was a black outline against the moonless sky.

"Cast off," Anicetus ordered the crew.

Slowly the boat left the dock and made its way out into the bay, vanishing from sight.

"Now we wait," he said.

XLIX

The hours passed. I was back at my villa at Baiae. Everything was just as I had left it—stools, tables, even scrolls and lampstands. But why shouldn't it be? The darkness outside was profound, in the moonless night. I lit only one lamp and it fought against the dark, unable to banish it.

Banish the darkness. Banish the darkness within and without. Oh, would that ever be possible? She was gone; it was done; I had done it. My trembling had ceased and a wooden calm pervaded me. The flame guttered and sputtered, like the flame of life, hers now extinguished.

A scuffling at the door, like wolf's claws, caused me to leap up. I flung open the door to find Anicetus standing there, sweat pouring down his face.

"It's failed!" he gasped out, panting. I pulled him in, closed the door. We were alone; the slaves were sleeping in their quarters.

"What?" All the horror of the deed, without the deed having been done?

He sank down onto a stool. His hair was in disarray, soaked with sweat, standing in tufts. "She got away. The boat did collapse, but after that everything went awry. Not everyone was in on the plot; there were too many sailors—it was too dangerous to let them all know. So the trained ones rushed to the listing side to try to capsize it quickly, while the ignorant ones rushed to the other side to try to save it. The boat then stabilized, although it kept sinking, but gently. One of your mother's ladies called out, "Help! I am the empress!" and was promptly beaten to death by oars and staves. So then your mother knew it was a plot to murder her; she jumped overboard and swam away, although her arm was injured."

"She swam?" She had been so plied with wine and food, how could she? "I didn't know she could swim," I said stupidly. "Where is she now?"

"She swam close to shore and was rescued by some fishermen still out in their boats. Or maybe it was merrymakers. Whoever it was, they rowed her to the shore by her villa at Lucrine. The beach was filled with onlookers who had seen the accident."

"Do they think it was an accident?"

"The people, yes. What else would they think? They weren't on the ship and couldn't see what happened."

"But she knows!"

"Yes, she knows."

Oh, gods! She knew, she knew, she knew, she survived and would pitilessly take her revenge. "She'll arm her slaves!" Worse pictures flew through my mind. "No, she'll come with a contingent of Praetorians! She'll have me taken prisoner! She'll then go to the Senate and incriminate me."

"Control yourself," said Anicetus. He took charge, calmed me as he had done when he was my tutor and I still a boy. "There is time yet. Send for Seneca and Burrus."

Their villas were nearby and if they thought it strange to be awakened in the deep of the night and ordered to the imperial villa, they did not show it and arrived within the hour.

"What is it?" Seneca asked. His clothes were rumpled and his hair uncombed, but that was good. It meant he had wasted no time but had flown to my summons for the task at hand. Anicetus told him all. Neither he nor Burrus seemed surprised about the plot. Perhaps it had seemed inevitable to them. Perhaps they had long expected it, or something like it.

They sat listening and took a long time to answer. Then Seneca turned to Burrus and asked calmly, "Can you order the Praetorians to slay her?"

He shook his head. "No. They are devoted to her and would never touch a hair on the head of the daughter of Germanicus."

Seneca said, "Then the task falls to you, Anicetus. You will have to follow through all the way, without flinching."

Anicetus nodded. "I take responsibility." He stood up. "I'll take a naval captain and a lieutenant who obey orders unquestioningly and scrupulously. You may count on me."

"This is the real first day of my reign," I said. It was true. I had reigned under her shadow all along. "A gift given me by a former slave, a gift more costly than any other."

"Now true loyalties are revealed," he said. "I take my leave. I must move quickly. In the meantime, you must think what to do if someone comes here with the same idea. Rouse the guards and slaves; be prepared. Do not be taken by surprise; fight back." In an instant, he disappeared out into the night.

Seneca, Burrus, and I looked at one another. "He is right," said Seneca. "She will send someone—perhaps several someones. But if you are prepared, you can not only protect yourself, but provide an explanation for all the rest, and what will follow. Remember you must give an account of all this to the people of Rome."

"Yes, yes!" Now suddenly fear and confusion seized me, turning my legs to jelly. So many things to consider. Keep calm. Think. My life in danger. My reign over. My mother gone, by my hand. I am alone. Too stunning, too staggering, too overwhelming for me to comprehend.

Only emotion filled me, dread and panic and the desperate need to survive.

If she did send someone to assassinate me, what if that were proved, what if intercepted, she the guilty one? Where was my dagger, the one I had kept about me always for safety? It wasn't here now—where had I left it? By my bedside. I hurried in to get it. I called for the guards.

The hours kept passing. No sign of dawn yet. Were the hours somehow held captive, blocked, so they did not progress? Seneca and Burrus sat calmly, statues. Where was Anicetus? What had happened? He must have reached Lucrine by now.

What if she was so well guarded he could not get through? What if even now he was lying dead?

A loud knock on the door. A slave opened it.

"A message from the Augusta!" announced a courier.

"Admit him," I said.

A short man came into the room, glancing at Burrus and Seneca and bowing to me. "I, Lucius Agerinus, have a message from my mistress, Agrippina Augusta, for the emperor Nero. Joyful news! There has been an accident at sea but by divine mercy and the emperor's own lucky star, the Augusta is unhurt. She wanted to reassure her son and tell him that although she knows he will be concerned, she is resting now and he should not attempt to visit her."

That meant she was gathering her forces! She meant to attack me. By daylight her troops, her slaves, would be here, surrounding me.

"Do you have a written message?" I asked.

"Indeed I do." He reached into his sleeve to retrieve it, and at that moment I dropped my dagger so it looked as if it had fallen out of his garment.

"Help! Help!" I cried. "Seize him! He was sent here to assassinate me!" Quickly the guards grabbed him, over his loud protests of innocence.

I turned to Seneca and Burrus. "You saw it with your own eyes!" I said. "She sent an assassin to slay me!"

They nodded gravely.

Still the hours passed slowly. The yelling courier was whisked away and silence fell over the villa. The darkness began to fade outside. The night was almost over. I sat rigidly, almost unable to move, listening for footfalls that seemed never to come.

A nicetus returned and stood quietly before me. "It is done," he said. Did I want to hear how? Could I bear it? If I did not ask, would I later wish I had? Could I stand it? "What happened?" I asked, in a whisper.

"When we reached the house we found it surrounded by curious crowds. They had been down on the shore and now had flocked to the villa itself. But they melted away when my armed column of sailors pushed them away. We surrounded the house, and then only I and the captain and lieutenant went inside. Are you sure you wish to hear more?"

"Yes." It was still a whisper.

"We pushed the slaves out of the way and came to her bedroom door. There was one servant inside, and she fled upon seeing us. Agrippina turned to her and said, 'Are you leaving me, too?' Then she was alone, with only one dim light by her bedside. She saw us and said, 'If you are visitors of goodwill, you can report that I am better. But if you are assassins'—and here she drew herself up—'I know my son is not responsible. He would not order his mother's death.'"

I shuddered. But I needed to hear it all. "Go on."

"The captain hit her on the head, and the lieutenant drew his sword. Then she pointed to her belly and said, 'Strike here! This is the womb that bore Nero!' And he did. And she died."

She had meant it, what she'd confided to me long ago and I had dismissed, forgotten. She had said to the astrologer doing my chart, *Let him kill me, so long as he rules!* She had promised herself to the gods, a sacrifice. And thus it had come to pass. The gods do not forget a vow, even one made recklessly. They collect their dues. By her last words, she was acknowledging this.

"And then?" I asked weakly.

"We cremated her on her couch. Her ashes are already buried nearby."

Mother. Ashes already. And now I did collapse, just as mocking birdsong ushered out the long night of horror.

L

The sun was merciless; it came up as it did every day, flooding the world with light, clear, hard light. A world without Mother in it, threateningly empty. I sat unmoving for so long that at length one of the slaves dared to touch my shoulder and shake me.

I moved with a shudder. What should I do? I had not thought beyond the night, beyond the boat. But now I must face the crowds, face Rome. The news was even now racing there, running faster than the fastest horse, the swiftest ship, with mysterious speeding wings that overtake all else.

I stumbled back into my most private room, where the shutters were still drawn and the hateful light shut out. I was shaking all over as if I had a high fever. I flung off the green silk tunic, dread keepsake of the night, and put on a warmer robe. I removed the snake bracelet and laid it carefully in a jewel box. No need for its protection now. I had survived.

Under the urging of Burrus, later that morning the captains and officers of the Praetorians came to me, knelt, and congratulated me on my escape from the designs of Mother. Then word came that people were flooding to the temples to give thanks for my safety. But what of Rome? What of the Senate?

Seneca and I composed a letter to be read to them, announcing the perfidy of the Augusta and the divine deliverance of the emperor from her plot. Upon learning that it had failed, she had committed suicide. Then he listed her former crimes, embellishing them to such a degree that she appeared worse than a demon. She had wanted to be coruler, to receive allegiance from the Praetorians, the Senate, and the people of Rome. Failing to achieve this, even with lavish bribes, she'd hated them all and contrived the deaths of twelve distinguished and innocent men and women. The scandals and follies of Claudius's reign were laid at her feet, as they were undertaken under her direction.

"How this will be received, we must wait and see," he warned me. He looked spent and beaten down. But, tellingly, he had not condemned my action or even hinted that it was wrong.

That first day over, night engulfed me again, plunging me into its dark depth. With the passing of hours, new terror gripped me, as images of the boat, her cries, and her bloody ending flooded my mind. I could see and hear it all. And her farewell—*Strike here! This is the womb that bore Nero!*—rang through my head. Was it true that an astrologer had predicted it? Or was that a personal mythology she had created to tell me? And to what purpose—to tell me in advance what I must do?

The torturous suspense of the past few days over, other emotions now flooded in. Was this real? Had it really happened? Was Mother truly vanished, gone, a pile of ashes? Had she ceased to exist? The reality of death did not grip me because I had not seen her; I had only heard of it from others. But I could not have borne to see her unmoving and dead. At the same time something even within myself had died; our dark and strong bond had snapped and I was alone.

I was lying sleepless in bed when eerie wails rang out from the direction of Mother's villa, shrieking ghosts. The Furies! I leapt up and looked outside, seeing only darkness. But they were there, pursuing me, swooping in to torment and punish me, to drive me to madness. I could feel them. Then dying sounds of military trumpets echoed in the hills. The dead cried out. Seeking vengeance? I must remove from this haunted place. I could endure it no longer.

Unsure of my reception in Rome, I did not go there. Instead I moved a few miles to Naples. On the way I had to pass Lake Lucrine, where Mother had lodged, and where presumably her ashes rested nearby. I resolutely looked the other way, out onto the sparkling waters of the bay, willing myself not to tremble. Just behind Lucrine lay Lake Avernus, with a portal where one could enter the underworld. But no, never! Mother would be waiting there, probably just on the near shore, not having yet progressed very far into the dark realm. And farther beyond that, the site of Cumae, where the famous sibyl gave prophecies, the last thing I wanted now. Once off the peninsula, we headed east to Naples, passing the sulfur-smoking Phlegraean Fields, a vast gray ashy expanse of gaseous vents and foul fumes. Truly this entire landscape was supernatural. I shuddered as I passed.

Naples, however, was resolutely human, warm-blooded and alive. It embraced me and soothed me, shouting, *Welcome! Welcome!* in a way that no other place ever had. Instantly I felt I had come home, to a home I had never known before but had paradoxically always known. And no wonder: it was founded by Greeks and was an island of Greekness in the heart of Italy. Every stone of it spoke to me, every lilting voice sounded perfect, speaking words precisely as they should be spoken. Music and poetry were celebrated here, onstage and even in the streets. I had come into my own land at last, washed onto a strange shore only to find myself at my own homecoming.

While submerging myself in the wonder of Naples, Rome never vanished as I waited anxiously to hear what my fate was to be there. And I did not dare to send for Acte. I was still in a state that was hardly normal; I could not explain to myself all that had happened, and it would be impossible to explain it to her. Oddly enough, it was not difficult to include Seneca, Burrus, and Anicetus in the secret, but they worked for me and their fate was tied to mine. They could know the worst about me, but I could not let Acte know the same. That third Nero—she must never meet him. He had been born as a result of Mother's drug and now he had grown, flourished. Perhaps he would wither away and disappear now that Mother was gone, but until then, I could not see her. I could neither lie to her nor be honest with her. And so she waited to hear from me and day after day I could not write to her.

Rome made her choice; she chose to believe my story and welcome me home. Seneca could mope about the servility of it, and he spoke true, but was eager enough to return home. So, five months after the Festival of Minerva, I rode back to Rome to be feted like a Triumphing general. Waiting at the city gates were assemblies of the citizens, the senators in gala dress with their wives and children, their cries of welcome ringing in the warm air. Along the streets tiers of seats had been set up to hold the crowds, throwing showers of petals on me as I made my way to the Capitoline and paid my vows to Jupiter.

There was more. Citizens proposed that there should be thanksgivings at every shrine for my deliverance. There should be annual games in honor of the discovery of the plot at the Festival of Minerva. There should be a gold statue of me and another of Minerva in the Senate. Mother's birthday on November sixth should be put on the roll of ill-omened days.

When the Senate read out these honors, only one man—Thrasea Paetus—walked out rather than vote for them. The rest applauded and now I knew true deliverance. And the third Nero grew stronger.

There were, of course, a few repercussions and mumblings. Oddly enough, it was Seneca who was condemned for his part in composing my explanation, rather than me for any part I had played in the action that he defended. The philosopher had soiled his robes, they felt. And there were silent, anonymous displays. A statue of Mother wore a veil (draped upon it until the statue could be removed from public view), and someone hung a placard around her neck reading, "I am veiled, but you should be the one to hide your shame." An infant was abandoned in the Forum with a tag on its neck declaring, "I do not want to raise you lest you grow up to slay your mother." Graffiti comparing me to Orestes and Alcmeon, matricides, appeared on walls. But no one dared to say anything to my face, and I did not ferret out the instigators of these attacks. Best to let it rest. To look the other way. To pretend.

LOCUSTA

Well, that was amateurish. I was appalled when I heard the details about the death of Agrippina. The rumors that were circulating were a mess of contradictions—it was a boat accident, an attempted assassination, treason, a suicide. Now, really. It was so obvious—to me, anyway—that Nero had taken matters into his own hands and bungled it badly. And the official cover story was equally amateurish. I suppose that man Seneca came up with it. Typical of a philosopher—complete nonsense.

Why had he not come to me? I could have managed it for him. Did he not trust me any longer? I have not seen him in a long time, although he has supported my academy and requested reports of my garden and trainees. But he has never accepted any of my invitations to come and see for himself. I am very proud of what I have built here—I even have rare plants from Arabia!—and have nothing to hide. Besides, I would like to see him again. I always liked him. I want to see for myself what he has become.

NERO

Actors. I was surrounded by actors. They wore masks as impenetrable as the ones in the theater, but these were of flesh. They smiled and greeted me cheerfully and respectfully, but what did it mean? Could I trust them? Did they really believe Mother was a dire threat that I had been providentially saved from?

No more of this, Nero. No more of this. Madness lurks here. I had to get myself in hand. The days were tolerable, but the nights . . . Mother's ghost came to me in dreams, pursuing, shrieking. *No more of this, Nero.* Since she corrupted my sleep as she had corrupted my body, I must stay awake and work. Work at my desk when everyone was sleeping, when there were no sounds but the crickets and owls outside. The light banished the dreams and gave me blessed peace.

I found, in that private space, a salvation as I laboriously began to collect my thoughts and sketch out my epic poem on the Trojan War, which had long been simmering in my mind. Art. Art was a portal that I could pass through, leaving ugliness behind. Describing ancient horrors was somehow an antidote to present ones.

By waiting (or was it hiding?) in Naples until September, I had spared myself the furnace heat of a Roman summer, and now the days were pleasant, the skies clear and the winds cool and refreshing. I must show myself to the people again, must launch the true beginning of my reign. It was time for the first shaving of my beard (which was not bronze, disappointingly), a ritual of great importance in the life of a Roman man. In my case, it would be the first time they had an emperor who was young enough to celebrate it.

"And what do you have in mind?" inquired Seneca. No deferential "Caesar." Beside him on a bench in my workroom, Burrus looked on me with furrowed brow.

If they expected me to be vague, they were disappointed. I had had much time to think about it in the inky hours of night. "A great exhibition, open to all. Using all the theaters and the Circus. Everyone will perform—senators and knights alike, and their wives. And I will perform, too. There will be trained elephants, and elaborate refreshments in the Grove of the Caesars . . ."

Burrus sat up straighter, if that were possible. "You will perform?"

"Yes. I have been training, and I think I am ready." *And Mother is gone, Mother who was ashamed of my art. Now I am free.*

"With all due respect, that would not be seemly," said Seneca. "It would destroy respect for the office of emperor. The emperor sponsors, the emperor observes, but the emperor does not participate."

"I intend not only to host the event but to appear onstage," I said.

"Never!" said Burrus. "This cannot be."

"I will not be alone. Everyone else will be performing, competing. Let Romans be free to show that side of themselves. That can be my gift to them."

Seneca smiled condescendingly. "I think they would prefer the lavish gifts you have showered on them in the past—money, gems, and horses."

"They shall have both."

Seneca and Burrus looked at one another, wearily. "The expenditure—"

I leapt up. "I have been saved! Can you not understand? I cannot count the cost of celebrating it in thanksgiving."

But they knew the nature of my being saved. They had seen me dispatch Anicetus on his deadly mission, had seen the staged dagger drop, had written the letter to the Senate.

"Perhaps it is best not to remind people," said Burrus. "Let it lie."

"No. That would imply guilt, shame." Which I was trying to exorcise. "Boldness is best." I sat back down and stared at them.

"Very well," said Seneca. "But perhaps, if you have no mind to spare expense, there should be two separate celebrations. The first could be called the Ludi Maximi, the Great Games for the Eternity of the Empire. You could preside at those, and watch the citizens of Rome performing, have the elephants . . . And then, following that, the celebration of the beard shaving. We can call it the Juvenalia, the Youth Games. Those can be private. By invitation only. After all, to see the emperor perform would be a special privilege, a highly coveted event. That way you can satisfy both segments of the population—the common people, and the elite who cherish and crave private events." He slumped back against the bench, looking exhausted from his presentation. He still had a quick mind, to have conjured all this up so quickly.

"This plan has its merits," I admitted. "But I *will* perform." Something was coming back to me, swimming out of the past. "Remember, my friends, 'There is no respect for hidden music.'" The cryptic words of the oracle, almost forgotten, suddenly were blazingly clear. I must not hide my art, my music. It was a mandate.

I immediately sought the guidance of my vocal coach, Appius, who had been teaching me songs for both the lyre and the cithara. I had progressed slowly but steadily, and the next step was to put voice and technique together. Mastering the instruments was a different matter, and my cithara training with Terpnus took place elsewhere.

Appius was a thin, intense, focused man, the sort who never forgot his papers or ran late. He expected perfection from me, too, which was what I wanted in a teacher. Although it is impossible not be swayed by the knowledge that one is dealing with the emperor (commander in chief of all legions, land and sea; supreme governor of all provinces; Augustus . . . and so on and on), Appius hid it well. He did not hesitate to reprimand me or give me an honest appraisal of my performance. I announced to him that I had taken the leap: I would perform in public.

"Where?" was all he said.

"At a private festival." I explained it all to him. "And so I need to strengthen my voice," I said. "I know there are regimens to do so, just as there are for running and wrestling."

He drew a deep breath and for the longest time did not reply. "It is always best to work with what nature gives us," he finally said. "You have a deep, husky bass voice, best suited for emotional drama, like Euripides. Unfortunately those are the most difficult musical pieces to master. But rewarding, if you can."

Euripides! "What do you think I ought to practice for this performance? It's my first—I don't want to disgrace myself."

"I am thinking something simple—perhaps just an ode set to the lyre? But at the same time, you could practice something more advanced."

"Could I write my own songs? Set to my own poems?"

His long, bladelike face widened in a smile. "Certainly, if you want to tackle everything at once, expose yourself like that, so that you are judged on many levels."

Yes. That was what I wanted. A clean, clear judgment where I could stand before men and know who I was, how good or bad my art was. "Fear and art cannot live together," I said. "Now tell me what I must do to strengthen my voice."

His instructions were to lie flat on my back and put lead weights on my chest, then speak loudly, to strengthen the muscles; to avoid apples, as they were harmful to the throat; to take a daily potion of chives in olive oil to soothe the throat.

"And have lots of sex, as that deepens the voice—at least, Aristotle said so." He allowed himself a smile. "Now, that's a pleasant regimen."

But one less available to me now than ever before. What was I to do about Acte?

. . .

Imust write to her, but the words, like cold honey, refused to flow. I sat at my desk late into the night, several oil lamps sputtering, illuminating the paper. I missed her keenly but at the same time found myself still reluctant to see her, as if I would keep her entirely in the past. The past, unchanging and preserved, sacred and cherished. To see her again would explode all that, bring her back into strange new territory between us. But I had to, or regret it forever.

My heart,

I call you that because that is what you have been and are. Six long months have passed since we parted, not knowing it would stretch so long.

Now what? Where to go from here? I chewed on the end of the pen, looking at the little yellow flame from one lamp as if I could read an answer there.

You know all that has happened in the interim, the great changes that have taken place.

No need to say more, especially on paper.

You belong here with me, and I implore you to return to me. As emperor I could send guards to bring you back, could line the streets with cheering people, have torches and arches all the way, but unless you come back on your own accord, because you want to, it would be meaningless. There are things an emperor cannot command, and your heart is one of them. I am equally helpless over my own, which longs for you. "Come to me now, then, free me from aching care." You remember that promise to one another, from Sappho's words.

How to sign it? Not "your emperor." Not "Nero." Not "your friend." What, then? I rubbed my eyes. It was late, and I was very tired, in spirit and body. Yes, let her free me from aching care—if anyone could.

Lucius

She would know who it was, and know I meant that she had known me before these other names and titles. *You know me truly,* it meant.

The letter dispatched, I did not feel like a lead weight was off me, only that I now had two: the plate that Appius had prescribed, and the suspense of waiting to see Acte again. I had a pallet of goose down made, and a flat lead plate weighing as much as a mastiff. I would lie down and ask a chamber attendant to lower the plate onto my chest and then have him stand at different distances in the room while I recited lines of poetry or rhetoric. The goal was for me to make him hear me even when he was in an adjoining room. It was very taxing, but I could feel my strength building as the days passed.

"I will have a chest as hard as a cuirass by the time I have finished these exercises," I told Appius. "So I won't need one when I go into battle."

"Were you planning to go into battle anytime soon?" He laughed. "Never, I hope."

"That is what people think," he said. "That the emperor is not interested in military affairs."

"I am interested, I just do not"—I had to stop and catch my breath; the plate had sucked it out of my lungs—"want to be a general myself."

"Perhaps if you had been a general, even for a short time, people would not look askance at your singing."

"Not you, too." I had to breathe deeply again, push up against the weight. "That is for Seneca and Burrus to say, not my voice master."

Would I have to don cuirass and helmet and ride out among the troops? There were no battles to fight now, in any case. The empire was quiet.

"That was just my private thought, not advice," he said. "The only useful advice I have to give concerns notes and breathing, not politics. I live as an ordinary man in Rome, not in the palace."

"True." As long as he admitted it.

But after the attendant had removed the plate and my aching chest could expand again, I brooded over his words. It was going to be necessary, at some point—and probably soon—that I play at being a soldier. But first the games.

I went to the Senate to announce the two sets of games and the difference between them. I wore my most regal toga, soft and rich double-dyed Tyrian purple, and sat between the two consuls, T. Sextius Africanus and M. Ostorius Scapula, as was protocol. Let all be in order, for what I would announce was beyond the normal order.

I rose. "I have called this session to make a joyful announcement." Two hundred faces looked at me expectantly but warily. "I invite you all to be my partners in celebrating two special sets of games. The first, the Ludi Maximi, the Great Games, will be to give thanks for the eternal empire of Rome, so recently preserved yet again from danger."

Still they looked on, impassive, bracing for what was to come. It was the cost they dreaded, I thought. Well, they could be relieved of that worry, as I would pay for it all. "A series of plays devoted to the eternity of the empire will be performed, and all Rome will be invited to attend, free. We will also have gladiatorial shows, dance exhibitions, and ballets, held in multiple venues—my new amphitheater, Taurus's older one, the theaters of Pompey and Marcellus, and the Circus Maximus. And"—I stepped down from the little platform and turned slowly to see everyone clearly, look at them one by one—"you, and your families, are all invited to perform, to be my partners in celebration. Yes! Men and women, boys and girls, old and young, from both the senators and the equestrians. You will be the entertainers, and I will provide your training at special schools. For those of you who are not up to the rigors of this, you may sing in a chorus instead."

A particularly crusty senator named Thrasea Paetus, who had refused to vote for the official thanksgiving for my escape from Mother, stirred and raised his hand to speak. "Gladiatorial games? You want us to fight as gladiators?"

"There will be no killing!" I assured him. "But how many of you have secretly wanted to put on helmets and nets and fight? You have watched these contests for years—is there anyone so craven he has not wanted to try his hand at it—once?"

Of course no one would admit to being craven, so they just nodded. "I will provide the equipment and the training there, too. And I promise a certain person will ride his elephant and perform such a feat that your grandchildren will never believe."

There was a low murmur, but all in all, they looked rather pleased and curious to hear what else might follow.

"As for the second set of games, they are private. I name them the Juvenalia, the Youth Games, to celebrate my first shaving. Unlike the first, open to everyone in Rome, beggars and generals alike, these are by invitation only and will be held in my private grounds and gardens across the Tiber. They, too, will rely on your performances, in both Greek and Latin, but they are theatrical only, no athletic exhibitions."

I mounted the step again and took my place back between the two consuls. "This is a personal event but one I wish you to join me in. As you know, the first shaving of the beard is an occasion. I am sure each of you remembers the day you did that, and the celebration your family had. You are all my family"—perhaps I shouldn't remind them of that, or why I had no family left—"yet at the same time I am also a dutiful son of the empire and will be dedicating the beard to Jupiter on the Capitoline Hill. And this is the first time you have had an emperor young enough to perform this ceremony while in office. It will also be five years since I became emperor. For five years you have trusted me to guide and protect you, and I pledge to continue to the utmost of my ability to serve the empire."

They murmured among themselves, but no one seemed displeased.

"There will be free feasting in the Grove of the Caesars, tents and booths providing food and drink and luxuries such as cushions and carpets during the festival, and all paid by me." Nearby, on the old naumachia of Augustus—where he had reenacted classic naval battles for entertainment—I would have boats where my closest friends and I could relax after the performances, while being slowly rowed around.

"And at the end of the festival, there will be an event even more singular than the elephant. That I can promise you, but I cannot divulge what it is yet. The mystery will be unveiled only on the final night."

Now they stirred, their eyes alert. I had them now.

The days flew, the venues were prepared—new awnings for Taurus's amphitheater, dredging of the naumachia—tokens with the prizes to be awarded were engraved, the elephant practiced his stunt, and the training schools were full. Many people attended them and seemed glad of the opportunity to indulge in a fantasy of another life—a fat old senator could be a gladiator, a young girl an animal tamer.

I had had no reply from Acte. Still I would wait, while earnestly composing the poetry and music I planned to perform shortly. I longed to be able to express the feelings that thronged my mind, but my words always fell short. Petronius had criticized one poet by saying, "His ideas surpass his execution of them." Oh, I knew that agony, the agony of all artists who know what they wish to express but cannot quite, a taunting prize just beyond our reach—or capabilities.

Seneca and Burrus regularly called upon me to report the progress of the preparations and the cost of them, and what had been overheard in the streets about them. To their dismay, it was mainly favorable.

"People are excited," Burrus admitted. "They are flattered that the emperor is lavishing such attention on them."

"They are also curious, of course, to see what surprises there are. And hoping always that they can make off with a prize of some sort. They are greedy, you know," said Seneca.

"No more than any other people," I said. "We are all greedy, just for different things." I looked particularly at Seneca, the shockingly rich Stoic. "Your older brother, Gallio—doesn't he like poetry?" I asked.

Seneca thought for a moment. "Yes, I believe he does."

"Ah, all of you Seneca brothers are so professorial," I said. "I'd like him to introduce me at the Youth Games. Introduce my performance, that is. I hardly need a regular introduction."

"Well, I can ask . . ." Seneca smiled wanly.

I laughed. "You should start wearing a theatrical mask," I said. "Your face gives away too much of what you really think. But you mustn't speak for others. Perhaps your brother would be honored. I have heard he has a gentle disposition."

"Yes, he does. It is a pity his health is poor."

"Another family trait," I observed. "But you all keep striving, keep working, in spite of it. Please do ask him. I would like to get to know him better."

The lead plates had done their work. My voice was much stronger, although I had not applied Aristotle's remedy in addition. I was waiting for Acte for that. I finally had my poem ready and was composing the music to accompany it. I also had gathered a large group of Alexandrians I named Augustiani to clap rhythmically at performances, as was done in Egypt. They made three different types of sounds: the bees (a loud humming), the roof tiles (staccato sharp claps made with hollowed hands), and the bricks (heavy, loud noises made with flat hands) to signal what their judgment was on a performance. I would seat them out in the audience to clap at the appropriate times.

My poem was inspired by Euripides' *Bacchae*, but it did not merely recite the plot. Instead I explored the theme, which was the struggle between the irrational forces of life and the rational mind, between freedom and control. It was the struggle going on within me, disguised here under the safe cover of a Greek myth. In the myth, the irrational destroyed the rational. But could there be no compromise? No way for those two forces to coexist within me? The daylight Nero, the Apollonian side who presided over the empire, and the Dionysian Nero who wished to explore the inchoate calling of creativity?

LIII

The day could not have been fairer. It was a replica of the one five years before when I first stepped out at noon, to be acclaimed as emperor. But, oh, the difference in me. I was sixteen then, now I was twenty-one. Then I could hardly believe myself an emperor; now it seemed impossible to be anything else.

I watched from a special balcony over the stage of the Theater of Pompey to see plays being enacted just below me, plays so realistic that the comedy *The Fire* by Afranius actually had a fire onstage, and the actors got to keep the furniture they rescued from the burning building. In the Theater of Marcellus, realistic mythological ballets were performed, in which the Minotaur was conceived onstage as he was in the story, and Icarus flew on wires, which unfortunately broke and spattered the audience with blood when he landed, although he survived, unlike the real Icarus. There were special dance exhibitions performed by Greeks, and when they were over I conferred Roman citizenship on all the dancers. At the same time, more entertainments went on in the Circus Maximus.

In my new amphitheater, I watched from the royal box as senators and members of the class just below it, the equestrians, battled in gladiator costumes with wooden swords and tridents, and "animal tamers" fought with trained "wild" beasts, and as every event ended I stood and threw out the engraved tokens to the crowd, this time for more extravagant gifts than ever before: a thousand birds, parcels of food, vouchers for grain, clothes, silver, gems, pearls, paintings, slaves, transport animals, trained wild beasts, even ships, apartment blocks, and farms.

At last, in the Theater of Marcellus, the promised surprise finale: an equestrian rode his trained elephant down a tightrope stretched from the highest tier of seats to the floor below. The rope sagged and swayed, but the majestic beast kept his balance, his enormous flat feet much more nimble than seemingly possible. It was a triumph of entertainment that brought the days of the Ludi Maximi to an unforgettable close. The cheers of the audience rang in my ears for days. I had done it—provided spectacle beyond anyone's expectations or experience.

Now I would rest and prepare for the Juvenalia, much more personal to me. It was late and I was practicing on the cithara for my debut performance, plucking the strings softly, relishing their melancholy sweetness. Whenever I stopped I heard the sound of crickets outside, and tonight, the faint notes of a nightingale, far beyond the window.

There was a light knock on the door, blending with the sounds of the night outside. Had I really heard it? I stood and walked over, listening again. Yes, a faint tapping. I opened the door and in the darkness saw Acte's face before me.

It seemed an apparition, called from the mists of the night outside. But no, she was real, warm as I pulled her into my arms.

"You came," I said, as if it were a miracle.

"Yes," she said. She pulled the covering from her head, and, arms around one another, we closed the door and she came into my room. We stood still, embracing, words suspended, awkward words that were difficult to frame.

"I am grateful," I finally said. "We must never be parted again."

What need for words now? They would only sully this precious moment. Let our bodies speak and our mouths be silent. And so it was.

• • •

The daylight stole into the chamber, the tawny October rays that bathed everything in gold. I watched as it crept across the floor, painting the squares of marble, reaching the bronze feet of a tripod, the square ebony legs of a stool. Gradually it touched our bed, but Acte did not stir even as the light lingered on her face. I studied that face as I never could when she was awake, marveling at its dear familiar contours, precious to me.

Acte was back. All would be well. The frightening anxieties that had descended on me—was this what the Furies really were, quieter and more persistent than the myth?—would be banished. The enormity of what had happened to Mother, which seemed to grow in my mind rather than fade away, would diminish. What was done was done and there was no undoing it. Her person could not be reconstituted from the ashes that rested in Baiae, although they seemed to blanket my mind, dark specks that swirled in my thoughts, clouding them. But Acte, my North Star, my constant, would hold me fast and anchor me.

She moved, opened her eyes, and in their dark depths I saw my world made whole again.

We prepared for the Juvenalia. I started to recount the events at the Ludi Maximi, but she said, "I was there. I saw them. Well, not all of them, as I couldn't be two places at once."

"You were there? Why did you not tell me, sit with me? Where were you?"

"In the stands with the common people. I wanted to see it through their eyes."

"What did you see, what did you hear them say?"

"I saw the 'gladiators' and the '*venatores*' fighting the toothless lions and the declawed bears and the fangless snakes, feeling very brave. Even toothless, a lion is dangerous."

Of course, professional *venatores* had been standing by in case of real danger.

"What else?"

"I was sitting behind someone lucky enough to catch a token. I have to say, your men threw them far, way up in the stands where the poorest people sat, and where they did the most good. The man who caught it near me shrieked with joy."

"Did you see what was engraved on the token?"

"Yes, it was a number four."

I smiled. "Ah, then he has much to shriek about. A number four was a sack of silver coins, mainly denariuses."

"I also saw the play with the burning house."

"Did you see the elephant?"

"No, I missed the elephant."

"Ah, that's a pity! We shall not see that again anytime soon." Now I must ask. "What were people's opinions of the games? You heard them, unfiltered."

"They were delighted. The common people love you; they feel you are one of them, that you care about them and share their passions. They love knowing that you support the plebian Greens rather than the aristocratic Blues, and that you spared no expense to give them these games. And that the tokens went mostly to the poorest, rather than the senators sitting in the first rows."

"Was there any mention of—Mother's plot against me?"

"No, none." She looked at me as if she expected me to speak of it. But I must not. No, the story must stay the same, the one that had been told to everyone, the official story; there could be no alternative version— not even to her.

The day had come, and the time-honored ritual of the first beard shaving must be carried out. I insisted that rather than a barber, Acte must do it in the privacy of my chamber.

"You have gentle hands and I trust you," I said. My beard was not very long, and truth to tell, it had been trimmed before. Had it not been, it would have reached to my navel by now. I had rather liked the short beard, but no Roman man was allowed to wear one—only barbarians had beards, the mark of the uncivilized. Oh, and some philosophers, but that was an affectation, and Romans did not trust philosophers anyway. So, above all, an emperor must be clean-shaven.

The instruments were prepared, laid neatly on a tray: a bronze scraper and polished steel knife. Acte picked up the knife, her hand trembling.

"Do not be nervous," I said. "Look, I am trusting you with a knife by my throat." Was there anyone else I could, unequivocally, say the same about?

She fluffed up the downy beard, still reluctant to attack it. "I suppose it is fitting that I do this," she said. "As I first met you before you had a beard."

"Yes, as a beardless boy," I said, using that popular phrase.

"Now you shall be beardless again," she said. Taking a deep breath, she proceeded with the scraping.

All done, the remnants of the beard were gathered up and put in a gold box to be dedicated to Jupiter later. I was closing the lid on my youth, offering it to the gods.

The ceremony on the Capitoline was watched by hundreds of people, as I solemnly laid the box at the feet of Jupiter's statue. It was a source of continual wonder to me how public ceremonies drew such huge crowds; it was as though they had a bottomless appetite for official occasions and formalities. And it was the emperor's duty to feed that hunger.

Now I would remove to my private grounds across the Tiber, near the Vatican Fields where the Juvenalia would take place. The racing track would be lonely, as all the events would be either in the gardens or in the theater; this was not athletics but art. And it was my first—but it would not be my last—attempt to change the thinking of Romans about art and drama, starting with the most influential people. Hence my insistence that they actually participate in the performances.

Strolling through the gardens I was pleased to see scores of people practicing. In the sunken garden, fifteen women were treading the stately steps of a ballet, moving slowly and deliberately, their costumes trailing on the flagstones. Oh, the suppleness of youth. They bent and swayed like willows in early spring, and they were early spring, too. But . . . looking closer at one of them, although she moved like the rest, I could see her face was lined and beneath her headdress gray hair protruded.

"Illusion, illusion, there is nothing like it," whispered my old friend and tutor Paris, the dancer, suddenly standing beside me. "Did I not show you long ago that a good actor can change ages?"

"Paris!" I had rarely seen him since I had left Aunt's. "Are you directing?"

He grinned. "Indeed I am. The ballet, pantomime, and the tragic drama. I leave the music and chorus to others." He nodded toward the older woman. "How old would you guess her?"

Her face and her movements were at different places on the age spectrum so I chose something in the middle. "Fifty?"

"No, my friend. That is Aelia Catella, and she is eighty years old."

"No, that's impossible."

"I swear it. Shall I bring her over and introduce her?"

"No, don't disturb her practice. But I am astounded. Ballet must be the elixir of youth, then. As you know, I've tried ballet. But I wasn't very good."

"No, I didn't know. But that does not surprise me."

"Why? Do you think I'm clumsy?"

"No, quite the opposite. The ballet is too slow moving for you."

"Ever the flatterer!" I clapped him on the back.

"It is an occupational hazard for an emperor, I fear. Hearing only flattery."

"A wise man once told me, if you want to flatter someone, tell him he hates flatterers."

"Who said that? I must remember it to quote it."

"I don't remember." Actually no one had said it. I had framed the words myself.

Leaving the sunken garden, we walked together through the open area hedged by myrtle bushes. In the middle a fountain splashed, filling a large circular basin bedecked with statues of Venus bathing, Neptune flourishing his trident, and a score of sea creatures—crabs, starfish, octopuses—crawling across the rim. The sun was still hot overhead, but nonetheless a score of men and women were practicing their chorus recitations in the wide-open space. The ages were mixed here, too, with elderly former consuls and aged matrons as well as comely youths.

"Paris, what do you think?" I turned to him. "All these people clearly have the desire and the talent to perform, and to appreciate drama. But what of other Romans? Do you think they are uninterested because it is foreign to them, or because it is inherently distasteful?" Before he could answer, I added, "For it is my wish that I can help bring an appreciation of all these things to the people of Rome."

He shook his head. "Tastes are particular to different cultures," he said, finally. "It is hard to transplant one from its native land to another climate."

"Customs aren't fruit trees," I said, "able to flourish only with one soil or altitude."

"But they are not always portable. What appeals to one population may leave another cold. It is hard to convert people—to *anything.*"

"But look, all these people—" I argued.

"They are here singing, acting, and dancing because they were ordered to by the emperor," Paris said.

"They were invited, not ordered."

"An invitation from the emperor is an order."

Not from me. Oh, surely not from me. I did not wish to be that sort of emperor, whose invitations were compulsions.

When I did not answer, he said quietly, "You know it is true. And I can speak freely because your old tutor has a special privilege—the privilege to speak the truth. Whenever and whatever you ask me, I will try to be honest."

"You old flatterer!" I laughed. But it was good to have an old friend, one who might be trusted. But I knew he flattered, too.

I turned and went my way to a shady trellised arbor, where several men were practicing tragic drama, all with masks. I would forbid them to wear masks in the actual performance—we wanted to see their faces.

"Off with the masks!" I said, startling them. They turned to face me and one by one stripped off the masks. There were two former consuls, several aristocrats, and one retired general. And, standing behind them, Gaius Calpurnius Piso.

"So I see you perform at last," I told him, signaling for him to come over to me.

He smiled, a smile that dazzled, and looked me searchingly in the eyes—something he must have perfected as a means of encapturing his audience. "Caesar, I perform only in private," he said. "You are giving me the chance to see how it feels to perform in public."

"This is a very select audience. It hardly counts as a genuine public," I admitted. "What are you performing?"

"The speeches from the scene in *Agamemnon* where he has just returned to Mycenae. 'Now I go to my father's house—I give the gods my right hand, my first salute. The ones who sent me forth have brought me home,'" he recited in Greek.

"Splendid," I said. A bit too slow in the delivery, but he did have something.

"I enjoy being someone else, even for a short time," he said.

As if he could know the true torment of being two, or three, other people, all at odds—but I liked him. "We should practice together," I said.

He smiled again. "I would be honored."

An invitation from the emperor is an order. "After the festival, let us choose a time."

"You could visit me in Baiae," he said. "My villa would welcome you. And the balcony there is a fine place to practice, with the sea gleaming below. Perhaps we could do *Andromeda* if we want a sea theme."

Baiae! A shudder went through me. "Thank you," was all I said.

Behind us the other actors were reciting their lines, melodious voices like the low murmur of bees. Did everyone see himself as a mythological character at some deep level? Far inside, an Agamemnon, a Perseus, a Jason? Was I giving them the gift of bringing it to the surface, revealing it in the light, if only briefly? "Well, I must not keep you," I said, releasing him back to the others.

On the other side of the garden a grove of plane trees offered winding paths beneath their shade. As I crossed over there, I was pleased that so many groups of people were practicing out in the open, availing themselves of my pledge to provide instruction. Once inside the grove, many people were enjoying the shade, strolling slowly along the pebbled paths. I spotted Seneca right away by his particular slow gait. There was another man with him.

"Teacher!" I greeted him. He swung around to see me and bowed.

"May I present my brother Gallio?" He coughed. His cough was getting worse.

"An honor, Caesar," Gallio said. He had a pleasant demeanor but seemed sickly like his brother.

"Gallio was with me in exile—er, relegation—in Corsica, and after that dreadful stint ended, we returned to Rome together, and then he served as proconsul of Greece under Claudius," said Seneca.

"But I had to resign early, because of my lungs." Gallio coughed, too.

"Literary talent runs in your family," I said. As well as weak lungs. "Your brother Seneca certainly, your father, Seneca the Elder, and I understand your nephew, who was a friend of Britannicus, is now in Athens. He used to attend my writers' group."

"You refer to Lucan," said Gallio. "The son of our youngest brother, Mela. Yes, he's now a furiously scribbling poet."

"I would welcome him back here in Rome. He could rejoin the circle of poets and writers I sponsor."

"He is—" Gallio started to say.

"He would be honored," Seneca interrupted.

An invitation from the emperor is an order.

"You shall write to him," I told Seneca. "Issue the invitation." I turned to Gallio. "I have told your brother it would be fitting if you introduced me at the Juvenalia. Your family's artistic standing would enhance the occasion."

"An occasion I have begged him to forgo," said Seneca. "He intends to perform onstage. Singing and playing."

"What is wrong with that?" said Gallio. Clearly the brothers had rehearsed this, knowing what I was going to ask. "Everyone else is performing. Why not you as well, brother?"

"Yes, I could perform, and it's no more wrong than other consuls performing. But he is the emperor. It demeans the office. He must not be onstage like regular men."

Gallio, a better diplomat, shrugged. "If one emperor did it, then other emperors would follow, and it would no longer be shocking. My lord, I will gladly introduce you. Now, tell me—how do you wish to be introduced?"

"Not as 'Caesar' or 'the emperor.' Let me take a stage name, as others do. Or let me for now be merely 'Nero.' I can choose a performance name later."

"And at what point does this performance occur?"

"It is last, of course," said Seneca. "For the shock value."

"No," I said, "that is not the reason. I wish it to be a surprise and the finale of the festival."

"The truth is you are nervous," said Gallio, winking. "Why not go first, then, and get it over with?"

"I don't want to overshadow the other performances. People will inevitably talk about it and that will be distracting. Let them talk about it later, not during the festival."

"Besides, this gives you the option of changing your mind," said Gallio.

I left them on the path, relieved to have met Seneca's brother and settled the matter of my introduction. It was a bit chilly in the grove and so I sought the sunshine. It was late enough now that the fiercest rays had passed, and the low light was turning benevolently golden, painting everything the distinctive Roman October glaze.

Along the far wall of the garden, small channels rippled with water, stirring water lilies on their surfaces, wafting their cloying perfume toward me. At the fountain-source of one of the channels, there was a woman moving languidly, like one of the slow-spinning leaves falling from the plane trees. She was completely alone, lost in her own dance.

As I approached, I recognized that form and face. Poppaea. The radiant beauty I had glimpsed, seen, met, but only in passing. I was drawn to her and stood watching as she practiced her steps, oblivious to everything around her, caught up completely in her art, a state all artists longed for but rarely achieved.

Suddenly she stopped, like a woodland creature that senses a human presence. She turned around, searching, and saw me.

I nodded to acknowledge my presence and walked over to her. She stood waiting.

I was used to beauty, for I saw it all about me in statues by Greek masters, in mosaics. Although I was surrounded by it, I was not inured to it, for beauty is supreme in its ability to wound. But few living persons can approach the heights of the beauty in art. Poppaea did.

"Pray do not stop," I said.

"I have come to a stopping place," she said.

Now I was close enough to speak in a lower level of voice. "What are you practicing?" I asked.

"A pantomime," she said. "Daphne and Apollo."

"Where are your leaves?" I asked.

"We will have them for the performance. They will be cleverly stuck onto my fingers. In the meantime, I am trying to capture the moment she becomes rooted in the ground and realizes she cannot move, and then sees her arms turning into branches. It must have been terrifying."

"I wonder if at that moment she suddenly wished she had just submitted to Apollo."

"It was too late then," she said. "The bark was already creeping up her legs."

"Now, if you were in her place, would you think it a worthy exchange—to be a tree with rough bark, forever, instead of a living woman?"

"It would depend on how I felt about Apollo," she said. She smiled. "Clearly Daphne had an aversion to him, but she is the only woman to have had that reaction to the sun god."

"Is Otho playing Apollo?"

"Yes," she said. "But you would be more suited to the role. Perhaps you can practice a few steps with me?"

"Where do you want me to stand?" I quickly asked.

"Here, just behind me," she said. "As if you are pursuing me and are just catching me."

An arm's length behind her, I felt myself drowning in the sense of her nearness. I reached out and touched her shoulder, grasping it like I imagined Apollo would have.

She shivered and writhed, throwing her arms up and twisting them. With her silent mouth she screamed—there is no voice in pantomime. I could almost feel her skin turning to bark, so well did she simulate the terror.

I stepped back. "Excellent," I said.

"Thank you for your help," she said. "It is difficult to practice alone."

"Why do you say I would be more suited to the role?" I had to ask.

She cocked her head. "Your hair, of course. It is golden like Apollo's. You ought to grow it out and wear it long. Then others could see what I see." She reached out and touched it. I was shocked at the familiarity with an emperor.

I touched my own hair, made sacred now by her touch. "Perhaps I will."

"You have other connections with Apollo," she said. "After all, when you were born, the sun anointed you with his rays before you ever touched the ground."

How did she know that? She must have studied about me. She had made it her business to know personal things about me. "So my mother told me," was all I would say.

"And is not Apollo the god of music? I have heard that your skill on the cithara approaches that of Apollo himself."

I laughed. "Hardly," I said. "But he does inspire me."

"You should not hide your gift."

There is no respect for hidden music. She understood. Or did she? Was this all just a clever ploy, a wife ingratiating herself with the emperor to help her husband?

So suspicious and wary had I become that the thought pierced the golden glow of the afternoon. But I banished it, choosing instead to bask in her beauty and aura.

"I do not intend to," I assured her.

LIV

The theater was prepared, draped with garlands. Each chair was fitted with cushions; servers were on hand to pass out goblets of drink. The invited audience filled the seats, dressed in their best, excited to have received a private invitation to the emperor's gardens. I sat in the very front, on an ivory chair, with Acte beside me. Seneca, Gallio, and Burrus flanked my other side. As each group performed, they would leave their seats and go onstage. So the audience would be at once performer and spectator, on a rotating basis.

I rose and faced the people. "Welcome, welcome, all! We celebrate today a happy milestone in the life of your emperor, crossing a threshold." They would think it meant the shaving of my beard, but by tonight they would know the true threshold I was crossing. "May all enjoy what we have prepared for one another."

After I sat down, Acte leaned over and whispered, "If they only knew. Are you sure you want to do this?"

I was sure. It had to be, and it had to be now. I nodded, slowly, keeping my eyes straight ahead so I would not see hers.

The first act, a silent, solemn ballet, performed by the older and more timid people, was rather dull. People tepidly applauded. The next, a chorus wailing about the fall of Troy, was an improvement and stirred the audience. In the meantime, the ballet dancers had filed back to their seats. A dance followed with the young daughters of senators, their gowns floating out behind them as they sought to depict the winds of early spring.

"The one on the left is about to trip over her gown," said Acte.

I was disappointed in her comment. She was not entering into the performance but focusing on the literal aspects of it. "I think the dance is graceful and moving," I said. "That is what I see."

"I see frightened girls," she said. "Terrified of performing."

Did she not understand? "That is what all true performers feel."

"I am not one of them, then, and never will be," she said. "I should count myself lucky to be spared such anguish."

Lucky or impoverished? Those who did not have the calling could never experience the ecstasy that followed the anguish. "You must content yourself with being the critic, then," I said. The critic: safe behind his wall, judging others. But without critics, there is no art. For art must be judged to be proved true.

I dug into a pouch I carried and fished out a rough-cut emerald, which I handed to her.

"Take this," I said. "It will help you to see better." In many ways, I hoped. Being shortsighted myself, I often put it up to my right eye to sharpen my vision.

She turned it over, puzzled. Then she laughed. "So this will make me see the way you do?"

"Perhaps."

She playfully held it up to her eye.

The next set of performances were the tragic dramas, and a number of actors left the audience and trooped up to the stage. One very aged senator acted the part of Tithonus, the man loved by Eos, the goddess of dawn, who asked Zeus to grant him eternal life but neglected to ask for eternal youth as well, so he withered away and was shut up in a room to chirp with his weak voice. The man's faded voice mimicked the enfeebled bleats of the very old, and their panic and fear at no longer being heard. He got a thundering applause.

The next was Piso, who strode onto the stage like a conqueror. But that was fitting, as he was Agamemnon. He declaimed the speech I had heard him practicing, and more beyond. For an instant I truly believed he was the doomed king, about to be led into a bath and butchered like a ram. His natural stiltedness worked in the role, for Agamemnon was pompous and rigid.

Acte was shaking her head. It distracted me, took me from the moment. "He wears a false face," she said.

"He isn't wearing a mask," I said. "No masks in these performances."

"I meant his real face," she said.

"Most women find it charming," I said. Men, too. He was universally popular. "The emerald isn't improving your vision! But keep it anyway."

More dramas followed; Oedipus, Hector, Hercules, all took their turns onstage.

Then the pantomimes—Odysseus and Nausicaa, the wanderings of Leto, Atalanta the lightning-fast runner, and then Daphne and Apollo.

Poppaea, wearing a bark-colored gown, fairly floated out onto the stage. Her movements were so fluid and graceful I felt prickles on the back of my neck. She enacted the happy life of the river nymph, bending over the stream where her father the river god lived. Then Apollo—Otho—appeared. He was wearing a short—too short for his spindly legs and knobby knees—tunic and a sun-rayed crown of divinity, which kept slipping over his wig, pulling it to one side.

The audience laughed. I felt embarrassed pain for Poppaea. But she gamely went through the rest of the performance. They got to the part I had enacted with her, and I watched as Otho's clumsy hand fell like a piece of overcooked mutton on her shoulder, at the very place where I had touched her.

She turned and, as she had with me, twisted and moved her arms upward, and just as she had promised, the leaves affixed to her fingertips gleamed green in the failing light.

The act received wild applause, but not the right kind.

As they were leaving the stage, Acte said, "Perhaps this will puncture her vanity a bit."

"What exactly do you mean?"

"She's very vain," she said. "So proud of her beauty. It's said she keeps a stable of five hundred donkeys to supply milk for her to bathe in."

"I haven't heard that."

"I had several months while you were away to hear what people in the street were saying. Everyone knows about the donkeys. And it's also said she shoes them all in silver."

"Five hundred asses," I said. "I know where the stable is. The Senate. There are certainly five hundred asses in the Senate."

Acte giggled, but Seneca harrumped.

I hardly saw the rest of the acts. For mine was coming closer. The moment was at hand.

As the last troupe of pantomimes were finishing their performance, I quietly rose and made my way back behind the stage. Gallio followed.

Behind the curtain, my cithara was waiting, along with my performance tunic. It was long and flowing like Apollo's. I removed my toga and short tunic, my heart beating so fast my fingers could hardly work.

A tempting pitcher of wine stood on a table to one side. I wanted to down a cup, to calm the trembling that was affecting my limbs, but knew I could not stifle my performance that way. Afterward, afterward, there would be wine aplenty. But not now, oh, not now.

Robed and holding my cithara, my hands still unsteady, I was asked by Gallio if I was ready. He touched my arm gently.

I answered for him then. "I am ready," I said, lying, horrified at how small my voice sounded. I clutched the cithara with sweaty hands.

Why am I doing this? Why am I doing this? I wanted to run away, to run into the rapidly falling night. What had possessed me to want to do this?

I took a deep breath, stilled my racing heart. An answer came. Apollo himself had possessed me; he had drawn me to him and commanded me to prove myself a worthy son by daring to do this. And he would protect me, empower me. I had to trust him.

"Let us go," I said to Gallio, holding out my hand.

Together we went out onto the stage.

There was a loud, collective gasp. In the dim light I could almost see the widening of eyes, their whites gleaming.

"My dear audience," said Gallio, doling his words out precisely—he was a skilled speaker, as his brother was—"I present to you tonight the pinnacle of the festival, a special performance just for you, here in private, a rare gift reserved for this company alone—your emperor, a citharoede of great but hitherto hidden talent, will sing and play for you." He stepped back. I stepped forward.

My heart was racing again. I commanded it, in the name of Apollo, to quiet itself. My mouth was dry, paralyzed. My hands were hot and wet and my fingers stiff. I held the cithara gingerly, afraid of it.

I recited the traditional plea of the performer to his audience. "My lords, of your kindness give me ear." For one awful moment there was silence, but then the trained soldiers clapped and the audience followed suit. "I will sing a poem of my own composition, 'The Bacchantes,'" I said.

I held the cithara as I had hundreds of times before, but this time, oh! so different. But then training took over, and the words of the song I had so labored over sprang forth, eager to be born, to be heard—*there is no respect for hidden music*—and my voice soared, my fingers magically mastered the strings, and the audience before me both vanished and at the same time throbbed through me, enflaming me with the creative fire of Apollo himself. The song rose clear and pure, my offering to him and to them and to myself.

Then it was over, the mystical wind that had sung through me passed on, and I stood on the stage hearing the audience crying out, "Glorious Caesar! Our Apollo, our Augustus, another Pythian! By thyself we swear, O Caesar, none surpasses you!" amid the trained and rhythmic clapping of the Augustiani.

I had done it. I had walked out where I feared to walk, shown what I had feared—yet longed—to show, and crossed the threshold. Now I was a true artist, having survived the initiation rite all artists must pass through. For *there is no respect for hidden music.* And only the fearsome initiation rite could uncover that music, reveal it. There is no other way.

Afterward I wandered in a strange altered state of mind. I saw the people around me, even (so I am told) conversed with them; I saw the bright torches being lit to illuminate the gardens and thought what a tender color a flame is; and somehow found myself (but I must have followed others, or been transported there) in the Grove of the Caesars, surrounded by milling people. They were speaking, but I did not register what they were actually saying. The trees were murmuring overhead, the booths with food and drink were closing, and two pleasure boats on the artificial lake of Augustus were waiting to waft us away. This was the private party, restricted to the emperor's close friends. I had looked forward to it as a relaxing reward for the tension of the day, but now, floating in exaltation, I hardly noticed what was happening around me. I welcomed them (I assume). I looked about and saw my friends and companions (although I cannot now tell you who was there). Of course wine flowed, and I availed myself of it, as I had promised myself I would when the performance was safely past.

Now the world spun more than ever, excitement and wine alike carrying me away. There was music, some sort of music . . . horns? Cymbals? It was loud enough to make conversation impossible. I found myself lying on the cushions spread out on the deck, next to rows of people likewise lolling. Laughter and poking. Bodies pressing up against me on both sides. Warmth. Complete happiness. The stars overhead wheeling. Part of me was numb, another part quiveringly awake. I felt a soft hand on my thigh, gentle, the brushing of a bird's wing. It inched up and down, sliding along the silk of my tunic. Someone spread a cover over the row of bodies, making a tent—a tent to veil activities beneath it. The person who was touching me—who was it? I shut my eyes. I did not want to know. It was better, more of a trespass, that way. The person—it was a woman—boldly made her wishes known by where she touched me and how she moved her hands and then, her entire body. A luscious and perfect body. Still I did not look, or speak. This was a gift directly from the gods (and perhaps was not even a real person), who would be insulted if I refused it. So I yielded to her. And never had I tasted a sweeter gift, never savored an act of love more.

The music was still blaring and bleating its high-pitched wails as I fell back to earth at last, slowly, deliciously. The world became real again, the wrinkles of the cushions under my back, the creaking of the wooden deck, the bumping of the side of the boat as it entered the narrow canal to the Tiber. And then, a familiar voice from the other side of me.

"Is she not supreme among women?"

Otho! I sat up with a jerk. He was lying beside me, smiling, his head propped up on his elbow, looking amused. "I knew you were curious about her, and told her to satisfy your curiosity. There is only one way to end temptation, and that is to give in to it. At least, that is my method."

I could hardly bring myself to turn my head and look on my other side. I knew what I would see, knew already, and I did not wish to confirm it. But I had to.

Poppaea was lying facedown, and all I saw was her unmistakable amber hair. I could not have borne it if she had spoken.

I could not speak to Otho, could not speak to either of them. I stood up and threw off the covering, then wished I hadn't: I had uncovered a row of other lustily coupling people. I flicked it back down again and walked off to the rail.

We were passing through the canal; we were almost back in the city.

My extraordinary day had come to an end, and I was stunned. I could not think, but without actual words I wondered how Otho could have done this. And how could Poppaea have complied? Or . . . whose idea was it, really?

That was the true temptation. To think Poppaea was the instigator, rather than her husband being a procurer. To imagine that she had wanted me first.

LV

You have had your amusement," said Seneca three days later. Outside, the debris from the Juvenalia had been swept away, the wilted garlands collected, the wooden stages collapsed and stored away. Inside, my crumpled citharoede robe was hanging on a peg behind my door, stained with wine, sweat, and scented balm.

If only you knew, I thought, and that lent a smile to my face as I looked at his stern one. Oh, if only you knew.

Poppaea had haunted my mind, my dreams, waking and sleeping, yet I could not even convince myself it had happened. The whole Juvenalia floated like a mirage in my memory, something precious and elusive, that might not even be real.

"Yes," I said. "And now it is time to work."

He looked surprised. Clearly he had never expected me to insist on that, or even to suggest it.

"I called you and Burrus here first, but the rest of the ministers will be joining us shortly, as well as some members of the Consilium."

Seneca looked at me expectantly. He was used to telling me what the agenda was and this turnabout puzzled him. Before I could speak, Burrus entered the room, spotted us, and strode over to the bench and took his place beside Seneca.

"Ah," he said, sinking down. "And what am I summoned for? Does the emperor, perhaps, have a new tune he wishes to preview with his faithful ministers?" He twitched his toga up to settle more comfortably on the bench.

I stared at him. How dare he mock me? "No," I said, and all the chill of deep winter was in that one word.

Burrus blinked and said, "I am disappointed, then."

"I am sure you are." The tone did not thaw. "But I wish to discuss matters far beyond the palace, beyond Rome, beyond even the Mediterranean."

Now they looked astonished, as if I had said a naughty word.

"Why, do you think I am not aware of that world? That I do not follow the dispatches, the reports of the generals there? For shame, if you serve a master so ignorant. For the fault would be yours, not the master's." Now that I had chastened them, I could proceed. They thought I was an ignorant, careless boy, content to leave the wider world affairs to them and see only my nearby music. But there was no reason why I could not do both—indeed, must do both. And I was no longer a boy. "The situation in Armenia is troubling, and the advice of soldiers like you, Burrus, for a military campaign there seems to be failing."

"Everything in Armenia fails," he said gruffly. "We have tried everything, ever since the days of Marc Antony. But they cannot be trusted, and if a region cannot be trusted, what recourse do we have but military action?"

Armenia sat between our traditional enemy, Parthia, and our province of Syria. Over the years we had installed puppet kings there, the Parthians had done likewise, and the only certainty was that any settlement there did not last. The latest round had recognized Tiridates, the half brother of Parthia's king, as our choice of ruler, but the man insisted on taking up arms against Rome, so I had ordered General Corbulo to pursue him. Next we appointed a pro-Roman collaborator, Tigranes V, to govern Armenia, and now the Parthians were at war with him.

"We should split the eastern command: secure Syria with Corbulo and appoint a new general to deal with Parthia," I said. "Burrus, who would you recommend for that post?"

He thought a moment, then said, "Caesennius Paetus. He has experience in that area."

I nodded. "Then we shall inform him. But I still think if there were some way to reinstate Tiridates, that would be preferable."

"Perhaps we should just annex Armenia and get it over with," said Burrus.

"Its mountains and remoteness make it a difficult terrain to conquer," said Seneca. "Not, of course, that a Roman army could not do it. But at what cost? And would it yield anything worth the cost of acquiring it?"

"Peace, perhaps," I said.

Burrus gave a barely suppressed snort. "And while we are discussing expensive ventures, useless provinces, what of Britain?" he said. "Is it worth tying four legions up there in perpetuity? It is ruinously expensive to maintain, and it produces very little."

I had thought the same. "Perhaps we should withdraw from there," I said. The only reason not to was that it was Claudius's main achievement, and I did not want to demote the reputation of my "father."

Seneca's face wrinkled with worry. "I have forty million sesterces out on loan there," he said. "I should call those loans in if you are thinking of abandoning the province."

I suppressed a sarcastic remark about the rich philosopher whose creed stressed indifference to material things, but who could make loans in the millions. Well, we are all a tangle of contradictions.

Now the others joined us: Phaon, minister of accounts and revenues; Beryllus, my former tutor, secretary for Greek letters; Doryphorus, minister of notes; and various scribes. I bade them take seats and had a slave offer refreshments, and then the meeting continued.

Phaon was the first to pull out his notes and report on the cost of the recent games and festivities, assuring us that the treasury had not been hurt by them. "In the goodwill of the people, it was a shrewd investment," he said. He had a broad, cheerful face and a booming voice that reminded me of an innkeeper. He seemed primed to report only pleasing news.

Dear Beryllus, quiet and contained, then rose and reported that dispatches had been coming from the governor of Syria, worried about the Armenian situation, but I assured him we were just discussing that and had settled the course of action to take.

Doryphorus, reporting on dispatches from lower provincial officials, launched into a long list of complaints from Portugal—the harbors were not well maintained; from Moesia—tribes from beyond the eastern borders were threatening; from Judea—purist zealots were increasingly restive over religious infringements. He was such an imposing, sculpted-jaw man and his looks were so arresting it was hard to concentrate on his news.

Now selected members of the Consilium trooped in and took their places on rows of benches around us. One, Thrasea Paetus, leapt in immediately. "Judea!" he cried. "The people there are a superstitious lot of heathen."

"No, Thrasea, you have it backward. They view *us* as the heathens. They say we desecrate their holy land by being there," said Doryphorus.

"There are Jews right here in Rome. Claudius expelled them, but they've crept back. In fact, I think there is a delegation from the high priest in Jerusalem here to see you," said Epaphroditus, my secretary for petitions. "Yes, forgive me for not arranging a meeting yet."

"How long have they been here?" I asked.

He hung his shaggy dark head. "Oh, a few years."

"That's outrageous!"

"I'll arrange a meeting immediately. Please forgive me, Caesar."

I then reported our decision about Armenia, and immediately a truculent senator named Nonius Silius decried it. "Force, force, that's all they understand. Send more generals, more soldiers. Beat them into the dust."

"Let us try one general first and see what can be achieved," I persisted.

"Germanicus, your great ancestor, would not have advised that," he said.

"Germanicus was obedient to his emperor, and so will my generals be. I am commander in chief and they must follow my orders."

He glared at me but said nothing.

Seneca now rose and said, "I have a proposal for exploration. If the emperor is amenable, we could send soldiers down the Nile to discover its source, and we could also send explorers far north to discover supplies of amber."

Amber. He knew I loved amber, and that we were forced to pay exorbitant rates for it from middlemen in the Baltic. And as for the Nile, its source was a mystery, a mystery I would love to solve.

"The Nile scouting expedition would be useful in planning an Ethiopian campaign," said Burrus. "We have spoken of provinces and adding new ones. Ethiopia is a promising candidate for that."

Ethiopia. Riches. Ivory. Ebony. Gold. I felt my heart beating faster.

"I would endorse such a plan," I said. And thus it was decided. "We will meet in a few days to discuss the details."

As they took their leave, I stood and poured a tall goblet of red wine. I was astounded. I had not thought of Poppaea the whole afternoon.

I spent several hours after the meeting poring over reports and studying maps. The two expeditions Seneca had suggested stretched far to the north and to the south, a slanted line almost three thousand miles long, from the icy seas washing the shores of barbaric lands to the hot dry desert, giving way to jungle in Africa. As at no other time, the sheer immensity of the empire struck me. The staggering responsibility for it lay heavily on my shoulders, although like any burden it is a day-by-day one that can be borne one step at a time. But the wisdom to guide such a vehicle—only with the help of the gods could any one man be wise enough.

I leaned on one elbow and measured the lands on the map spread out before me. I had said that the empire was large enough, that it should not expand. But beckoning beyond the Mediterranean—now referred to as "a Roman lake" in popular parlance—lay the Black Sea. We already had provinces on the nearer, western, side of it—Moesia, Thrace, Bithynia, and Pontus—but the eastern side was tantalizing. There was the troublesome Armenia, but there was also the Cimmerian Bosphorus with its fields of wheat, which Rome could use for its ever-growing population. And Ethiopia, east of the Nile—if the Nile went that far south—would be a worthy addition to the empire, a provider of such luxury items as incense, gold, and gems.

Judea. My eye fell on that small country and I remembered what I had heard about the troubles there. For such a tiny place it produced an outsized amount of upheaval. It did not rate a governor of its own, but a lesser appointee, a Roman prefect. He lived in Caesarea Maritima, a city on the coast, to stay away from Jerusalem, the religious capital filled with violent zealots and anti-Roman insurrectionists. Their anger usually had something to do with their temple or theological disputes between the sects. Caligula had set off a riot when he wanted a statue of himself put up in the temple. They had a prohibition against art depicting humans and animals.

I looked over at my small statue of an athlete tying his winning ribbon around his head, a celebration of the sheer beauty of the human form. What fools those people were! I shook my head. But fools or not, their deputies should not have been detained here so long without a hearing. I must investigate this.

The empire. Just glancing around the room I could touch the far-flung places where we ruled. The floor had multicolored marbles— yellow Numidian from North Africa, red porphyry from Egypt. The walls had inlays of green-veined Carystian marble from Euboea and purple Phrygian from Asia. The scrolls were of papyrus from Egypt. The bitumen for my imperial seal was from the Dead Sea. On my tray was a precious goblet of murra from Persia, translucent, with a delicate scent. I drank only my special snow-cooled boiled water, my *decocta Neronis*, from it. Wine might stain it. The empire was almost impossible to comprehend, except through tangible objects like this.

I commanded all this. I was a boy no longer, despite that lingering impression with Burrus and Seneca. Perhaps it is impossible to ever see one's former pupil or child as anything but that. But the bonds and inexperience that had restrained me now fell away. Mother was gone; the prohibition on pursuing art had been smashed at the Juvenalia; the Senate had proved itself spineless and docile with no power to rule me. The world now beckoned, saying, *Come, come, stride out and take command.*

There was one bond yet to sunder. I would end the marriage to Octavia, the marriage that was no marriage but a forced yoking of two victims in their childhood. Neither of us was a child any longer; I would cut this Gordian knot in one blow.

LVI

Bursting with newfound purpose and surety, I retired to my bedroom at the back of the vast imperial quarters. The sinking sun was washing its color over the already painted crimson walls, creating a livid red made up of unworldly tints. The shadow of my head made a black profile as I passed through the rays.

I hoped to find Acte there, but the chamber was empty except for the usual slaves. She had her own rooms nearby, but we usually spent the night in mine. Eager to see her, I walked to her chambers and found her busy arranging a set of scrolls.

As always, when I first saw her, I felt a wave of contentment and peace.

She looked up, smiled. "The meeting took a long time," she said. "But the more people, the longer it takes. I trust the senators were not obstructive."

"No, they are tame as kittens these days." I took her hand, her slender fingers unadorned by the heavy rings favored by the wealthy. "The world is mine—ours. Perhaps the first shaving of the beard is just a ceremony, but it has marked a line in my life. The true end of boyhood."

She slid her arm around me. "I have watched you all these years. Do not denigrate your boyhood—keep the best of it all your life."

I would have said, *Come, walk with me in the gardens*, but what I wanted to tell her should not be done in the open. Instead I said, "Let us retire to our inmost room." It was the one where we kept our favorite jewels and gold, at the very end of a corridor where access was limited.

She probably thought I was going to present her with a necklace or earrings, pearls and emeralds. Had I not been so excited about my private decision, I would have noticed her disquiet.

In the room at last, I asked the attendant slave to close the door and leave. Now we were alone. I looked at her dear face, the face I wanted for my empress. Now it could come about. But I found it hard to speak.

"What is it?" she asked gently.

I took a deep breath. "It is this. I lack one thing to complete my happiness. You know what that is."

Instead of smiling and saying, *Yes, I know,* she looked sad. "That can never be."

"You have said that before, but that is in the past. Now it can come about. I am prepared to proceed with the divorce from Octavia." I thought for a moment. "I haven't even seen her in months. For all I know, she has taken a lover."

Now she laughed. "That is unlikely, knowing her."

"In any case, she is no impediment to us. I can wait no longer to have you as my empress."

"I do not wish to be an empress."

"That is one of the things—but only one of them—that makes me love you. You are the only woman in the empire, I would venture, who would not wish to be an empress."

"I can claim no virtue in that," she said. The smile had faded from her face. What was wrong?

"Then don't be an empress," I said. "You can be my wife without taking that title."

"I cannot be your wife," she insisted.

"You know we have solved the problem of your so-called unsuitability. You are now an attested daughter of the royalty of Pergamum. The papers are all signed. They have been for some time and have just been waiting to be used."

"It isn't the legality of it, or my bogus pedigree, or the title of empress. I cannot be your wife because things have changed between us—you have changed."

Yes, I had. Had I not just said I had changed from a boy to a man? I said as much.

"There is a distance between us. You have not been the same since you went to Baiae last spring."

Hardly. Oh, if only you knew—the same words I had said to myself just hours earlier, when I was with Burrus and Seneca. I had become entangled with differing versions of events that I must not let others know. And she could not know the truth about Mother. That could never be.

"It was a shock about Mother." Yes, that was certainly true.

"But it is eating away at you. Did you know you have nightmares and scream, calling her name?"

No! What did I say? "Is that—all?"

"I can't make out all the words. You mumble them and even the words I can understand are out of order."

Oh, thank the gods. "In spite of all our disagreements, she was my mother," I said piously.

"You aren't mourning her in your sleep; you are afraid of her."

"Ghosts . . ." My voice trailed off.

"Not *any* ghost, *her* ghost."

Now I had an opening. I took both her hands in mine and looked deeply into her eyes. "We must not let a ghost, no matter whose, destroy our happiness."

"It isn't the ghost, Nero, it is you. Your remoteness, your secrets."

"Secrets? I have no secrets from you." Except one. Or two.

Tears formed in her eyes, spilled down her cheeks. "So you lie now. You choose to lie even when you have the opportunity to be honest."

I pulled my hands away. "I don't know what you mean."

"I know what happened on the boat last week. How oblivious do you think I am? That my love means I see, hear, nothing around me?" She wiped the tears off her cheeks with an angry swipe. "I was lying almost beside you. Not only could I hear you, I could feel all the movements."

A jolt of shock went through me, and I felt as though a thunderbolt had struck me.

"It was disgusting! How could you do that to me?" she cried.

"I didn't do it to you. I didn't know you were there. It had nothing to do with you. I was not myself." That was true.

"That is where you are wrong. You were yourself. This is you, a side of you I refused to recognize. But now I see, and I don't need an emerald for my eye to do so. I would not marry you; I do not want a liar for a husband, even if he is the emperor."

"But the years we have had together—can you not forgive one error on my part? How can one night cancel out years?" I could not believe it.

"Why must you make me say words that will hurt you?" she said. "I love you. I will always love you, no matter what you do. But I cannot be your wife. I am going to buy a villa of my own outside of Rome and live there."

Now I truly was in shock. "You are—leaving me?"

"I am moving to Velitrae. I will never leave you. I told you, I will always love you."

"But you won't marry me, won't even live in Rome! And now who has secrets? You must have been planning this move to Velitrae for some time. Looking for a suitable place to live. Well, buy the best. I am pleased to pay for it. Never say I am cheap or want revenge."

"I knew you would react this way. But I will never be truly separated from you, and when you need me, call for me and I will come. But this new Nero will not need me for long. Or for a long time, I should say."

"When will you leave?"

"I can leave tomorrow."

"Then let us spend one last night together, as if we were still young and innocent."

I hoped that that would persuade her and when the morning came she would change her mind. But although we made love, it was bittersweet, no, painful. The joy was gone. And the next morning so was she.

I could not bear the morning light, and I closed the shutters, as if that would stop time from moving forward. *Stay, stay, time! No, go backward, let last night never have happened.* But it was utterly in vain, and I sat slumped in misery and with an actual pain in my chest. If I could not stop time, I tried to smother the torturing thoughts that raced through my mind. But that was equally fruitless. So I sat helpless and let them wash over me.

Time did not obediently stop, but I had no sense of it as I sat captive. At length (but after how long?) there was a knocking on the door and urgent cries of "Caesar! Caesar!"

I ignored them, but they grew more insistent, and then there was the sound of someone beating against the door, trying to break it open.

They thought I had come to harm. I had, but not in the way they feared. I rose and shuffled to the door. Two guards were standing just outside, one with his foot raised to kick the door.

"Caesar! The day was at noon and you had not appeared. It was our duty—"

"Yes, I know," I said. "But I am quite safe." I started to close the door, to be alone again in my sadness. But standing right behind them was Epaphroditus, my secretary. "The Judean delegation," he said. "They expected you this morning." He looked at me. "Shall I tell them you are unwell?"

They had already waited years. I could not make them wait longer. "No, I will come. Tell them I will be late but will see them this afternoon."

I let my chamber slaves dress me. So this was what it would be, life from now on. I would do my duties, perform as required, but that distance I had created between myself and others that had driven Acte away would remain, as it must. No one could know the truth about me and trust me, let alone love me. The only way I could approach others safely was to disguise myself through art.

I received the Judeans in the smaller of the reception halls. It was chilly in the mid-November afternoon, so I had braziers lit. The small group was huddled together in the middle of the hall, their translator standing by.

"Great Caesar, we are grateful for your attention," he said, bowing low.

"I understand you have been waiting for some time," I answered.

They murmured among themselves, then the translator said, "Yes, Prefect Antonius Felix sent us here."

Felix! He had been out of office for almost two years already. "What is the nature of your embassy?" I asked. Looking at them more closely, I wondered why they were so thin and pinched. Were they not being fed?

"We represent the high priest of the temple in Jerusalem. Our temple is the holy center of our Jewish religion, built according to the specifications of our god—whose name we cannot utter except in prayer or study, forgive me, Caesar. King Agrippa built a tower on his palace that allowed him to see into the inner yard of the temple, so we built a wall to block his view. He ordered it torn down, but we resisted. Finally Prefect Felix said this should be decided in Rome, and he sent us here."

What a silly and petty thing to be placed at my feet to decide. Why could they not have settled this themselves? I said as much.

Epaphroditus whispered to me, "The tensions between the strict Jewish believers and the compromisers there are high. They quarrel over a straw. Felix did not wish to ignite anything, so he passed it on to Rome."

"He is rightly retired, if he could not manage better than this," I muttered. Then I turned to the delegation. "You may keep your wall," I said. "I regret that it has taken so long for you to get resolution on this matter."

As soon as the translator passed on my words, smiles broke out on their thin faces. "Caesar, we are deeply grateful," they said.

The business having been briskly dealt with—years of waiting settled in only a few moments—I asked them about their homeland.

Their leader, a man named Jehoram, said, by way of the translator, "To be honest, Caesar, these are frightening times. We are plagued with assassins who go about attacking anyone they perceive as being part of the oppression or the opposition."

"What is the difference?"

"The oppression is, forgive me, Caesar, Rome. The opposition is all those Jews who will settle for anything less than a pure Israel, utterly obedient to the law of Moses. That means anyone who has adopted Roman or Greek customs. So there are foreign enemies and home enemies."

"The zealots create terror everywhere as part of their opposition to the Romans—in the marketplace, the streets, even in the outer courts of the temple," another man said.

We would have to control this. I would inquire to Felix's replacement, Festus, about it. "I assume you are not part of the group that has assimilated," I said.

"No, although some accuse the high priest himself of being corrupted that way. But we have subsisted on nuts and figs since we have been in Rome, because we are not allowed to eat meat that might have been sacrificed to your gods."

"You *are* purists, then," I said. "I will fetch you meat straight from the pens that has never been presented to any god."

They looked uncomfortable. "With the greatest respect, we will wait until we return home and can have the meat properly butchered according to our ritual law."

What a strange, stubborn people! "Then I will make sure you have the best apples and grapes we can offer, along with the nuts and figs. And good wine. I assume you can drink that?"

After the delegation left, bowing low on their way out, I pulled Epaphroditus aside. "I need a report on exactly how unstable that region is," I said. "I want to know more about all these factions. We have a military fortress in Jerusalem with a garrison, but our prefect lives on the coast. And what is going on in the land in between?"

"Nothing good, we can assume. Lately there has arisen yet another group from this volatile stew, a group of Jews who worship a criminal that a former prefect put to death about thirty years ago. The regular Jews hate them, and so do the Romans."

"Are they violent?"

"No violence has been reported concerning them, except between themselves. They, like the regular Jews, argue about doctrine and ritual."

Oh, how tiresome! I could not imagine sensible Romans or Greeks getting into fights over Zeus or Hercules. I shrugged. "Get me a report," I said.

Back in the privacy of my rooms, all thoughts of Jerusalem faded away and I sat watching the sun's rays ebbing and withdrawing from the wall they had bathed so richly the day before at that time. The day before, when all was intact, when my world had not been shattered. But it was not truly intact, I told myself. It was already destroyed, I just had not known it.

The slow dripping of the water clock on a table nearby made time tangible. On and on it went, in one direction only, and not all the will in the world—not even the emperor's—could make the water drops flow upward and back into the clock.

LVII

There are so many prescribed remedies for pain—distraction, action, numbing oneself, escape—and I can attest that none of them work absolutely, but some work partially better than others. Perhaps I should write a treatise on this rather than the Trojan epic I am creating. Writing, itself an escape, has been a balm. The distraction of matters of state has been a blessing. Action has not been possible, as I have been too enervated. As always, music has soothed but in some ways actually worsened the pain, as it strikes so deep into the heart.

But everything ebbs in its time. Nothing is forever—not winter, not summer, not youth or even the long, slow decline of age.

People came and went; dinners were held, the Senate met, my secretaries for correspondence brought dispatches daily. There were more conferences about the Jerusalem problem, and my councilors were eager to debate it.

"The legion in Jerusalem isn't allowed to show the eagles or the images on the standards because of the prohibition against graven images in the Jewish religion," said Beryllus with a nervous laugh. "We have coddled them and mollified them in ways we never would have done with any other people. And still they complain."

"It's in their nature," said Otho. He was sitting as calmly in my council as ever. "My wife knows a lot about them. In fact, at one point she was so taken with them she thought of converting."

"Why didn't she?" asked Doryphorus.

"They make it very difficult to join them. Too many barriers. It isn't as bad for a woman as for a man, though. The men have to be circumcised."

All of us winced.

Otho said lightly, "Caesar, I am sure Poppaea would be willing to talk to us about this sect, if we invited her."

I ignored the suggestion. I resented his jaunty dismissal of what he had brought about on the boat, as if it were of no importance. Perhaps it was not to him. Or to her. It was as if he had erased it from his mind, expecting me to do the same.

"It can rest for now," I said. "What of the situation in Britain? The king of the Iceni in southeastern Britain has died and left Rome half his legacy and the rest to his two daughters."

"His will is illegal," said Seneca. "Roman law does not permit women to inherit their father's estate."

"But he isn't a Roman," I said. "What is the law in the Icenian tribe?"

"What difference does that make? He was a client king of Rome's, and the will was written to be administered in Rome," said Burrus. "Client kings retain their independence only for their lifetime. When they die, it all reverts to Rome. He knew better."

"I've called in my loans there," said Seneca. "I don't foresee any trouble, but it is too far away to have money lent out. After it's been collected I'll invest closer to home."

"We have four legions there," I said. "I've ordered one, the Fourteenth Gemina, to go west to Wales and wipe out the Druids on Mona Island. That's the heart of any future resistance to us."

Phaon, my minister of accounts and revenues, said, "I will have our agents go and collect the Icenian king's treasure and announce to the daughters that they retain none of it."

"Isn't that rather harsh?" I said. "Can we not leave them their personal jewelry and money?"

"Very well," said Phaon. "There will not be much of that. They are a simple people."

"What of the queen? Or was the king a widower?"

"There's a queen," said Burrus, pulling out his notes and thumbing through them. "Her name is Boudicca."

The days grew shorter and darker as my birthday approached. My birth was at the low point of the year, the turning point for the sun's return. I would be twenty-two. The age did not matter to me. I was not like Caesar, comparing myself to Alexander at his age. There was no other ruler like me, no one I could measure myself against. None who was an artist as well as a sovereign.

Saturnalia came on its heels two days later. Usually I hosted a party in the palace, but this year I had not planned anything; my lassitude excused me. But I received a cryptic invitation to a celebration at Petronius's villa on the night of the full moon, which fell in the middle of the Saturnalia. The invitation was delivered in a sealed box with a band that had to be cut; within was a rolled paper with instructions:

Tell no one.
Password: *Venationes.*
Bring: Your imagination.
Leave: Your inhibitions.

I turned it over and over, puzzled. But in the end I decided to go.

I made ready, choosing a warm long tunic and cloak. My hair had grown long, and it framed my face in waves. I liked Poppaea's suggestion; I no longer wanted to clip it off in imitation of Augustus. As I said, there was no one I need model myself on.

The villa was just outside the boundaries of the city, where the darkness would have been very deep if the searching white moon had not illuminated the countryside. Sharp shadows etched the reaped fallow fields and the boundary stones, making every detail visible. Around the walls of the villa torches flared and guards watched. At the gate, my head hooded, I gave the password and was allowed to pass inside.

An aisle of torches led to a huge structure—a facsimile amphitheater, made of plaster and wood. I was ushered inside, where a large group of similarly hooded and cloaked figures waited silently. The moonlight showed a number of stakes, the sort that bound prisoners in the amphitheater who awaited execution by wild beasts. Large cages were placed around the perimeters of the space.

Petronius stepped into the middle. "Greetings, all. I am honored that you have accepted my invitation to this Saturnalia celebration. And as you know, in the Saturnalia all things are reversed. So here we have a wild-beast show, but the wild beasts are—you." He gestured to his slaves, who rolled a big cart out into the arena, heaped high with animal pelts. "You may choose your animal. You can be bears, wild boars, leopards, panthers, crocodiles. But there can be only one lion." He extracted a lion skin and approached me. When he was close, he whispered, "Your hair is looking leonine these days, so this is appropriate." He draped the skin over me, arranging its maned head over mine. Then he turned back to the others. "I am the master of these games, and I make the rules. Bound to these stakes will be tonight's criminals, men and women. They will be unable to move and must wear flimsy robes, the better to be parted or ripped. Then you, the animals, will attack them, wherever you wish, but I would suggest—" He pointed to his crotch. A nervous titter spread through the crowd.

Who were these people, my fellow celebrants?

One by one, as they shed their cloaks and masks and assumed their scanty costumes, their identities were revealed. There were senators and their wives; Tigellinus; the young poet nephew of Seneca, Lucan; Senecio; Vitellius; Doryphorus; and Piso and his wife; as well as twenty or so others. Last of all to unmask were Otho and Poppaea.

"Again, at a Saturnalia, all things are reversed. The *venationes* take place in the morning, but this is night. The emperor goes first, but here he shall go last. So, let us begin. To your cages!" He led five men, including Tigellinus, who had chosen to be a bear, to their cages. They crouched down and entered. In the meantime, other guests, several men and women, had been bound to stakes, draped in filmy gowns and tunics. Petronius signaled and a gong sounded. Slaves opened the cages and the men crawled out, growling and snarling.

They seemed truly transformed into beasts and leapt upon the captive people, going for their necks, which they bit and sucked, then they clawed at their clothes, tearing them away. They licked and chewed on them everywhere, while the victims shrieked in false pain, but really (it soon became clear) in squealing ecstasy. Finally the beasts collapsed at the foot of the stakes, fully dispatched, and the prisoners were untied and carried away, limp from their pleasure.

Others took their places and the procedure was repeated. Lucan was a leopard and he twined himself sensuously around Piso's wife, Atria, while Piso himself, a crocodile, fondled and slobbered on one of the other senator's wives. Perhaps he had always wanted to.

Slowly the number of waiting people dwindled, and those who had finished were drinking and watching. Flickering torches and the moonlight competed to lighten the ground, red tinting the bright white light. Finally the last were led out to the stakes. Poppaea was bound to the middle one. Otho, who had not donned an animal skin, stood watching from the side. The other "victims"—an elderly senator; a slender slave girl; a burly legionary; Marcella, the wife of a senator—did not interest me. All I could see was Poppaea, crowned in silver light, her head held high.

I was included in this round as an animal, and I crouched in my cage, waiting for the gong. Then I emerged, first on all fours, approaching the stake slowly, deliberately. I could see her bare feet, smooth like a statue's, at the base. Then I rose up, not quite a leap, and went for her throat.

The touch of her skin against my lips set something off within me. Part of me wanted revenge for what she and Otho had done to me; another part ached to repeat it. She stood still, not responding at all, truly like a statue, but a warm one.

"How dared you?" I breathed in her ear.

But she did not answer or indicate that she had even heard me. Cruel goddess. Since I had leave to do whatever I wished, I pressed myself up against her, the heavy lion's pelt I wore cushioning whatever I could have felt. Under cover of the pelt, I kissed her belly, her thighs, all of her. I was intoxicated by her. But in the end I pulled away and motioned for one of the *venatores* to slay her while I stood by.

"And that, dear friends, brings to a conclusion our executions by wild beasts," said Petronius as the victims were freed from the stakes. "But, oh! That is not the end of our entertainment. No, no. For tonight you are privileged to witness a wedding, the like of which you have never seen."

He motioned to his slaves to bring out a chest, which they set down on the sand. With a flourish, he opened it and brought out a wedding veil, flowers, and a ring. To my shock, he approached me with them.

"In the Saturnalia, there is no male or female, no emperor or slave, no bachelor or married man, no virgin or whore. All is fluid. Therefore, I invite you to become a bride." He held out the marriage veil to me. "And you, Doryphorus, will marry this lovely maiden."

Why not? I put on the flame-colored veil, went through a mock ceremony with Petronius officiating, and afterward, when we were led to a little shelter, gave loud shrieks and cries like the proverbial virgin on her wedding night. Other people also went through mock ceremonies, men marrying men, women marrying women, and already married people marrying others. Whether they carried the pretense further and consummated the marriages I cannot say, for false yelps and moans sound like the real thing.

I saw Poppaea and Otho by the refreshment table and walked over to them. Surely now they would finally say something about that night. But no, they just smiled at me and said nothing. I wanted to shatter their infuriating equanimity. Were they partners in tormenting me? They had cost me dear.

"That was interesting," I said. "Otho, you did not participate."

"I prefer to watch."

"There is a name for that," I said.

"Doubtless," he said, still smiling.

"Poppaea, I would like to speak to you. Come to my palace apartments tomorrow."

Otho's smile faded. But Poppaea's expression did not change.

The night was far gone by the time I returned to the city, but I arose at dawn and called for certain record books, which I pored over, searching for particular information. When I was satisfied with what I had found, I asked Epaphroditus to fetch me some things from the archives and treasury. Then I went to the baths to steam all the impurities out of my skin, extract the fatigue from my limbs, and spread invisible balm over my overwrought brain. Floating in the hot water, I kept at bay the question: why did I ask Poppaea to come see me? What could possibly be achieved by that? I was tempted to send a messenger, canceling the appointment, but that would make me seem indecisive and unreliable—not ideal traits for an emperor. I would see her and end this strange silent tormenting ménage à trois between her, Otho, and me.

She appeared in the late morning, was announced by my secretary, and walked in as if she was strolling on a country road, not the marble floor of the palace. "I am here," she announced needlessly, untwining the thin veil that covered her hair and face.

"So I see," I said, rising to meet her. She retained no hint of weariness or lack of sleep, and, so I noted, no trace of any marks on her neck.

She waited, saying nothing further. Outside, a crow gave a rasping caw and then choked, and we both laughed.

"He ate too much," she said. Without asking, she went to the window and looked out. The crow was madly flapping to retain his balance on the branch. We laughed again.

"I've seen some senators do just that," I said. "And they don't always get back on their feet."

Our laughter died. I sat down and motioned for her to do the same, then held my silence. Usually that made people nervous and gave me the upper hand, but it did not seem to affect her. "I was reading some reports on Moesia," I said, as if it was the most natural topic in the world, "and came across mention of your illustrious grandfather who served as proconsul there under Tiberius."

She continued to look calmly at me. "Yes?"

"I wanted to learn more about the province. Rome is considering expanding farther into the surrounding area. The reports from those years are spotty. Did your family, by chance, ever discuss it? Do you retain any correspondence from those years?"

"My grandfather died when I was five, and he died in Moesia. We visited him once there, but I have no memories of it, or of him. But my mother, if she were alive, could tell you more."

"The elder Poppaea," I said. "A victim of Messalina. I, too, was a would-be victim of Messalina, but she failed with me." Poppaea's mother had been forced to commit suicide over the false accusations of Messalina.

"Those were bad times," she said. "But we survivors have a common bond and can rejoice together to be walking this earth, while our enemies Messalina and Sejanus lie beneath it."

"Your grandfather sent items back from Moesia over the years, and these were deposited in the archives and treasury of Rome." I handed her a box of coins, minted in Moesia during the time her grandfather had been governor. A second box held a gold honorary Ovation medal that had been awarded to him by Tiberius for putting down a revolt in Thrace.

She took them, opening the lids with a graceful motion, and stirred the coins with her finger. She stroked the medal. She smiled. "Thank you. It is very thoughtful of you. Now I shall have to think of a gift for you, but what can a simple person give an emperor?" Her eyes seemed to bore into mine.

"A tour of Pompeii," I said hastily. "Is not your family from Pompeii? Sometime when I am in Baiae"—but when would I ever want to go there again, even for her?—"perhaps you can show your hometown to me."

"Gladly," she said.

The meeting was ended. There was nothing more to say or do. I had failed to change anything or end anything or even understand anything between us three. Impulsively I added, "Otho says you know a great deal about Judaism. Perhaps I shall consult with you about that." That would be useful, at least.

"I would be pleased," she said. On her way out, she said, "In answer to the question you did not ask, I did want what happened on the boat back into Rome, and I have not forgotten it, nor ever will. In answer to the other question you did not ask, I do love Otho." She was almost out the door when she turned and added, "I am pleased you took my advice about your hair. It flatters you."

LVIII

New Year's Day, and once again I sat on the Rostra in the Forum with Octavia and accepted the pledge of loyalty from the legions far and wide. We wore the customary white robes with gold thread and accepted the pledges, our breath making white puffs in the cold air.

Octavia sat stiffly; I might as well have put a statue in her seat. I had not seen her in many months. I looked over at her and attempted a smile; she gave me a tentative one back. Then we continued sitting in silence.

It was painful to sit next to this person who had shared much of my childhood and was bound to me by politics now obsolete and super-seded. But she was not the innocent that people assumed. There was her attempt to murder me, let me never forget. But in the world we lived in, that was just business as usual. We were not like other people; I must not forget that as well. Something that Acte could never understand, to our sorrow.

Ranks and ranks of legionaries and their centurions stretched before us, in lines straighter than any plowed field, their precision a reflection of their organization and training. And these were just a token, a sample, of the entire army. I felt a surge of surprising excitement wondering what it would feel like to lead such men, to be a conqueror. I did have the blood of Germanicus in my veins, as well as Marc Antony. Some of it had survived to pulse strongly through me now.

I leaned over to Octavia; under cover of the trumpets sounding the end of the ceremony I said, "It is necessary that we divorce."

She turned and looked at me. "As far as I am concerned, we are already divorced."

"Not in the eyes of the law," I said. "We need to formalize what has long since happened in practice."

"I concur," she said. And she turned away to look at the troops again, presenting her clean profile to me.

Burrus and Seneca did not concur. Meeting with them one chilly morning in my warmest small business chamber, I was unpleasantly surprised when Burrus crossed his arms and said, "Then give her back her dowry!"

"Gladly," I said. "Whatever it was, lands or gold or gems, I will happily grant so we can be free of one another."

"Her dowry is her inheritance as the emperor's daughter," said Seneca. "Her marriage to you cemented your claim to the throne, which was shaky."

"Shaky? I am a direct descendant of Augustus."

"So are Decimus and young Lucius Silanus of the Torquatus family. And Rubellius Plautus comes close to that, being descended from Octavia and Tiberius. But only you were the son of the reigning Augusta and the adopted son of the emperor and his son-in-law as well. That is what put you where you are. Do you want to jerk that foundation out from under yourself?"

That and a dose of Locusta's poison put me where I am, I thought. "All that is in the past. I have been emperor now for over five years; my position is secure. Whatever is, people come to accept it."

"Some people," said Seneca. "Others see an opening for themselves. As I said, there are many descendants of Augustus."

Too many. Augustus was a brilliant statesman, giving king-phobic Rome a king under another name—Princeps—First Citizen. But by pretending there was no monarchy, there could be no official line of succession. Instead, the throne went to the cleverest manipulator with the right pedigree—as Mother had proved. And that meant that within a certain circle, there were many potential contenders for it. The habit of the noble families' intermarriage only deepened the competition, as at every generation the pool of descendants of either Augustus himself, his sister Octavia, or his wife Livia increased. They had to be constantly watched and guarded against, lest they make a threatening move. And many were eliminated by means both fair and foul. It was dangerous to possess that blood.

"I cannot be bound to this forever! I am only twenty-two! If I live as long as Tiberius, that means another sixty years of this sham marriage."

Burrus gave a cough and rubbed his throat. "It is a small thing to endure. You can have any mistress you want. Or several."

"I don't want a mistress, I want a genuine wife. I want a legitimate heir, not a bastard from a mistress. Octavia cannot give me a child. She is barren." Not that I had given her much opportunity to prove otherwise.

Seneca frowned. "Since boyhood, you have had foolish and romantic notions. So far none have cost you much—the singing at the Juvenalia did not damage you—"

Damage me! It created me anew!

"—but this is different. She is popular with the people, and divorcing her will alienate them."

"The people don't know anything about her. She is a cipher to them."

"The better to project their own ideas onto her, then," said Seneca. "That is what people do—what they imagine is more powerful than what is really there."

He sighed. "I am tired. I would like your leave to retire. I have served Rome for many years and now would like to spend my remaining time in quiet seclusion and study." He did look old and hunched.

"I am not ready to release you," I said. "I still value your wise counsel."

"But you don't take it," he said.

◆ ◆ ◆

Other meetings followed, as the days slowly warmed. I let the divorce simmer; sooner or later the two old councilors would come to accept it. I put the word about that it was being promulgated, as much to test public reaction as anything else.

Seneca's hopes of retirement quashed for the time being, he and Burrus turned their attention to matters outside Rome, and there were three of them—Britain, Armenia, and Judea.

I made it my business to gather all the information I could about Britain, reading reports in the archives, studying the correspondence, and interviewing military commanders. Just as I did with legal cases I had to judge, I wanted to garner knowledge on my own before further consulting with others.

Although we claimed that Julius Caesar had conquered Britain over a hundred years before, he had merely landed and done some reconnaissance. Caligula had planned an invasion that never happened. It was Claudius's generals who finally got Roman troops across the channel and staked out Roman territory there, roughly the southern third of the island. What we found there were tribes who farmed and raised livestock, drove horse chariots, made jewelry, had a structured aristocracy and royalty, but would still be judged barbarian. Eleven tribal kings had submitted and pledged loyalty to Rome, and we had set up Camulodunum in the east as our Roman capital and headquarters. There was also a town on the river Thames, at its first crossable point, called Londinium and another north of it called Verulamium. Retired soldiers settled at Camulodunum and soon the town had Roman amenities, such as a theater, forum, and a magnificent temple dedicated to Claudius. We appointed two Britons annually to serve as priests in the temple. This had worked well in Gaul, binding the native temple priests to Roman culture.

Although there were a multitude of tribes, there were three main ones with jurisdiction over the others: the Iceni and the Regni in eastern Britain under Rome, and the Brigantes outside our territory in the north.

We had four legions stationed there: the Fourteenth Gemina Martia Victrix, the Second Augusta, the Ninth Hispana, and the Twentieth Valeria Victrix. All was quiet, or relatively so, except that the native religious cultists, the Druids, were violently hostile to us. Their stronghold was on their sacred island of Mona in northwestern Wales.

Their priests perform human sacrifices in the groves where they worship their gods. They butcher their victims on an altar for augury and study their entrails. They collect booty and tithes from far corners of the island. They employ powerful magic and are the lawgivers and judges of tribes. Noble sons are sent to study with them, and followers make pilgrimages to the sacred island from as far away as Gaul. They give resistance fighters sanctuary.

Thus said a report filed in the archives. I shuddered. These Druids were the main source of resistance against Rome, and Augustus had made it illegal for Roman citizens to follow the Druid religion; Claudius had banned the religion entirely, for citizens and noncitizens, throughout the empire. But it still held power in Britain.

So I had ordered our governor, General Gaius Suetonius Paulinus, to go to Mona and wipe out the Druids once and for all. He led the Fourteenth Legion west as soon as the spring mud had subsided and we were now awaiting news of his campaign.

In another region of the island, the southeastern, there had been the unfortunate business of the Icenian king Prasutagus's death and his invalid will. Presumably the agents of the procurator, Catus Decianus, had delivered the unwelcome news and transferred the title to Rome and settled with the family. I reviewed the case and thought it possible that we could restore some independence to the Iceni rather than so abruptly terminating the tribe's rule. The widow, Boudicca, should be approached. But we had had a difficult time dealing with another British royal widow, Cartimandua of the Brigantes, so perhaps it was not a route to be pursued.

I remembered the fair-haired Britons brought here for Claudius's

Triumph, pale skins and icy blue eyes. But from the reports, many others were ruddy, bushy bearded, and freckled. And with a penchant for body painting in lurid colors, running about bare chested. I opened a box stored in the archives with objects from Britain and spread them out before me. There were bronze drinking cups, with handles of swimming ducks with inlaid red enamel eyes, exquisitely modeled. Did they drink wine or beer from them, or some native intoxicating beverage? I turned one over in my hands, trying to imagine who had held it over there. There were silver coins with horse, boar, triangle, and portraits of people. One of them was labeled by its Roman curator "Prasutagus." He looked young. Now there would be no king to mint Icenian coins. This was the last. There were three heavy, rigid gold necklaces, circular except for one opening, labeled "torque." Apparently the tribes there used them to signify their wealth, and indeed there was a lot of gold in them. I was tempted to take one, but I had no woman to bestow it on. Not now. Acte was gone, and she did not fancy gold in any case. It could not win her back, to my sorrow. But once I held it in my hands I could not put it back. It possessed a power of its own. Perhaps I would wear it myself. Apparently they were worn in Britain by both men and women. I took it back to the palace, its smooth gold arc warm in my hand.

I had planned to visit the baths that afternoon. Since their opening they had been enormously popular, and the especially hot water I had ordered for the *caldarium* had proved a draw. After that I would exercise in the yard next door, happy that warm weather allowed us outside again.

But as I was instructing my slave to gather up the bath items, the strigils, oils, and towels to take along, another slave appeared at the threshold—one of Burrus's.

"Caesar, my master urgently requests your presence in the council chamber."

Damn! If only I had already left. I was yearning for the waters of the baths.

"Tell him I will come in the late afternoon," I said. I would not be deterred.

"It is most pressing," he said. "My master is distraught."

Burrus? Distraught? Never in my experience. "Very well," I said, sighing.

Burrus was pacing the room when I arrived. His choppy hair was mussed as he was running his hands through it aimlessly. His riveting blue eyes stared at me, almost unseeing. Only after I looked around the room did I see the dusty military messenger sitting on a stool. On the worktable were dispatches, unrolled and held open with weights.

"What is it?" I asked the messenger, as Burrus still had not spoken.

"Britain," he said. His voice was a croak. "Rebellion. Massacres. Bloody." He pointed to the dispatches. "All the details."

"Tell me first," I ordered. "It will take too long to read them now. Just relate the main story and I will then read the details. Burrus, come here and sit down." I motioned to the slaves stationed around the room. "Bring us some wine."

Stiffly, Burrus obeyed and sank down on a stool.

"Now, one thing at a time. The beginning," I ordered the messenger.

"Last autumn procurator Catus Decianus sent agents to the Iceni to take their property and transfer it into Roman hands," he rasped. "Queen Boudicca refused and resisted. So they confiscated the property of the other leading families and returned later with a larger contingent of enforcers. They then stripped the queen—"

"What? They stripped the queen?"

"It is the standard punishment for resistance." Burrus finally found his voice. "Stripping and beating with rods."

"So they stripped her and flogged her in front of her people," the messenger continued. "And then they—they got carried away with vengeance—and raped her two daughters. Then they arrested all the king's male relatives to sell into slavery."

"What?" Could I be hearing correctly? "They raped the princesses? Girls under the protection of their mother, a queen?"

"It is un-Roman," admitted Burrus. "Except when they are slated for execution, as it is illegal in Roman law to execute a virgin."

"Execution? *They* shall be executed! I want the names of the men who did this. They will be punished—executed for shaming Rome so. No stripping and flogging for them." I was so angry I would have strangled them myself.

"They are probably already dead, Caesar, so there can be no vengeance from us. Not on those men. But it is almost certain they have paid the price."

"Explain yourself," I said.

"The bloodied queen pulled herself up from the dirt and vowed revenge, calling on the war goddess Andraste. And quietly, over the winter, she gathered forces from not only her own people but from the neighboring Trinovantes and other tribes who also had grievances against Rome. They resented the very presence of the huge Temple of Claudius and being taxed for it, and the two persons selected as priests there had to bear the expenses of the office that they didn't even want. Furthermore, the agents had demanded repayment of the money Claudius had distributed to them when they submitted, renaming it a loan rather than a gift. And, last, Seneca's calling in his huge loans so suddenly was more than they could pay."

Burrus pointed to something in the report. "She was very clever. She knew all the movements of our troops, even which legions were filled with raw and inexperienced recruits, and exactly when they were due to replace the veterans who would retire, taking their expertise with them. She waited until Paulinus and the Fourteenth were tied up in Wales, far away, to strike."

"How many people does she have?" I asked.

"One place in the report says one hundred and twenty thousand to start with," said Burrus, who seemed to have recovered his wits and was once again the soldier.

Oh, gods! "And us? Were we not at four-legion strength?"

"Were," said Burrus. "No longer."

"The Ninth—" began the messenger.

"Let me tell it now," said Burrus. "In the proper order." He took a deep breath. "Boudicca's army consists of chariots, warriors armed with massive shields, made of oak planks covered with hide, and spears. They are not trained to fight in formation but en masse. They descended on Camulodunum, our colony and capital, which had no defenses—we trusted the people!—and savagely destroyed it. The retired soldiers of the Fourteenth and the small guard left behind barricaded themselves inside the Temple of Claudius, along with townspeople. Boudicca surrounded it and, acting on informers' information, her warriors overran the temple, set it on fire, and burned the people inside alive. Then they attacked the town, killing men, women, children, Romans, yes, but anyone who had been associated with Rome."

He reached for the wine and downed a cup before continuing. "Prisoners were taken to an open area and tortured and killed. Some were burned alive, others crucified, others hanged. Men and boys had their genitals cut off, women had their breasts cut off and sewed into their mouths, then were impaled on stakes. The British women who had married Romans, particularly centurions, got the worst treatment. But children suffered the same as their parents." He poured another cup of wine as if to rinse out his mouth. "Then they had a wild sex party, in the name of their war goddess Andraste." He spit out the wine into a saucer.

"But that is not all," said the messenger. "Next they went to Londinium, where there were also no walls or defenses, and repeated the massacres. The Romans had abandoned the Londoners and they had to fend for themselves. All the merchants left, so there was not a single ship in the docks. Only the old, sick, and stubborn stayed behind. Meanwhile, the procurator Decianus abandoned Britain and fled to Gaul."

"Is that all? Are you finished?" I asked. I was beyond stunned. Now I knew why Burrus had been speechless.

"No," said Burrus. "The Ninth Hispana came down from a hundred miles north to help Camulodunum but were ambushed by Boudicca and annihilated." He winced and rubbed his throat. "And the Second Augusta, ordered to meet up with Paulinus's Fourteenth, refused the order and stayed put in the far west. So all we have to face Boudicca, whose army has now grown to well over two hundred thousand, is the men of the Fourteenth. She has destroyed Verulamium about thirty miles north of London, as she has anything in her path. Altogether seventy thousand people have been killed. All of the province now lies in the hands of the insurgents. The only thing standing between us and the total loss of Britain is Paulinus's Fourteenth and the soldiers of the Twentieth that are with it. Perhaps ten thousand men—against two hundred and thirty thousand. Odds of twenty-three to one."

LIX

Clutching the dispatches, I reeled back to my apartments, seeing the burning towns and hearing the screams of the victims—victims whose only crime was to be Roman, or to have cooperated with Romans. I rushed into my innermost room, the one where no one could enter or disturb me—unless Boudicca herself stormed them.

Boudicca. Who was this woman, to lead an army? Feverishly, I unrolled the scrolls and scoured them for information about her. The dispatches were detailed, and I would read every word later, but for now I sought only to know my adversary. For she was my adversary as surely as if we faced one another in person. And so far I had never been vanquished by an adversary; I had always outsmarted or outmaneuvered every one of them. But this was different.

Finally I found a description. It said she was tall, fierce, and uncommonly intelligent. That she had masses of waist-length tawny hair and wore a gold necklace (like the one I had brought from the archives?), brightly colored patterned cloaks, and brooches. That she had a harsh voice, which she used to address her followers. A speech was included—she was a stirring speaker.

As I read it I had to admit she was a born leader. She would make anyone want to follow her, as she spoke meaningfully about liberty and freedom, and she knew how to appeal to the people not as their queen but as a fellow sufferer under the yoke of Rome. To aid her speech in effectiveness, she brandished a spear.

I am descended from mighty men! But now I am not fighting for my kingdom and wealth. I am fighting as an ordinary person for my lost freedom, my bruised body, and my outraged daughters. Nowadays Roman rapacity does not even spare our bodies. Old people are killed, virgins raped. But the gods will grant us the vengeance we deserve! The Roman division which dared to fight is annihilated. The others cower in their camps, or watch for a chance to escape. They will never face even the din and roar of all our thousands, much less the shock of our onslaught. Consider how many of you are fighting—and why. Then you will win this battle, or perish. That is what I, a woman, plan to do!—let the men live in slavery if they will.

It moved *me*, the enemy she was facing. I read on.

Have no fear whatever of the Romans; for they are superior to us neither in number nor in bravery. Indeed, we enjoy such a surplus of bravery that we regard our tents as safer than their walls and our shields as providing greater protection than their whole suits of mail.

But these are not the only respects in which they are vastly inferior to us: There is also the fact that they cannot bear up under hunger, thirst, cold, or heat, as we can. They require shade and covering, they require kneaded bread and wine and oil, and if any of these things fail them, they perish. For us, on the other hand, any grass or root serves as bread, the juice of any plant as oil, any water as wine, any tree as a house. Therefore, let us show them that they are hares and foxes trying to rule over dogs and wolves.

She then practiced some sort of divination by letting a hare loose from folds in her cloak and, interpreting it as favorable, thanked Andraste.

I thank thee, Andraste, and I call upon thee as woman speaking to woman; for I rule over no burden-bearing Egyptians as did Nitocris, nor over trafficking Assyrians as did Semiramis, much less over the Romans themselves as did Messalina once and, afterward, Agrippina, and now Nero, who, though in name a man, is in fact a woman, as is proved by his singing, lyre playing, and beautification of his person—

My eyes bulged out when I read this. Calling me a woman!

I pray thee for victory against men insolent, unjust, insatiable, impious—if indeed we ought to term these people men who bathe in warm water, eat artificial dainties, drink unmixed wine, anoint themselves with myrrh, sleep on soft couches with boys for bedfellows—boys past their prime, at that—and are slaves to a lyre player, and a poor one, too. Wherefore may this Mistress Domitia-Nero reign no longer over me or over you men; let the wench sing and lord it over Romans, for they surely deserve to be the slaves of such a woman after having submitted to her for so long.

I almost dropped the scroll. I wanted to say, *How dare she?* But this was war, and any invective must serve to be marshaled against the enemy, as Augustus had done to Antony. But to say I was a poor lyre player—! Oh, she was clever and, like all great warriors, knew exactly how to wound. We each commanded thousands, but she had made it personal, one enemy staring down the other across all the miles, the armies behind us fading to pale in the background. She would see what this lyre player could do, and regret her words.

I had more of the temper of Germanicus and of Antony than I had recognized. Now all hinged on the confrontation between the two armies in Britain. For the first time ever, I longed to lead troops, to clash with the enemy. But all that was out of my hands. I had to rest my trust and hopes on what resources I had already placed there. There was no time even to send reinforcements from Germany; in fact, the battle may have already taken place.

And if it had? If we had lost? Then I would be the first emperor to lose a province. Oh, the shame of it. It was not to be borne. We could not lose. We could not lose. We could not lose.

Days passed; days in which we waited for a messenger bringing news. It would come by the swiftest military post possible, but it would still take nine days at best. I had memorized the dispatches, memorized every detail of the battles—the tactics, the chronology, the geography. The question was, where would the armies finally come to engage? Paulinus was a cautious but steely general and he would try to find a way to neutralize the great numbers of his foe. That had been done in Greece, in the battles of Salamis and Thermopylae against the Persians. The trick was to get them into a position where they could not maneuver, where their numbers conferred no advantage, rather the opposite.

But the countryside of Britain was mainly flat, with a few rolling hills, and forested, except in cleared farmland. It would be difficult to find a place to box them in. And would Paulinus retreat, withdrawing back toward Wales, luring them on? If he retreated too far, he would have the Welsh at his back and be trapped.

But the farther he lured her, the farther she would come into unfamiliar territory and lose her advantage of intimate knowledge of the terrain. He must find exactly the right balance. It might take a long time to play out.

Any commander knew to choose the site most advantageous to his strengths, and any foe knew to prevent this. But knowing is not doing.

I hardly slept during those days. For it was days and days—twenty since the first news—before a trembling messenger knelt before me and handed me a sealed dispatch. I took it, oddly calm, and withdrew into my rooms. I put it down on the marble table, where it rolled a little way before stopping. The brass container glinted in the morning sun. Within that vial lay the truth. Such a small and innocent-looking instrument, with momentous contents. But the same can be said for a bottle of poison, or a gold box with an enormous ruby.

I let it sit there for several moments, as if to touch it was dangerous, as if it housed a ferocious creature. Which it did: my future, and the pride of Rome. Finally, chiding myself, I opened it. Unrolled it. A very long missive. Words, words, words.

> *Better for us to fall fighting bravely than to be captured and impaled . . . frontline standard-bearer . . . Jupiter Best and Greatest, protect this unit, soldiers all . . . tree-lined plain . . . Cavalry . . . Form wedge . . .*

My eyes raced down the scroll, searching, leaping over the phrases, till, breathless, I read:

> *The day is ours. Casualties: four hundred Romans, seventy thousand Britons.*

I put it down, let it rest, still unrolled. We had won. Britain was still ours. And I would not be remembered as the emperor who lost a province. I thanked the gods, at first wordlessly, then murmured, "Jupiter, Mars, I am grateful forever, forever and ever."

With Burrus and the Consilium and senior officers of the army, all the details were discussed and recorded. The battle had taken place some ten days after the burning of Verulamium, twenty to thirty miles farther north. Paulinus had been searching for the right terrain to take his stand and another day's march northwest would have put him too close to Wales. He found what he was looking for: a narrow defile with a dense forest in back of it and a wide-open plain before it. He would place his men in the narrow part, after having secured the forest behind him. The forest would preclude the use of the British war chariots, and the narrow defile would cause a bottleneck and prevent the large army from spreading into a frontal array.

"He was damn lucky to find that spot," said Burrus. "Britain isn't like Greece, with its handy hills and gorges."

Boudicca's army had not only its warriors but the families of the warriors, who had followed in wagons. These drew up in a semicircle at the back of the plain.

"And here was where the gods proved they were looking out for us and not them," said Senator Vibius Procolus, a former army legate.

The Britons had employed their usual procedure: In her chariot, Boudicca rode around the army with her last instructions and exhortations. In the front rank of the fighters were the chariots, then the tribesmen. Paulinus had ordered his troops not to move until the chariots had come and gone. At Boudicca's signal, the charioteers raced forward across the plain and launched their spears at the Fourteenth, who were waiting stolid and motionless for them, a line of soldiers across the defile with the cavalry filling the remaining gaps on either side. When those missiles were spent, hurled fruitlessly against the wall of Roman shields, and the chariots wheeled away, the tribesmen rushed toward the Romans, yelling unearthly cries and wails.

Under Paulinus's orders, the Romans waited until the Britons were fairly close before they threw their first javelins, felling many. The Britons kept coming, and now the Romans threw their second, heavier javelins, felling even more. Still the waves of Britons kept rushing forward, but now there was a barrier of the newly dead piled before them.

Then the trumpets blared the signal and Paulinus cried, "Form wedge!" Next the trumpets sounded, "Advance!" and slowly, methodically, the front line moved forward, three wedges, wading out into the enemy.

"The wedge is the secret," said Burrus. "It can slice through anything."

And indeed it had, dividing the Britons into smaller sections, sections that could be attacked from either side of the wedge. The Romans kept protected behind their shields, slashing with their swords around the shields, marching ever forward, stepping on the dead, pushing the Britons tight against one another, where they could not free their spears or shields or even move, while the Roman cavalry used their javelins as lances to hem them in. Back and back they were forced, until they hit the still-oncoming warriors. Then they were halted, and the back line began to retreat, seeking space, but there was none to be had.

"Their wagons trapped them with nowhere to retreat. They were hemmed in, pushed up against their own families, while the Fourteenth kept coming, bodies falling all around them," said Senator Quinctius Valerianus, rereading the dispatch, shaking his head.

"The wedge is formidable," said Burrus. "But it requires rigorous discipline and training, which the Britons didn't have. They were brave, yes, but bravery alone can't win a battle. Discipline and practice will."

The entire tumultuous and consequential battle had taken only an hour or two. At the end the corpses lay strewn all over the field. The Romans did not bury them but left them for a warning.

"Boudicca," I said. "What happened to her?" That had not been in the report.

"She disappeared. No one knows," said Burrus.

That was fitting. I would not want to see her in chains, paraded in Rome as a prisoner. She was too fine and fierce for that. A worthy adversary, one I admired. I wanted to imagine she survived and could rest in the knowledge that she would be legendary.

But the lyre player had won.

Perhaps I would compose a song about her. She had surely earned her poetic remembrance, even if she would not have wanted it from me.

LX

I was proud to address all the Praetorians, and indeed all of Rome, announcing our victory. For their courage and steadfastness I pronounced the Fourteenth Legion Rome's "most effective," transforming them into Homeric heroes. From then on, admirers would flock to them when they marched, flinging flowers and gifts in their path. Highest honors went to their commander, Paulinus, the man who'd saved a province.

"Just by the skin of our teeth," said Tigellinus, as we sat discussing it in my office. "A near miss. But now we will grasp it firmly, squeeze it until it gasps for air and goes limp."

That was already an issue of contention. The general pattern of Rome was to be vindictive in victory. We burned cities, turned the inhabitants into slaves, plundered and looted. In Britain we had lost seventy thousand people, and Paulinus had seen it with his own eyes. In such a case, it is almost impossible to be magnanimous; the siren song of revenge calls. But the Britons were suffering from a severe famine as well as the loss of so many people.

Paulinus and militant Romans argued that if the Britons were starving, it was their own fault, for they sowed but did not reap their crops; they made war instead. But all these harsh reprisals would merely sow another crop—one of festering bitterness that would break out into rebellion again. I believed the way to terminate opposition was not to oppose and punish it but to smother it with a gentle hand.

"Terrible as it is, we are even in our losses," I reminded Tigellinus. "They lost seventy thousand, we lost seventy thousand. Now that we have mourned them, we must learn to live together."

"Bah," he said. "The only thing a vicious dog understands is beating. Break its spirit so it doesn't attack again."

"People are not animals. They can plan ahead, and, unlike a dog, if they cannot get revenge, they can teach their children to do it after them."

He shrugged. The tough horse trainer saw life only in the simplest direct terms. But I had decided that if Paulinus did not alter his course, I would recall him and replace him, hero or not. I wanted this to be the last rebellion in Britain. And I would gamble on my conviction of the way to prevent it, just as Paulinus had gambled on his battleground strategy. There was no point in winning a battle, as the saying goes, if we ultimately lost the war.

The people of Rome rejoiced at the news of our victory in far-off Britain and celebrations erupted all over the city. Graffiti appeared on buildings trumpeting our triumph, made all the more jubilant by the closeness of defeat. Wherever I went I was hailed as Imperator— Victorious Supreme Commander—and I would be lying if I said I did not relish it. So this was what it felt like to be a conquering general.

There would be no Triumph, though. There had not been one since Claudius's all those years ago, and before that, none for some thirty years, when Germanicus had one. Although the saving of the province was vital, I did not think it seemly to claim a Triumph. Someday, perhaps, I would ride through the streets in the chariot of Augustus and look down at the spot where I had stood as a child watching Claudius pass, but it would be for a different place. And I must first have set foot in the land I was claiming.

October again, now the sixth anniversary of my accession. And it was time, time for me to inaugurate my program of bringing Greece to Rome. I announced, as a celebration of my accession, Greek games modeled on the Delphic and Olympic contests, to be named the Neronia and treated as a sacred occasion. This new festival would be a five-year occurrence in Rome from now on.

There was the usual grumbling from Burrus and Seneca, but for the most part people were enthusiastic, even the Senate. The festival would be divided into three parts—athletic, artistic, and equestrian. Athletic would feature racing, jumping, wrestling, and gymnastics. Artistic would include music, oratory, and poetry. Equestrian would of course have chariot racing, with two-, four-, and six-horse teams. Ex-consuls, drawn by lot, would preside; I would merely attend. Formal Greek dress was required for the audience. It was time to free ourselves from the restrictions of the toga. Loose, free-flowing tunics and cloaks would replace Roman garb, with its stripes and colors indicating rank and class. I myself would wear a linen tunic in sea blue, a far cry from imperial purple.

I had invited my old instructor Apollonius to join me for the athletic portion of the Neronia. I had not seen him in many years and was relieved when my invitation found him, and found him in good health. I was sitting with the senators and hailed him as he arrived, delighted to see his face again. He stood and looked at me; the years showed on him but he was by no means old.

"Little Marcus," he said with a grin, "how you have changed!"

"And how you have not," I said, showing him his seat. "Welcome."

"You fooled me all those years ago, and I am not easily fooled," he said, shaking his head. "My pupil the emperor."

"I did not deceive you," I said. "I was—I still am—earnest about athletics."

"But your competing days are over," he said.

"I am not sure of that," I said. "It is difficult to watch something I love and not participate."

"They have to be over," he said. "No one can win against the emperor."

"Then perhaps I will have to disguise myself."

"There is no disguise that is not revealed," he said. "No one will risk beating the emperor. So you are doomed to never truly know your worth on the field of competition."

His words were cruel, and true. As they had always been. He truly had not changed. "Honest, as always," I said. "But you must know, when little Marcus trained with you, he was not an emperor or anything beyond a little boy who had scant happiness except what you gave him. Remember that always—I do."

"You were my best pupil," he said. "As you said, I am honest and that is true. I was sorry when you had to leave, but I understood why."

For those few minutes I was back there again, in those dark days when my only two lights—Crispus and Apollonius—left my life.

"Do you like being emperor?" he asked suddenly.

What a strange question, with such an obvious answer. "Yes. Of course I do."

The gymnastics contest was beginning, and the Vestal Virgins took their designated places in the front row. In homage to the priestess of Demeter, who observed the Olympic Games, I had invited them to come.

"I think you are cruel," whispered Apollonius. "To make these virgins sit and look at shining muscular male bodies for hours."

"They are supposed to be above such longings," I said.

"Perhaps you are still a bit naïve, Marcus," he said, laughing.

The wrestling was especially exciting, with the two contestants evenly matched.

"It is going to be a dustless victory," said Apollonius, meaning a bout in which no one was thrown and got sand on his body.

I leapt up and went to the edge of the ring to watch more closely. I stayed out of bounds, but it was almost as if I was in the ring myself.

"I am sure your looming over them distracted them," said Apollonius later. "But I can see that you long to get back in there yourself."

It was torture to just sit and watch. He knew me very well. I nodded. And contented myself from then on to watch the events from a distance. But I enjoyed being in the audience. I looked around. I was pleased; surrounded by crowds in Greek clothing, I could almost believe I was in Greece itself. Someday I would go there, but for now, this must do. And it gave me great satisfaction to know I had created the occasion, transplanted it intact from its native land.

The chariot races were a great success, and a team from Sicily won the prize for the four-horse race, the most popular one. The charioteer was exceptionally skilled and he handled the horses as if they were extensions of himself. It was a pleasure to award the crown to him.

There were fewer six-horse teams and they were slower, but they required more strength and dexterity to control them, so they made for good races. Being wider, they took up more space on the track, so the number competing at any one time was limited, hence more heats. The opposite applied to the two-horse races, the fastest of all.

The last contests were the artistic, slated for the final three days. I enjoyed the oratory contests; listening to a polished speaker is always a pleasure. Odd how all men can talk but few can speak in an entertaining or attention-getting manner. That is a gift few are born with; the rest have to train.

Next came the poetry contests. Several from my literary group competed, including Lucan, Seneca's nephew. He had returned from Athens (on my "invitation") and rejoined the group a few months back. I was impressed with him; his talent was much more imaginative than Seneca's and his words soared where Seneca's walked earnestly on the ground. He often wrote about nature (and particularly, of all things, snakes), so I was taken by surprise when he stood onstage in Pompey's theater and announced that the title of his poem was *"Laudes Neronis"*—"In Praise of Nero."

He made a handsome figure as he took a deep breath and began reciting his poem. His praise of me made me blush. I felt I shouldn't be there listening.

> *You, when your duty is fulfilled*
> *and finally you seek the stars, will be received in your chosen palace*
> *of heaven, with the sky rejoicing. . . .*
> . . . .
> *every deity*
> *will yield to you, to your decision nature will leave*
> *which god you wish to be, where to set your kingdom of the universe.*
> . . . .
> *But already to me you are deity, and if I as bard receive you*
> . . . .
> *you are enough to give me strength for Roman song.*

Thunderous clapping and stomping filled the theater, and he was awarded the crown for poetry. His words were surely masterful, but they were an intoxicating beverage dangerous to consume—for an emperor. Yet they could be written only for an emperor.

The next day the musicians would compete, bringing the festival to a close. I was keen to see this, especially to take note of the expertise of other citharoedes. I knew, of course, the mastery of Terpnus but had little opportunity to hear other players. As they took their places, appropriately costumed, and tuned their instruments, I was as nervous as if I were competing. Why? Did I fear embarrassment for them, that they were poor players? Or did I fear they played better than I?

As the succession of players performed and then stepped off the stage, I kept gripping the arms of my chair, exhausted as every muscle stayed tensed. But now I had heard them all. They were good, but none as good as Terpnus, as it should be.

The judges huddled, then one of them took the stage to announce the winner. I would have chosen the man in the yellow robe who had sung of Antigone. But the judge looked around at the audience and cried, "We award the crown to the emperor Nero, who as a performer is superior to all these others, making it a mockery to award it to any lesser talent."

All eyes turned to me. What was I to do? I did not want a prize I had not fairly earned, but to spurn it in these circumstances would be considered rude. I stood and said in a loud voice, "I accept the crown, but only to lay at the feet of the statue of Apollo before the house of the divine Augustus." I ascended the stage and took the oak leaf wreath, holding it as if it were made of precious metal.

As we left the theater, Piso came over to me. "A fitting conclusion to the Neronia," he said. I could not tell from his tone—he was, after all, an actor—whether he was sincere or not.

"A surprising conclusion," was all I allowed.

"I hereby invite you and all our friends to Baiae for a week of relaxation and sport. Surely you have earned it, what with Britain and now this festival, and you need to celebrate the victory in both."

Again—was he mocking?

"This is an official invitation," he insisted. "I, Gaius Calpurnius Piso, invite Emperor Nero Claudius Caesar Augustus Germanicus and his friends to come to my villa in Baiae—oh, say, next week?"

Baiae. Was I ever to set foot in it again? Would any other occasion prompt me to do so? Either I said yes now or I knew that it was no forever.

"Very well," I said.

That evening, in my citharoede robe, I entered the gymnasium to be enrolled as an official member of the artist guild of citharoedes. Although I would not keep the crown, the award entitled me to join this fraternity, the first step on the road to being a professional performer. My hand trembled as I signed the paper that admitted me to this brotherhood of musicians, a recognition precious to me.

The next day I made my way, with a procession of witnesses, to the house of Augustus on the Palatine. His house also incorporated a shrine to Apollo, and outside stood a statue of the god dressed as a citharoede, which he was—the divine model of one. I addressed him reverently, thanked him for what skill he had bestowed on me, and dedicated the winner's wreath to him. I laid it at his feet, knowing he alone had earned it for me.

As I turned to go, I saw the sacred laurel grove of the Caesars on one side of the house. I made my way over to it. How long ago it had been that my sprig had been planted, handed ceremoniously to me by Mother. Mother. I shuddered. *Mother, I am returning to the scene.* To both scenes. This one, and Baiae.

I stood before the arbor. Claudius's tree had now withered away, to join the stumps of the deceased others. But mine was healthy and bristled with sleek green leaves and was already twice my height. It flourished. I flourished.

LXI

Piso's villa was astounding, as luxurious as any ruler's. It perched on the edge of the Bay of Naples, with a further extension of the house on pillars so it overhung the cliff. I could stand on it and be directly above the waves. A stiff breeze ruffled the water, making whitecaps. In late October, the pleasure boats on the bay had mainly vanished; only working boats remained.

Piso strolled over to me, his robe floating around his long legs. "Is it not what I promised?" he said, indicating the bay, as if he owned it all. I nodded. "And there will be pleasures galore for my esteemed guests. The warm sulfur baths, of course—we will partake of them in my private bathhouse. It's best in the early evening, when the torches are lit all around the periphery. And then the feasting, and then—the girls. Or boys, whichever you please."

Wasn't he married? And supposedly fond of his wife, Atria? Where was she? Or was she to indulge in the delights of a young soldier?

"Petronius will be master of ceremonies. He's so good at this."

"He has had a lot of practice," I allowed.

Everyone was there—Petronius, Senecio, Vitellius, Lucan, many other friends of Piso's. But not Otho, oddly missing. Nor Mother. Oh, never again Mother, except in the images that stole into my dreams. Would I feel her presence more strongly here? But she had never been in Piso's house, and so far I had not encountered her shade.

"And then, for those of us who like theater, there will be recitals and performances—by ourselves, that is. During the day. Then at night, back to the baths and the girls."

His "entertainments" lived up to their reputation. The daytime dramatic readings and performances by guests were a safe way of practicing without fear of ridicule; the sulfur baths were soothing and reeked—and not only because of the strong vapors—of the indolent east and our provinces there. Their very city names conjured up sensual escape—Damascus, Antioch, Palmyra. Scented oils, smoking incense censers, carpeted tents of pleasure, bejeweled lanterns, all the objects of fantasy. Someday, perhaps, I would visit them, these far-flung provinces. For now this Roman imitation must suffice.

As for the girls—after my long abstinence they, not the preceding dinners, were the feast. It is true—it had been a long time since I had permitted myself to venture into that realm. First it had been the desolation over Acte's absence, then the strange teasing arousal of Poppaea that rendered anyone else tepid, then the fearful watch over the rebellion of Britain that killed all other senses. All combined to make a celibate ruler, probably the only one in history who was not sixty years old. Well, Piso cured that ailment. After such an extended denial anyone would have seemed desirable, but these girls—women— were in a realm of their own. (Where did Piso get them? I should have inquired.)

Not only were the women delectable in myriad ways—in their youth, in their glistening skin from dusky to pearly, in hair of shades from inky to silver, thick curly to shimmering curtain of straight strands— but they embraced sex as a pure gift of Venus, to be exuberantly celebrated, enjoyed—and shared.

Yet the more I indulged, the higher I heaped this plate of human pleasures, the less sated I felt. Always there was something out of reach, just beyond, a fruit I could not seize, like Tantalus in the underworld, a completion ever receding beyond my grasp. And pale lost faces, Acte's and Poppaea's, even Boudicca's, floated above them all.

I had to do it. I had to walk again the steps I dreaded. Telling my host that I needed to inspect my own villa for the day, I made my escape. His villa was some distance from my own, which I did not actually intend to visit. But it was closer to Mother's, and to her grave.

I wore a heavy wool cloak against the chill winds of late autumn, pulling it up to warm and hide my head. A pair of silent slaves accompanied me, for protection. The waters of the bay were dull under the cloudy sky, and some of the villas lining the shore looked shuttered for the season. As I walked I felt each step a sort of meditation. A meditation on time, on the past and the future.

In the distance I could see the shore of Lake Lucrine, that small body of water barely separated from the bay. It was along here that Mother had been set down by the fishermen who had rescued her. Just here, on this pebbled shore, I imagined. Then she had walked to the villa, pushing through throngs of people in the darkness, who had all been alerted to the mishap.

But today in the daylight I could not picture them. I could see only the villa ahead, which I trudged toward. Just along this path she had come, and later Anicetus and his henchmen had marched, forcing their way through the crowd.

I stood before the villa. It was closed and had begun to look unkempt. Paint was peeling on the shutters, and vines were climbing up the walls. Not derelict yet, but tending that way. Should it ever be opened again? I could never use it. No amount of fresh paint or new furniture could erase its essence for me. So it should be sold; let some new person with no memories take possession of it.

Mother, I thought, *you went in here but never came out.* The enormity of seeing that closed door made it more real for me than it had been all this time. I grieved, but silently, grieved that it had been as it was, and by my decision. Yet I would not—could not—change it.

There was a small mound on the other side of the road, surrounded by a low stone wall. I knew before I went there that that was where her ashes had been interred. I walked over and peered in. Just a patch of grass. Not even a bare spot to mark her presence. Creepers and grass had grown over her.

"Mother, rest your shade," I whispered. "I am here." I put one of the out-of-season flowers I'd brought with me from Piso's on her grave. "Your son is here."

That night at Piso's I declined the girls, although I did go to the baths: the baths, where supposedly all the poisons in our skins were leached out. The steamy fog that enveloped me, so that I could see only the vague outlines of others, seemed something emanating from a witch's cauldron. The poison in my skin was gone, but what of the poison in my mind? Had the afternoon expunged it? I did not spend long there and, swathed in a towel, was making my way to the dressing room when I saw Lucan. I must say something to him, but, oh, my mind was not there that night. But this was the only time we might be alone to speak freely.

"Lucan, your poetry is exquisite, but I blushed at the accolades you awarded me at the Neronia."

He pulled the towel down off his head, showing his dark wet hair standing up in spikes. "But it is true," he said. "You are a deity to me."

I shook my head. After my afternoon, I felt the need to speak plain. "We are alone here; no audience, no requirement to be other than we are. We poets know of poetic license, but there is a limit we must not exceed."

He grinned. He had pretty, white teeth. "I stand by my words about your giving me inspiration for Roman song. You are an inspiration to me; that is truth. And I am humbled that you permit me to join your literary circle at the palace."

I laughed. "You are the best of them all, so it is no favor on my part."

"Thank you," he said. "May I show you my verses sometime in private? I am going to write an epic of the civil war between Caesar and Pompey and would value your criticism."

"Gladly. And if you want access to the archives for research, I can arrange that."

"Oh, this is not a real history, but my imagination. My interpretation of what happened."

"Then you have grasped what it is to be a true artist," I said. "There are so few of us."

I lay on the sumptuous couch appointed for my bed—a curved head like a fern waiting to unfurl, bulbous ivory-inlaid legs ending in brass lion paws, a downy coverlet of white wool from the sheep of Baetica. The silk curtains puffed and billowed on the open windows, catching the pattern of light from the sea below. My room was right over the sea and I felt suspended in air. Restless, I got up and pushed the curtains aside.

The moon, almost full, shone down on the bay, making slashes of silver, unlike the night Mother sailed upon it with no moon at all. The dark silhouette of Mount Vesuvius reared itself in the distance, and the far shore of the bay twinkled with torchlight from the villas and towns ringing it. The breeze carried with it a tang of sea creatures, and a promise of winter.

I returned to bed. I was tense, wide-awake. So it seemed real when Mother stood before me, silent and frowning. There was no blood on her gown, which was an everyday one, strangely plain and austere. She did not speak; I did not speak. She made no gesture but to gaze at me, her expression almost blank. Then she leaned forward and handed me a small piece of paper; when I took it she withdrew, vanishing into the Stygian shadows at the far corner of the room. I looked at the paper, but it was too dark to read the writing. I would have to read it in the morning. Oddly untroubled, I let it drift to the floor. I heard its soft brushing sound as it settled on the marble. In the morning. I would read it in the morning.

When I awoke, the sun was already coloring the horizon, dyeing the sky the shade of a new peach skin. Vesuvius was visible now, no longer a black outline. Luxuriating in the spell of dawn, I suddenly remembered the visitation of the night and scrambled to find the piece of paper where it had fallen beside the bed.

But of course there was no paper. I felt all along the cool marble, looked everywhere it might have landed, but it was not there. It never had been. It was only a dream, and Mother had passed back over the Styx, having visited me in the only way she could. I never should have sought out her grave; I had called her forth. But now I knew I would never be free, never forgiven, always hounded and pursued, if not by the actual Furies, then by she herself.

As if in mockery, a messenger came to my door shortly thereafter.

"A letter for you, Imperator," he said, holding out a heavy envelope with a seal. It was real; much more substantial than the spectral one I had been looking for. The wax seal bore a signet stamp I did not recognize. I broke it open and read, so easily, the words written there in dark ink.

My most gracious Emperor and friend,

You made a request of me some time ago, which I promised to honor but have not yet done so. That was to see my home in Pompeii. It has come to my attention that you are nearby in Baiae and if you would find yourself amenable to traveling to my villa, I would welcome you with all joy.

Poppaea Sabina

One letter canceled out the other; dread and sorrow of the one was replaced with eager anticipation and excitement by the other.

She had not mentioned Otho. Was he there? Did she issue the invitation for both of them? Whichever way she meant it, I would be surprised when I arrived. That much I knew for certain, knowing how she played with me, always obliquely.

The messenger was waiting, standing stiffly beside the desk. I shot a look at him. "Tell your mistress the *domina* that the emperor accepts her invitation." I would not wait to write out a formal answer; let it be done verbally. "I will arrive as soon as I may." Let her wonder when that might be. He bowed smartly and took his departure.

Yes, I would go to her. But on the way I would pay a visit to the Cumaean sibyl, hoping to learn something of the future. The detour would give me time to think.

The villa was stirring to life and Piso greeted me as I came into the atrium.

"Ah, how fresh you look! A night off from the girls has been restorative!" he said with a wide grin.

I had a desire to tell him that a night spent with ghosts was not restful. Instead I smiled and said, "I must take my leave today. Some business has come up in Rome, and I also wish to visit Cumae."

"Oh, can the business not wait?" He looked genuinely disappointed. "And as for Cumae, Petronius calls that region home and he could show you—"

"No, I prefer to go alone. I would not cut his visit here short." Trying to be companionable, I added, "His pleasures here are more compelling than a visit back to his hometown."

One by one the others emerged, joining us, and the slaves brought out pomegranate juice and bread, olives, and cheese, and the sleepy-eyed partyers munched slowly. Senecio, who had put on weight, rubbed his growing belly as if he were pleased with it.

"Our guest of honor is leaving today," Piso announced. Everyone made *tsk-tsk* noises.

Senecio, his dark hair still uncombed, shook his head. "Too much indulgence, then? Back to Rome and the straight path of virtue?"

"Yes," I said. Why tell them otherwise?

"But you will miss our dinner honoring the late lost Serenus," cried Vitellius. "His absence leaves an empty place on our couches of debauchery."

"But out of respect, we will serve no mushrooms," said Piso.

Serenus had perished from eating a poison mushroom, but unlike Claudius's, this one was natural, and his death accidental. Suddenly I thought of Locusta, thankful I no longer needed her services. But I heard that her special academy was flourishing. I should request a tour of her garden of lethal plants; I was curious to see it. She would undoubtedly be pleased to welcome me.

But no! Why should I chance reawakening the third Nero, who had been sleeping, dormant? Let him slumber on, undisturbed. Let him never rise again. Locusta must remain in my past.

And in answering the summons of Poppaea, which of the Neros was being drawn there? She had caused me to lose Acte, who would always be the guardian of all that once was best in me. That Acte would always be a part of me, buried deep within, she who had known the first two Neros but fled from the third. The third one even I wanted to flee from.

But enough. Enough of this. I go forward, not backward.

Petronius, joining us, did not look the worse for wear, but perhaps, while maintaining his reputation for debauchery, he secretly paced himself, the better to create awe and admiration for superhuman endurance. He looked at me. "Next year, then, we will meet at your villa. And outdo ourselves. You will have to work hard to top what Piso has offered this time."

"I have plans for remodeling it." In fact until that moment I had not thought of it. But now that I knew I could reclaim Baiae for myself (the ghost would always be there, but I would not flinch), I could think of improvements to the imperial villa high on its hill. "I will put in large fishponds and oyster beds so that we can feast heartily," I said. "They can reach all the way down the hillside to the sea."

"You will have such an excess you can sell them," said Vitellius. "If the imperial treasury needs a boost." He laughed, rubbing his plump cheeks.

"It never refuses a donation," I admitted.

I took my leave, making extravagant compliments to my host. I would send him a shipment of wine in thanks—another claim on the imperial treasury. The emperor was expected to be generous.

Riding north, I headed for the Phlegraean Fields, an eerie gray expanse of smoking vents, acrid sulfur vapors, and volcanic dust. On my right was the dull blue of the autumn bay; straight ahead lay the fields, the Lake of Avernus, and Cumae. A miasma of the underworld clung to the area; Virgil had sited the entrance to Hades at Lake Avernus, and people believed that lethal vapors from its depths kept birds from flying over it. Here Aeneas and Odysseus had entered to encounter their dead.

As I rode past it, its bright blue circular beauty seemed to belie its lethal reputation. But such is often the case in life; they say some poisons taste sweet, and snakes lurk under the most fragrant flowers.

Now on into the fields themselves. The powdery gray dust was easily stirred up by the horses' hooves—mine in front, my guards' behind—and soon the sun was hazy, obscured in the ash cloud. The foul fumes of the smoking vents, mixed with the swirling ash, made us choke and hold our breath. By the time we emerged, our clothes stank and we were light-headed from the breath-holding.

Up to this point, the sights around me had been so arresting and demanding that I had not been able to think about Poppaea and what would happen, but now I could. I seldom was so uncertain, not only of what someone else would do but of what I would. Perhaps I should not think about it. Whatever I predicted would likely be in vain.

Beyond the stench of the fields, on a high rock overlooking the area, we stopped to eat. Piso had provided picnic fare and we spread out the food and ate slowly, enjoying the late-autumn warmth of the sun on the rock. Ahead lay the cave of the sibyl, where Aeneas had taken refuge. The ancient sibyl's prophecies had been inscribed in several books, kept in Rome—now in Augustus's shrine to Apollo on the Palatine. They were consulted when the state was threatened or decisions had to be made about policy. But the sibyl also gave individual readings, like the famous oracle at Delphi.

It was a short distance now to the hewn rock cave where the sibyl sat. We rode on, the sea visible on our left. Umbrella pines spread their flat branches overhead, making round shadows on the ground around us. A stiff breeze swayed the branches, making the shadows shiver.

We reached the top of the hill, with its steps winding down to the entrance of the cave, and left our horses there. The place seemed deserted. As I descended the steep stairs, the wind tried to push me back against the rock, and the force of it made the crevices sing. Finally I reached the flat bottom, where the entrance beckoned.

A long walkway, cut through the rock but still open to the sky, led to an actual doorway. On each side the rocks, green-hued with moss and creepers, funneled my vision toward that dark cave ahead. There was not a sound from within.

It had been years since I'd visited the oracle at Antium and received the then mysterious saying *There is no respect for hidden music.* But now the meaning of that had become clear. I needed further guidance; I had followed the first. I should have been nervous but felt oddly serene. I was emperor and needed every bit of information about myself and what awaited me that I could obtain. My fate was not solely mine but affected millions of other people. It was my duty to know it.

Nearby, birds were twittering in the bushes, but that all ceased at the door of the true passageway. I stood on its threshold, seeing a series of archways lit from slits on each side, each archway a replica of the other, looking smaller and smaller as they receded down the long passageway, like boxes fitted inside one another, each framing the next.

The portals were a series of trapezoids, unlike any doorways I had ever seen. The eerie light illuminating them, tracing their outline, made them glow in the surrounding darkness. The passageway was very long, at least three hundred feet, and as I passed through each portal, the vista of those yet before me seemed infinite.

Finally I came to the last of them and was in a dark, rounded, natural cave. The light was dim; there was no slit window to the outside. A faint scent of both incense and a subtle wet rot filled the cave.

It was silent. Was anyone there? My eyes grew accustomed to the dimness and I could see a little alcove hidden behind a half wall.

"Is anyone here?" I asked.

Suddenly a figure rose from behind the wall, seeming to grow to outlandish size as she stood. She was draped in black, veiled, and beyond that, wearing a mask.

Her rising stirred the mossy smell.

She did not speak.

"Are you the sibyl?" I asked her directly.

Still no answer.

"Have I come all this way for nothing?" I persisted.

There was a soft chuckle, or perhaps a muffled gurgle. I could not tell which.

"I deserve an answer," I said.

Another soft laugh, then, "You will get what you deserve, Emperor."

How did she know I was the emperor? But before I could be awed, I reminded myself that my portrait was on coins that everyone saw. "Tell me what that is, then," I said.

"You are fortunate. Not everyone gets what he or she deserves, but you will." Her voice was cracked, as if she seldom used it.

"And what is that?" I asked. Now I would know.

She stood taller. She towered over me; was she even human? "Fire will be your undoing," she finally said.

"Explain further," I said, knowing that usually the enigmatic statements were not explained.

The mask tilted as her head moved. "Flames will consume your dreams and your dreams are yourself."

"Which dreams?"

She laughed, an otherworldly, high laugh. "If you do not know, how can I tell you?"

"If you do not know, how can you prophesy?"

"No more questions, no more answers." She turned her back on me and sank back down behind the wall, out of sight.

I waited. Perhaps she would speak again. But no. Finally I turned and retraced my steps through the series of trapezoids. Flames. Fire. I passed through the first portal. Undoing. Loss of my dreams. Through the second. What I deserve. Through the third. My dreams are myself. Through the fourth. As I trudged through the portals I kept repeating the phrases, until at last I reached real daylight and returned to the real world.

Like the flames she described, her words burned into me, but I did not know what to make of them or how to guard against them. Shaken, I mounted my horse and left that place.

LXII

The sun was nearly setting by the time we left Cumae and headed toward Pompeii, back past Lake Avernus, darkening now, and along the shore toward the east. Vesuvius was fading, turning purple against the sky. Now pinkish clouds shot out around the sunset—daggers of flame?

I must put it out of my mind. As time passed, the meaning would be clear. I could recognize real fire when I saw it. But "fire" and "flames" could also be used as metaphors, and perhaps that was what she meant. Oracles were by tradition deliberately misleading and tricky.

We passed Naples, then approached Herculaneum in the shadow of Vesuvius. It was full dark before we reached Poppaea's villa, not actually in Pompeii but west of it, closer to the foot of Vesuvius. The villa lay in the heart of extensive gardens, their trees visible now only as dark forms on either side of the walkway, the leaves rustling. Torches lighted the wide paved path, showing a tall, colonnaded entrance before us. Guards stepped out, emerging from the sides of the pillars.

But they did not question me. Like the sibyl, they recognized me.

"Enter, Caesar," they said.

I walked into a large reception room, lit only by a candelabrum in a corner. The high ceiling was lost in shadow and as dark as a starless night. All along the side stood ghostly statues, guarding the room. One of them moved and came toward me, its filmy drapery stirring.

She was pale as the dawn and too beautiful and perfect to be alive. I reached out to touch her shoulder, expecting it to be cold and smooth, confirming that it was marble. After the sibyl, everything today could be otherworldly.

But it was warm.

"Poppaea," I said, half expecting her to answer, *No, I am Aphrodite . . . no, I am a dream . . . no, I do not exist.*

"Welcome," she said. "I did not know what hour to expect you. But expect you I did."

"The journey was . . . demanding," I said.

"How so? I always found the scenery between here and Baiae quite lovely."

"The scenery, yes, the scenery was striking."

She looked at me, puzzled, tilted her head the way the sibyl had done.

"But much of my trip was in darkness," I hastily explained.

"Come," she said, taking my hand and leading me through the large room. "We will dine together, although it is late. The dinner is all prepared."

She led me into the triclinium, the dining room, where the couches were covered in plump shining pillows and a gray-veined marble table awaited the food. Slaves appeared out of nowhere and washed my feet, dusty from the travel, and my hands. I was handed a napkin of the finest Alexandrian linen. More lamps were lit around the room, brightening it and showing the wall paintings, their colors vibrant even in the yellow light.

There were only the two of us. The guards melted into the shadows in the corners. Where was Otho? I should ask. Or shouldn't I? It didn't matter. If this was a trap to embarrass me, I would do nothing to warrant it. Let him lurk in the next room. Let him hear every word I said.

The silent slaves brought in the platters, heaped with enough food to serve a cohort.

"In the morning when we have light, I will show you the villa and all its treasures," she said. "But for now, we can be content with just this room."

All I wanted and desired was in this room. Here I could stay forever.

We spoke little, as if to do so would shatter the perfection of the moment. The light played on her features, caressing them. The clink of the spoons on the silver serving platters made its own music; the steam from the baked ham and figs in pastry loosed a succulent culinary perfume. Our goblets were refilled with different wines as the dinner progressed, each fitted to the proper dish: sweet, tart, slightly smoky for the finale of hot African sweet-wine cakes with honey.

When it was over she rose, wordlessly, and took my hand again. She guided me out through a labyrinth of passageways and turns, coming at last to a doorway. "This is your room," she said, stepping into it. A slave following us quickly lit several lamps and the room opened up before my eyes. But it was dark, a cave, lightened—like the passage to the sibyl's—only by thin ribbons of yellow, in this case painted on. The room itself was utterly black.

"Am I in Hades?" I blurted out. The shiny black of the walls was erotic and threatening at the same time.

"Don't you like it? I had it decorated especially for you," she said.

"Why would you decorate a room for someone who might never come, and decorate it in such a . . . a singular style?"

"I knew you would come," she said. "I willed it."

I was not stupid enough to ask, *Why?* "Then your will is very powerful. For I was drawn here. Remember, I first asked to see it."

"If you did, it was because I willed you to ask it."

The slave withdrew. "Stay with me," I said. "Tomorrow is time enough for you to seek your own rooms."

I held a goddess in my arms in the midst of Hades, and this time there was no subterfuge, no mistaken identity. It was deliberate and knowing; the only discovery was that a goddess is no less a goddess for being fully human as well. The blessing of the black room—for we extinguished the unhelpful lamps—was in hiding her beauty so I was not blinded by it, as Anchises was by Aphrodite.

She truly was wise in the ways of Aphrodite; the goddess herself must have tutored her, how to please in ways beyond the mortal. But I did not need such extraordinary skill; her mere touch was enough.

In the begetting of Hercules, Zeus made one night into three, and this night felt like three as well. There was no way of measuring how the hours passed; they seemed to stretch and stretch, pulled lengthwise by invisible hands, holding us warm within them. All my life I had contended against boundaries, the forbidden, but only in public actions—not wearing a toga, singing before an audience, growing my hair long—but I had never transgressed the code of the body that Romans obeyed, the sex rules about who could do what to whom, and with what, all having to do with rank and power. But she taught me to surrender all that and throw aside the artificial restrictions that told us what we could and could not do.

"There is nothing forbidden to the emperor," she whispered, "but likewise nothing forbidden to his lowest subject. In the garden of Eros, we are all equal and all free."

The garden of Eros . . . we chased one another through it, tumbling, turning, caressing, clutching, exhausting ourselves, then resting under its perfumed branches, only to awaken and drowsily begin again while the threefold night enveloped us.

The black room kept the morning at bay, and the sun was flooding the rest of the villa when we at last emerged, blinking. I shielded my eyes.

She sighed. "But remember there are no boundaries. We need not obey the rule of the sun."

I pulled her to me. Truth to tell, after such a night I was content to let the daytime restore me. The sun would set again; we need not be impatient.

After a quick breakfast, enchantingly served in the small enclosed garden with its dwarf trees and frescoes of birds and flowering plants, she said, "I will show you the rest of our villa. It has been in my family for many years."

For all her talk about the lowest subject of the emperor, she came from a prominent and aristocratic family. Perhaps she identified with the poorest subjects, as someone whose safety, like theirs, was always provisional, but she was hardly one herself. Her family had been buffeted by winds that blew only through the aristocracy. Her father had been convicted and executed with the purge of people associated with Sejanus and his plot against Tiberius, and her lovely mother had been forced into suicide by Messalina. Such was the stain on the family name that she had taken her unsullied maternal grandfather's name, Gaius Poppaeus Sabinus.

The villa was stunningly huge. It would seem to belong to a king or pharaoh, not a citizen, even an aristocrat. It was larger than the palace on the Palatine and boasted an enormous swimming pool some two hundred feet long. She proudly led me into her favorite room, on the west side of the villa, which had a spectacular view of the Bay of Naples. Exquisite frescoes made the walls an art gallery, set off by the contrast of the white mosaic floor.

"It is here that I like to spend my time," she said.

I walked around, inspecting the frescoes with their brilliant golds, sea greens, and reds. One wall had a depiction of the Temple of Apollo at Delphi, with the tripod of the oracle on the upper section.

I started to tell her about my visit to the sibyl the previous day, but something stopped me. Instead I said, "Have you ever visited the oracle?"

"No," she said. "I do not really want to know my fate."

"Are you or your family especially devoted to Apollo?" I asked.

"Yes. Why do you think I see Apollo in you? I know him well."

"Although you enacted Daphne, who would have none of him, I assume you do not feel that way?"

"Obviously," she said. "I spent last night with him."

We walked through other rooms. The original atrium in the back side of the villa had frescoes of magnificent architectural structures, in a city that never existed save in the artist's imagination. Two small rooms on either side had depictions of tragic masks. The gaping sad mouths and heads with their weary ivy leaves spoke of despair.

"I saw another tragic mask off to the side of Apollo's temple," I noted.

"We are fond of drama," she said.

Oh, everything she said mirrored my own self.

"Come," she said, "we must go to the baths!"

There was a bathing complex incorporated into the villa, and after the previous day I was yearning for the baths. Silent slaves stood by to assist us as we shed our clothes in the first room, then went to the cold room and plunged into the pool there.

November having arrived, the water was cold enough to leave me gasping. I hurried into the next room, the tepid one, and jumped in. Poppaea followed, and the warm water felt even warmer after the chill of the first bath. From there it was into the hot bath. The walls here, with a background of yellow and red, were adorned with frescoes of Hercules in the garden of Hesperides. A gloomy-looking Hercules was clutching a tree trunk and gazing upward. Two recovered apples rested on a rock nearby. Above this dominating fresco was a deep orange-red panel with a citharoede in the center. He was framed by two wreaths and seated, holding his instrument on his lap, gazing out at us. He was utterly alone, but composed.

It was me. It was me sitting there, looking at myself.

"Yes, it is you," she said. "But you are much better looking." The citharoede himself was rather forgettable, but perhaps his music was not.

We swam toward one another and entwined our bodies in the hot water, turning and turning, trying to find our footing on the slippery mosaic and laughing as we twirled and splashed.

Out of the hot bath, we returned briefly to the warm one and then onto the tables to be massaged and oiled by the still-silent slaves. As they poured the warm oil over my back and pressed their skilled fingers into my muscles, my skin and body sang with the pleasure of it.

Poppaea turned her head and looked at me. There was in that look a yearning and a promise of disclosure, as if at last we had come to that point where all distrust had fled. She reached her hand between the two tables and took mine.

We hurried back across the passageways to the black room, where the sun's rays could not follow us. We threw off our robes and embraced, our freshly oiled and slippery bodies pressing together.

"I told you we need not wait for the sun to go down," she whispered. "I knew I could not wait that long."

In our absence the slaves had brought fresh linens for the bed. We slid into them, everything clean, reborn, and hungry.

We have outlasted the sun," she said, as we emerged just in time to see the purple stain of the departing sun on the horizon.

Now it was time to return to the triclinium for dinner. But how different from the night before. There were more lamps lighted, and this time the slaves spoke. The enchanted day and night were done, the spell broken. The food was not a seeming apparition but solid fare. We could talk normally. But although we could freely chat, it was not until the dessert of fricassee of roses in pastry had been served that I said, "Where is Otho?"

"I sent him away. To Rome to attend to our house there." She twirled a stripped stem of grapes in her right hand.

"Did he know why you were sending him away?"

"He didn't ask."

"If he had, what would you have told him?"

"The truth."

"And what is that?"

"That I like to be by myself sometimes. Does not everyone need that?"

Her answer disappointed me. "And if he asked you now?"

"I would tell the truth."

"And again, what is that?"

"That I have entertained Apollo."

"That is hardly the truth."

"It is to me."

"But not in reality."

"What is reality? Only what we believe."

I shook my head. "There is a concrete reality, and the reality is that you have been copulating with the emperor for a night and a day."

"You put it in crude terms."

"I am putting it in the terms Rome will put it in." No mythology now, no poetic license, but in the coarsest words, the words our critics would use.

She looked distraught, and goddesses are never distraught.

"I've upset you," I said. "I did not mean to."

She stood up and made her way to the door. She did not look back at me or ask me to follow. But I did, catching her arm as she left. A slave standing in the corner eyed us. "We cannot have this conversation here," I said.

"Very well, we will go elsewhere." She walked to her own room on the other side of the triclinium, avoiding the black room.

Her own room was painted in greens and blues and featured landscapes. Her bed was draped with silk and was so high it required a footstool to mount it. A dressing table, with many glass perfume bottles and polished silver hand mirrors, stood in a corner. She sank down on a chair, gripping the arms, and looked at me.

"Poppaea," I said, "we must decide where we go from here. I was only pointing out what awaits us when we leave. What of Otho? You told me once that you loved him."

She bent her head. "I do. But I am . . . enthralled . . . taken . . . with you. Ever since you danced that practice ballet with me. I knew we were made of the same stuff, that we understood one another in a way beyond the ordinary, on many levels. It sounds so . . . fanciful, but that is what I felt. And I believed you felt the same way."

"I did. I do. But you teased me. You and Otho together."

"It was because I thought if I could just have one experience with you I would be released from my . . . my obsession with the idea. I told Otho about it and he agreed. Dear Otho. But the opposite happened after the boat episode. The desire grew, rather than withering away."

Here she was before me, baring her soul. Impulse took over and, ignoring caution, I said, "There is only one thing for us to do. We must marry."

"We are both already married," she said.

I laughed. "Don't pretend to be so innocent," I said. "You have been divorced once already."

"Otho is a good man."

"So was your first husband, Rufrius Crispinus, as I recall."

"But what about Octavia?"

"I have already asked her for a divorce. I wanted to be free, regardless of anyone else." I hadn't pursued it, though, and I didn't mention that. I leapt up, came over to her. "This conversation is not as it should be. These things are trifles. I have just asked you to marry me. What is your answer?"

"You should have asked in a more loving way, not 'We must marry' as if I were a pregnant farm girl."

"You are right. I did not mean to sound so pragmatic. But it is hard to speak the words I would really like to, for they sound like those of a besotted schoolboy, not an emperor." I began again. I looked at her breathtaking face and said simply, "Poppaea, I have waited all my life for you. You know all the sides of me, I can feel it, even the sides I keep secret, that you haven't seen yet. At last a person I can truly show myself to, can be at one with. I want you beside me every day, every night, for the rest of my life. Come with me."

She sighed. Then smiled. "Ah, that's better," she said. But she gave no answer.

"You cannot not give an answer to such a request."

She stood up, pulled me toward her couch. But I refused to budge. "Not in a bed you have shared with Otho."

So we went back to the black room, and as soon as the door closed, she threw her arms around me and said, "Yes, yes, I will."

And we spent the rest of the night celebrating it, a night more magical and erotic than the one before, for we were no longer strangers.

LXIII

The air the next morning was ringingly clear and crisp. After our restorative breakfast in the enclosed garden, she said, "Now I can show you the rest of the villa, the grounds, and gardens."

I rose. Would we mention our intentions of the previous night, or were they so firm they need not be spoken of? While I was pondering this, she said, "We are resolved in our decision?"

"*I* am," I said. Never had I been more resolved in anything.

She took my hand. "As am I." She glanced around the private garden. "I will send for Otho. We will tell him." She breathed deeply. "Until he comes—at the soonest, some six or seven days—we have the villa to ourselves. Perhaps our last privacy."

I nodded. "There is no privacy in Rome," I agreed. "And I will want you there with me." Suddenly I could not bear the thought of being without her nearby, something I had never felt before for anyone, not even Acte.

"Then let us bask in our seclusion for now," she said.

The villa was even larger than I had thought the day before. It faced the bay on the west side, its grounds almost level with the shore, so the expanse of water spread out like a plain before us, and a salty breeze tinged the air.

On the other sides extensive gardens and orchards spread. Rows of bare fruit trees stood in orderly formation on the east side, awaiting the spring to burst into bloom. "They bloom in order," she said. "First the plums, then the cherries, finally the apples. If spring is late, though, they bloom all at once. And their perfumes mingle and scent all the rooms inside the villa."

"We can certainly leave Rome to be here then," I said. I would not want to miss it.

"But they make me sad," she said. "For they last such a short time. And if it rains and strips the petals just after they have opened, they are barely here at all. The ground is littered with the fallen blossoms that never got their allotted days."

"Like some people," I said. And what were a person's allotted days? How could you know? "You must write a poem about it."

"I have," she said.

How many more things would I find us alike in? I marveled. "I should like to read your poetry," I said.

"It is mostly about the passing nature of things," she said. "I find it almost unbearable that beauty must perish, and yet I must bear it."

Looking at her in the morning sunlight it was impossible to believe such beauty as hers must also perish. But not today. Oh, not today.

The north side flanking the entrance to the villa had the largest gardens, along with groves of plane trees and olive orchards; citron and oleander lined the paths. Many of the gardens were planted with beds of flowers to make chaplets and garlands: cyclamen, cornflower, hyacinth, iris, lily, violet, all dormant now. Then other beds provided green leaves to weave with the flowers: periwinkle, ivy, myrtle.

"And here is my favorite," she said, pointing to a large bed of roses. "They take a great deal of care, but they are worth it," she said. "I have three shades of red—very deep, bright like blood, and pale, almost a blush. You will have to wait to see them." She clasped my hands and her face shone like a child's. "Oh, there are so many things I will show you," she said.

Farther from the villa were the necessary buildings—the barns, the granaries, the blacksmith, the winepress, the fishponds, and the stables. As we strolled past the stables, I asked, "So where are they? The five hundred asses you keep?"

She stopped and looked indignant. "There aren't five hundred!" she said. "There are only two hundred."

I burst into laughter. As if extravagance and vanity could be finite and controlled. "And when do you bathe in the milk?" I asked.

"Usually in the morning," she said.

"I apologize for keeping you from your routine," I said. "We must not interrupt the ministrations in the temple of beauty. May I watch?"

"If you like," she said. "Or you could join me."

"I think not," I said.

"Otho does," she said.

At once the mood changed, like a shadow passing over the sun. "He is known for his vanity and effeminacy," I said. "So it does not surprise me."

"You should try it," she said, undaunted. "It is very good for the skin. You are out in the sun too much and it will age you."

"I suppose you would like me to wear a comical sun hat like the pale Augustus did? No, thank you."

Now she laughed, and the shadow passed, the sun's warmth returned.

The day was bright and warm enough that we spent most of it outside, wandering the gravel paths and inspecting the buildings. The winepress still smelled of dank acid from the recent pressings. The vineyards themselves stretched out on the lower slopes of Vesuvius, climbing up the gentle rise.

"The soil is one of the best for grapevines," she said. "You can see the whole mountain is covered with them." Indeed, as far as the eye could see, rows of vines were clinging to the slopes. The top of the mountain was still sunlit, but where we stood it had already fled, and the evening shadows were creeping upward.

"I feel as if the mountain is keeping watch over us, protecting us. It is our guardian."

The oncoming night beckoned us back inside, first to dinner and then to the black room.

When would Otho arrive? Not knowing made each day suspenseful, although it would have been impossible for him to arrive before at least five days had passed. So we used those days, understanding they were the last we would ever have of true privacy and the treasure of our secret.

I did watch her bathe in the asses' milk, floating in the creamy white liquid, although I doubted it was responsible for her perfect skin. She laughed and splashed me and asked, "Where shall we stable my donkeys in Rome?"

"We will find a place," I said. We would find a place for everything. We would want for nothing as long as we were together.

Otho came on the sixth day, dapper and smiling. He said, "So you were able to come," as if it were an ordinary visit. I wondered how anyone could be so compromised as to pretend thus?

"Yes," I said.

After a dinner in which much small talk was made—gossip about Piso, about the lion who had escaped from a pen at the amphitheater, about a senator who cheated at dice—we rose and went into one of the large reception rooms, where we could sit on comfortable cushioned couches. Otho was still chattering away when Poppaea rose and said, "I request a divorce."

He looked struck, as if he had never considered it. "But why?" he asked, looking plaintively back and forth at us.

"Because I wish to marry Nero," she said calmly.

"But can we not . . . continue as we are?" he asked.

I was astounded. How abject could a man be? But in his love for her, no humiliation was too great if it allowed him to retain her. Thus was the strength of her spell. "No," I said. "I do not wish to share her."

"But I am willing to," he said. He reminded me of a wheedling merchant.

"It cannot be," I insisted.

"Poppaea?" He appealed to her.

"It cannot be," she repeated.

His eyes darted back and forth, taking our measure. "Very well, then," he said. He looked at me. "She will not come cheap." Now he *was* a wheedling merchant, rather than a wronged husband.

"I am not surprised," I said. "I can give you an enviable life, but not in Rome."

"What?" he cried. Then: "Where?"

"Portugal," I said. "You can be governor of Portugal."

"So far from Rome," he said.

"Yes, very far from Rome." That was the purpose.

"So far," he repeated.

"It will have its compensations," I said.

"It must be pretty to be emperor and have everything you desire, even another man's wife," he said. "To be able to grant any gift to any person."

"No one has everything he desires, not even the emperor," I said. But right now I could not think of anything I wanted that I did not have.

"Perhaps I'll be emperor someday, and see how it feels."

He would never even be consul, I thought, but said nothing. Besides, he was not of the imperial family, not even remotely. Such a man was not eligible to be emperor.

He turned to Poppaea, who had remained silent. "Is this your desire? Do you want this?"

"Yes," she said.

"Why? So you can be empress? Have power? For surely you don't love him. You don't love anyone, not really. I was content knowing that. Will he be?"

I waited for her to contradict him.

Instead she said, "You slander and insult me. This proves you do not really know me, and so you are no longer worthy to be my husband. So here it ends."

Otho stood up. He glared at me and I felt a sinking sense of loss, for our friendship that had spanned so many years, for his company that I had always enjoyed, for his loyalty and good-natured camaraderie. For a fleeting moment I almost wished it were possible for us to continue as we were, as he had offered. But no. It would be monstrous.

"Farewell," he said. "May your rule continue in prosperity."

With a dignity he had not shown heretofore, he straightened his back and left the room.

I lay quiet in the black room, in the deepest dark of night, black held within black. Sleep was impossible, knowing I had embarked on yet another perilous journey striking out into the unknown in my life. I loved Poppaea, sleeping beside me. But in what way? Was she a work of art I wanted to possess, like my priceless goblets of murra? Was she a reflection of myself, a wavering image I thought I recognized? Was she the shelter from ugliness I had sought all my life?

And what was it Otho had said? That she loved no one. If that was true, then I loved an object that was incapable of returning that love. He accused her of wanting power, which she would get by her proximity to me. That was undeniable. I was the source of fortune and reward for many people, and the closer they stood to me, the greater the bounty they might reap.

I never know what someone sees when he sees me . . . a person or a cornucopia of riches to pour out upon him. I never know if I am beloved or only tolerated, despite the assuring words of companions.

But such was the innate condition of being emperor.

If you cannot bear it, cannot live with the uncertainties, then you must relinquish your station.

No, never.

I was aware of Poppaea's soft breathing beside me, could feel the warmth of her back, a peaceful presence, a reassurance.

I could bear it, could bear the uncertainties that awaited me, while this moment was blessed.

We had several more days in the villa, which we spent quietly, talking as lovers do who are hungry to know every little thing about one another. The most inconsequential preferences—does she like pistachios?—seem monumental and revelatory. The smallest incidences of childhood—she wandered away on the beach once and could not find her way home—take on the contours of a Homeric tale. It is as if we seek to capture all the aspects of the loved one, even the days before we knew her. We are jealous even of the past. The present and the future are not enough for us. We must have the whole.

We went into Pompeii one day but did not linger. The streets were crowded and busy and it seemed too much like Rome.

The last day I was there, the villa trembled slightly. We were standing in the large room that overlooked the sea when the floor shivered under our feet. There was a slight groaning from the walls but nothing else, and it passed. It had felt like the shiver one gets sometimes and the common people say, "Someone just walked over your grave."

Poppaea steadied one of the vases. "We have these tremors every so often," she said. "Lately they seem to be increasing. There was some structural damage in Pompeii at the last one. The upper story of one house collapsed, and a crack appeared in one of the side streets."

"Was anyone injured?"

"No. Luckily no one was home when the house was damaged."

Now I would worry about her safety here. "I have something to protect you," I said. "Something that suits you as well as me." I went to my room and took the snake bracelet. The old skin still gleamed unfaded inside the crystal. I held it out, put it on her arm. "Messalina killed your mother as a grown woman, and she tried to kill me as a child. But a snake—divine or not?—averted my fate. It slithered out from under my pillow just as her assassins were reaching for me."

She stroked the dome of the crystal, puzzled.

"This is the shed skin of the snake. I have worn it for protection ever since." I omitted the fact that my mother had ordered it. Thus do lovers hide their secrets from one another, even while vowing to be open and reveal all. "I want you to wear it, so no harm will befall you while we are apart."

"But what of you? Now you are vulnerable. No, take it back." She tried to pull it off, but I stopped her.

"I am more concerned for your safety than for mine."

"But you are going back to Rome, the most dangerous place in the world."

I smiled. "Hardly. It is not the swamp of Ethiopia, where my explorers down the Nile have run into a choking sea of weeds, ferocious mosquitoes, and biting flies. The dangers of Rome are softer ones."

LXIV

The plan was that I would return to Rome and immediately move for the divorce from Octavia and present Poppaea's request for hers from Otho. Poppaea would wait for me at the villa. As soon as it was done, we would marry and I would bring her to Rome as my empress. It seemed straightforward.

But the climate in Rome had changed in the time I had been away. As I approached the city along the Appian Way, with its sepulchers and tombs looming on either side, throwing shadows across my path, I sensed something was afoot. Once back in the palace, even the familiar floors and appointments could not banish the unease that pervaded the atmosphere.

As soon as I had bathed and resettled myself, I sent for both Burrus and Seneca. Seneca did not appear until late in the day.

I was shocked at his appearance—he seemed to have withered like a stalk struck by an untimely frost.

"Forgive my lateness, Caesar, but I had to come up from my country villa," he wheezed. "Rome has grown too noisy for me, and since you were not here . . ." He spread his hands.

"Yes, yes. Please sit." It could not be soon enough; he was tottering.

"My lungs have worsened, as you can see," he said. "But when the body declines, sometimes the missing fire goes to the mind. This has happened to me. I have done a great deal of writing in my quiet country home."

"I am pleased to hear that. I know that is your first love." In his face I saw, fleetingly, all the times we had passed together. I remembered the picnic by the side of the Tiber, all those years before, when he had stepped into the vacant place left by the father I had never known.

"Indeed, and I wish to discuss that with you," he said. "The truth is, I am weary and wish to retire. I have served in court for many years, and I feel I have spent long enough in the traces."

"Do you consider yourself a mule?" I said, laughing, hoping to lighten the mood. But he did not smile.

"In some ways, Caesar," he said.

"Can you not call me just Nero? Of all people you have the right. Or even Lucius, if you want to go further back."

"Very well—Nero. It has been hard to continue in these traces as I sensed I was becoming more and more irrelevant. You paid little heed to anything I advised; I was only ornamental, like one of the brass fittings on the harness of a mule."

"So you felt even less than the mule itself?" I tried to laugh again.

"I am afraid that is accurate. So, Cae—Nero, I beg leave to retire, truly retire, to my estate and come no longer to the palace."

I had not expected this, had not prepared for it. It was true I no longer followed all his advice, but his presence was somehow soothing, protective, and beneficent. "I see," I said. That old feeling of being betrayed, abandoned, crept up and tried to seize me. I beat it back. "Although I can command armies and fleets, I cannot command your heart. So I release you, but with sadness."

"Thank you," he said, rising. He stretched out his feeble arms and embraced me. I clasped him, feeling what was left of his body inside the layers of enveloping robes.

"But not yet," I said. "I still want to talk to you about my divorce. I am determined to divorce Octavia and will petition for it immediately."

He shuffled back to his chair, his face sagging. Release was not yet, then. He had to earn it. "We have already discussed that, why it would be inadvisable. She is the daughter of the last emperor, she inspires loyalty, and furthermore if you divorced her she might remarry someone with a lineage that could challenge your rule."

But none of that was important now. Poppaea would be my wife, and that was all that mattered to me.

"I don't care," I said.

He sighed. "That is why I can't continue serving you. It is pointless for me to remain when I cannot offer you any advice you heed."

"Give me advice I can use," I said. "Advice about how to manage the opposition I may encounter. Advice about what to do with Octavia once we are divorced. In the name of Zeus, give some practical advice about how to manage what I want, rather than finger shaking about what might befall."

"You want an executioner, not a philosopher," he said. "Someone like that Tigellinus, utterly without scruple and ready to obey your every command. Or Anicetus, your old tutor. He certainly didn't hesitate to literally execute your command."

How dare he remind me of that? It was not to be spoken of. "I need someone who can think, not just perform."

"Very well, here is something to think about. You are embarking on this course at a dangerous time. A comet appeared while you were away, and you know what a comet presages."

A change of regime. A new emperor. "Have many people seen it? It wasn't visible where I was."

"People in Rome have seen it," he said. "It has a very bright tail and is visible even in the daylight."

I shivered. But if my reign was in danger, would not the sibyl have mentioned it? Instead she talked of flames and fire. But could she have meant the tail of the comet?

I took a deep breath. At that moment I seized my future and steered away from the safe shallow shore. Come what may, I would not alter my course. "I will proceed anyway," I said. "And where is Burrus?"

"Dying," he said. "He has a throat ailment that has progressed to the point he can no longer eat. He lies in the Praetorian commander's quarters at the camp."

Seneca gone. Burrus gone. I sent physicians, restorative broth, and medicines to him, and asked to come see him, but he refused, via a note. Since he could no longer talk, and was so weak, he wished me to remember him as the robust man he had once been, not this diminished person. I had to respect that.

I drafted a legal letter to Octavia telling her I wanted a divorce, had it witnessed and copied, and then left Rome. The law required only such a letter to establish a divorce. I would have to return her dowry, but that was a pittance compared to the treasury I had. Augustus had instituted strict marriage and divorce laws if a wife had committed adultery—she must be divorced, surrender half her dowry, and be exiled to an island. But we would not have to resort to that. If questioned, I would claim she was barren, which she certainly was. That should suffice.

I sought the escape of Sublaqueum, my mountain villa retreat. In the years since I had built it, I had furnished it with every luxury and many works of art. But as I walked into it, what was there now melted away and the rooms seemed bare, as they were when I first built them, and Acte was by my side. When I was very young. Where was that young emperor? Apollonius had said I was still the boy in my thinking, but that was only in a very few areas that I guarded and treasured, my private passions and youthful yearnings that did not fade.

I sat alone at the long black polished marble table, my arms and face reflected in the surface, savoring my solitude. Outside, the wind was rising and dark clouds chased across the sky. Suddenly a flash of lightning ripped through the room, hitting the table, splitting it. I was thrown backward onto the floor, unharmed. But so shaken I could barely rise. The table was smoking, shards of it lying on either side of the crack.

This was an omen, a warning from the gods. It had to be. But damn the omens. They did not frighten me.

The storm passed swiftly. The sky cleared and the stars came out. I walked out to the lakes I had created from the dammed streams. In the darkness it was hard to see their extent, but I could just make out the ripples moving across their surfaces. I had envisioned their contours with Acte standing beside me. When I was truly young and believed I could bring about anything with no opposition. Now I knew better, but I also knew how to counter and overthrow opposition.

Bright white against the sky, I saw the comet. It hung in the heavens, its tail twinkling.

Do your worst. I do not fear you.

When I returned to Rome, I found that gossip about the lightning bolt at Sublaqueum had already spread. Since Sublaqueum was near Tibur, the familial estates of Rubellius Plautus—a descendant of both Tiberius and Octavia—people took it as a sign that the gods were pointing to him as the next emperor. Then, when a statue in Rome inexplicably fell and toppled in that direction as well, they took it as confirmation of the divine will. So the gods sent this message? I would prove how powerless they were, or rather, how preposterous the interpretation of their message was. Rubellius Plautus had been an irritant and a threat for years. Mother had even threatened to marry him at one point, and together to oust me from the throne—one of her many plots and schemes. Anyone else would have executed him right then, but instead I sent him to his vast estates in Asia where he would be far away. A fresh bit of unwelcome news I now received sealed his fate—rather than the so-called omens: he was attempting to convince my general Corbulo, currently serving in Syria and fighting the Parthians, to aid him in an uprising. I gave orders; they were carried out, and at last Plautus was no more.

The Senate obligingly expelled him from their number and erased his name from their annals. That once august body was my obedient creature now.

With the loss of Burrus, I would need a new Praetorian prefect. I decided to revert to the old system of having two, to act as checks on one another, and also to share the increasing demands of the office. I appointed Faenius Rufus, a man who had been trustworthy and resourceful in the demanding job of managing the city's grain supply and distribution. For his partner, it would be Tigellinus.

When I informed him, he grinned and said, "What would Claudius say, eh? My wheel has turned. And I am content to be the spokes of *your* wheel."

That was what I needed. Spokes that turned my wheel, not grit that kept it frozen. "Keep that promise," I said.

I received a message from Octavia. She had signed the divorce papers and was agreeable to the terms. We had to appear before a set of lawyers with our statements, and then we could part. But she wanted to see me in person first.

I had not seen her since our obligatory appearance together on the Rostra at New Year's. As she came into the room, it struck me as inexplicable I could be married to a stranger. She was recognizable as someone known since childhood, but not as someone who had traveled beside me, like Seneca or Burrus.

"Husband," she said, walking toward me. "I address you thus for the last time."

"I hope you will continue to call me friend," I said. I couldn't say the word "wife" to her.

"Of course," she said. Then, with a sad glance, she added, "I wish it could have been otherwise. But we had little say in what had gone before us."

"It is my hope that our futures give us more choices."

"Yes," she said. There was nothing left to say. "Good-bye. I will see you at the hearing."

I stood before two solemn lawyers and a scribe and gave as the reason for the divorce that Octavia was barren and could give me no heir. The lawyers nodded and signed papers. Octavia stood with downcast eyes, enduring the embarrassment of my accusation. She would have been justified to cry, "All women are barren if their husbands keep them in celibacy." But she wanted to be free of me as much as I wanted to be free of her. And so she kept silent.

I gave her the estates of Burrus and she moved from the palace. I jubilantly wrote to Poppaea that all had gone as hoped, that we were free. But I reckoned without the people of Rome, who were Octavia's vocal and aggressive partisans. A mob marched on the palace, demanding that I take her back. I was glad to have Tigellinus to make sure they did not breach the grounds and to disperse them.

Afterward, it was Tigellinus who came to me and said, "The civil and polite divorce is not convincing to the people. They do not accept it. They are howling that you must take her back."

"Then let Octavia tell them she is not interested in coming back," I said.

"They won't listen to her," he said, clenching his wide jaw. "People decide what the truth is and stop their ears. It is up to us to open them again."

"How?" Seneca would have counseled Stoicism, Mother murder.

"You will have to change the terms of the divorce and accuse her of adultery."

I laughed. "No one will believe that."

"Oh, yes, they will, when they hear the details." He then went on to outline them; clearly he had been thinking. Anicetus would swear before the Consilium that she had seduced him, thereby trying to subvert the fleet and harness it for her treasonous designs. The law of Augustus would then demand that she be exiled to an island. "Out of sight, the people will soon forget her."

I shook my head. Ingenious, but anyone that ruthless was frightening, even if he worked for me. "Exiled to an island—it seems extreme."

"Nothing less will free you of her."

Still I balked. He suggested changing the accusation to having an Egyptian flute player in her household as a lover. But no. People would think she was hardly to be blamed since I did not visit her as a husband. So we went back to Anicetus and the attached treason accusation. I sent for him.

Sitting before me, he smiled widely. I would have welcomed the opportunity to spend the day with my old, and seldom seen, friend, had it not been for the business that had summoned him.

We exchanged news about the fleet, the recruiting, the legions, and especially the Fourteenth, which had excelled in Britain. Then, gingerly, I made my request. He looked dumbfounded.

"What? I have never seen her alone. I've seldom seen her, period."

"You are my only hope," I said. "The only one whom I can rely upon utterly, and who did not fail me in my hour of greatest need." By mutual tact, that hour was not specified, nor need it be. It could hardly be forgotten. "This is simple in comparison."

"It causes me to perjure myself," he said. "And injure an innocent person."

"All these matters are merely legal formalities. They are not to be believed, but must be on record in order for it to be official. Besides, having you for a lover would be a benefit for Octavia's reputation. Her next husband could assume she was experienced." But he didn't laugh. And I, knowing that in exile there would be no second husband, was ashamed of my attempt to whitewash it.

He looked pained. He twisted a paper in his left hand, turning it over and over. "I don't know . . ."

"You can retire to Sardinia, to huge estates that I will grant you, and never have to endure Roman gossip."

"No longer be admiral?"

"You have been a stellar admiral, but are there not other things you would like to do? Things you have put aside while you were anchored—pardon me—in Misenum, hardly an exciting place."

"Yes . . ." he admitted. "I would like to have the leisure to enjoy a retirement when I am still young enough to appreciate it."

"Well, then . . ."

He did it. He stood before the Consilium and solemnly swore that he had been Octavia's lover and that she had tried to persuade him to commit treason against me, to turn the fleet to her own purposes. He should have been in Athens, competing in an actors' contest. He surely would have won the wreath. Who knew he had such talent?

LXV

Poppaea obtained her divorce with no delay, as there was no opposition from any quarter. Otho departed for Portugal, and all was tidy. He came to the Senate for his formal leave-taking, but I chose not to be present.

Octavia had likewise departed for the island of Pandateria, after a particularly unpleasant interrogation by Tigellinus, in which unsavory accusations about the details of the adultery took place, culminating in her maid telling Tigellinus that the private parts of her mistress were cleaner than his mouth. He excused himself by claiming that it was necessary that such an interview be on record. I chided him for it, but he assured me that he had seen to it that in compensation she had comforts in her new setting. Special foods, dainties that would be brought from the mainland twice a week; the best couches and tables; an abundance of lamps and torches; books. Guards who were well educated and could discuss poetry or history equally.

"They should stay away from history," I said. "Pandateria has a gloomy past as far as women from the imperial family are concerned." Augustus's daughter, Julia the Elder, had been sent there, and her granddaughter Livilla as well; Tiberius had sent Agrippina the Elder there. I hoped the amenities that were provided for her would soften the contours of life in her new home. If only this had not been necessary. After the furor died down I would bring her back; Augustus had allowed Julia back. People had a short memory and soon the clamor for her would fade away. Then it would be safe for her to return.

But, freed, I could now look forward to my marriage to Poppaea. I made arrangements to return to Pompeii and spend several weeks there with her. Tigellinus and Faenius Rufus would be in charge in Rome; I finished the business that needed my seal before departing. One item was to replace Paulinus in Britain with the consul Turpilianus; it was time to implement a policy of clemency there.

"I have made it easy for you two," I said. "All is quiet. Lesser problems that arise, you can deal with yourselves. Anything major, send news by the swiftest messengers." But I hoped there would be no such disruptions.

Tracing my way back down toward Pompeii, I no longer felt the unease that had enveloped me heading into Rome. It was now spring; this time it was the lavish villas lining the road I noticed rather than the tombs. The piercing new green of the fields and leaves, the high-pitched birdcalls, the winking starry white of meadow wildflowers—all called me to my new life. Happiness, so long elusive, would be mine.

Poppaea was waiting, hurrying down the broad entranceway toward me as I rode up. I leapt down and embraced her. "How did you know I was just arriving?"

"I felt it," she said. "I knew it would be today."

For a moment it seemed the sun circled dizzily around my head and I felt unsteady. I buried my face in her thick, glorious hair, with its faint musky scent. I took a strand of it and held it up to the sunlight, where its rich amber glowed red-gold-brown.

"I shall write a poem to your hair," I said. "True amber." We turned and walked together on the wide path toward the colonnaded entrance, arms around one another. "Amber," I said. "Did I tell you I heard from my agents sent to get amber from the Baltic? They have located a large source, so soon Rome will be floating in it." I had been pleased at their success.

"I hope not literally," she said.

"Oh, I plan to have the gladiators' nets and shields decorated with it," I said. "Among other things. And because it is the color of your hair, I cannot have enough of it."

The villa's front room, familiar but where I yet felt a guest, was bright now with the spring sun. It gave it a different feel, open and warm. I turned to her. "Where will we marry? Not the black room—although that would be the most symbolic."

She laughed. "I thought in the inner garden," she said. "The real flowers are lovely now, and the painted ones never change."

We stood together in the warmth of the enclosure, the sun touching our heads, a gentle breeze stirring the lilies blooming along the wall. She wore the traditional saffron wedding veil, with a wreath of flowers sacred to Juno and Venus she had gathered at sunrise that morning—roses, narcissus, and hyacinth—twined through her braided hair. Several of her Pompeian relatives were invited as witnesses, and they stood quietly watching as we faced the priest of Jupiter, holding hands to show consent and chanting the ancient marriage vow *Quando tu Gaius, ego Gaia*—Whenever and wherever you are Gaius, then I am Gaia—and I gave her the wedding ring, made from gold of Lydia and stamped with our two hands clasping. Now the priest turned to the wedding altar we had set up against one wall and made an offering to Jupiter, a honey cake. He then broke it and gave us each a piece to eat. With that last ritual completed, we were married.

She had no mother to dress her, no father to give her the traditional wedding dinner, no wedding procession from her father's house to mine. Instead she led me, and the guests, into hers, where the dinner waited. She mingled with her relatives, thanking them for coming and promising to visit them in their homes. I could not take my eyes from her as she gracefully insinuated herself between the guests. She seemed to hang in the gathering twilight like a luminous opal.

Night had come, and now the guests would escort us to the bedroom in a version of the traditional wedding procession from house to house. They trooped behind us, carrying the flaming hawthorn wedding torch. I stopped before the bedroom entrance and slowly pushed open the door, staring in. It had been completely redone; the old bed was gone. All was new. I took her in my arms and lifted her up, stepping over the threshold.

Behind us the guests crowded in, and one of them kindled the wedding fire on the hearth with the torch, although in the warm weather we did not need more heat. We both looked toward the bed, heaped with silk and pillows. Then back at the guests.

"Good night, all," I said firmly, pointing toward the door.

When the last of them shambled out, I could hardly wait to close it behind him. Then I turned to Poppaea. "It is done," I said. "You belong to me. Forever."

"We belong to one another. Forever," she corrected.

We passed the next few days in delight, savoring our new life. We had no family, but we would make our own. We would have children. We would avoid the horrors of our original families. We would never desert or disappoint our children, but give them a heritage they could be proud of.

"What would you like?" she asked drowsily one night, after one of these conversations, lying in bed while the warm, pine-scented air stole through the open window. "A boy or a girl?"

"Why do I have to choose? Cannot I have both?"

"Not this time," she said. "It is not twins."

"What do you mean?" I sat up.

She giggled and covered her mouth. "I am trying to tell you that I am pregnant." Before I could rush and say anything, she said, "I have known for a while, but I did not want to tell you until you proved you wanted to marry me without any such coercion."

"But—I should have been told!"

"Sometimes it is wiser to wait awhile, to make sure there are no mishaps." Now she sat up. "And your divorce from Octavia was complicated. I did not want to add to that."

"But I would have had longer to be happy." I sighed.

"This is my true wedding present to you, better than any carving or silver."

"Yes. Yes, it is. It is priceless." I was to be a father. A son or a daughter. If a son, then an heir. If a daughter, then with Poppaea's beauty. I said so, taking her face in my hands.

"I want us to have a long life together," she said. "Many sons and daughters. But at the same time I have long prayed that I would die before I lost my beauty, and that is not compatible with the first wish."

"You will never lose your beauty," I said. "I promise. I will always see you as beautiful."

"Yes," she said, "but others will see me with clear eyes and not share your vision."

"We don't care about those others," I said. "Let them see what they see. Oh, I am too happy to think of anything but us together, and our child."

LXVI

ACTE

I prayed that he would not marry that woman. I beseeched Ceres, the goddess I honor, begging her to prevent this. I sought out her shrine and made my offering, as generous as I could afford, and dedicated a plaque in my name. I did not care who saw it or reported it. I only cared that it do its work.

She would ruin him. I knew what sort of person she was—vain, greedy, amoral, using her looks to propel her into power. She had had her eye on him all along, and the shameless act on the boat meant that she meant to have him.

In spite of his seeming sophistication, he was still an innocent about people. He thought betrayal only came wearing a sign, only came with poison or dagger. But that he was the anvil on which all men tried to hammer out their desires he seemed unaware.

His attempts at secrecy with me were clumsy, but the fact that he wanted to keep secrets was the damning thing. So I had to leave him. But I will never truly leave him. He is with me every day, in my mind, and I keep the clumsy emerald eyeglass he gave me as a tangible tie to him, feeling that it somehow still binds us together.

In the three years since we parted I have made a comfortable life for myself here in Velitrae—more than comfortable. I now have a pottery factory in Sicily that turns out expensive ware, sold in Spain, Italy, and Gaul, and it has made me rich. I live the life of a respected and powerful *domina*, mistress of an estate. Men have come calling, thinking I might be needful of a mate. They have ranged from honorable, young, and handsome to scheming, old, and ugly. They come in almost as many styles as my pottery.

In Rome, despite all the divorces, a woman who has been married only once, such as Agrippina the Elder, is revered, called by a special name, *univira*—perhaps because she is so rare. Although we were not formally married, I feel bound to Nero forever and find my eyes do not wish to look elsewhere.

O Ceres, hear my prayer. Deliver him from her!

LXVII

NERO

We spent those halcyon days enjoying not only the villa but the wide blue bay sparkling under its summer sun. As she promised, Poppaea visited her relatives in their Pompeian homes, bringing me along as if I were an unknown person from out of town. I rather enjoyed it—the whole game of pretending not to be emperor but just the well-to-do husband of a local girl.

Her family had been patrons of the town and endowed many public buildings and events over the years. As we strolled through the streets we noticed cracks and damage from the recent tremors. Plaster had fallen from some walls, one of the pillars in the Temple of Isis had toppled, and a fountain had ruptured, so water was trickling out at its base. But these were minor harms, and the town basked under a benevolent sky, its vine-entwined arbors, stocked fishponds, and flowery gardens exuding contentment. The thought of returning to Rome dampened my mood. I was not ready; I wanted to stay here longer, where life was easy and steeped in pleasantries. Where there was no Senate, no petitioners, no spies. I even enjoyed reading the exuberant graffiti that festooned the walls in bright red—slogans, caricatures, poems. I laughed out loud when I saw a cartoon of myself.

"Not a bad likeness," she said. "And look at the words under it—'Imperator Felix'—Fortunate Emperor."

"No one more fortunate," I said. And indeed that was true.

* * *

Of course there was still business to attend to and we did that in the mornings at the villa, when scribes and secretaries stood by to take dictation, and messengers were waiting to deliver letters. Poppaea, an astute businesswoman, had much responsibility for her property and commissions. She had her own signet, her own secretary for correspondence, and her own messenger service. I kept my own separate and worked in a different room. Tigellinus and Faenius kept a steady stream of notices coming to me, from the most trivial to the more important. There were encouraging reports from General Corbulo in Syria in his campaign against Parthia, and my Nile explorers had sent a new summary of what they had found so far: heat, stinging insects, snakes, and crocodiles. But not the source of the Nile. Following one of the forks of the great river below Meroe, they were stopped by a huge marsh that stretched in all directions. After traveling fifteen hundred miles south, they had to turn back.

In with these innocuous messages came another: *Crisis. Octavia is dead.*

In an hour came more information. She had died, some said, of her own hand. But other reports were that she had been murdered. Her guardian soldiers reported seeing two strangers land on the beach. Octavia went out—alone—for her regular midday walk that day but never returned. A knife was found by her body, and her veins had been opened. Then, on its heels, a third message with more details. Her body was found in the warm bath so she would bleed more freely, the knife on the floor beside it.

Octavia dead. I put my head in my shaking hands. How could she do this? But she was proud and perhaps could not endure what she envisioned as life there with no escape. I had never conveyed my plan to bring her back—indeed, how could I safely at that point? But I was unable to imagine that she had taken this route. It had to have been murder. Murder. But who would have the authority to order this? She was Claudius's daughter and the first wife of the emperor. That could not be ignored or set aside. So whoever had done it was bold and had access to means to intimidate anyone who would question the order.

Suddenly I realized: the instigator had pretended the order came from me. No one else could be obeyed for such an order.

Who would dare? Who had access to my signet or my messengers? Even Tigellinus and Faenius were not empowered to use them.

As I sat there, the sunlight playing merrily on the walls, I knew. Poppaea.

For as long as an hour I sat there nursing the dreadful knowledge, not trusting myself to go to her. Perhaps it was not true. Perhaps I was utterly wrong. That she would deny it, I knew. But as the minutes passed, the truth grew stronger, sinking deep into me. Finally I stood and made my way into her *tablinum*—workroom—where she was bent over her desk, writing.

The curve of her neck as she wrote was as graceful as a swan's; her beauty was a shield that deflected any evil aura. But this evil had come from behind the shield, not outside it.

"Poppaea," I said. She turned and looked at me, a smile on her face, tendrils of hair falling on her cheeks. "I have something for you." I thrust the three letters into her hands.

She read them slowly, her expression not changing. Then she laid them down and stood up. "A tragedy," she said. She reached out to touch my shoulder and I shrunk away. Never would I have predicted I would ever recoil from her touch. "I know you will grieve for her."

"You did it."

I expected a denial or an evasion. Instead she lifted her chin, looked me right in the eyes, and said, "Yes. I did. I did it not for me, or for you, but for our child. It must be safe; it cannot have rivals or enemies. She was your enemy, though you never would have admitted it. She was plotting to be rescued from the island so she could marry one of the remaining descendants of Augustus. Their child would have eclipsed ours."

"She wouldn't have had a child."

"Now you've come to believe your own story about her being barren," she said. "She was barren because she had no chance to conceive. But Mr. Augustus-Descendant would have put that right."

"How do you know she was plotting?"

She gave a small laugh. "You have your spies, I have mine. I tell you, this is the truth."

It was impossible to prove. But not impossible to believe. It could have been true. But *could have been, might have been, probable, not impossible* are not the same as *true*.

"I did this for our child. And I would do it again—will do it again—if I see a threat against it." She cupped her hands protectively around her belly, pressing the material down to reveal her growing shape. "Here!"

Suddenly I saw, in that gesture, another from the past.

Mother. Clutching her belly. *Strike here! This is the womb that bore Nero!*

The womb that bears an emperor . . . I had struck once; now Poppaea had done likewise. My act to preserve my own life, hers to preserve my child's.

Hesitantly, she reached out for me again. This time I did not push her away.

Now I knew why I had seen my own self in her. That dark side of me, the third Nero that I had repudiated, yet could not flee, the side that I could not reveal to Acte, was reflected in her. We were truly the same, for better or worse, made of the same material. If I embraced her, I was embracing myself. And I did, uniting all my sundered selves.

LXVIII

The beauty of Pompeii palled on me. The glittering water nearby was only a reminder that similar water lapped the shores of Pandateria, its blue surface the last lovely thing Octavia had seen. The water, the water . . . waters that Mother had sailed on, waters that surrounded Octavia. Rome was inland. To Rome I would hurry back, even though the summer heat was mounting.

Tigellinus and Faenius were relieved to see me. Tigellinus, whose worry had stamped two deep lines on his forehead, grinned and let out a laugh. "Welcome, Caesar, and just in time. We want no mobs, no riots, no marching on the palace. Your presence can mollify them. We have withheld the information about Octavia, but it cannot keep much longer. This will give you a chance to make up a story."

"What, do you—even you—think I ordered this?" But people would think as I had—that no one else had the authority. Or the daring to issue a false order.

He looked puzzled. "Didn't you?"

"No!"

He nodded. But his calm acceptance signaled that he had interpreted my denial as a routine one, meaningless. "Then who?"

I had to pretend I didn't know. But that would trigger an investigation. "I don't know," I said. "Someone who wants to blacken my name." Let them look for this bogus person.

"You will have to calm the people," said Faenius. "They will be angry and sorrowful that she is dead. And it would help if you could name whoever's guilty and have them punished. Just to . . . er . . . clear yourself."

The old adage *Cui bono?*—who benefits?—usually lighted a trail to the guilty one. Obviously Poppaea benefited most of all. But I must protect her.

"That family was doomed," I said, to deflect suspicion. "Messalina executed, Britannicus felled by epilepsy, now Octavia struck down by assassins." Not to mention Claudius poisoned by Mother. But I would not mention it.

"Yes, very sad," said Tigellinus briskly. "Very sad."

Faenius shook his head in concurrence.

For now, we made no announcement of Octavia's death; and the news leaked out very slowly, so by the time everyone knew, it had lost its immediacy. The demonstrations and mobs did not materialize; it was as if they had mourned her once, when she first left the palace, and then put her out of their fickle minds. I was her only mourner, as the person who knew her best and also the one who had, by happenstance beyond our control, blocked her chances of happiness in her short life. And it was short. I could remember the little child clinging to Messalina, and that was not so long ago. A small window in time to have opened and then shut so quickly.

When at length the death was formally announced, the official story was that she had committed suicide, after its being revealed that she was plotting an escape and allying herself to a traitor seeking my overthrow. The Senate duly issued a decree of national thanksgiving at the timely exposure of the plot and at my deliverance. Just as they had for Mother's "plot."

The Senate . . . should it change its name to "Your Obedient Slave and Minion"? For that best described what it had become.

+   +   +

As the heat—both real and political—of the summer subsided, Poppaea joined me in Rome, and our marriage was announced. This time she was received warmly, and when I named her Augusta, the obsequious Senate applauded us. Livia had received the title only after the death of Augustus; the lady Antonia, only after her own death; and Mother, only on account of her lineage in addition to her marriage to Claudius. Poppaea was not of that class or rank, but this time—unlike with Acte—I was able to impose my will on anyone who might object to her elevation or claim that she was not worthy.

When her pregnancy became known, we basked in excited approval. There had been no baby born in the ruling imperial household since Britannicus, more than twenty years past. In providing the people with something to anticipate, we guided their eyes to focus on what lay ahead, not behind.

Poppaea settled easily into the palace but shunned Octavia's quarters. "I don't want to go there," she said. "An angry presence is lurking there to fasten itself on me and revenge itself."

"You are thinking of the Furies," I said. "But she is no Fury. Really, her demeanor was always gentle." However, she had plotted to kill me in her gentle manner.

"In life, yes," she said. "But people change in death."

"Yes," I said. "Into nothing."

"What of ghosts?"

"Ghosts are not people. They are something else. I know not what— remnants of the person?"

"I hope I come back as a ghost. Better that than obliteration."

"Better eternal fame than being a ghost," I argued.

She put her arms around me. "Why are we talking of these things? They are far in our future. Yet . . . I do not want to die wrinkled and old."

"Enough of this. We have a child to look forward to. A child coming first thing in the new year. A favorable omen. The beginning of a new life for us."

Only a few weeks after this, Pompeii was hit with a severe earthquake. Unlike the tremors that had rumbled when we were there, this one was violent and caused extensive damage and many deaths. We first learned of it in Rome when a vast tidal wave generated from the quake raced north and swamped two hundred grain ships anchored in the harbor at Ostia. Then news came of what had happened in the city. Every public building had been damaged—some were in ruins—even the great Temple of Jupiter, a copy of the one in Rome. Pipes and aqueducts were shattered, leaving the city without water and many people homeless, wandering the streets in a daze. The cries of distress were heartrending, and I sent agents posthaste with relief funds and supplies for rescue and rebuilding.

Poppaea's villa suffered from some collapsed walls, and the roof over several rooms near the baths fell in. It would cost a great deal to repair. But no one had been hurt. Some of her relatives had sustained minor injuries and house damage that would be costly to repair. But the weather was still warm and there would be time before winter to take care of the most glaring devastation.

As distressed as we were by the damage in Pompeii, Rome presented a never-ending parade of concerns vying for my attention. Some were more diverting than others, and so to end the backlog of prisoners waiting on appeal to me, I decided to spend several days hearing them. Any citizen had the right to appeal to the emperor, but that did not mean the hearing would be speedy or even that the emperor would hear the appeal in person. Usually I assigned members of the Consilium to hear the appeals and render judgment, reserving only a few for myself. This time I asked Epaphroditus, recently promoted to become my head secretary and administrator, to select a few he thought would interest me. He presented a list of ten men with a variety of cases, from smuggling (could be interesting) to contested wills (possibly interesting, depending on what was being fought over) to religious clashes (why would that be interesting?). I pointed to that name and request.

"Paul of Tarsus—why is he on this list?" I asked Epaphroditus.

"I thought you were interested in affairs of the east," he said. "He is a good representative of some of the oddities that flourish there. Of course, if you'd rather not—"

"What is he here for? All it says here is 'religious clash.' Did this happen in Tarsus?"

"No, the original arrest happened in Jerusalem, under the jurisdiction of Prefect Felix. After his arrest, Paul appealed to Caesar for a trial in Rome, as all Roman citizens are entitled to do. He was transferred to Caesarea for his own safety, as the Jewish zealots were baying for his blood. Once there, Felix ignored him and Festus inherited him when he replaced Felix as governor."

"But why was he in danger in Jerusalem? Why would anyone want to murder him?"

"Apparently he is an itinerant preacher who goes all over Greece and Asia talking about a Messiah for the Jews. Everywhere he goes, there are riots. In Ephesus he tried to disrupt the worship of Artemis— imagine!— right in the shadow of her temple. Well, of course they tried to kill him. It's the same story everywhere."

"Who is this Messiah? Why isn't *he* here, arrested, if he's the root cause of the trouble in the province?"

Epaphroditus laughed. "He can't be here. He's dead. Executed by the prefect of Judea for instigating rebellion with his band of followers."

"Just now?"

"No, years ago. Thirty years ago."

"Then how can he be the Messiah?"

"Because he rose from the dead." Epaphroditus kept a straight face.

"This is ridiculous. I won't waste my time with this. Give him to a deputy."

"I agree, a dead man as Messiah is ridiculous; but this man, this Paul, has been causing trouble in his name all over the eastern provinces nonetheless."

"How long has he been here?"

"He's been waiting two years to see you. He's under house arrest but has a lively stream of visitors—believers and new converts to his cult. He even claims there are some in the imperial household who have embraced this belief. I really think you ought to acquaint yourself with him." He paused. "Gallio had dealings with him in Corinth ten years ago. He was causing a ruckus, as usual."

"I will send for Gallio, and we will hear him together. It will be helpful to have a knowledgeable witness present to help examine him."

When I told Poppaea about the impending interview, thinking it a light topic that would make her laugh, she sat up straight. "I want to be there!" she said. "I want to see one of them."

"One of who?"

"One of those people who are insulting Judaism, trying to destroy it."

"I do remember now that you are partial to Judaism, that you have studied it. So you have heard of this man?"

"Not this man, but of the grotesque distortion of Judaism that this—I won't dignify it by the word 'religion'—heretical sect presents. It must be destroyed, like the cult of Baal long ago!"

She was trembling. I hated to see her so upset. And over something as preposterous as the dead so-called Messiah. "Calm yourself. It is of no matter, just a ripple in the stream. Judaism has survived the pharaohs, the Babylonians, and the Assyrians; it can survive a crazy preacher."

"I want to be there," she insisted. "I want to see the face of the enemy."

Epaphroditus was right. This man stirred up strong feelings wherever his presence was felt. "Very well," I said. In the meantime, I sent for papers to give me a better background for understanding this controversy.

I would hear him in the chamber reserved for trials: a large one on the ground floor of the palace, appropriately decorated with paintings of famous trials in history, with Socrates in the center. Gallio, hastily summoned the night before, sat on a folding chair; a secretary stood by to record the hearing; Poppaea sat on a chair beside me. A large chair awaited the prisoner, who would face us both. The proceeding would be conducted in Greek; I assumed his Greek was better than his Latin, and I wanted no hindrance to his ability to speak freely.

The door opened and a small bald man with spindly legs walked in, flanked by two tall, muscular guards, who hardly seemed necessary.

"The prisoner Paul, also known as Saul, from Tarsus," the secretary announced, pointing him to the waiting chair. He took it as if it were a privilege. And perhaps it was, since he had been waiting two years to sit in it. No, four, if his incarceration in Caesarea was added to the time in Rome. Still, he did not seem angry or waiting to spew out complaints about his treatment. He glanced briefly at Gallio.

"I am grateful to be allowed to speak to you, Caesar," he said. His voice was weak and reedy. And he was known for his preaching? He would not cut much of a figure among Roman or Greek rhetoricians.

"I do not hear many cases in person, but I chose yours," I said. "The Augusta is also interested and asked to be present." I motioned toward Poppaea, who was staring at him. "Now, tell me of what you are accused and why you have appealed to Rome." I indicated the papers detailing his case. "I want to hear your own side of it."

Now his dark eyes danced at the chance to speak.

"I am interested only in the legal aspects, not a primer on your religion," I instructed him.

"They are hard to separate, Caesar, as they are entangled together.

Still, I shall try. I have traveled tirelessly in the east on behalf of my belief, the truth that was revealed to me twenty-five years ago—"

The year I was born. A shiver went through me. But I steadied myself. What of it? Many things happened that year. "You need not explain the truth, merely tell us how it led to your actions."

"I sought to correct the errors in my familial religion, Judaism. As there are Jewish communities and synagogues all over the east, I traveled to these places to preach there. But although some listened and believed, others were offended and tried to harm me. It happened over and over again, in Antioch, in Iconium, in Lystra, in Philippi, in Beroea, in Corinth, in Ephesus, and in Jerusalem."

I laughed. "You are a persistent fellow, to have kept on the same path facing hostility everywhere you went."

"I had to. I could not let my brothers perish because of their blindness."

I felt Poppaea bristling beside me, but I touched her arm to restrain her. "I have here a witness to this, someone who observed one of the riots in Corinth. Proconsul Gallio, please speak."

Gallio rose. "I remember you, sir. Yes, indeed. You were the one the Jews brought to me, complaining that you were blaspheming against their religion, or some such nonsense. As if I could rule on that! I told them it wasn't in my jurisdiction, just a theological quarrel they should settle themselves. I cut them off before you spoke, sir." He turned to me. "There was no need for him to, or for me to listen to their charges."

"And then what happened?" I asked. I had a feeling I knew.

"I—I don't recall," said Gallio.

"I do," said Paul. Now his voice did not sound so weak. "Proconsul Gallio let me go, but immediately the crowd turned on Sosthenes, an officer in the synagogue sympathetic to my message, and beat him near to death right in front of Gallio."

"And what did you do, Gallio?"

"I, er, I let it take its course."

I was astounded. "You, the highest Roman authority in Corinth, let them beat an innocent man in plain sight right before the courthouse, the symbol of justice?"

"I . . . was afraid to interfere."

"You were unconcerned, not afraid," said Paul.

"Who's on trial here?" asked Gallio. "We are here to examine him, not me."

"Perhaps we should reverse that," I said. "You may leave, Gallio. No further questions—for now."

He rose and left, holding his head high, glaring at Paul.

"I can see that, whatever this belief of yours is, you will not be deterred by wind, fire, or water," I said.

"By water!" He laughed. "I have been shipwrecked three times, the last on my way here to Rome. And as for wind and fire—the only fire I know of is the flames of the spirit that lighted on the earliest believers just ten days after our leader left us. But I was not there; I am a latecomer to the belief."

"Fire—don't you believe that a great fire will destroy the earth at the end of days?" Poppaea suddenly spoke. "And aren't you all waiting for this fire?"

"We are waiting for our leader to return," he said. "He promised to return shortly, and yes, when he does, it will be the end of time as we know it. That is why it is imperative that my message reach people before it is too late." His voice was becoming more and more compelling, like a bird that takes a long time to soar but, when it does, flies high above other birds.

"But there's fire at the end of the world," Poppaea persisted.

"Some people may believe that, but Jesus said only that we cannot know the end times, but that it will come suddenly and unexpectedly," Paul said.

"I've heard that he told his followers that he had come to cast fire upon the earth, and that he wished it was already kindled," Poppaea said.

"He had many followers and one hears many claims about what

each of them heard. Sometimes they are directly contradictory. I was not there; I didn't hear him say any such thing."

"How can you preach about this Jesus?" She turned to me. "He was executed as a traitor to Rome. Anyone who supports him is also a traitor to Rome." She pointed at Paul.

"Jesus is dead. He has already been tried once and found guilty; no need to try him again. Paul has not preached sedition to Rome, from what I have read." I patted the papers. "In fact, he preaches cooperation and compliance with Rome. Apparently"—I picked up the paper and thumbed through it—"he has been grievously mistreated as a Roman citizen—unlawfully beaten three times, jailed without trial, stoned once and left for dead." I turned to him. "It seems you have a case against us, not we against you. You are a forgiving man."

"I follow Jesus in that," he said. "It is an order from him."

"But still—why do you do it? Preach everywhere in such danger?" What would drive a man to do that?

"May I rise, Caesar? I would like to address you personally." After I nodded, he stood and took a step closer to me. "You are an athlete, and a competitor. You know what it is to train, to put all of yourself to the test. There are many runners in a race, but the prize goes only to the winner. But you compete for a wreath that will wither; I run for a crown that will never wilt, a crown imperishable, one awarded by Jesus himself. We both disregard the body in pursuit of our goal. That is what drives me, as well as what drives you. We are fellow competitors, brothers in dedication that others cannot understand."

He knew me. For a moment I was speechless. How had he that insight? Finally I found words. "I see no fault in you. You are free to go. I only regret it has taken us this long to meet."

"All time is in his hands," Paul said. "He brings us where he wants us at any moment."

Who? Jesus? God? But I didn't want a sermon about his god. I was content that another human being understood what drove me—the same thing that drove him, a rarity among men, a gift and a curse.

• • •

Back in our apartments, Poppaea turned on me. "You let him go!"

"Ah, don't revert to Latin so soon. Keep speaking Greek—it's so much more seductive," I said, reaching for her. She was most enticing when she was angry. Perhaps it was the challenge of trying to calm that tempest that lured me.

"I don't care to be seductive now," she said in Latin. "You promised to take measures against this vile sect. Instead you smiled and freed him, after listening to a catalog of his tribulations."

"I had already ascertained the story of his ministry, and I never promised to punish this sect. You are being unreasonable."

She sat down on a bench and leaned back, putting me on trial. "You were clay in his potter's hands. He fashioned his words to what would fall favorably on your ears. They say he is an expert at that, tailoring his message to his audience."

She was challenging his honesty in his personal address to me. I resented that. "Everyone does that, every time he speaks to anybody. Except you, right now. You are deliberately provoking me."

"No, I am demanding that you give me the same courtesy you gave him. Listen to what I can tell you about these people, then see if you regret letting him go. He's free to do more of his mischief, converting people to this heresy."

"One person's heresy is another man's orthodoxy," I said. "What difference does it make what these people believe?"

"It isn't what they believe, it is what they do. They are subversive, a danger to the state." She plucked at her gown, choosing her words, speaking more slowly now.

"Convince me." I crossed my arms.

"First of all, they break the law every time they meet. It is illegal to hold meetings not sanctioned by the state. You know that measure was enacted by Augustus to prevent secret clubs from operating. And the

Law of the Twelve Tables, set up by our ancestors, forbids night meetings. But these people meet secretly in houses, at dawn and at night."

She had a point. Secret meetings were the essence of conspiracies.

"They are a foreign cult, undermining the Roman religion. First it was the Dionysians, then the Isis worshippers—we have tried to outlaw them, but they keep creeping back to Rome. The Attis devotees, whose priests mutilate themselves—all those foreign cults are bizarre and decadent versions of true religion."

"You forgot the Jews in your list."

"The Jews are different."

"You say that because you favor them. But aren't they eastern like the others? Don't they also have strange secret rites? Don't they also exclude outsiders?"

"Their rites aren't secret; there are synagogues all over the empire, and anyone is free to attend. Anyone can convert if they are willing to go through the process. Anyone can read their holy book. They pay their taxes. They are good citizens."

"Ah. So as long as they pay taxes, a religion is permitted? Don't these people, the Paul converts, pay taxes?"

"I doubt it. They are mostly from the lower classes, slaves and criminals and misfits."

"So your main objection to them is that they are at the bottom of the social hierarchy?"

"You make me sound like a snob."

"My dear Poppaea, you *are* a snob. I love you, but you are a snob. You don't like the common people who flock to the games and races, or my spending time with them. But I prefer them to the senators. They are honest; the senators are not. So a religion that appeals to them must have something to recommend it."

She stood up. "You are impossible! Stubborn, closing your ears and eyes!"

I stood up likewise. "I would say rather that it is your prejudice that is closing *your* eyes and ears. Your favored people, the Jews, don't like them, therefore they are bad. Come, come, Poppaea. You are better than that."

"That's right, let them flourish. Why, you heard it yourself—there are some in our very household. But do we know who they are? No, they keep that secret. If it is a harmless belief, why the secrecy? They should be proud of their group, not hiding it shamefully—unless it *is* shameful."

"Perhaps they don't care to run afoul of you," I said. "To be on the wrong side of the Augusta is a fearful thing. So they pour your water, arrange your flowers, scent your gowns, and keep their beliefs to themselves. I fail to see how what they think about this dead Jesus impairs their ability to perform these tasks."

"Oh!" She shook her head. "I cannot reach you. There is none so blind as he who will not see, as your beloved common people say. And that will be your undoing."

She turned and walked away, into her own set of rooms, leaving me in the chamber, standing on the exquisite multicolored marble floor, surrounded by marble and bronze statues, alone with my art, which never failed or deserted me. It was indeed the crown I strove for, and Paul had understood that.

LXIX

The face of autumn that year was brisk; other years she wore a heavy, drowsy persona, ripe and mellow, but now she hinted of the coming winter and her winds had an edge to them. I needed heavier tunics and cloaks, and for a fleeting moment thought that Augustus was not entirely preposterous to wrap woolens around his legs against the cold.

Poppaea had ordered a new wardrobe, with gowns woven of finest wool from Galatia and pallae edged in leopard fur. She'd had her ivory combs inlaid with lapis, and she and her hairdresser had created a new style, with her hair piled high on her head and a few stray curls around her neck.

"You should try a new hairstyle, too," she said, tilting her head to look at me. "You should impose some order on it. Make a row of waves across your forehead. It would, of course, require a curling iron."

I shrugged. As long as I did not have to wield it, I did not care. "Anything to please you, my exalted empress."

She moved on her cushioned stool, turning her back on the table of perfumes, creams, unguents, and eyeliners. "You only say that to humor me now," she said.

"I do not deny it." She was in her sixth month of pregnancy and I would pamper and protect her like a glass vessel. "But pleasing you is pleasing me, and so I am happy to do it."

Happy. An insipid, pallid word to describe the joy I felt every day with her. Other, stronger words—ecstasy, delight, bliss, rapture—carried within themselves the sense of being momentary, passing. Sturdy "happy" was a condition that could endure day after day. Yet it felt inadequate. And it is almost impossible to describe happiness because it is the absence of pain, of loneliness, of despair, yet it is infinitely more than just an absence of anything. It resides in small moments, moments that lose their power in the telling but pin themselves fast to our hearts.

I had passed the stage of being struck motionless by her beauty; like anything that we grasp continuously, it becomes our everyday, freeing us to see deeper than that. I found more and more of that mirror of myself within her, but unexpected, foreign things, too, that captivated me.

I reached over her head and picked up one of the flasks. Its flat glass bottom was heavy, and its long, slender neck was stopped with a carved alabaster swan. I opened it and sniffed. A cloud of lilies escaped from the bottle. I stoppered it quickly. I took another one, a squat container that proved to have a rose garden inside. "Summer captured forever," I said.

"Not all of it," she said. "Just one little vestige of it."

I grabbed another jar. Inside was a thick white cream; this smelled faintly of almonds. "What is this?"

"It's my own beauty cream," she said.

"What, did you boil down the asses' milk?"

"No—this is made from swan's fat, ground oyster shells, and almonds. It is the closest I can come to guaranteeing eternal youth. And as for the asses' milk, I don't think they like their stable here."

I had brought the whole herd up to Rome and found them quarters across the Tiber near my grounds there. "Why not? Have they told you so?"

She laughed. "Yes. I know how to talk to them. But, seriously, they need thicker grass than grows near their stable."

I would order baskets and baskets of whatever grass they wanted, even if it had to be fetched from Sicily, so besotted was I by her. "I will find something to their liking," I promised. "And yours. If their milk preserves your skin, then no price is too high."

"You could do something else to please me," she said. "I have been thinking, I would like to have a leopard cub."

"What?"

"I fancy a leopard cub," she said. "Oh, I would only keep it when it was small."

"No," I said. I had seen too many in the arena and knew what they could do. "Too dangerous. They cannot be trusted, even the little ones."

"But—it would be on a leash."

"Not good enough. A leash leaves room for movement. No, I cannot let any danger near you and our child." Before she could pout, I said, "Perhaps we can go out to the arena holding cages and see what animals they have on hand. Some other animal might appeal to you." The wild beasts transported to Rome for the arena were held outside the city and the pens were full of lions, bears, leopards, snakes, stags, ostriches, and bulls, as well as smaller animals such as porcupines, foxes, and monkeys. But by definition those small wild animals were all dangerous, too.

"Are you giving games to celebrate the eighth anniversary of your accession? The pens must be full if you are."

Eight years. I had been emperor for eight years. But aside from a small formal ceremony at the Forum, with the legions pledging allegiance, I had not planned anything. "No, not this year. We will soon enough have something to celebrate, and too many celebrations earlier would dull the edge of it. Just be patient."

She was disappointed but acquiesced. She looked at me again. "Perhaps it is just as well. You will need to look your absolute best when you celebrate the royal birth. I hate to say it, but you are starting to put on weight. Nothing that you can't lose by January, though."

The morning of October thirteenth was clear and cold. The sun streamed through the window, shadowed only by the branches outside, rapidly losing their leaves. Eight years since the dawn had come and Claudius lay propped in bed while acrobats danced before his corpse. While Mother held Britannicus and Octavia captive so I could walk forth unhindered. All of them gone now, gone to join Claudius. And where was the young Nero who had assumed the purple that day? Where had he gone?

I held up a large polished bronze mirror and studied my image. I had heeded Poppaea's suggestion that I adopt a new hairstyle, one that gave me a row of waves across my forehead, the opposite of the straight, forehead-hiding style favored by aristocrats and old people. I thought it a welcome change. But was my face fatter? I turned it this way and that, trying to see it from different angles. It was hard to tell if I was gaining weight. I certainly was not going down to the market and getting onto a food scale to find out. My tunics and togas were loose fitting so I couldn't measure any expanding girth by their fit. But perhaps she was right. I would have to resume the athletic training I had let slide in recent months.

"Yes, it is becoming, and you are by any measure a striking emperor." Poppaea had entered the room silently and watched me consulting the mirror.

"I've had a few critical remarks from old senators about the hair," I admitted, "but I barely hear their mumbles anymore." I put my arm around her. She leaned up against me, her firm, hard, swollen belly a reassurance and a promise.

"Even if you do not choose to formally celebrate your accession, I am here to do it privately."

"We will hear the loyalty oaths from the legions this afternoon," I said. "They renew them on this anniversary and at New Year's. But that is all I will do publicly."

"I have an idea," she said, smiling slyly. "Something to mark this anniversary."

It would be something on a large scale, and she did not just now think of it, that I knew. Still I played her game. "And what might that be? Perhaps a fine dinner? A concert by a new musician you have discovered?"

"A place where dinners and musicians can indulge in grandeur."

"Will you remodel the villa? Now is the time, since it is still undergoing repairs."

She snuggled within her warm palla. "Not the villa." She walked slowly across the floor to the balcony and opened the door, stepping out into the cold. "Look straight out. What do you see?"

I joined her. "I see the Forum below us. The Temple of Vesta, and the House of the Vestals. Off to their left, the Temple of Castor. And—"

"No, no. Look beyond that."

"I see the Esquiline Hill, and to its left, the Viminal Hill."

"And on those hills?"

"I don't see that well!" I laughed. "You know I am shortsighted." I still used a large cut emerald to try to see at distance, but I had trouble nonetheless.

"The Gardens of Maecenas," she said. "Look, they spread across part of the hill, next to the Lamian Gardens."

"I take your word for it." What of it?

"The Gardens of Maecenas are imperial property, are they not? Did not Maecenas give them to his friend Augustus?"

"Yes." Again, what of it?

"You inherited this palace from Claudius, who inherited it from Tiberius. Few changes have been made. It is old-fashioned and beneath you to settle for this. Should you not have a palace worthy of your imperium?"

"It is an improvement over Augustus's," I said.

"That goes even further back," she said. "Even while he lived, it was more a shrine than a home. No, you need something new and opulent, befitting your own splendor. I propose that we extend this building and link it to the Garden of Maecenas and other imperial property between them."

"But the gardens are a good mile away from this palace."

"Is that a stumbling block to the emperor, the most powerful man in the world? What is a mile to him?"

"It's a lot of mosaic, marble, workmen, and expense, that's what it is to the emperor."

She stood on tiptoe and took my face in her slender, cool hands. "You must learn to see the greater stage you are set upon. To expand your vision. Do not hold back. Little people hold back. Not heroes."

"Heroes often come to a fiery end." *Fire will be your undoing* flashed through my mind, a warning.

"But with a glorious finale, a blaze that burns in memory forever."

"Let's go back inside." I detached her hands from my (expanding?) cheeks.

She prevailed. I was anxious to please her; with the coming child, she must be kept calm and placated. But as I thought of it, the idea took hold of me, burrowing into my dreams and waking thoughts, rising up like a phantom beckoning me toward it. A new palace, incorporating the latest styles of painting, flooring, and architecture. Just the linking of the two sites would be a challenge, a creative venture, for this would be no ordinary building. Soon she and I were consulting with my favored architects, Celer and Severus, who had executed the difficult design for Sublaqueum. Beginning at the edge of the original palace, built by Tiberius, the new one would have a sunken garden with a long, colonnaded fountain fed by a series of waterfall steps. At one end would be a dining pavilion to eat and relax either in the cool of the evening or in the midday heat, because it would be shielded from the sun and cooled by the flowing water. A set of marble stairs would lead to a higher level of the palace, the part that would snake across the hill and hollow and climb up to the Garden of Maecenas.

We had a large container of marble samples for the floors. We put various squares next to one another to see how the colors complemented one another, and Poppaea sketched designs for the patterns. She favored twining, circular, curving ones, and we both liked the purple porphyry set against variegated white and black marble.

"With a touch of green serpentine to set it off," she said.

"But we don't want too many colors."

"But a little yellow to frame the green," she said. "Tunisian limestone is a good stone for that." She laid the samples side by side. "Do you see?"

"Yes," I admitted. "It does show the green to advantage. Now, about the rooms coming off the sunken garden, and the vaulting of the sunken portico that will stretch to the Esquiline—the background of the wall paintings should be white. Pure white."

"White? But no one does white."

"Red is the common color, but it is passé."

"What about black?"

I ran my hand over her shoulders and whispered, "You know I am partial to black rooms. Or rather, one black room in particular. But no, white is what we must use here. The paintings can be delicate and show up well against it. And it will lighten the entire space, make it seem airy and open."

"The fact that no one does it means it is not suitable. What about yellow?"

"Even more passé than red," I said. "And the fact that no one has done it only means no one has thought to try it. We will bring it to the world."

Immersed in our planning, we were close partners and the days flew. Building began on the new palace, so quickly that everyone was stunned. But the noise and dust from the construction rendered the old palace unpleasant. So I decided that we would move to Antium, and the baby would be born there. In the same room where I had been born.

LXX

With winter closing in, we did not take the sea route to Antium, but traveled by land. It was a pity we could not land at the new extension of the palace I had built by the seashore, but safety was now the most important thing and I would not chance a sea mishap. The Senate had called down heaven's blessing on the pregnancy and made vows of loyalty to the coming child, and I beseeched all the gods to protect us.

Poppaea seemed to delight in the villa, almost skipping through the rooms with the paintings that had so intrigued me as a child. When I was a child . . . and did not know the things I knew now. When Mother brought Crispus there and told me she was marrying him, and I never sensed any danger for him, whereas now I knew it lurked under the most innocuous plant. But I would bar the door to it; it could not enter here, just as Hercules fought with Death at the palace of Admetus, choked his cold neck, crushed his bony fingers, and turned him away.

The airy, light-filled room where I had been born and where my child would be had been refurbished and shone with anticipation. The balcony overlooking the sea had new marble tiles, and the row of eastern windows were draped in sheerest silk, pale as the dawn. Gilded benches lined the walls, and the bed had ivory fittings. Poppaea exclaimed over it and said, "Surely this is a sacred place."

"That is going a bit far, but it has been a fortunate place."

"It is sacred because you were born in it," she said. "I loved the story I heard long ago about how the sun shone on you before it touched anything else."

"It may or may not be true," I said with a smile. "I certainly don't remember." Stories attach themselves to events and cling like mists, true or not.

All was in readiness. There were two physicians and three midwives, all the expertise, herbs, and instruments that could be mustered. Poppaea did not seem worried or fretful, but I was. New Year's passed, then the Festival of Carmentalia, honoring the guardian of pregnancy and patron of midwives, an auspicious sign. Seven days after that, Poppaea's pains began and she took to the chamber, surrounded by a swarm of attendants.

I waited in a room that had various paintings of the Trojan War, remembering what Anicetus had told me long before, explaining about Helen of Troy and her unattainable beauty. But I had attained her; I had held her in my arms, and now she was bearing my child.

Hours passed. The sun was sinking, splashing the sea with fiery color before it disappeared. Servants kept bringing plates of food—cheese and eggs and dates—but they sat untouched. The stillness in the outer room was oppressive, but there were muffled cries from the birth room. I wanted to run into the chamber but knew that was foolish, perhaps even harmful. But how much longer could I stand this?

It was full dark, and torches had been lit, before a sweaty and exhausted midwife, flanked by an equally depleted physician, emerged. I jumped up and ran to them. "Yes, yes, what?" I cried.

The midwife pushed her damp hair off her forehead. "Caesar, you have a beautiful daughter."

A daughter! "And her mother?" Was she safe?

"Well, and resting."

"I must see them!"

The physician tried to restrain me. "Caesar, perhaps you should wait."

"No, no!" I could not wait, it was impossible. Leaving them behind, I ran into the room.

In spite of the torches and lamps, it was rather dark, as the room was large. But I saw Poppaea lying in bed, propped up on a pillow, her hair matted with sweat and her face still unwashed. But never had she been more beautiful to me. Her eyes were closed. I took her head in my hands and covered her salty face with kisses, unable even to talk. My joy was beyond expression.

"Here is your daughter," one of the midwives said, holding out a wrapped bundle. I took it—it was so light!—and peered down at the face, enveloped in its coverings. Its eyes were shut fast, and then they opened slowly and looked right at me, a blurry stare that burned into my soul and bound me to her with hoops of love.

"Claudia," I said, pronouncing her name for the first time. Claudia! Claudia! The most beautiful name in the world, Claudia my daughter.

The Senate decreed a day of thanksgiving and celebratory games in honor of Claudia's birth, and a temple of fertility to be dedicated to Poppaea. Ten days after the birth, the entire Senate came to Antium to pay their respects and be present for the formal naming. By then Poppaea had gained strength and was resplendent in a gown of sea green. Little Claudia's eyes were bright and open, deep blue and fringed with dark lashes; her hair was golden and promised to be wavy. She looked around alertly when the room was crowded with visitors.

There were so many of them—nearly two hundred—that I held the audience in the largest room, the one nearest the edge of the bluff. Outside, the blustery winds sought entrance into the room, and the pounding of the wintry sea below rang in our ears. I welcomed them, looking around at their faces, all seemingly benign and well-wishing. The only one who had seemed hostile to me and my reign, Thrasea Paetus, I had forbidden to come. I would have no apple of discord at this gathering. I announced the baby's name and then added, "And her title is Augusta, like her mother's."

None could keep the shock from his face. To name an infant Augusta, that exalted title for a woman of power and distinction, was scandalous. They stared back at me but did not dare to murmur any dissent. One, in fact, said, "Glorious, O Caesar! To have two Augustas in his household! Blessed be Caesar and Poppaea Augusta and Claudia Augusta."

Well, they would get used to her title. They would have to.

After they departed—we housed and fed them for two days—I sat with Poppaea in *the* room, the room that had opened the door of ultimate joy to me. Drooping in her chair, she moved to lie on her couch.

"These days have exhausted me, worse than the birth itself," she said.

"The Senate will do that," I said with a laugh. I took her hand and kissed it. "You gave them every hospitality. It was honorable of them to make the journey. A vote of confidence for us and our dynasty."

"We don't know what they are really thinking," she said.

"We never know that about anyone. All we can say is, they came."

For the remainder of January and all of February I stayed at Antium, held captive by my adoration of my daughter. I never tired of looking at her, holding her, trying to see, by a miracle, how she would look as she grew up, what her character would be.

"For one so young," said Poppaea, holding her, "it is impossible to know what she will be. Will she like music? Reading? Will she be shy or friendly? It takes so long before that is revealed." She handed her to me.

"We know she is not fretful or troublesome," I said. "She seems to have a quiet soul. A contemplative baby."

"Contemplative!" Poppaea laughed. "Only you would choose to assign that trait to a baby."

Claudia started to wiggle and turn. I looked down at her face, changed from the red flush when she was first born. Her skin was pale, her lips rosy. "Her skin shows the colors we chose for the new palace— white and red," I said.

"Do you know how comical you sound?" asked Poppaea. "Really, you are worse than a love-soaked poet."

"I am love soaked!" I said. "And, if you must know, I have composed several poems for her and am setting them to music. I shall sing them soon."

"Alas, no sun shone on her when she was born, as it was at night."

"The moon did," I said. "I saw it outside the window, rising just as they called me in."

She smiled indulgently. "Even if it did not, I am sure you saw it."

Affairs of state called me away in March. By this time the seas had opened and I took a ship back to Rome, landing at Ostia and then sailing up the Tiber. Spring had begun; green fuzz outlined the tree branches and already the fields had cast off their winter brown. Overhead, in the clear sky, flashes of white from the wings of returning birds winked at me. The world was reborn, and at long last I belonged to that world and its rebirth. The ugliness of my inheritance and lineage were put to rest, and the future flashed bright like the birds' wings.

Striding into the palace, I saw that workmen had completed a great deal of the new construction, but it was still not ready. The mounds of dirt had been cleared away, but the pavement had yet to be laid and the final artistic touches were missing.

By summer, though, we should be able to use it.

I had been called back by urgent news about the eastern campaign in Armenia. When Burrus was still alive, the Consilium had hewed to an aggressive military policy, dispatching General Domitius Corbulo and General Caesennius Paetus to fight against the Parthians in hopes of annexing Armenia outright and putting an end to the tug-of-war between Rome and Parthia over this country in the middle. I had misgivings but allowed this stratagem to continue.

Now my misgivings had been justified. General Paetus had been soundly beaten by the Parthians, surrounded north of the river Murat, captured, and, to gain his freedom, forced to agree to the Roman evacuation of Armenia until the Parthian king Vologases and I could settle the matter. Once free, Paetus behaved in a dishonorable fashion, abandoning his wounded troops and rushing back to Rome at the phenomenal rate of forty miles a day, as if a demon was chasing him. Now this disgraced general awaited me in the palace.

For this audience I would wear a toga, as I had for the reception of the Senate in Antium. I would receive him in one of the reception rooms designated for the purpose. It had frescoes of Achilles in various battles on all the walls, a silent rebuke to the cowardly warrior I would now meet.

He stood in the middle of the room, wearing civilian clothes. Perhaps his military garb had been surrendered to the Parthians as a trophy. Or perhaps, even if he still retained it, he did not think himself worthy to wear it.

He fell to one knee as I entered. "O most exalted Caesar, I prostrate myself before you," he cried, flinging himself flat on the floor.

I stood looking down at him for several long moments, letting him taste the full measure of his abjection. Then I said, "Arise."

He picked himself up and slowly stood upright. His hair had mussed itself and stood out from his head in asymmetrical tufts. He looked terrified.

"You have returned to Rome, after having grossly humiliated your country, your army, and your emperor," I said. "Rome's Eagles, captured by the enemy! Your wounded, left to fend for themselves, against all decency in a commander. Agreeing to abandon territory to the enemy."

His mouth was quivering so badly he could hardly form words. "I—I—they—it—it is all true, Caesar." He then bowed his head as if he expected a sword to strike it off.

"What punishment could be worthy of this?" I asked.

He kept his head bowed. "What—whatever Caesar decrees," he said.

I let him wait. Then I said, "I pardon you." His head jerked up, his eyes wide in shock. "I am telling you this first thing, since you are of such a weak and anxious disposition any long wait to hear your sentence might prove too much for your delicate nervous system." I hoped he heard the slap in my explanation.

"I—I—"

"You are dismissed, General," I said. "There is nothing more to be said."

He backed out of the room, his knees still shaking, bowing all the way. Once outside he took to his heels.

Now I would call the Consilium and get down to the real business—what to do about Armenia. I had let Caesennius Paetus go to make my point to them—that their military policy had failed and would continue to fail, not through the fault of any one general but because it was untenable. It was time to try my policy—diplomacy.

It took several weeks, but after an initial meeting of the Consilium and messages to our remaining general in the field, Corbulo, an agreement was reached between me and Vologases. Vologases's half brother Tiridates would be king of Armenia, recognized and supported by both of us. In recognition and submission to this, Tiridates laid his diadem at the foot of my official statue, where it was received by General Corbulo and sent to me. Tiridates would travel to Rome, where I would restore the surrendered diadem and crown him publicly before the entire city.

At last, in May, I received and held Tiridates' bejeweled strip of majesty and turned it over and over in my hands. What it cost him in pride to surrender it I could only guess. But the cost of the surrendered dreams of conquest by my generals and war supporters had been higher, harder to part with. Tiridates would get his diadem back. We would have magnificent ceremonies to welcome him and mark the occasion, but none could be great enough to truly salute this momentous agreement—peace with Parthia after over a hundred years of war.

Parthia had been Rome's enemy far back into the Republic. It was to conquer Parthia that Julius Caesar was leaving Rome when he was assassinated. It was considered a campaign that only someone of his genius and skill could win. Now I had won it, not with swords but with words and ambassadors.

When I returned to Antium, spring was already past and early summer whispered in the gardens. This time I alighted at the sea entrance, where the waves lapped near the buildings on the shore. I was delighted to find Poppaea in the cool pavilion overlooking the sea, shading her eyes as I walked up the pavement. She sprang up with excitement and we embraced; I lifted her up off her feet and swung her around until we were both dizzy.

"I heard! I heard!" she said. "Your achievement! Rome's success!"

I put her down. "Now you rob me of the joy of telling you. But gossip flies faster than ships sail."

"You can still explain about it all. I heard only the barest facts—that Armenia is settled and war will end."

We sat under the vine-covered arbor and I related everything that had happened, all the arguments and the letters and negotiations between the two sides.

"How long have we waited for this?" she asked. "A hundred years? More?"

"Crassus was murdered there more than a hundred years ago," I said. "Yes, it has been a long time. And they supported Brutus and Cassius. But that is over now, buried at last."

"I hope you will get your due as the emperor who ended this."

"I will get my due," I reassured her. "And we will get an event the equal of a Triumph when I welcome Tiridates to Rome and crown him. Rome has not had a Triumph in a long time—not since Claudius's, which I saw when I was a child."

"Now your child will see *your* Triumph—or what is similar to one. Oh, you haven't seen her in weeks!" She motioned to a slave to bring Claudia down to us.

In a few moments the baby was placed in my arms. She was heavier than the last time I held her, and much more alert. "Oh, I have missed you," I said, stroking her cheek. Inexplicable how I could miss someone who did not recognize me or talk, but I had. She was bone of my bone, flesh of my flesh, as no one else was.

For a moment I wondered if Mother had felt the same about me. I had not understood her professions of our unity, thinking they were just another of her ploys, but now I did. Perhaps it is always the parent who feels it and the child who fails to recognize it.

That night Poppaea and I lay in the bed in the large room with the windows open and listened to the sea. The rhythm of the waves below, coming in regular intervals, held us in a drowsy web. We had made love after the long absence, all the more precious because of the separation. I floated on a sea of lulled content, safe at last. Then the sound faded and I slept.

I awoke to a scream. Poppaea was not beside me. It was just before dawn: light was blue and diffuse in the room. In one corner I could see a dim figure, arms outstretched, holding something inert. Her hair was long and streaming, like a madwoman's. Still I couldn't see, and another scream tore through the air. The figure tottered over to the bed and laid something on it. Something that did not move.

"She's dead, she's dead, she's dead!" It was Poppaea beside me, Poppaea screaming.

A cloth was over the bundle. I pulled it away to see Claudia's face, blue like the light in the room. I touched her cheek, as I had only hours before. It was cold.

An actual shock went through me, as if I had been struck by a bolt. I trembled; I turned cold. Poppaea collapsed on the bed, facedown, sobbing. I touched her, but my hand, cold and clumsy, could offer no comfort.

I touched Claudia again, as if this time it would be different. Her blue eyes were open and staring, seeing nothing. Horrible. I closed them, pushing the eyelids down. Her perfect row of dark lashes lay against her cheek.

I pulled Poppaea to me and let her sob against my chest. I could offer nothing besides holding her close. No words could help; no words heal; no words soften. We would never know if she would have grown up to be contemplative.

LXXI

There were questions; there were no answers. Waking early, Poppaea had gone into the nursery and found the slaves sleeping peacefully by Claudia's cradle. Claudia, too, was peaceful; there was nothing to have wakened her attendants. It was thus that she found her, dead sometime during the night. Hysterical, Poppaea had taken her into our room.

My physician Andromachus gave Poppaea a potion to calm her and ordered her to lie down. He took the lifeless bundle that was Claudia and examined her.

"I see no reason she would have stopped breathing," he said, carefully refolding the covering. "Everything is well formed, and she bears no marks of injury. But how was she lying when Poppaea found her?"

Groggily Poppaea roused herself and said, "She was lying on her stomach."

"Ah." Andromachus thought for several long moments. "I have heard of this in other instances. The child stops breathing for reasons we do not know, and it happens more often if she is lying facedown. It does not happen once a child reaches a certain age, around one year." He touched my shoulder. "I know it is difficult, Caesar—"

"Difficult?" I cried in anger. "Difficult?"

"I do not belittle your loss," he said. "But what can be done to alleviate it? Nothing, I fear. We do not know the cause."

But I did. My family was cursed, targeted by the gods for destruction. And this child, who was to be a new beginning, cleansed of all the taints of the past, had been snatched by them, as too pure and good for this earth. They had taken her to be with them on Mount Olympus. There she would take her place with Hercules and Psyche, mortals welcomed by the immortals and given the cup of ambrosia. But she would never take her place by my side, by mine and Poppaea's.

They say my grief was immoderate, just as my joy had been. Great joys, when stolen, call forth great grief. I had no choice in the matter; I did not choose to be laid low by sorrow so heavy it felt like an enveloping fog, overlying everything, darkening everything. For days I shut myself up in a room far on the other side of the villa, curtains drawn to keep the summer daylight out, reliving over and over again what had happened, castigating myself for the time I had spent away from her in Rome. Had I known those precious days were already numbered, I would not have parted from her, no matter what the cause. The desire to hold her in my arms again was so acute they ached.

Even when, days later, I left the chamber, that fog still hung over everything. The bronze lamps, the meadows in their dancing summer flowers, the drip of the water clock—everything was altered, not right. Her absence tinged the world.

As I emerged back into that world (now distorted and smudged), I had to endure the pitying looks and tiptoeing, the false, stiff expressions of sympathy, as if for anyone else to smile was to betray me. Fools. They had not lost anything and to pretend otherwise was a lie. And I despised pity. It was a loathsome position to be in—the pitied. And the irony of it: to pity the emperor!

The Senate returned to Antium to pay their respects. I received them wearing the dark toga of mourning. They likewise had put on mourning togas. I accepted their condolences and thanked them for coming. Then I announced to them that Claudia was a goddess and would henceforth be known as Diva Claudia. They showed no sign of surprise and even told me her image had been voted a place on the gods' ceremonial banquet couch—the pulvinar—that was honored in the Circus Maximus. I proclaimed that she would have her own shrine with her own priest in Rome.

I then informed them that she had been embalmed, rather than cremated. I could not bear to consign her to the flames. She would be interred not in the Mausoleum of Augustus but in the tumulus of the Julian family, where Caesar's daughter had been buried a hundred years before, where his own ashes lay, and where the embalmed body of my great-grandfather Drusus Germanicus lay. I myself would see to the honors when I returned to Rome by and by.

The first raw transports of grief wore away like chalk marks on a sidewalk, rinsed by rain. Made blurred and faded, but still legible. Now it was something I wore, something that was branded on my soul, like the brands forced on runaway slaves. As summer waned, I put off the mourning toga and made ready to return to Rome.

The city I beheld seemed duller of hue, louder, and meaner, or perhaps I was drained of life force and therefore saw only its unpleasant properties. The climb up the Palatine Hill took me away from the congestion and heat of the streets, and once in the palace I felt more at home. The new adjoining building was almost complete, I was pleased to see. I descended the marble steps to the sunken garden and stepped on the pavement Poppaea and I had designed. It was still shiny and untrod. I poked my head into one of the adjoining rooms. A painter was busy at work, his brush tracing delicate red twining borders ending in stems and flowers, framing the white that would serve as background for the paintings. He worked methodically, intently, his hand steady, his eyes focused only on his task.

He would create the paintings within the white space waiting for them. While he was doing it, he would be in that world, not in the one where he wore heavy, paint-stained sandals and sloshed his brushes in grimy water. Art. It was the only antidote to the grief of life, the only solace and escape, for him and for me.

Poppaea came up behind me. "You were right about the red and white," she said.

Only at the sound of her voice did the painter stop and notice us. When he realized who we were, he immediately put down his brush.

"Don't stop," I said. "Continue your work. I was just admiring it." I quickly moved away and back out into the garden.

"Is the tunnel finished?" Poppaea asked. A dark arching way stretched before us.

"I don't know," I said. "Let us see." We stepped into the space. It was not entirely dark because of small slit windows cut along the way, and the white plaster made it light. "You were right about the white in here, too," said Poppaea. "The paintings here aren't finished. They will need scaffolding to do the ceiling."

"The ceiling will have gold, glass, and lapis worked into the frescoes," I said. "I may have been right about the colors, but you were right to suggest the entire project. What shall we call it?"

"The Domus Transitoria," she said quickly. "The House of Passages, of Transition. In many ways that is what it is—what it will be for us."

Together, holding hands, we walked the distance through the tunnel and emerged in the Gardens of Maecenas. The sunlight hit us as we came out, dancing motes of light. The gardens, quite extensive, were set on a series of terraces marching up the hill. Ornamental fruit trees filled one terrace; in another, winding paths snaked between arbors and shaded stone benches; a third was open to the sky, with only low-growing flowers like irises, roses, and peonies in geometrical beds. Butterflies flitted and swooped among them. At the very top terrace was an elaborate marble and mosaic fountain, spewing water in four directions and filling a round basin, to overflow in gentle waterfalls to the terrace just below. Tall umbrella pines shaded it with dappled light.

"Now we have true privacy," Poppaea said. "We can visit our gardens without traversing the crowds in the Forum."

I stood silent, not wanting to share the somber thoughts I had. For the first time, the future was not bright and beckoning to me. It looked shadowy and murky and I did not know where it was leading. The House of Transition—where was it taking us?

LXXII

ACTE

I was saddened to hear of the death of his little daughter, and even more saddened when I saw how crushed he was by it. I do not wish him any pain; I always felt that was what Poppaea would bring in her wake, but I did not wish it.

The funeral ceremony took place later, and, drawn to witness it, I made my way back to Rome. There I stood unrecognized in the crowd gathered before the Julian family tumulus to watch him place her there. He looked careworn and forlorn, but he spoke his words with dignity and then turned away, swallowed up by his attendants, and he was lost to me once more.

LXXIII

NERO

My absence from Rome had done no harm as the empire basked in a quiet period. I had replaced Paulinus as governor of Britain with a more conciliatory official, and the island was recovering from the recent grisly disruption of war. My ambassadors had set out again to Armenia, this time to arrange for the official journey of Tiridates to Rome, and Vologases was keeping his vow to uphold the settlement. General Corbulo now retreated back to Syria and there were no skirmishes.

The Praetorians had finally returned from their trip down the Nile, bringing back priceless information about that region. The Nile, they said, split into two branches south of Meroe. They'd followed the inland branch because it looked wider, but then ran into the impenetrable swamp and were lucky to find their way out. They reported that there were no ebony trees, one of the things I sought, in the area. There were trees that had ebony-like wood but the trees were crooked and thin, not useful for much except perhaps small carvings. They handed me samples and I had to agree. As for gold, they hadn't found any. There was, of course, gold in Nubia but nothing south of that.

As emperor there were innumerable—or seemingly innumerable—formal events I had to attend or preside over. The Ludi Victoriae Caesaris, ten days in July celebrating the military victories of Caesar. Feriae Augusti, the entire month of August dedicated to the triumph of

Augustus over Antony and Cleopatra, with horse races and a respite for all beasts of burden, the donkeys, mules, and camels. The Consualia in August, dedicated to the god of granaries and featuring horse, mule, and donkey races in the Circus Maximus. The Volcanalia, honoring the god of destructive fire. And on and on all year, so to miss some, as I did this summer, does not lighten the burden. How dreary, how plodding, to lead these ceremonies year in and year out, like the donkeys they celebrated. Few people can grasp just how many tedious tasks an emperor is required to perform, all the while acting as if he relishes them.

At night, the robes laid aside, the glittering gold removed from my arms, I took refuge in my poetry. Before, it had been a pleasure and a diversion, a means of personal expression. Now it was my salvation and sanctuary. A still place, eternal and unchanging. There was Sappho, of course, who knew all the stabbings of human emotion, and many other poets, mainly Greek. They dwelt on death and loss but could also turn to the joys of the moment, reminding themselves—and me—that that was all we had to balance sorrow.

> *Yet against this incurable misery the gods*
> *Give us the harsh medicine of endurance*

wrote Archilochos seven hundred years ago. Well, I would endure. I had no choice.

> *I love and yet do not love.*
> *I am mad yet not quite mad*

wrote Anakreon a hundred years later, capturing the playful side of human existence.

> *Our powerful destiny comes from the gods,*
> *And whichever way the scale of Justice*

Dips, we shall fulfill
Our determined fate

wrote Bakchylides a hundred years after that.

I found great solace in reading and translating these works, remnants of events long forgotten, preserved only in the poets' words. It inspired me to write my own words. I brought out my neglected manuscript about the Trojan War epic, my *Troia*. Before, I had focused on Paris and his love for Helen, but now other aspects of the story called to me. Paris's abandonment by his original family and his later reunion with them. The attempt to forestall the prophecy about his destroying Troy, only to have it fulfilled regardless. *We shall fulfill our determined fate . . .*

After I had written enough to feel comfortable again as a poet, I reconvened my old literary coterie, adding some new names. We would meet for dinners, then stay on for a working literary gathering—a version of the Greek symposium but with the twist that we would be composing and criticizing one another's works.

The new sunken garden's pavilion proved to be the perfect setting. The twelve columns served as sturdy supports for us to lean against, drape ourselves around, declaim from, once the food and tables were removed. The whisper of the long fountain nearby provided our applause.

Petronius came—I had not seen him in a long time. As he was Otho's friend I had hesitated to seek him out, but he seemed perfectly at ease with the change in marriage arrangements. Lucan came, and Piso, and Spiculus, a gladiator who wrote poetry, or was he a poet who fought as a gladiator? In addition, there were several young men who had shown a passion for writing, sons of senators and librarians. As appropriate to the Muses, we put on wreaths of ivy to keep our heads cool even with the wine. And I had provided choices of wine to suit all tastes: dry or sweet Albanum, aged fifteen years; Calenum, lighter than Falernian; sweet golden Spolentinum.

"Spolentinum," Petronius asked the serving slave, "but only if it is cooled with melted snow from the Alps."

"Sir, we have only snow from the Penniculus mountain," the slave said.

"Oh!" Petronius looked as if he had just spotted a large rat on the floor. "In that case, I will have the Calenum." He turned to me. "You need a better supply of snow. There's a slight tang—a funny taste—to the Apennine snow, haven't you noticed?"

No, I hadn't. And the differing taste of various melted snows was not important to me now. I shrugged. "If you say so, my arbiter of taste." Just to make a point, I ordered the Spolentinum with the local snow.

Just then the musicians arrived—an aulos player and a barbiton player, to provide soft music to blend in with the murmur of the fountain. I was most intrigued by the barbiton, which was a bass cithara. I would like to learn to play it.

For this first meeting, I asked everyone to tell us what he was writing, and where he hoped for criticism or comments, and suggested that we could work together on troublesome lines.

"I am still working on my civil war epic," said Lucan. "I will not finish it for a long time. I have three books of it done, up until Caesar's siege of Massilia." He lolled on the floor on cushions laid down over the marble.

Piso sank down beside him. "Nothing so weighty for me," he said. "I like light verses, satires."

Spiculus was still standing, not leaning against a column. "I like composing love poetry," he said. How at odds with his looks. His bulging muscles would not have been out of place on a bull.

"How did you come to writing poetry at all?" I asked.

"Like many people who live by their bodies, my imagination longs for another avenue," he said. "My training takes so much time but leaves my mind starving. So I feed it with poetry as I feed my body with meat for strength."

The others volunteered that they liked epic, lyric, song, and satire.

"And you, Petronius?" I asked.

"I am writing a novel," he said.

"What's that?"

"Well, a novel is . . . something novel. It's a story, like *The Odyssey*, but it isn't in verse. It's just in prose, everyday language. And it isn't elevated. The hero of my story is trying to escape the wrath of a god, like any good epic hero. But not Neptune, Jupiter, or Juno. No, the god he is trying to appease is—Priapus, the Lord of the Phallus."

Everyone hooted.

"So you can imagine what Priapus puts him through."

"Read some of it! Read some of it!" they all cried.

"Very well," he said, pulling out his manuscript.

The torches were flaring and the wine flowing as the company sat entranced by the scurrilous adventures of the hero. Their faces grew flushed in spite of the protective ivy wreaths. Finally Petronius rolled it up and said, "I have stopped here. Suggestions as to where the hero should go next?"

"A brothel?" one of the young men asked.

"Too predictable," said Petronius. "After all, where do you expect Priapus to lurk?"

"What about a ship?" asked Lucan. "With a debauched captain?"

"Not bad," said Petronius. "I shall think on it and next time we meet continue the story."

Now they all looked at me. "I am composing an epic about the Trojan War," I said. It sounded unimaginative, coming in the wake of Petronius's mock epic. "Especially the theme of fate." I fetched my manuscript. "But there are some lines here that perhaps need revision." I unrolled it. "Yes, as I set the scene, what do you think of this?"

The Tigris first drawn down by earth in covered depths is plunged
And holds a secret course; then born again
Flows on unhindered to the Persian sea.

"Too wordy," said Lucan promptly.

Lucan should talk. His writing was florid beyond measure. But I wouldn't point that out.

"But he has the meter right. It's difficult," said Spiculus.

"What do you think of this simpler line: *You might think it thundered 'neath the earth?*" I asked.

"Better," said Lucan.

The evening went on until it began to grow light in the east.

"Ah, dawn's car is approaching," said Petronius. "I shall stay poetic till the end! But really, it is time for bed. Time for my bed, as I prefer to sleep during the day!"

After they had stumblingly taken their leave, I leaned on the table holding the wine—or what was left of it. I had not felt sad during those hours; they, and poetry, had banished the black mantle of grief, if only for that brief time.

LXXIV

Determined to reclaim the side of myself that had run like a lifeline through my earlier years, and given me definition, I turned back to my music and athletics. Once again I pursued the lead plates and the diet and the practice; once again Appius came to teach me. My voice had deepened since the Juvenalia, even though it had not been exercised much, and my vocal range increased.

"That is what is known as happy chance," said Appius. "Usually people do not improve when they do not practice." He refrained from scowling, but he didn't need to; I could see the invisible lines on his forehead. He stood rigidly beside the bronze table that held my cithara.

"I have had little opportunity to perform," I said. "Practice with no hope of performance is a dull exercise."

"But necessary," he said. "Necessary! All art is anchored in discipline."

"As you say," I said. I needed to embrace something that would consume my being, to keep the darkness at bay. "I want to perform before an audience!" I suddenly said. "A real audience, not a handpicked, private one." That would be the real test; that would be the true nerve-shattering artistic debut.

He frowned. "Where in Rome could this be?"

"Not in Rome!" I remembered hearing about a music festival in Naples. Yes, Naples, that Greek-inclining city, which was amenable to the finer arts. "Naples. There's a theater there—they have a music event in the spring—I could train for that and be ready—find out about it!" My words tumbled out.

"You will have to work hard to be ready in only six months," he said. "You are a long way from flawless."

Good. That would call forth the utmost effort from me, an effort that would blank out other things, leaving only the sweetness of pure concentration on a high goal.

As for my athletic reclamation, I sought out Apollonius, whom I had not seen since the Neronia. We met in my gymnasium training yard in the Campus Martius.

"Much has happened to you since I last saw you," he said. "I give you my best wishes for your marriage, and my condolences for the loss of your daughter."

I winced. But it was necessary for him to mention it, I knew that.

"I am ready to go back to what once brought me such gratification," I said. "I need your advice and teaching." All around us men were exercising and shouting, making a din, wearing almost nothing. I had stripped, too. No one but Apollonius glanced at me; such was the license of the exercise yard.

He looked me over. "When I first knew you, you were a boy, a sapling. Now you are a man, an oak."

"What you mean is, I have grown stocky." I laughed to let him know his words had not displeased me. Obviously Poppaea's observation about the weight gain was shared by others.

"An athlete cannot choose his event until his body chooses it for him. Yours has chosen wrestling. You are well suited for that. But you will have to leave racing behind, I fear."

I knew as much. "So, I will train again for wrestling. And I wish to go back to chariot driving. And eventually racing them. I was quite good at one point."

"That is not my expertise. I think your prefect Tigellinus is the man to help you there."

Yes, Tigellinus. I would see him about that. But for now—"I am ready to begin today!" I said. "Give me some exercises." My slave stood by with the olive oil for my body, used by all athletes in training.

"Always eager—too eager. You jump ahead of yourself. Build slowly and the foundation will be firm."

I nodded, but I did not concur. How could I tell him I had a sense of time pressing, of my race ending too soon? Like Claudia's.

The ninth anniversary of my accession; the occasion was an invitation to brood on my dynasty and its future. My first (earlier) wild surmise that it was cursed had abated but not disappeared. In the past, I had rarely visited the ancestor room in the palace, in my eagerness to put the past behind me and build my own future, but now I found myself drawn to it, as though the solemn busts of my predecessors had wisdom to impart to me. To be an emperor was the sublime good fortune so many sought and only four before me had attained, but every one of those four had been dogged by disasters.

I eyed the bust of Augustus on its pedestal. He was wearing a crown of flowers and looked divinely serene. "But appearances are deceiving, eh, Great-great-grandfather?" I challenged him. "By the reckoning of history you were superlatively successful in establishing the empire, and you lived an astonishing seventy-six years to cement it. But not so lucky in your family, eh? No sons, and forced to rely on nephews and grandsons to inherit, and they all died and left you. What an extraordinary roll call! All of Julia's sons, and Octavia's son! All four! Just bad luck? I don't think so." I left his snow-white marble bust and found Tiberius's, one of black basalt. The gloomy man stared at me as if he would have said something nasty if his mouth was real instead of stone. But he was condemned to remain still while I scrutinized him.

"Miserable man," I said to him. He kept silent. "Cheated of the wife you loved and forced to marry Augustus's daughter. Your son poisoned by his wife, the mistress of your betrayer. Forced to adopt your nephew Germanicus, who was more popular than you. He was conveniently poisoned and removed from the scene by an unknown, but you were blamed for it. Great-great-uncle, can you argue that you were not blighted in everything you held dear? And you didn't even get to be emperor until you were in your fifties. Just bad luck? Again, I don't think so."

And next was Caligula. His big ears stuck out from his triangular face on the alabaster bust. His eyes looked dead, but then, they were only empty stone sockets. He was harmless now, the man who had tried to drown me but had killed so many others. "You were young but went mad early. Madness is sent from the gods. Just bad luck, again, Uncle? No."

Then there was Claudius, reduced to a genial bust. "From the beginning the gods inflicted humiliation on you, with your impediments and defects. But, being truly cruel, they did not leave it at that. No, they gave you two wives who betrayed you, one of them my mother, who murdered you. And an adopted son who became the enemy of your natural son and put an end to him. And now that adopted son, also your great-nephew, stands here and asks, what can the gods have in store for me, when they have dealt so harshly with those of my blood?" If I expected Claudius to reply, I was disappointed. I had, rather, expected the gods to hear me and give an answer.

But they were silent, speaking only through the stories and legends they had left us. Of the House of Atreus and its curse through five generations. Was theirs any worse than ours? The only crime missing from the Julio-Claudian House was the Atreus House cannibalism. Until now none of us had baked children in stews, but wives had murdered husbands, brothers had murdered brothers, untimely natural deaths had stolen the hopes of parents. And I was part of this parade— the deadly fifth generation.

My child had been taken away, as I thought, because she was too pure for this family. But I must have an heir, to redeem the dynasty and change its fortunes. Surely there was a way to reverse the curse. But

Poppaea had not conceived again, as if in mockery of the first time, which had happened so swiftly and effortlessly. Was I to be the last of the line? Was it to be snuffed out?

There was only me to carry on. Recently the last remaining descendants of Augustus, Decimus and Lucius Silanus Torquatus, had been found guilty of imperial ambitions against my throne (it ran in the family) and Decimus had committed suicide. I faced the Augustus bust squarely and said, "I would have pardoned him. He never gave me the chance, just killed himself before I could respond. This one was not my fault!" As for Lucius, he had fought against his executioners and died like a warrior.

The Naples festival I aimed at was the Greek Anthesteria, celebrating the early spring. Like my Neronia, it also featured drama, dance, and poetry, but I was concerned only with the music contests, which honored Dionysus. Some of the other contests awarded monetary prizes, but the music recital awarded a sacred wreath, and that was what I wanted.

Poetry had sustained me through the dark days of grappling with my heritage, searching for an answer. Finally the lines of Kallimachos on his dead friend pointed the way out.

> *Dear Halikarnassian friend*
> *you lie elsewhere now*
> *and are mere ashes;*
> *yet your songs—your nightingales—will live,*
> *and never will the underworld,*
> *destroying everything,*
> *touch them with its deadly hand.*

Paul of Tarsus was wrong. It is the wreath of art that is imperishable. If I sought it and won it, I would never die. It is the wreath of the Caesars that fades; only through art could I transcend the curse of the family.

◆   ◆   ◆

I stood on the stage of the theater in Naples, dressed in the loose robes of a citharoede, my hair long and falling down my neck. As an enrolled member of the guild of professional citharoedes I was entitled to enter the main music contest. The moment was here, the moment I had spent hours and hours preparing for. (Is any preparation ever enough?) This contest was in the form of a recital and I had one song of my own composition as well as several in the common repertoire.

The nervousness had not seized me yet and I calmly looked out at the audience. There were eight thousand seats, all filled, and crowds were standing in the back. I had brought my Augustiani clappers and they were in one section, recognizable by their bushy hair, their elegant clothing, and their left hands devoid of rings. Anyone who wanted to come was admitted and the crowd was a mix of the general public, Romans who had traveled all this way to attend, and local Greek aristocrats. My competitors were lined up beside me. I did not dare to look at them; they must not exist for me. Still, as the first one was called to perform, I could not help but admire—and hate—his artistry. No, no, I told myself. Do not compare. You are not a judge. You cannot judge. Listen only to yourself and hear only your own music. And then the next came out, and he sang in a clear, supple voice that could lure serpents from their dens. And the next, a virtuoso on his cithara, his fingers moving swiftly but almost invisibly as the fluid notes filled the air. There were more, each seemingly better than the last.

Suddenly I was alone out on the stage, the last one called. Now agitation seized me, the old familiar spasm of fear, wondering why I was there—how could I escape? I gripped the cithara, tuning it to buy myself time. I cleared my throat a few times, panicked that I had not had a chance to sing earlier and loosen my vocal cords. I was afraid only a squeak would come out.

The judges were stirring impatiently. I had to start. I did, boldly, and after the first few notes all fell into place; I had entered the groves I had traveled before and my voice and fingers knew the way unerringly. And I soared, leaving the stage and all those faces below, seeking out Apollo himself.

When it was over, the applause was deafening. People leapt to their feet. Was I really better than the preceding singers? How could I know, not actually hearing myself? Now the rhythmic clapping of the Augustiani provided its own percussive music.

The three judges rushed forward to award me the wreath. The imperishable wreath of artistry.

I retired to dinner with my friends—for some had come to Naples to hear me, and of course Poppaea was there—and relaxed at last. Then we returned to the theater to hear the other contests. As soon as I entered, people began chanting and calling on me to perform again. But really, I just wanted to hear the others, be an attendee now. They kept up their noise and finally I stood up and said in Greek, "After I've had a drink or two I will give you some songs to make your ears ring!"

How could I refuse them? Otherwise they would complain the next morning that the emperor was standoffish and selfish. So I drank two or three cups of wine, and then took to the stage again. This time I did not have to be careful of my phrasing or my timbre; the wine allowed me to enjoy myself and sing however I pleased.

It seemed to please the listeners as well, for once again the response was loud and emphatic. They demanded more and more and, buoyed by the wine and my success, I sang on and on, until the moon shone down into the theater. Then I held up my cithara and said, "Good friends, my cithara and I need to rest, and the night is calling you to other entertainment, to taverns or to—?" I winked. They all laughed and began to file out, the theater emptying at last.

It took me a little while to gather up all my belongings—the cithara case, the handkerchief for wiping sweaty hands, the jug of sweet wine to soothe the throat—and most precious of all, the wreath of laurel. Yes, its actual leaves would fade, but its glory would not. As I was walking out, I felt the ground quiver, a feeling I recognized from Pompeii. A tremor, a shiver, a shudder.

"Run!" I called to Poppaea and my friends who were waiting. "Run!" I took her hand and sprinted toward the exit, my friends close on my heels. As we reached the outside, a mighty rumble rang out behind us. "Don't look! Don't look!" I cried, pulling them along farther. We rushed out into the flat open space around the theater, in time to see the walls sway and buckle and the entire theater come crashing down. The stones tumbled like a child's blocks, the smaller ones flying even to where we stood, panting.

"Take cover!" I shouted, seeking the trees ringing the open pavement. The branches would shield us from the worst of the flying debris. The collapse continued, columns tilting, roof beams falling, until a heap of stones, surrounded by a halo of dust, illuminated by moonlight, was all that remained of the theater.

We were stunned, as survivors always are immediately afterward. Then Spiculus said, "It's an evil omen." Lucan nodded.

"No," I said. "Can't you see? It is a favorable omen. The gods spared us, and the entire audience. They kept us safe, holding back the earthquake just by a few moments."

"If they are so benevolent," said Petronius, "why do they send earthquakes at all?"

"We need to thank them, not question them," said Poppaea, squeezing my hand.

I would; I did. I composed a poem about it, and later the Senate voted a thanksgiving for our safety. Once again, our safety.

LXXV

Grateful for my deliverance from the sudden destruction of the theater, and also that I had reclaimed my music vocation, I returned to Rome now eager to pursue the other calling I had neglected: chariot racing.

I had never lost my fervent interest in it; I still attended the races in the Circus Maximus and followed the careers of the charioteers, their horses, and the racing factions. But I had not driven myself in a long time.

Tigellinus grinned when I asked him to initiate me again.

"You don't need initiating," he said. "You are not a neophyte, just out of practice."

"As Praetorian prefect, you don't have time to instruct students," I admitted. But I knew he would be keenly involved in my progress and we would bond again as we had way back. Our incessant duties had kept us at a distance from one another. I had missed him, even though I saw him every day.

"I'll find a good charioteer to brush you up." He thought for a moment. "Why don't we go out to the horse farms and select your team? That way you can learn on the team you will be competing with."

"You're an old horse trader from Sicily," I said. "So I will defer to your expertise. But I will accompany you."

⸱   ⸱   ⸱

We went to a horse farm run by a friend of his, Menenius Lanatus—a fellow Sicilian. It lay some ten miles outside Rome, and it was a pleasant ride there in the May sunshine. Huge barns stretched across the fields, circling the training yard with its paddock, with a practice racetrack running alongside the stables. Inside the paddock a number of horses, mainly chestnuts and bays, were being led.

Lanatus welcomed us. "So you're here to put together a team," he said. "Only the best for my old friend Tigellinus!" He shot a look at us, then cocked his head. "And who is this?" As if he did not know.

"Guess," said Tigellinus.

He scrutinized me. "Can it be—is it Apollo himself, come to select a new team of horses to pull his sun chariot?"

Tigellinus roared. "You old ass. The emperor will never buy horses from such a charlatan."

Now Lanatus laughed, too. "I'm no charlatan, just mocking the fawners. I am sure he gets enough of that. It gets tiresome, doesn't it?" He looked familiarly at me.

"How would you know?" said Tigellinus.

"People fawn over me because of my horses. The best in the land. Oh, you would be surprised—or maybe you wouldn't—at what people will do to procure the horse of their dreams."

"We are here to get four such horses," I said.

Lanatus whistled.

"The emperor is of a mind to put together a four-horse team, train them, and race them."

"Who do you have in mind as your charioteer?" he asked.

"Me," I said.

He smiled patronizingly. "I can get you a team of gentle horses," he said.

"The emperor has driven chariots before, and acquitted himself well. Now he wants to become truly competitive," said Tigellinus.

"There are many charioteers," said Lanatus, "but only one emperor. Why would you want to trade places with them?"

"You, a horseman, need to ask that?" I challenged him. "Because there is nothing like it in the world! And because I have been consumed with interest in horses since boyhood. Then, I was forbidden to act on it. Now, there is no one to forbid me anything." What a world lay in that last sentence.

"But it's dangerous. If we should lose you, Caesar, Rome would suffer. When a charioteer is thrown and gets trampled and dies, it's entertainment. If that happened to the emperor, it would be his people's tragedy."

"Oh, I see, Lanatus. You don't wish to sell us horses. Well, Caesar, let us go on to Augurinus's."

Lanatus grabbed his arm. "I didn't say that!"

"You bet you didn't, because who in his right mind would forgo the honor of supplying the horses for the imperial chariot? Now, show us what you have. And no gentle nags, but the finest."

"All mine are the finest!" he protested.

"I am sure some are finer than others," I said. "How many horses do you have in your stable?"

"Oh, at least a thousand." He led us over to a smaller paddock and asked the groom to bring out several he specified. "I'd recommend Sicilians," he said.

"Out of loyalty?" I asked.

"No, because they are very fast." He nodded as two dun-colored horses with black manes were led over to us. "These are five years old and have been trained for two. They are ready to go." He patted their necks. "I train my horses up to a certain point and then it is up to the charioteer to complete it, so that the personal preferences of the driver are met."

Tigellinus laughed. "There was one team in the Circus so well trained it finished the race itself when its driver fell out at the starting gate. And won, too! That wasn't one of yours, was it?"

"No, more's the pity." He continued stroking the horses' necks. "What do you think?"

"What else do you have?" I asked. "What about Iberians?"

"Ah, you know your horses. The Iberians are the fastest, but they have no endurance and they have soft hooves. They are only good for short races."

"Couldn't an Iberian be the pacesetter and pull the rest along? The Circus is not so long."

He had a beautiful cream-colored animal brought out, with wide-set, intelligent eyes. "Fast as the wind," he said. "Nothing can catch him."

"But I wouldn't have all Iberians. What about a Cappadocian?"

"Not as fast as the other two but with tremendous competitive spirit and will to win. Would make a good outside horse, the *iguales*, to pull around the turn in a four-horse team. I'd put the Iberian on the inside, giving him the *funalis* spot, requiring both speed and sure-footedness for the tight turns." A sturdy black horse was led out.

"And the other two?"

"I'd recommend Mycenaeans," said Tigellinus. "They pull well with others and are a nice balance of speed and endurance. Stay away from Libyans, unless you have a long trek in mind. They have hard hooves and great endurance, but that's not what you need for the Circus."

"I'd stick with the Sicilians," said Lanatus.

"They're fast but tend to be unpredictable," retorted Tigellinus.

"How about one of each?" I asked.

"You've heard of the gods harnessing bears and lions together, but unless you are a god it is better not to have too many different breeds on one team," said Tigellinus.

"It would be more of a challenge that way," I said.

"Isn't being a chariot-racing emperor challenge enough?" asked Lanatus.

In the end, after looking at many horses of each breed, I settled on the cream-colored Iberian and the dark Cappadocian, a chestnut Sicilian, and a gray Mycenaean. They looked mismatched, but I believed their strengths would complement each other. And that was all that counted.

In preparation, I went to the races nearly every day, watching intently. My beloved Greens were doing well, and one day I ordered all the sand colored green to salute them. I was excited to begin my training as soon as the horses were settled in their new stables near the Circus.

Wandering through the Forum one afternoon, paying my respects to the shrine to Caesar, passing the Curia and the Basilica Julia, I decided to visit the Temple of Vesta. This round marble building housed not only the Palladium, brought by Aeneas from Troy to Rome, but the sacred flame that symbolized the Roman state. It was cool inside, a relief from the afternoon heat, and surprisingly light because of its roof opening. Beneath that opening was the sacred flame, which flickered and jumped. A Vestal Virgin sat nearby, watching it. It must never be allowed to go out.

I sank down on a bench, staring at the flame. It looked so vulnerable, so unstable. But the empire and Rome itself were neither. They were strong and secure.

And I, their emperor, was strong once again, restored to life.

The blessed coolness in here was soothing. The Dog Star had not yet risen, but the scorching heat of midsummer was already upon us. We planned to return to Antium shortly, to flee the baking inland. We would enjoy the sea breezes in the newer part of the villa at sea level.

Suddenly the flame wavered before me; I could barely see it through a mist. Then a blanket of darkness enveloped the whole temple, dropping down, blinding me. My limbs trembled and I could not make them obey. And a chill seized me. A pervasive, jolting fear engulfed me, coming not from within but from somewhere else.

Then it passed. I stood up, feeling limp. Whatever the mysterious force that had flooded the temple, it had passed on. But all my peace of mind, so slowly and painfully restored over the past few months, was swept away. This was an omen, striking at the very heart of the essence of Rome. But an omen of what?

* * *

For the next few days I was skittish, expecting something to happen. But gradually my vigilance subsided, although I did mention my apprehensions to Tigellinus without actually confessing the incident in the temple.

"Have you heard anything, any rumors, any disquiet, in the city?" I asked him. We were sitting on the balcony of the palace, where any stray breezes would be funneled. Slaves had brought pitchers of pressed melon juice and we held cooled goblets in our hands.

He took a long swallow and squinted. Very few men look attractive when squinting, but he did, which was probably why he did it often. "No," he said. "But this is an uncomfortable season for the people. The insulae must be stifling. They have no balconies to sit on and cannot retreat to a villa in Antium like their emperor."

"They have the races," I said. "They can spend their time outside for those. And speaking of races—"

"No, you can't race in the Circus Maximus," he said, reading my mind. "You don't belong to a faction. You should try the smaller tracks in Rome; there is plenty of competition there. When you are ready, that is."

"My grandfather was a renowned charioteer," I said. "I have it in me."

Tigellinus grunted. "Yes, I know. I knew him, remember? When I was in your father's household. I saw him race. You are not there yet. You still need a good deal more training before you are ready to compete." He held out his goblet to be refilled, and instantly a slave did so. Muscles bulging as he bent his elbow and brought the goblet to his lips, he downed the liquid quickly, then wiped his lips. "We should provide a treat for the people; take their minds off the heat and the bugs. We should entertain them—'The emperor invites the people of Rome to party with him.'"

"What—into the palace?"

He leaned back, putting his hands behind his head, tipping his chair. "No. But you will be the host nonetheless. In name. I shall be the actual host." He turned and looked at me, his eyes dancing mischievously. "Leave it to me. I shall provide an entertainment never to be forgotten."

W hat is this all about?" asked Poppaea as we were dressing for the grand event ten days later. "I don't know what to wear!"

"Tigellinus has kept it a secret, and I must say, I do not think his lips could be sealed as tightly with Arabian glue. No word has leaked out of the particulars, but the people have been invited to come to the Lake of Agrippa in midday, prepared to stay. It seems that I, the emperor, am hosting something. What, I do not know."

"You give him too much power," she said.

"He obeys me," I said.

"So far. But a servant can turn quickly into a master."

"Ah, that's why we have two Praetorian prefects," I reminded her. "It's a check to the power of each."

"But Faenius Rufus is practically invisible. I don't see much checking going on."

"Stop worrying," I said. "Let us go to our party and be as surprised as all the rest."

T he Lake of Agrippa had been dug some eighty years before, as part of his baths and other public buildings in the Campus Martius; it was fed by an aqueduct and surrounded by a wooded park. Our litter deposited us by one bank, and when we stepped out I protested that they had taken us to the wrong location. None of this looked remotely familiar. But walking closer I saw that it was the original lake, now transformed. The banks were lined with temporary pavilions and taverns, and in the middle of the lake a large flat pleasure vessel floated on huge empty wine casks.

Just then screeching in the trees nearby revealed fighting monkeys, and a brightly colored bird preened and called. What were these exotic animals doing here?

"Hail, Caesar!" Tigellinus emerged from one of the pavilions, hitching up his tunic. He strode over to us and said, "Would you care to partake, before being rowed to your vessel?"

Oh. The pavilions were brothels. "I see you already have," I said.

"A good host always tastes his own wine and food before offering them to guests, so I was following that principle here. These pretend brothels are stocked with real prostitutes and others who just want to be a prostitute for a day. You know, it's a common fantasy that women have, and in this entertainment we strive to answer all secret wishes. The services are all free, of course."

"To the guests, you mean. I assume we are paying for them?"

"Of course. Come, the boat is docking." He motioned for us to follow him as he walked down to the water's edge.

The heavy raft was towed by two little barges gleaming with gold and ivory fittings. The rowers were pretty boys, *pueri delicati*, the sort Tiberius liked, and they towed our clumsy barge out to the middle of the lake.

Tigellinus had created a pleasure garden on the deck of the boat. A sandalwood screen arched over us, shading us delicately from the sun, dappling us with playful shadows. Pots of cascading flowers waved their petals in the breeze. Soft patterned rugs and silken saffron pillows invited lounging. Perfumed incense smoked from braziers, and murrhine cups, each worth a fortune, were handed round as if they were clay, filled with wine Tigellinus claimed was a hundred years old.

"Oh, I doubt that," said Petronius. "More like twenty, I'd wager."

"You'll lose," said Tigellinus. "I can prove it."

Poppaea lounged with her cup, draping herself over one of the pillows. "Faenius Rufus," she said, spotting our elusive prefect. "We were just talking about you. Where have you been hiding yourself?"

He had a boyish demeanor that made anything he said sound innocent. "Doing my duty," he said. "It keeps me busy." The rebuke to Tigellinus was quietly targeted.

"And I've stocked the groves with imported animals and birds,"

Tigellinus said, seeming not to hear him. "I want people to feel they are no longer in Rome. Not today, and not tonight."

"How many people are coming?" asked Faenius.

Tigellinus shrugged. "I invited the whole city. So we'll see."

A gasp of disbelief went through our group. "Are you insane?"

"It's the emperor's bounty," he said. "He cares for his people and wants to show it in the plainest way. They will never forget this."

As night fell, torches began to flicker among the trees, and the grove echoed with song and noise. People fell on the taverns for the free food and swamped the brothels. "Hail to Caesar!" they cried. I could hear it clearly across the water. "We love him!"

"I told you so," said Tigellinus, bending over and speaking in my ear. "A good investment, my lord."

Poppaea curled up next to me on a slippery pillow. "I remember the other boat ride," she whispered. I held her to me. Yes, the other boat ride. The common people may have found the night's activities transgressive, but they were tame compared to that boat ride back from the Juvenalia, at least for me.

LXXVI

We stood on the deck of the ship bringing us to Antium. On our left the shoreline streamed past fields and hills baking brown in the midsummer heat. On the right the open sea, mischievous and whitecapped, flung spray in our faces, stinging but refreshing. I grasped the rails and enjoyed the ride.

"It is a pleasure to sail this time of year," I said. "Smooth voyage and no dangers. If only we could say the same for the other half of the year."

Every year ships were wrecked making their way up the coast to Ostia, assaulted by wild winds and high waves and driven onto the shore.

"When do you estimate the Avernus–Tiber canal will be finished?" asked Poppaea, drawing her scarf around her head; the playful breeze whipped it all around so it seemed to be flying.

"It's been started, and the diggers have made good progress, but with a hundred and twenty miles to go—"

"How far have they gotten?"

"They've begun at the Avernus end and gone some five miles," I said. "Some Caecuban vineyards in Campania have been affected, unfortunately, by the changed water drainage. Some of the best."

"Petronius won't like that," she said.

"Neither do the vineyard owners. But I have recompensed them. We must have this canal; it will ensure safe passage for the grain ships. No more food losses."

A wave of spray hit us, and we laughed like children.

"You have a grand vision for projects," she said. "A pity you meet resistance at every turn."

"Some people see only the loss in something, not the gain."

She smiled. "Are we speaking of the august Senate?"

"We are indeed." But the project *had* been audacious. And many were fearful of disturbing Lake Avernus, which still had the legend of Aeneas and the underworld clinging to it. People also remembered the disastrous Fucine Lake incident in Claudius's time, the bungled engineering and the flooding. But I saw it as a way of solving the perennial problem of the sea passage up to Ostia, and if a few vineyards were lost, or the level of water in Avernus went down, so be it.

We were on our way to spend July at Antium, until it was time to return for the annual Feriae Augusti games. I was also eager to see what progress had been made there; my renovations, transforming the villa into two parts—the higher, original one linked by descending terraces to a new one at sea level—had been well under way when we left the last time.

"Will the theater be finished?" Poppaea mused.

"I hope so." My grand plan was for a long terrace linking the natural grotto at one end of the harbor to the breakwater at the other end, a place open to the public with gardens, fountains, and a drama theater. The population of Antium had grown, because I had named it an official Roman colony, and now many retired soldiers and their families had settled there. Of course the original town, with its homage to Aeneas, was still there, just swelled by the newcomers.

"If it is, perhaps you can officially open it with a performance."

Ah. That would be gratifying, to have another chance to perform in public, but not in Rome. Not yet. "Perhaps," I said. "Perhaps." And how fitting, to sing near the place where I had first received the (then) mysterious mandate *There is no respect for hidden music.* Of course, there were some who didn't respect my unhidden music, but it was my higher duty to obey the oracle.

. . .

It was dusk when we sailed into the artificial harbor at Antium—another of my projects. When I had become emperor, the harbor was a small natural one; I had enlarged it with two breakwaters extending far out to sea so that Antium could now boast the third-largest harbor, coming only after Ostia and Naples. The Roman invention of concrete that hardened underwater made such maritime engineering possible. Antium could now serve as emergency shelter for distressed ships not able to make the rest of the journey farther north. Of course, the new canal should make that situation obsolete, but that was still in the future. One engineering project rendered the last one outdated; such is the inherent nature of progress.

I was proud to stand at the rails, sailing into the welcoming harbor I had created, its breakwaters and towers painted pink now by the last rays of the sun. We stepped off onto the dock, glad to be on solid ground, and made our way into the seaside pavilion.

This time we would stay in the lower part of the villa, leaving the original part, with its now-painful birth room, empty. The new quarters gave us a new beginning, one with no memories. Our enormous bedroom looked west, out across the sea toward Sardinia and Corsica, though, at close to two hundred miles away, they were not visible; the horizon seemed endless.

Later that evening, having settled in and dined, we strolled along the waterfront. The waves, tamed by the breakwaters, lapped harmlessly against the quay. A half-moon was rising, its light spilling down and coating the water and the walkways.

"Oh, look!" Poppaea pointed to a rounded shape farther down. "It's the theater!"

In the moonlight we inspected the exterior. "I think it is finished!" I said. "No one told me—what a happy surprise."

"It's a good omen," she said, sliding her arm around my waist.

That night we inaugurated the new bedroom of the villa, throwing open the windows so the briny air swept through the chamber, rustling the curtains and stirring the clothes we had discarded and draped over the chairs. All during the long sail down from Rome I had been afire to be alone with her, to touch her and hold her. Now we were together on the bed, made luxurious with perfumed sheets and pillows of swan's down. Unlike the first time in the black room, when we were both frantic and hasty with desire, we had all the time in the world. I brushed her hair away from her forehead and caressed her face. I could barely make out her features in the dim light of the burning oil lamp nearby; it had the hazy contours of something seen in a dream. I could hardly speak for the desire welling up in me.

"Whenever and wherever you are Gaius, then I am Gaia," she murmured. She framed my face in her slender fingers. "That odd vow in the marriage ceremony haunts me. I think it means that we are the same person now."

Yes. We were. It was hard to say where I left off and she began. There was no part of me that she did not share, and no part of her, I hoped, that I did not share. All through my life, separated from and wary of others, I had not hoped to find this—a harbor safer and more mine than any I had built in Antium.

I buried my head against her smooth, sweet shoulder. She ran her hands down my back, tracing patterns, sending tingles all over me. The breeze blew over us, and, rather than cooling us, it heated us until we could bear it no longer.

I have said we were not frantic, but there was urgency in our lovemaking, as if losing this chance would lose it for us forever. Foolish, but reason played no part in it. The more precious something is, the more we fear to lose it, even when we are clasping it tightly.

The hours passed in a way difficult to measure, except in how many times we made love and how varied it was—not because we were trying to be inventive but because there was no perfect way to express exactly what we felt; each one fell short in some way, even as it was unsurpassed in pleasure.

The night nearly spent, the oil lamp burned out, and Poppaea sleeping quietly, one arm hanging limply down over the side of the bed, I quietly slid off and walked to the open window. The half-moon was now shining directly into the room, bathing everything in a clear white light. Her sandals, my tunic, a three-legged bronze table, all were etched in sharp detail. An ivory inlay on a couch was turned a dazzling white rather than the muted cream color it normally was. I looked back at Poppaea's face, touched by the unsparing white light. Even that could not diminish her beauty, transforming her into the finest marble.

We ventured to the upper portion of the villa the next day, climbing up the terraces to survey the new construction from a higher vantage point. It spread out along the edge of the sea, and people were strolling through the colonnades and gardens, lingering before the fountains.

"Just what I had hoped for," I said. "It should be open to the people. My gift to them."

The gardens on the upper grounds had expanded since my boyhood venture there. They now covered a wide, flat area and boasted not only roses but also larkspurs, poppies, irises, and grape arbors as well. In the center of the rose garden a mass of peonies bloomed. I bent over and picked several stems for Poppaea, sticking one of them in her hair, which she protested.

As I parted the peony stalks, I saw the patterned back of a tortoise, dug in and resting in the shade of the leaves.

"Oh, no!" I said. Could it be? I lifted him up and, sure enough, carved on his underside was PATER PATRIAE. "It's the Augustus tortoise!" I said.

"What do you mean?" Poppaea asked. "It's just a tortoise."

"He's very old," I said. "I saw him as a boy. The gardener told me the words were probably carved to commemorate the day a commission came here to tell Augustus he had been named Pater Patriae—Father of His Country. At the time it just irritated me, because I was so tired of Augustus, and even here he appeared in the guise of a tortoise. Now I'm just glad to see the old fellow."

"I am glad you have gotten over your hostility to Augustus."

"I got over it when I realized I did not have to emulate him or be measured by him. Besides, they offered me the same title and I turned it down."

The balmy days sped by at Antium, and we busied ourselves with overseeing the finishing touches on the construction. Now it was the artists who arrived to complete the work and make it wondrous. The people crowded around to watch, then thronged the buildings when they were declared open. I also took Poppaea to the Temple of Fortuna and the cove where Ascanius had landed.

"I was awed by these when I was a boy," I told her. We were standing off to the side watching suppliants approach the statue of the goddess and receive their fortunes, as I had—the fortune that had shaped my life.

She twined her hand in mine. "One of the happy moments in your young life," she said. "Or were you ever young? Can anyone in the imperial family be said to be truly young?"

"At that time I was nearer being ordinary than I would ever be again," I said. "I was not predicted to be emperor. I was but one of several descendants of Augustus, and only through the female line." And where were those others now? Done away with in the ruthless pruning of the imperial tree. I myself had wielded—at a distance—the pruning shears. Now there was just me.

"But your mother had plans for you," she said.

Nearby on the seashore, a line of visitors was approaching the statue of Aeneas, chattering away. Their leader was pointing to it, lecturing, doubtless, on the noble history of the former Trojan. One of the unruly children tried to jump into the water washing the base of the statue. We laughed.

"Ambitious plans," I said. "Audaciously ambitious plans."

"And she managed to carry them out."

"Yes, when it came to scheming, she was a genius."

But not as good as I. The pupil had, in the end, surpassed the teacher. But I did not wish to think further on that. "The imperial line has narrowed to just me," I said. "We must help it branch out, provide it with new leaves. Healthy new leaves that will carry on the line of"—I pointed toward the statue—"the Julio-Claudian House."

"Then we should retire back to the villa this noon and carry on the project," she said, laughing, leaning against me.

Here in Antium, I was able to concentrate on my Trojan War epic. Perhaps it was being away from Rome that lent itself to creative work; perhaps it was the sound of the sea, or the scent of ocean air, or even just the memory of myself as a child roaming the halls and cliffs, bursting with curiosity, learning from Anicetus and Beryllus, watching in wonder as my world expanded with knowledge, that launched me further in my attempts to make an old story new.

The Trojan War . . . I had finished the first part, the opening when Paris is rediscovered by his family. His identity is revealed when he defeats Hector in a wrestling match. I took contrary pleasure in this. The Paris of *The Iliad* was dreamy, ineffectual, irresponsible. But my Paris was stronger than the vaunted warrior Hector. What Homer valued and celebrated I might not; Paris had gifts that I would laud. Paris had said something along the lines of "What golden gifts the gods give us we must not refuse, even if we would not have chosen them in the first place." Paris's gifts had not been appreciated in Homer's version of Troy, but they would be in mine. And why could a dreamer not also be a formidable warrior?

But since my daughter's death, I had found myself drawn more to the last days of Troy, to the ending of things, the stern visage of fate that signaled destruction. And now, suddenly, the horrors of the fall of

Troy, the killings, the destruction, the burning, haunted me as never before.

Sitting at my work desk, I put aside the earlier sections of the manuscript and went directly to the last night of Troy's existence. When one is longing to write something, one has to obey that command and leave the rest.

I would start work when the sun rose and immerse myself so much in the faraway event that the sun had set before I stirred. Later I would return to it, writing furiously by lamplight. I was there; I was truly there. When the last stone fell and the city was consumed in flames, I was drained and grieving. I let the paper curl before me. I had said all I could. Now a melancholy swept over me. It was done. I could never write that scene again. And Troy was truly gone.

D o you think you will perform it for the drama festival?" asked Poppaea, standing over me. I had fallen asleep at the table, my head resting beside the manuscript. Sunlight was streaming in, hurting my eyes. Before me the yellowish paper lay where I had left it.

"The drama festival?" I shook my head, trying to clear it. The screams of Troy still resounded in my ear, but they were fading.

"The opening of your new theater! They are performing in three days, when the moon is full, calling it an homage to Diana."

"Oh." I looked at the manuscript. Did I want to expose it to others so soon? There was a part of me that wanted to clasp it to myself a while longer. But it would be fitting if I, the patron of the theater, participated in its first performance. "Perhaps."

P oppaea had been so patient while I abandoned all else to submerge myself in my writing that I had ordered a gift for her, something to express my gratitude for her understanding. Truly she was that rarity, a person who sensed the needs of another and stepped graciously aside to honor them. So I consulted with a trader from India to design a necklace for her that would be unique, at least in Rome.

"In India we have a special necklace based on astrology," he told me. Rome had a lively trade with India and formerly exotic goods were flooding in. "We call it the nine-gem necklace—oh, another word in our language, but the Latin describes it. There is a stone—and it must be a perfect stone, no flaws or blemishes—for each of the heavenly bodies. We believe it has a sort of magic when the stones are brought together, linked as they are above us in the heavens."

"What way? What are they?" He had my curiosity up.

"Ruby for the sun, and it must always be in the center of the design, since the sun is the center of our heavens. Pearl for the moon, cinnamon stone for the waxing moon, and cat's-eye for the waning moon. Red coral for Mars, emerald for Mercury, yellow sapphire for Jupiter, diamond for Venus, and blue sapphire for Saturn."

"Aside from the sun in the center, are you free to arrange the others any way you please?" Perfect specimens of all those stones would be wildly expensive, but so be it.

"Yes, there is no set pattern, as all the planets and the moon move constantly."

Immediately I saw the arrangement I wanted. "A wide collar with the ruby in the center, and lower. On each side, red coral and emerald. Then the pearl above the ruby—as the moon is above the earth and sun. Then the orange-brown cinnamon stone balanced by the cat's-eye, for the moon's phases. Next, on either side, the yellow and blue sapphires. Finally, hanging beneath the ruby, the diamond. For the moon and Venus are the fairest in the night sky and should have a prominent place."

"Caesar, as you wish. I can procure these stones."

"I want the ruby to be larger than the others, as the sun is larger than the rest. And I want it set in finest gold. The bright kind, from Nubia."

"Caesar, as you wish. I can have it for you in two months."

"No, I want it in three days." I wanted to present it to her the night of the theater opening, and of the full moon.

He was silent a moment, thinking. Should he admit it was impossible? Was he remembering one already made but not in that design, that perhaps he could offer instead? "I—I—" He took a deep breath. "Caesar, as you wish."

"I will pay triple for your speed," I assured him. "I value your professionalism."

He looked a bit less troubled, as the bill would be a whopping one. That was a consolation.

I would recite my "Fall of Troy," I decided. I did not feel quite ready, but this was fate. The festival called out for my participation, and I had the new work ready—if not quite polished. The theater was festooned with garlands for the occasion, and word had got back to Rome about it. So I was not surprised when I saw several senators and magistrates out in the audience. Curiosity had drawn them, and probably a hope that the emperor would do something that would lend itself to gossip.

I was pleased with the performances of the local poets and musicians, and when my time came to mount the stage, I welcomed everyone and thanked them for coming. I praised the local artists and announced that the theater was open to all, as my gift to the city of Antium. "I know there will be many more such festivals, enriching the culture of the town, and I am proud to be here."

I then took up my cithara—I had hurriedly written the music to accompany the poetry—and began, no nervousness this time. The audience was small and local and friendly, except for the visitors from Rome. And they did not bother me. That was past. As I recited and sang, though, Antium vanished and Troy rose before me, blazing and doomed. That was all I saw, all I knew, until I finished the last notes and let them die away.

There was a great stillness, and I knew it was not for my artistry, for that was still raw, but rather for the tragedy of Troy. Even my rude art had captured enough of it to move people.

Then came the applause, but still subdued. It was not appropriate to cheer when Troy had been so gruesomely ruined.

I let the audience depart before Poppaea and I left. For a moment we were alone in the theater.

"It was magnificent," she said.

"*You* are magnificent," I replied. "Without you, I could not compose a word. There is no way for me to express it but—"

"How can a poet have no way of expressing himself?" she teased, putting her arms around me.

"Without words," I said, pulling out the elaborate carved presentation box for the necklace that I had hidden inside my cithara bag. I handed it to her. "This speaks for me."

Surprised, she carefully opened the hinged box. The necklace, in its glittering splendor, lay spread on dark cloth. She actually gasped.

"It mirrors the heavens," I said, and I explained what all the stones meant. I took it out of its box and draped it around her neck, fastening it. Then I stood back and looked. Oh, it was lovely beyond even what I had imagined. Her hands flew to it and caressed the stones, smooth and rounded beneath her fingertips.

"I have no words, either," she said, kissing me.

As we left the theater, the full moon shone down on us, catching its light on the pearl.

The next day I had set aside to relax and recover from my furious creative sprint and subsequent performance. The sun rose in a cloudless sky, and the day promised to be quiet and restorative. We sat out on the shaded terrace and for a while watched the horizon. It was soothing and still. And I relished the mindlessness. No thinking. No thinking. Just sit with closed eyes and drift, reliving the night before.

Attendants brought us food, placing the trays down on a stand— platters of cold ham and mullet, pine-tree honey, bread, eggs, olives, and cherries, with juice or Tarentinum wine to wash it down. Lazily I reached out and took a handful of cherries.

Poppaea was so enthralled with her necklace that she wore it that morning, hidden under a scarf. "For I can't take it off just yet," she admitted. She had insisted on wearing it to bed, where the cool gold and bumpy gems felt peculiar against my chest when we embraced, and kept it on through all the rest, like a charmed object from a myth. But in the myth the hero would have insisted on her removing it, only to doom himself with a curse or some such. I simply enjoyed the singular experience.

I was just passing her the platter of eggs and olives when a panting, dusty, sweaty messenger was hurried out to us, flanked by two of the villa guards. His face was set in a grimace, matched by the expression on the guards' faces. I stood up.

"Caesar, Caesar!" he cried, falling to his knees and clasping his hands piteously. "I come from Rome, from Tigellinus." His voice was a croak.

"Well, what is it?"

"Rome is on fire! Rome is on fire!" he shrieked. "It is burning out of control!"

I rose, still not taking it in. "On fire?"

"Yes, yes! It started in the Circus Maximus, in one of the shops at the far south end."

"When?"

"Night before last—and the northerly wind fanned the flames so they swept fast down the length of the Circus and then started climbing the hills around it."

Rome was a firetrap, and we had had many fires in our history. To guard against this, Augustus had created the Vigiles Urbani, a fire brigade of seven thousand men. Serenus had been head of it, and now Nymphidius Sabinus had replaced him.

"What of the firefighters? Are they out?"

"Yes, but helpless to stop it. The fire is spreading faster than they can contain it. The sparks jump over roofs and fields and flare up in new places. It was starting to climb the Palatine!"

I turned to Poppaea. I felt numb, not at all able to truly believe this. "I must go," I said. "We'll ride together," I told the messenger. "A fresh horse for you."

It was midday when we set out, but darkness had fallen before we approached Rome. All along the ride I felt myself becoming more and more agitated, hoping that the messenger had exaggerated, or that the fire was already contained, or that it had not destroyed much besides the shops in the Circus. *Calm, calm, Nero, you must keep calm, think clearly.* But inside another picture was emerging—of Rome destroyed, people dead or destitute, historical treasures lost forever, all when I was emperor, all happening while I was responsible for the safety of my people. *Rome was ruined under Nero, the city incinerated, nothing left but ashes.*

As we neared the top of a hill near Rome, before we could see the city itself, a lurid color stained the night sky, orange and red and yellow, ugly fingers reaching up into the heavens, pulsating. Then we crested the hill and I gazed down on the city aflame. Billows of smoke roiled upward, and spurts of color, clouds of sparks, and bursts of exploding stone and wood punctuated the darkness. The brisk wind blew ashes in my face, carrying the stench of burning cloth, garbage, and things unnamable.

It was true, all true.

"It's worse!" the messenger cried. "It's still spreading! It's much bigger than when I left. Look, it's engulfed the hills!"

Rome was being devoured. Suddenly I knew what the strange threatening portent in the Temple of Vesta, the hearth of Rome, meant. And I understood the meaning of the sibyl: *Fire will be your undoing. Flames will consume your dreams and your dreams are yourself.*

I stood at the turning point of my life. This was my battlefield, the battlefield I had wondered if I would ever face. My ancestor Antony had faced his twice: at the battle of Philippi, when he crushed the assassins of Caesar, and the battle of Actium, when he himself was crushed by Octavian.

Either Rome and I perished together, or we survived together.

But no matter the outcome, there was only one choice, to go forward, to wade into battle.

"Come," I said, urging my horse forward. "Rome awaits."

And we descended the hill, heading into the maelstrom.

AFTERWORD

This novel is my mission to rescue a gifted and remarkable young ruler, who was only sixteen when he became emperor, from what historian David Braund, in his essay "Apollo in Arms: Nero at the Frontier," calls "the extensive fog of hostility, which clouds and surrounds almost all the historical record on Nero" and "makes historical analysis extraordinarily difficult."

From being accused of fiddling while Rome burned to being the Antichrist to being Hollywood's favorite over-the-top emperor, Nero has suffered badly at the hands of popular culture. This is ironic, as Nero himself embraced and cultivated popular culture and was probably the first public persona to thoroughly understand and manipulate image control on many levels. I was drawn to him as I sensed the vast gap between the perception of him and what he really was. It is possible, with the help of modern historical analysis, to blow the fog away and see a different person standing before you, not the madman who fiddled, the pyromaniac who burned Rome, the violent sex fiend and debauched tyrant, but a man of considerable talent, a visionary in many ways—in architecture and urban planning, engineering projects, diplomacy, and artistic freedom. He also was a man of integrity, ingenuity, and generosity.

How did his reputation become so tarnished that in popular memory he became a monster? Suetonius said that Nero longed for immortality and undying fame, but what he has today is not what he had in mind.

Much of the blame can be laid at the feet of the authors of the three main surviving histories that cover his reign—Tacitus, Suetonius, and Dio Cassius. There were many other histories, some favorable to Nero, but only these hostile three remain. Not only do the writers assign motivation to him for his actions, they invariably interpret every motive as malign, rather than just reporting the facts. They were not contemporaries of Nero, and two of the three histories are incomplete. The first two were written at a time when the Nerva-Antonine dynasty had recently come to power and it was in the new regime's interests to tar the ones it had displaced, the first of which had been founded by the revered and deified Augustus, Nero being its last representative.

The first of these histories, Tacitus's *Annals of Imperial Rome*, was written around AD 115, about fifty years after Nero's death. The account breaks off at AD 66, missing the last two years of Nero's reign. Tacitus is a genuine and thorough historian (especially by ancient standards if not by modern ones), but he still colors his text with his proaristocratic biases, and he is a moralist. To him, the entire Julio-Claudian dynasty was corrupt, whereas the aristocrats of the old families of the Republic, and the senatorial class, were noble. He saw their continuing decline of power, with the rise of the emperors and their freedman administrators, to be a national tragedy. So Nero could do little right in his eyes and he lost no opportunity to make covert smears or outright attacks on his actions, while also supplying his own interpretation of Nero's motives.

Suetonius's history, *The Twelve Caesars*, written more or less at the same time as Tacitus's (around AD 120), contains much information—some probably pure gossip—arranged by subject rather than chronologically. This has made it difficult to date the material or put it in context. Suetonius's work was the basis for Robert Graves's book *I, Claudius* and the subsequent miniseries, which titillated modern audiences to no end.

How much is true? We can never know, but Suetonius must be taken cautiously and with a grain of salt. His magnificent tale of the last hours of Nero reads like a Shakespearean tragedy—but is it accurate? What is the source of his information?

The last one, Dio Cassius's *Roman History*, came some one hundred and fifty years after Nero (around AD 230). We do not even have the complete text, just an extract produced by Byzantine monks in the Middle Ages, redacted for what seemed important to the summarizers. Dio was a fervent partisan of the Senate and judged Nero by how well he cooperated with it.

As imperfect as these sources are, we have to rely mainly on them for our knowledge of Nero. But with modern methods of analyzing material, we are able to shift the lighting and see between the cracks better. We are also helped by other evidence, coinage and archaeological, that adds another dimension. It remains, however, a challenge—how to find the real Nero?

The last step in his cultural evolution was joining an elite group of rulers who were thought not really to be dead but poised to return one day to rescue their respective countries: King Arthur, Charlemagne, Frederick Barbarossa, Constantine the Great. After his death, no fewer than three Nero imposters appeared and gathered a substantial following. Suetonius says, tantalizingly, "There were people who used to lay spring flowers on his grave for a long time . . . pretending he was still alive and would soon return to confound his enemies." (This in itself testifies to his popularity with the common people, regardless of Tacitus's spin, for disliked rulers do not inspire imposters and no one wishes for their return.) In addition to that, by the end of the first century he had been assigned the role of the Beast in the Book of Revelation, which was written castigating Rome as the Whore of Babylon. The spelling of Nero's name in Hebrew numericals adds up to the "666" of the Beast. From there came the identification as the Antichrist, who was also supposed to return to battle with Christ at the end of days.

Nero himself is a creature far different from the stereotype. The "fiddling while Rome burned" saying didn't arise until the seventeenth century. He wasn't violent—he even forbade killing in the amphitheater—wasn't debauched, wasn't a sex fiend (considering what was available to him, he was pretty restrained), and doesn't fit the usual description of a tyrant. He took action only against those who directly threatened him, and only among a small circle of people, affecting very few, not the population as a whole, for his own safety and that of Rome. Would people today be surprised to learn that he was athletic, affable, and tolerant? That as a composer and musician he was quite good? That his projects were futuristic? That he had a bond with the common people, whom he preferred to the aristocrats, and that his successor, Galba, admitting the admiration was mutual, said, "Nero will always be missed by the riffraff"?

Actually he was a lot like his ancestor Marc Antony—generous, impulsive, dramatic, emotional, athletic, with a passion for the stage. Just as Antony did not fit into the proper Roman mold, neither did his great-grandson. Later the emperor Hadrian was to embrace many of the same things—Hellenism, extensive building projects, dabbling in the arts, wearing his hair long—and be admired. But Nero paid the full price of being ahead of his time.

It is also good to remember that Nero did not operate in a vacuum. He came from a murderous family, suffered a series of psychological shocks in his childhood that surely would have left their mark on him, and lived in an environment where murder was often the only means of survival. The track record of the preceding emperors was even more steeped in blood, but we don't hear as much about that, because the murders were not so spectacularly theatrical, and because there was not a posthumous campaign to blacken their names to legitimize a new dynasty. In the case of Augustus, the opposite dynamic was at work: to expunge anything derogatory about how he came to ultimate power in founding that first dynasty.

The historian Edward Champlin, in *Nero*, sets out to answer the question "Why is Nero so fascinating?" He concludes, "Our image of Nero was reworked for eternity by hostile sources and by the popular imagination, but they did not create it. It remains so vivid because it was created by an artist." By his last words, *Qualis artifex pereo* (What an artist dies in me), Nero chose his own epitaph as that of an artist. He was above all an artist who happened to be an emperor, and it is this Nero I wanted to bring to you.

I have never written a novel in two parts before, and I hasten to assure my readers that the story will continue just where it left off in the next volume, although each book can stand alone. Nero's life was so extraordinary it is impossible to get it all under one roof without stinting on important events, and since this work seeks to be fair to him, it seems only right that he should be given the space he needs to tell his story. I am eager to go on, because, as unbelievable as it may seem, what comes next is even more unprecedented and unforgettable.

In writing this I had to be mindful that I was writing a novel, not a history, and for a twenty-first-century audience. For that reason I have at times used modern terms—such as Naples instead of Neapolis and Portugal instead of Lusitania, as that name makes most people think of the ship sunk by the Germans in World War I. I also use the English versions of names if that is how we generally know them: the playwright Terence instead of Terentius, Marc Antony instead of Marcus Antonius. I use the modern terms "emperor" and "empress" although they were not used then. I use feet and miles as measurements because the Romans did, albeit theirs were not quite the same as ours, and it feels less jarring than meters and kilometers.

In chronology, I have made some adjustments for continuity—for example, I moved the date Otho was sent to Portugal and the date Nero built his baths and his gymnasium, closed a very slight gap between the death of Caligula and the birth of Britannicus, and changed the time of year the theater in Naples collapsed and the earthquake hit Pompeii.

And I have combined the two historical Jewish delegations to Rome into one, for simplicity. In addition, I moved the dates of the deaths of the last Silanus descendants of Augustus back a bit and merged the years AD 56–57 and AD 60–61, but without omitting anything.

It is my custom never to knowingly go against a known fact, but in the case of ancient history much is fuzzy. I adhered to that standard here as much as I could. The chronology of Nero's childhood is a bit vague, but we have the contours of it in external events around him. All the characters named are historical, except three men I invented to appear only once to do a minor action: the senators Nonius Silius, Vibius Procolus, and Quinctius Valerianus.

At times I have had to fill in when information is missing, where the modern reader would be confused, or where the story demands it. For example, from what I understand, divorce was a simple matter in Rome. It may not have required the statements and questions I have here, but apparently they were asked in some context, because they are recorded in the histories.

As I stated earlier on the reliability of the ancient historians, much that was rumor was reported as fact. Whenever someone died there were always whispers of poisoning, and many deaths were laid at Nero's door when there would be no plausible reason for it. So I have Burrus dying a natural death, which he probably did. On the other hand, I don't whitewash Nero by omitting things he did; I have included all his escapades and actions, such as his disguised night crawls and brawls with his friends in Rome, the engineered death of Britannicus, and, of course, the most famous, the theatrically managed death of Agrippina. But many of his actions considered shocking by Tacitus, such as chariot driving and stage performances, to us seem rather tame and hardly scandalous. Undignified for an emperor, perhaps, but hardly worthy of being described as "the wildest improprieties." From this image comes our Hollywood emperor, with the type of improprieties left up to the studio's imagination.

I have been blessed with many outstanding books and sources for my work. First, of course, are the three histories I mentioned earlier: Tacitus, *The Annals of Imperial Rome* (London: Penguin Classics, 1985); Suetonius, *The Twelve Caesars* (London: Penguin Books, 1986); and Dio Cassius, *Roman History, Books 61–70* (Cambridge, MA: Harvard University Press, 1925). For biographies, I found the oldest (and still the longest one in English), Bernard W. Henderson's *The Life and Principate of the Emperor Nero* (Philadelphia: J. B. Lippincott, 1903), was very good in providing many small personal details that helped make the book intimate. Michael Grant's *Nero: Emperor in Revolt* (New York: American Heritage Press, 1970) served as a basic go-to book for clear explanations and all pertinent facts. Miriam T. Griffin's *Nero: The End of a Dynasty* (New Haven, CT: Yale University Press, 1985) proved to be a treasure chest of information and analysis on him and the period. Stephen Dando-Collins's book *The Great Fire of Rome: The Fall of the Emperor Nero and His City* (Philadelphia: Da Capo Press, 2010) also has much more information than on just the fire, but it is excellent on that; and his *Nero's Killing Machine: The True Story of Rome's Remarkable Fourteenth Legion* (Hoboken, NJ: John Wiley & Sons, 2005) covers the war with Boudicca. Richard Holland's *Nero: The Man behind the Myth* (Stroud, UK: Sutton, 2000) is good on the psychology of Nero; and Edward Champlin's *Nero* (Cambridge, MA: Belknap Press of Harvard University Press, 2003) is superlative in analyzing the person inside the myth, and the method in his madness—if indeed it was madness. Last, from editors Emma Buckley and Martin T. Dinter, *A Companion to the Neronian Age* (Chichester, UK: Wiley-Blackwell, 2013) provides invaluable information on a variety of facets of Nero, military, mythological, artistic, and psychological; their book contains the David Braund essay.

Two excellent Seneca biographies, James Romm's *Dying Every Day: Seneca at the Court of Nero* (New York: Knopf, 2014) and Emily Wilson's *The Greatest Empire: A Life of Seneca* (New York: Oxford University Press, 2014), were very helpful. For Seneca's direct words: *Seneca: Dialogues and Essays* (New York: Oxford University Press, 2008).

On some other topics, Patrick Faas's *Around the Roman Table: Food and*

Feasting in Ancient Rome (New York: Palgrave Macmillan, 2003) is just what it says it is; Linda Farrar's *Ancient Roman Gardens* (Stroud, UK: Sutton, 1998) is a wonderful source for information on private and public gardens; and Roland Auguet's *Cruelty and Civilization: The Roman Games* (New York: Routledge, 1994) tells you all you want to know about the arena. T. G. Tucker's *Life in the Roman World of Nero and St. Paul* (New York: Macmillan, 1936), although written in 1910, has the most complete coverage, along with diagrams, of any book I've seen for details of daily living.

Cicuta virosa (Poison Hemlock)